The Weight of Time

THE WEIGHT OF TIME

CHRONICLES OF ETERNITY II

J. A. GORDON

DERWEN PUBLISHING

PEMBROKE · DYFED

First published in Great Britain by Derwen Publishing 2009.

Derwen Publishing
3 Bengal Villas,
Pembroke, Dyfed
Wales, SA71 4BH

A CIP catalogue for this book is available
from the British Library.

ISBN 978-1-907084-02-7

This is a book about the people who fall between the cracks of history. Much of
what appears here is recorded history and the names of those persons, places and
events have been used unaltered but the names of the other persons are not
necessarily those which they used at the time.

Design and production by David Porteous Editions.
www.davidporteous.com

Printed and bound in the UK.

PROLOGUE

The room was warm and the subject lay on the deeply uphol-
stered sofa. The woman's voice was calm as she said, 'Do you
know what year it is?'

The subject thought for a few moments and said, 'Not exactly –
I know that Nero is the Emperor… but we, my century and I, are
nowhere near Rome. We're in the middle of nowhere… at the
edge of the empire.'

'Is anything happening at this scene?'

'Not especially – it's just the normal evening scene with the
men laughing with each other and the smell of food being
cooked, but I feel happy. I feel really content.'

'Excellent. Now I want you to go to the next scene. An
important scene in that life. Take your time, there's no hurry.'

The subject's eyes moved rapidly under their closed lids –
searching, searching, searching. The candle guttered in the
breeze coming through the gaps in the shutters.

'We're on a beach.'

'Good,' said the woman. 'Who is with you?'

'My century, well, most of them anyway. My son is here. My
son – I have a son! He's young and strong and he has bright
blonde hair. He doesn't look like me in any way but I know he's
my son and he is the apple of my eye.'

'Do you know where the beach is? Is it a sandy beach?'

'No, it's mostly pebbles, and there's a path up the cliffs to the
headland. It's somewhere in this country. It's not abroad.'

'Why are you there? Have you just landed?'

'Yes. We landed just after dawn – we have an important job
to do inland.'

'Why have you come to this scene in that life?'

'I don't know. I'm feeling relieved that we've landed safely.
I'm with the people I know and trust and I have my wonderful
son with me.'

'Look around you. Can you see anything that tells you why

you came to this scene?'

The subject's eyes scanned the scene, searching under closed eyelids.

'Well, I feel that something – or someone – is missing – it's more what I cannot see that is confusing me.'

'What is it?'

'I'm not sure… I'm looking out to sea and… something's wrong… I'm very concerned.'

CHAPTER ONE

Graecus was not sure what was bothering him the most. It could have been that he was hungry and thirsty but then again it could have been that he needed to empty his bowels. And then again, if he were truthful with himself, he would have to admit that what was really worrying him was that he had no idea where Acerbus and his men were and he had even less of an idea whether they had managed to cross Ocean or whether their ship had foundered on the rocky coast in a more tragic working of the drama which had recently attended Graecus's journey and that of his men.

They had landed from the navy ship, Nauplius, early that morning after a foggy night, gratefully putting their booted feet onto the pebbles of Britannia's shores a few miles north of Dubris and Graecus, having satisfied himself that Acerbus's ship was nowhere to be seen, had wasted no time in ordering his men up the cliff path onto the drovers' road which would take them to the main port but the men had been marching for a couple of hours now and, feeling his horse tire beneath him, Graecus decided it was time that they had a rest and that he took stock of their situation.

He raised his right arm signalling the column behind him to halt and, having heard the footfalls behind him cease, Graecus dismounted and turned to face his men.

At the front of the column was the century's standard bearer, Graecus's adopted son, Germanicus, now standing to attention next to the horn-blower, Solitarius, and in front of Graecus's old friend, Felix, the best cook in the Roman Army – bar none.

Graecus had been feeling isolated sitting on his horse, riding alone at the front of the column but now that he looked at his son and his old friend, his face softened into a smile and he said, 'It is time we broke our fast. We shall take some time to rest and refresh ourselves. Felix, please supervise the feeding of the men.'

The men broke from the column, shaking the tension from

7

their arms and legs while Felix made himself and those of the men whom he trusted with the cooking pots busy with lighting fires and making the porridge which would put warmth in their bellies. Magnus, the century's medicine man, was looking at a livid gash on a young soldier's leg and was taking something from the pouch around his waist to apply to the wound.

Graecus watched this activity from the corner of his eye – he was looking forward to the porridge and hoped that Felix would be able to find some honey with which to sweeten his dish but, before he could enjoy his food, he needed to make himself comfortable.

Standing nearby was Pneumaticus, one of the most seasoned campaigners in Graecus's century, and Graecus motioned to him to come forward.

'Brother,' he said, 'I have need to void myself and wish you to stand guard for me,' and then he and Pneumaticus walked a hundred or so paces from their colleagues to an earthy area with a conveniently situated bush.

Graecus unpinned his scarlet cloak from his shoulder and gave it to Pneumaticus before stepping behind the bush.

As he squatted, he said, 'Pneumaticus, you are from Britannia, tell me, is this part of the country well-populated?'

'Domine, I was not raised in this region but I know that these coastal areas have many small settlements where the people make their living by fishing as well as growing their crops.'

'And are the tribes here friendly to the Romans?'

'It is many years since I lived in Britannia and much has changed but I think it is the case that many people in this area have prospered under Rome's rule and they are more likely to view Rome and its emissaries more favourably.'

Deprived of the convenience of the wet sponge on a stick with which to clean himself, Graecus made do with several handfuls of large leaves before rearranging his clothing and now he reappeared from behind the bush, and taking his cloak from Pneumaticus, he said, 'I am encouraged by what you have said and I hope that if Acerbus and his century were shipwrecked close to the shore then the people of this place will have looked kindly on them and helped them in their distress.'

'I am sure that you speak for us all, Domine. We all fear for the safety of our brothers.'

'Indeed, and I would be a much happier man if we were sharing this march with them, but in their absence, the only course open to us is to make haste to Dubris where we shall be given fresh orders.'

'Do you yet know where we shall meet up with Suetonius Paulinus and the Legions?'

'No. I suspect that it will depend on where Boudicca and her tribal armies are and where Paulinus thinks they will strike next.'

'Strike next? Is it not sufficient that they have already sacked Camoludunum and Verulamium? How much more carnage are they to be allowed to inflict on our peaceful citizens?'

'We are here to put a stop to her, but even though she is a barbarian, you must give her credit for having chosen the best moment to start her rebellion – just when Suetonius and all his men were away on the other side of the country putting down the Druids.'

'Yes, she is clever and she has the support of many of the other tribes from that area. I suppose that they must have felt that Rome was taking too much from them in taxes and land.'

'I would imagine that was the reason for their rebellion, it usually is, but that is no excuse for the atrocities they committed in killing innocent citizens, nor for the outrages her men visited on our noblewomen, and we are honoured to have been chosen to reinforce the legionary troops. But now, old friend, let us go and see what Felix has prepared for us.'

They walked back to rejoin their comrades and found them sitting on the ground with bowls on their laps and spoons in their hands, enthusiastically shovelling porridge and bread into their mouths.

Graecus rinsed his hands and took a bowl from Felix who said to him, 'I have put some honey in it for you. I kept some in my bag, for ease on the journey.'

'Thank you, my friend.'

9

'Father,' said Germanicus, 'how far are we from our destination?'

'About an hour's march, I think. Why do you ask?'

'I wondered whether I should allow Zig to do some hunting now, in case we might need some food for the pot later.'

Zig was the small, grey, hound-like dog sitting at Germanicus's side. He had come to their camp in Lower Germania as a stray but had been adopted by Germanicus and given the name Exiguus, meaning very small but this name had, long ago, been shortened to Zig. The little animal was looking around him with bright intelligent eyes and sniffing excitedly at the new scents in this foreign country and, at the mention of his name, Zig gazed adoringly at Germanicus.

'I do not think it will be necessary my son, for we should be safely quartered in Dubris long before nightfall and I am confident that our barracks there will be properly supplied with all that we need.'

'Yes father. When will we meet the enemy?'

'That is a very good question. I do not know yet but I am sure that we shall find out soon enough.'

'Father, why did we land so far away from Dubris, did Xanthippus fail in his navigation?'

'No, Xanthippus is an able mariner. I do not wish for you to tell everyone but, since you have asked, I shall tell you – Xanthippus purposely took us several miles off course so that he could avoid the ship coming into port.'

'But why would he want to do that father? Why would he want to disobey his orders?'

'Well, you have every reason yourself to recall that vile captain Jejunus's strange and cruel behaviour; Magnus and I are sure that he is insane, so, at my instigation Magnus gave him something to calm him down. That is why he was asleep for most of our journey.'

'Yes, but why would that mean that we did not land in port?'

'Because the harbourmaster at Dubris is Jejunus's brother and when they are together they encourage each other to indulge in all kinds of debauchery which does nothing to improve

Jejunus's temper and this is bad for Xanthippus and anyone else who has the misfortune to sail with the captain.'

'Oh, so Xanthippus landed us miles away so that he could keep Jejunus from his brother?'

Yes, my son. That is what I have just said, is it not?'

'Yes, father. Father, what kinds of debauchery do Jejunus and his brother get up to?'

By now, Graecus had had enough of his son's questioning, and, anyway, Germanicus was still young enough to be innocent of some of the world's baser activities and he wished to shield him from them as long as possible, so he said, 'I am afraid that Xanthippus did not elaborate and I did not have the time to ask him. Now, please go and give Perdix some water.'

Germanicus walked away and untethered Graecus's mare to take her to the cart which held the fresh water. Graecus looked around and saw that the men had finished their porridge – Solitarius, as usual, standing apart from his brethren, observing them– and that it was time to move on so they extinguished the fires and packed up their pots and formed up in their column behind their Centurion.

Germanicus put on his helmet, covering his shock of unruly bright blonde hair, then the wolfskin which was the mark of his rank and picked up the century's standard. The helmet and wolf-skin put his face in shadow emphasising the deep scar in his cheek where some years before he had had an argument with a wild boar which had detached part of his face and had left him with not only the scar but also a slight lisp.

Graecus smiled at his son in memory of the awful thought that day that he might have lost him and gave silent thanks that he had not and then mounted his chestnut filly and they moved off, marching in perfect time.

About an hour later, having passed through some rolling countryside, they came to the crest of a hill and Graecus called a halt.

'Men, you see below you the port of Dubris. I wish you to brush the dust from your clothes and clean your faces of any dirt so that we arrive in good order. Take ten minutes.'

While his men were brushing themselves down, Graecus dismounted and sat on a nearby rock. He took off his helmet and ran his fingers through his dark hair.

He was not a Roman; not having ever known his real family he was unsure quite what he was, but he spoke Greek and had been given his nickname 'The Greek' on that account but he was probably not pure Greek because he had grey eyes. He pushed back the lock of hair which fell onto his brow and allowed himself a few minutes' quiet thought.

His mind turned again to the question of Acerbus and what had become of him and his century. Graecus tried not to think of what it would mean to him if they had perished but he could not help it.

He thought of how he would manage to be a good Centurion for his men in this dangerous land and with a new commander whom he did not know and he thought how it would all be ten times more difficult and challenging for him without his mentor who, in being older and more experienced than him, and above all, by being a well-connected Roman, knew so much more about politics and the subtle ways of the Roman world than did he and was not only his closest colleague but also his lodestone in these delicate matters.

Graecus had found his early command a lonely existence until Acerbus and his men had joined them but then there had been several peaceful, almost idyllic, years in the fort in Lower Germania when they had all lived and worked together in harmony and Germanicus, the dirty little orphan, had grown up among the men, leading an ideal life for an adventurous boy – hunting, running, swimming and learning the ways of the army from good soldiers who were proud to uphold the values of the Emperor, the Senate and The People of Rome.

Graecus had taught his son Latin, the most important tongue in the world, and had delighted in explaining the different tenses and moods of the verbs, their conjugations and the declensions of the nouns. Graecus loved words and he had enthusiastically explained the deponent verbs, the mysteries of the ablative absolute and all the subtle ways in which the language was a richly potent tool which could and should be used with precision. Germanicus had been an apt pupil, soaking up the knowledge and the vocabulary like a dry sponge. But sadly, he had not embraced mathematics with the same fervour and had preferred to gossip with the men rather than do his sums.

Graecus was pondering all this when he heard a loud sound and looked up to see Germanicus, his head thrown back, laughing wholeheartedly at something which Pneumaticus had just said and he smiled as he looked at his wonderful adoptive son, who for the past eight years, since he had been given to him, aged about ten, by a slave-master, had been the object of his love and attention. He looked again at him and felt a pang because he realised that he envied him his carefree joy.

And that was another thing. As Germanicus opened his eyes and Graecus again saw his piercing blue gaze, he thought of the secret which he shared with Acerbus and their General, Flavius. The secret of Germanicus's parentage.

He shuddered at the thought of what he knew and that there were others who knew who would not hesitate to use this knowledge to their advantage and he decided that it was best put to the back of his mind as there were more pressing things to attend to at the moment, and if Flavius were as good as his word and kept them as far away from Rome as possible, then no harm would come to Germanicus.

Graecus shook his head to dislodge these thoughts, pushed back the errant lock of hair and put on his helmet.

'Line up men. We're marching into Dubris and we're meeting our brothers from the legions so I want nobody falling out of step. When we get to the barracks I want to give the best impression possible so with your best foot forward, MARCH.'

The column descended the hill and into the town.

As they were arriving from the landward side, Graecus did not quite know where they would find their quarters but he took the column towards the sea and quickly found the group of buildings which comprised the Roman administrative section of the port.

Then he found the largest building and ordered his men to halt outside it.

Having done that, he thought that he should go and find the most senior officer present so, dismounting, he told his men to stand easy and, after motioning to Germanicus to accompany him, entered the building.

This was a tense moment for Graecus as it was at times like these, when he was faced with making his presence known in unfamiliar surroundings, that he felt most keenly his lack of pedigree and that, although he was a Centurion which was a most respectable rank, he was a mere auxiliary and not one of the legionaries. In these circumstances, it was Graecus's dread that he would unwittingly wander into a situation which would cause him to be reprimanded and be shamed in front of his men.

This would always have been dreadful but was worse now that they had Solitarius in their century. He had been appointed directly by their cohort commander, Gnaeus Claudius Verus, whom Graecus for good reasons cordially disliked, and the new horn-blower could be relied upon to report anything of interest to him.

Given this feeling of apprehension, the interior of the building gave him no comfort for there was a long dark corridor ahead of them with smaller, darker corridors going off on either side and not a man in sight. Graecus took a deep breath and started down the corridor with Germanicus at his side, their hobnailed boots making such a clatter on the tiles that Graecus thought the noise would summon at least someone. Clatter, clatter, clatter they went and then they had reached the end of the corridor, and his eyes having adjusted to the gloom, Graecus could see, sitting in a niche in the wall opposite the building's entrance, was a large bust of the Emperor Claudius, the real conqueror of Britannia. It was done in black marble and was, insofar as a quick glance could discern, a magnificent piece of sculpture but Graecus shuddered and quickly turned to Germanicus and said, 'My son, I think it would be better if Magnus accompanied me, so please go back to our brothers and wait with them and send Magnus to me.'

'But why father?'

'Because I have changed my mind and because I am order-ing you to go back to our brothers.'

'I do not understand father, but I will obey.'

With a puzzled look on his face, Germanicus turned on his heel and marched smartly down the corridor.

Within a few moments, the tall broad-shouldered figure of Magnus appeared, looking as puzzled as Germanicus but Graecus just clapped him on the shoulder and said, 'On reflec-tion, I felt it more appropriate that you should be with me when we meet these people for the first time. Let us see if we can find someone down this corridor to the left here.'

Magnus smiled his quiet smile and followed his leader down the corridor.

Graecus walked slowly ahead but there was no indication as to what lay behind the various doors so he was forced to stop and think what to do next. He knew no-one in this place and he did not wish to burst in to someone's quarters unannounced, especially if that someone were an ill-tempered superior officer in the legions.

Graecus was pondering this when he heard the sound of a raised voice somewhere in the distance. He stopped thinking and started listening. There it was again. It seemed to be coming from a room on the left at the far end of the corridor so he motioned to Magnus to follow him and crept down the corridor and put his ear to the door.

Then suddenly throwing caution to the winds, without knocking, he threw the door open... and saw the back of a Centurion, a Centurion with very skinny legs. He was leaning over the desk of a naval officer and bellowing at him, 'I'm not bothered who you are, you aren't being helpful to me. In the name of all the gods, will you stop going on about your 'broth-er.' I don't care what's happened to 'your brother.' What I want to know is what's happened to my colleague and his century.'

'We are all safe, and ready to join with you in defeating Rome's enemies,' said Graecus and was delighted by the joy on the man's face as he swiftly turned and recognised him.

15

Seeing Acerbus's honest toothy grin again was a great relief for Graecus and the two Centurions enthusiastically embraced before turning back towards the desk and the man of about 40 sitting behind it. He was very ugly – his square bald head seemed to be joined straight onto his sloping shoulders without any intervening neck and his eyes bulged glassily from the corners of his head, reminding Graecus strongly of a frog sitting on a lily leaf, and when he spoke Graecus almost laughed, for his voice croaked huskily. 'And who might you be, young man?'

Insofar as he knew, Graecus was about thirty five so being addressed as 'young man' was either patronising or an insult to his virility so he pulled himself up to his full height, which he knew was taller than most Romans,' and said, 'I am the other Centurion of the Auxiliaries from Lower Germania who have come to reinforce Suetonius Paulinus. We arrived this morning from Gesoriacum in the Nauplius.'

'Ah, so you sailed with my brother?'

Before Graecus could answer this, Acerbus said, 'In the name of all the gods will you stop wittering about 'your brother'? I'm not bothered what happened to that mad, vicious, bastard. There are more important matters at the moment.'

Graecus knew that, in the normal course of things, Acerbus had a very sharp eye but the man in front of them was such a haggard version of Jejunus that Acerbus could be forgiven for not seeing any resemblance.

The Frog looked angry and started to splutter, 'I'll thank you to keep a civil tongue in your head when you mention my brother…' but Acerbus had had enough, and turning, leaned over the desk to grasp the Frog by his shoulders, saying,

'If you mention that once more, I'll…' while Graecus decided that he must intervene and pulled Acerbus away from the Frog by the back of his armoured torso.

Graecus turned Acerbus round and firmly said to him, 'May I speak to you outside, my friend?'

Acerbus saw that Graecus was serious and allowed his colleague to lead him from the room then closed the door behind him. Magnus was still standing in the corridor and Graecus motioned to him to keep quiet before whispering to Acerbus, 'The harbourmaster is Jejunus's brother.'

'Well, I know they're both in the navy, but…'

'No, no, I mean that he's his brother in the sense that they actually have the same mother and father.'

'Oh. So he is his brother?'

'Yes. Isn't that what I've just said? And you've just called him a bastard – and a mad vicious one at that.'

'Well, he is a bastard, you know that as well as I do.'

'Yes, that's true but it's obvious that they are close as brothers and Xanthippus told me that, when they're together, they vie with each other to see who can be the more depraved.'

'Well, having seen Jejunus take the whip to that young man's back on the boat before we left Gesoriacum, I would have thought that he'd easily have come first in that game but this brother of his looks so seedy that it could be a close run thing. Did the young man survive by the way?'

'Yes, he did, his name is Gideon and it was a miracle. I will tell you all about it when we have the time but what we need to do now is find out where we're billeted and who will give us our orders and the only person we can find here for the moment is Jejunus's brother so we need to be civil to him.'

'I will admit that you are correct but it rankles with me to be all sweetness and light with these lunatic navy men.'

'In that case, you do not need to say a word. I shall speak for both of us.'

'All right.'

Graecus pushed open the door to reveal the Frog excavating his filthy fingernails with the point of a knife, and all three soldiers entered the room. The Frog stared at Graecus in a challenging manner while he put on his best smile, showing his excellent teeth, before saying, 'My colleague here meant no harm. He was concerned that my men and I had perished in the crossing. We landed safely several miles north of here and Nauplius turned back for Gaul once we had disembarked. Your brother is in good health and is probably half way back to Gesoriacum by now.'

'Well, that was a pretty speech after listening to the other one's sour words but what am I going to do with the women I've laid on for tonight? I paid good money for them and even I can't service them all on my own.'

'Well, that is a refreshing admission from a navy man. We thought that you were all capable of satisfying any number of women – in your dreams, at least,' said Acerbus.

'I can guarantee you one thing, you skinny upstart, and that is I won't be seeing *you* in my dreams.'

This was not turning out as Graecus had hoped and he wondered how he could engage with the Frog. He would need to try something different, so he said, 'My friend, I have just the thing for you. My colleague here,' indicating Magnus, 'has a most effective preparation for those times when a man wants to be at his most active. It is absolutely guaranteed to ensure that you will not leave any of the ladies unsatisfied.'

The Frog now looked very interested and eagerly leaned forward to hear more but Graecus said, 'So, if you will just tell us where we need to go to meet our new officers and get our new orders?'

'Oh, all right then. You need to go to the Army barracks which is about half a mile from here, turn right at the statue of Nero at the exit here. The duty officer at the barracks will put you in touch with whoever it is you need to meet.'

'Thank you. Now, Magnus, please give our colleague enough of the magic mushroom preparation to help him with his problem.'

Magnus began fishing around in his waist-pouch looking for the dried mushrooms which he had brought all the way from the forests of Lower Germania where their amazing analgesic and hallucinatory properties had come in very useful during the century's stay there and where their aphrodisiac side-effect had, some years back, rendered Felix senseless to all around him for three days after he had merely inhaled their vapour from his cooking pot.

Bearing this in mind, Magnus handed to the Frog the smallest speck of the dried fungus and said, 'This will produce the effect you want but you must be very careful with it – it is extremely strong so you need to put this piece of fungus in a beaker with some hot water for a few minutes then take out the fungus and dilute the water with another two parts of cold water and then sip it slowly during the evening's entertainment. On no account must you eat the fungus or drink the water undiluted. Do you understand?'

'Yes, yes, yes, I understand but I expect you are being over cautious – I have the constitution of an ox and the appetites of a bull. Just leave me another dose of the mushroom in case I need it another time when we get a new delivery of fresh female slaves.'

'I will gladly give you another dose but you must remember to be very careful, this is a powerful drug.'

Having been given what he wanted, the Frog now looked bored and waved his hand dismissively at the soldiers but there was one matter which was nibbling at Graecus's brain, and as he turned to leave the Frog's room, he said, 'Tell me, my friend, where is everyone today? This building seems to be deserted. Why is there no one here other than you?'

'Oh, had you not heard? I suppose it happened while you were making your way here over Ocean. Boudicca and her troops have sacked Londinium. There is hardly a building left standing nor a citizen left alive. They have laid waste to the place and everyone here is running around trying to decide what to do.'

CHAPTER TWO

Graecus and Acerbus exchanged a horrified glance before looking back at the Frog who seemed unperturbed by this appalling news. Indeed, the Frog was now staring with awe at the speck of dried mushroom in the palm of his hand and was clearly more interested in his forthcoming night of debauchery than this latest affront to Rome's reputation as an invincible military power. To the soldiers, it was almost inconceivable that not one, not two, but three of Rome's major settlements in this island had been destroyed by an ill-disciplined rabble, but even worse, the rabble was led by a woman. They could not understand the Frog's calm demeanour and they all stared at him in disbelief before Graecus found his voice again and said, 'This is not the best place for us now, we need to go to the army barracks as soon as possible and find out what is happening in the light of this new development.'

'Agreed' said both Acerbus and Magnus and they all turned and strode from the room simultaneously without saying farewell to the Frog.

As they marched back to the front of the building Graecus said, 'Well, we have not yet had official confirmation that what he said was correct but I see no harm in telling our men now that we have heard informally that Londinium has been sacked. What is your view?' to Acerbus.

'I think you are correct. They may as well begin to get themselves accustomed to the idea that this Boudicca woman is no pushover and that defeating her will be a real challenge.'

'Those are my thoughts also.'

They had now reached the steps in front of the building and looked out at their men (who had managed to rendezvous while their officers were looking for each other in the building) ranged in front of them, their expectant faces all upturned in their direction. Graecus spoke first. 'Men, we have had some disturbing news just now. For the moment it is unofficial but we have no real doubt of its truth. The news is that Boudicca and her tribesmen have sacked Londinium, razing it to the ground and massacring its citizens.'

Here he paused and Acerbus said, 'Make no mistake, we have underestimated these people. We have relied on the fact that they have been lulled into servitude by Roman baths, Roman wine and Roman ways but they have had three victories and they are made bold by their successes. It is now our job to show them they are wrong to think that they can drive Rome from this island.'

At this, all the men raised their arms in the air and shouted 'Aye. Aye' and cheered their leaders.

Graecus mounted Perdix and, sitting next to Acerbus on his horse, he ordered his men to leave the naval dockyard marching side by side with Acerbus's men.

The two Centurions rode in silence for a while and Graecus had the opportunity to give thanks to the gods for the fact that he had been reunited with his colleague and mentor and to contemplate that, much as this latest news was disquieting, it was nothing compared with how he would have felt had he learned that Acerbus had been lost crossing Ocean.

The columns of men passed through a rough town to its outskirts and there was the military camp. This was a welcome sight to both Graecus and Acerbus and, it could be guaranteed, every man behind them after their recent experiences with crossing Ocean and their unpleasant encounters with navy personnel. The organisation of the Roman army was the same throughout the Empire and this meant that every man would recognise the layout of this camp and its routine so that he could immediately feel at home and immediately make himself useful.

Graecus and Acerbus halted in front of the gatehouse and Acerbus shouted 'Hail' to whoever was on duty.

A ruddy-faced young man, a legionary, came out, saluted, and looked them up and down and said, 'Good afternoon, gentlemen. Who are you and how may I help you?'

Acerbus said, 'I am Marcus Caelius Caldus, Centurion of the Auxiliaries from Lower Germania and my colleague here and I and our men have been sent to reinforce Suetonius Paulinus and his men in their fight against Boudicca.'

'Well, gentlemen, you are very welcome, I'm sure, and you have arrived at just the right time, she's been on the rampage again.'

Feeling that the situation was urgent and that they needed to find a superior officer as soon as possible, Graecus did not wish to engage in conversation with the young man any more than was necessary so he said, 'Yes, we heard. She's destroyed Londinium.'

'Oh, it's worse than that. She didn't stop at Londinium, she laid waste to several outlying estates as well, you know, estates belonging to Roman sympathisers, so the message's clear to all the tribes – fight with me against the Romans or be annihilated. Not much of a choice is it? Seems as if she's unstoppable, if you ask me.'

Graecus was shocked by the young man's incautious words and concerned that they could undermine his men's confidence, so his voice was sharp when he replied, 'I am not aware that we did ask you and I'll thank you to keep your defeatist opinions to yourself, especially in front of me and my men. Now, be so good as to tell us where we will find the duty officer.'

The young man stood to attention and, dropping his earlier conspiratorial manner, spoke straight ahead saying, 'He's in the bunkhouse at the moment sir, we've got an attack of stomach trouble in the camp and the infirmary's full so some of the sick are being treated in the old bunkhouse.'

'What is the officer's name?'

'Miseryguts, sir. Oh! I'm sorry, sir, that's his nickname. His proper name is Afranius, sir.'

'Thank you, soldier, now let us through the gate and mind your language in future – Boudicca hasn't reconquered Britannia yet and if we have anything to do with it, nor will she.'

'Yessir!' said the young soldier, standing aside to let the columns of auxiliaries into the camp.

Graecus had been wondering why this very young man seemed to be on duty unsupervised by anyone more experienced and when they entered the camp he immediately knew that all was not as it should be. There was none of the hustle and bustle of a busy camp – true there were a few men going about their business but there was a most unwholesome and dejected air about the place which he found unsettling.

Graecus turned in his saddle and looked at Acerbus who returned his gaze and said, 'Something's really wrong here. I don't like the look of this place.'

'Nor do I. But we must go and find the duty officer.'

They dismounted, told their men to stand easy then made their way to a building which looked as if it would be the old bunkhouse as, alone among the white painted, tiled roofed edifices, it remained, in effect, a log-cabin with a thatched roof.

Graecus and Acerbus approached the building and knocked at the door before entering.

The stench was overpowering.

There were sick men lying everywhere in a tangle of arms and legs, all of them sweating and groaning and some of them, presumably in the later stages of whatever it was which afflicted them, calling out in delirium.

Graecus, ever a stickler for hygiene and cleanliness, took off his neckerchief and held it to his nose. It smelt of his own sweat but that was infinitely preferable to the fetid stink of the room. Nearby, a legionary who looked to be in his late thirties, and who would otherwise be an imposing hulk of a man, leant from his bunk to be sick in a bucket. Then looking up, he saw the two Centurions and said, 'What are you staring at? Never seen a man vomit before?'

It was a gross infringement of army discipline for a soldier to speak to officers in this way but neither Graecus nor Acerbus knew quite what to do in this situation as the man might well be hallucinating and they were busy looking at each other for inspiration when a voice at Graecus's elbow said, 'Thank Jupiter, you must be the reinforcements. Hail brothers, I am mightily glad to see you.'

Graecus looked down and saw a very short man, a legionary

and a Centurion like himself. So this must be Miseryguts.

'Hail, brother. We are glad to have arrived safely at your camp but we have just learned of Boudicca's latest outrage and it is obvious that many men here are very sick. What ails your men?'

'I do not know. This sickness came with all the vigour of the Furies behind it four days ago. We've lost upwards of forty men so far and it shows no sign of abatement. Some of the first to die were our physician and our medical orderlies so I am at a loss to know what to do.'

'You say that *you* are at a loss to know what to do? Surely you are not the most senior officer here? Where is your Camp Commander? Where is the Senior Centurion?' Graecus fired these questions at Miseryguts from behind the safety of his neckerchief.

'Our Commander died last night and the Senior Centurion is very sick – he's in isolation in the infirmary. The legate left camp a week ago with three centuries and some cavalry to join up as reinforcements with Suetonius Paulinus but we've heard nothing from him in that time – for all I know, they could have perished by now in an ambush laid on by Boudicca or one of the tribes friendly to her cause.'

'It is a very black picture you paint,' said Acerbus.

'Well, it was bad enough before, what with the attacks on Camoludunum and Verulamium but then there was the attack on Londinium, and now this terrible sickness. Morale here is very low and the men feel they're sitting targets for attack.' Here, Miseryguts wearily wiped his hand across his eyes before con- tinuing, 'The problem is that Boudicca has been so successful that even the tribes in this part of the country, which have been faithful to Rome so far, are beginning to waiver in their loyalty – they see that it is possible that Rome could be expelled and they could be relieved of the burdens of taxation and tribute – at this moment, even those tribes who have been staunch allies of Rome, can no longer be counted on.'

'My friend,' said Graecus, still from behind his neckerchief, 'that is an interesting subject and I would like to discuss it with you further, but for the moment there are urgent matters. I will send our medical man to help you and my men will set about cleaning up the camp as best they can. We shall need to be here for a short while to re-provision before we set out for our rendezvous with Suetonius Paulinus and we shall do our best to help you while we are here.'

Graecus gratefully turned to leave the bunkhouse accompanied by Acerbus. When they were outside they both stood for a few moments taking in gulps of fresh air in the hope of driving the stink from their nostrils.

'Ye gods,' said Acerbus, 'what a mess we are in here in this barbaric land! We have too few soldiers, too many enemies and a plague of sickness to contend with. Sometimes I almost wish I were back on my aunt's farm supervising the olive harvest. But then I would be bored to death, so I suppose the gods have their little joke with me by ensuring that I am never bored in the army.'

'Well, that's a blessing then,' said Graecus, and they both laughed at the ironies of life then walked back to their men.

'There is grave sickness in this camp,' said Graecus to the men, 'and we must ensure that it does not spread to our ranks. We will not, therefore, be billeted in the camp buildings but will pitch our tents just within the perimeter fence and will keep our drinking water and our ablutions separate. Now, I need Magnus to come with me, and you, Impedimentus, I want you and Felix to organise our camp.'

Impedimentus, a small man in his late thirties, broke from the ranks and stepped forward. Unusually for an auxiliary, Impedimentus was a Roman, something of which he was very proud and sometimes, to their great annoyance, used as a weapon against those of his comrades whose ancestry was less certain. It was Impedimentus's job to look after the century's equipment and Graecus knew that he could rely on him utterly in this respect.

Felix, of course, would ensure that the men were properly fed and that their food would be kept away from the contaminating influence of the sick men.

Magnus and Graecus walked swiftly back to the bunkhouse and opened the door. Magnus reeled as had Graecus and Acerbus

25

but he stepped inside and smiled warmly at Miseryguts.

'Tell me, what is the problem here? What are the men's symptoms?'

'It starts with stomach pains and sickness but then they suffer from terrible sweats and delirium. And, of course, there is the awful diarrhoea.'

'How long ago did this begin?'

'The first men fell ill four days ago and then many more fell ill and then the first deaths occurred two days ago.'

'Is there blood in the faeces?'

'Yes, there is. How did you know?'

'Because I have seen this sickness before. In Pompeii, actually. The local physicians called it the bloody flux.'

'What is the cure?'

'There is no known cure, but it is important to give the patient as much liquid as possible to replace the fluids being lost.'

'It is difficult for us to do that here at the moment as there are so few men untouched by the sickness.'

'We shall do our best to help you, but firstly, tell me – where will we find lavender or rosemary or myrtle bushes nearby?'

'Well, the Camp Commander's wife has lavender and rosemary bushes in her kitchen garden. Why do you ask?'

'Because we need to bring some of the branches in here and burn them to clear the air, then the men can breathe more easily at least. I will ask one of my colleagues to cut the branches.'

'Please ask him to do it quietly as the Commander's wife also has the sickness and is in her room. The Commander died last night but she is so delirious that I doubt she understood when I told her of his death.'

'I will ensure that he does it silently. Now, tell me where shall we find garlic plants?'

'There is wild garlic in the fields surrounding the camp.'

'Good. I will have some brought to you.'

'Why?'

'Well, I assume that you do not wish to catch this dreadful sickness.'

'Of course I do not wish to catch it.'

'Then you must take a large piece of raw garlic and rub it on the soles of your feet three times per day to ward off the sickness.'

'Does that work?'

'I have used it myself these many years to ward off all kinds of contagion and I have never yet known it to fail – it is one of the most enduring gifts from the gods, so we need as much of it as can be found, and I will be able to use it myself and give some to the rest of the men'

'I will send someone immediately.'

Miseryguts left the bunkhouse and Magnus began looking at the sick men there. Some were in the early stages of the illness and, with proper care, might recover, but some of them were too far gone with the sickness and would most likely die, even if they had been big strong men before it struck. It occurred to Magnus that this would not be the death they would have chosen for themselves – miles away from their homeland and as lacking in glory as it was possible to be. He shook his head and hoped that his own death, whenever it came, would be more glorious than squeezing his life-blood into a shit filled slop-bucket.

Miseryguts returned with the garlic and, taking some from him, Magnus rubbed it on his feet demonstrating the method to the still sceptical Centurion but the threat of catching the illness was obviously strong for Miseryguts removed his Centurion's shoes and followed suit.

Magnus now picked up the rest of the garlic and, leaving the bunkhouse going in search of his comrades, he passed by the camp's kitchens. Having half an idea in his head seeing the place now deserted, he wandered in. All appeared to be in order. There were the usual large pots and cauldrons, the knives, the chopping boards, the plates, the skillets, the containers for fire, etc. etc. So much for his half of an idea – there was nothing to indicate that he might have been correct.

He turned to go and was walking out of the building when, out of the corner of his eye, he saw a pile of something next to what appeared to be a heap of rotting turnip peel. He walked over to the mounds of rubbish and found what he sought – a huge pile of empty oyster shells.

'Ah ha!' he said to himself, and went to find Felix.

The men from his century were at the edge of the camp busy putting up tents and digging latrines. Felix was standing at a makeshift chopping board, quickly and expertly dicing root vegetables for a stew.

'Brother, I have a few questions for you.'

'If you want to know if there's anything other than vegetable stew for supper, the answer's the same as I've told everybody else and it's no.'

'That wasn't what I was going to ask you.'

'That's all right then because I'm fed up with people whinging about their bellies.'

'Well, what I want to know is connected with that in a round-about way… what I wanted to ask you is what, if anything, you know about the bloody flux? I mean, have you heard of it and where?'

Felix stopped chopping and began stroking his chin. Magnus, who had known Felix for many years, knew that this was a hopeful sign as it meant that Felix was searching in his memory for some little useful snippet of information, so he stood quietly while Felix stroked and then scratched his chin and then stroked it again.

'Hmm!' said Felix. 'Is that what the poor blighters here have got?'

'Yes. I think it is.'

'Been eating shellfish have they?'

'Felix! You are a marvel! There is a huge pile of oyster shells behind the kitchen. How did you know?'

'Because I heard it from an old cook in Brundisium. Do you remember, we were stationed there for that summer about twelve years ago… I was a slim young man then, and as handsome as they come….'

'What did he tell you?'

'He said that the fashion for serving shellfish raw was a big mistake and he reckoned that it gave people the bloody flux.'

'How interesting! I have had similar thoughts myself. Well,

thank Jupiter that we know better in our century and I know that
we shall never be given anything unwholesome by our trusted Felix.'

'The others are complaining that our diet's been so bland
since we came to this wretched island.'

'Well tell them that bland is better than the bloody flux.'

'I will.'

Magnus now went in search of Graecus and found him under
the extended flap of their leather tent which was serving as an
awning, seated at a campaign desk on a folding stool poring over
pieces of parchment. Next to him sat a slender young man. The
parchment was covered in close writing and it looked as if
Graecus and the younger man were trying to decipher it.

At Magnus's approach, Graecus looked up and smiled – rubbing his eyes to adjust their focus. He then turned to the young
man and said, 'That will be all for now, Incitatus. My eyes are
tired with the strain of looking at this small script. Let us try to
make sense of it tomorrow – the light now is not good enough.'

'Yes, Domine,' said the young man and walked away with a
light springy step, his feet hardly touching the ground. Graecus,
with a satisfied smile on his face, watched him walk in the direction of the men doing weapon training.

'Yes,' said Magnus, 'he is really one of us now, isn't he?'

Magnus was referring to Incitatus's unpromising start in the
Army; he had been rescued from certain death in a 'gladiatorial'
contest at a mediocre circus in Germania when Graecus had been
so disgusted by the relative skills of the combatants – a huge,
muscular beast of a man from Britannia and the slight boy who
had pissed himself through fear – that Graecus had taken on the
bully himself and quickly brought him to his knees before taking
the boy away from the baying crowd. Graecus had then had to
endure the comments of the men about 'waifs and strays' before
the miraculous discovery that Incitatus was an amazing runner
who could keep going all day over hills and valleys and at a great
speed. This talent had been honed in the hills of Sparta where
Incitatus had grown up and it was a source of amusement to
some of the men that the skinny boy came from the place which

29

was a by-word for valour. But Incitatus was, to Graecus's delight, also very learned and had studied Law with a famous jurist in Mediolanum. Graecus valued learning and it was a comfort to him to have someone so cultured and well-read in his century.

But now, after five or six years with the Army, not only had Incitatus more than earned his keep as a messenger and scribe, he had grown into a fit and sinewy man who, albeit not one of the best swordsmen in the century, could hold his own in most types of combat, and it was at this transformation that Graecus was now smiling – it made his heart feel good that he had saved a frightened boy from an ignominious death and had given the brave man a worthwhile life

'What is it you wished to tell me?'

'That the men in the main camp got the bloody flux from eating raw oysters. There is a pile of shells behind the kitchen and Felix confirmed to me that it is a known phenomenon that raw shellfish can bring on the illness.'

'I never liked raw shellfish anyway.'

'In that case, your body is wiser than the fools who have made it fashionable. Now, if it is not secret, please tell me what was the document you were studying with Incitatus.'

'It is not secret, quite the reverse. It is our copy of our General Standing Orders. Now that we know that the camp is in disarray without a senior officer present, we have a problem with our orders as Acerbus and I were expecting to receive new orders from someone here but there is no one to give them to us.'

'I see. Can we not just go and find Suetonius Paulinus?'

'Yes, I think it will come to that, but I will be happier if I can find some reference in the orders to justify that course of action.'

'Well, I'm sure that Incitatus's training is very useful in finding the meaning of all those dry regulations.'

'Indeed it is, but then there is the other problem of actually finding Suetonius without running into Boudicca and her hordes on the way.'

'We must trust in the gods to give guidance to our enterprise.'

'Yes, we must…'

At this moment, whatever Graecus was about to say was drowned out by a terrible cry of pain and rage coming from Pneumaticus, who was crossing in front of Graecus's tent flap with a large plank in his hand when he tripped over a hammer someone had left in his path and fell flat on his face, landing heavily on the plank.

'Ouch!' said Magnus in sympathy and ran over to his prostrate colleague. And then kneeling on the ground next to him, said, 'Turn over carefully so that I may see what damage you have done to your face.'

Pneumaticus turned over very slowly, and with such effort that it was painful to watch him. Now that he was lying on his side on the ground, both Magnus and Graecus could see that he had bruised his right eye and cut his lip very badly. The lip was bleeding and Magnus did not know whether this was from the cut or whether Pneumaticus had lost any teeth so he said, 'Open your mouth, I need to make sure that your throat is clear.'

The injured man slowly did as he was asked and Magnus looked in his open mouth and put his finger in to check Pneumaticus's teeth.

'Hmm,' he said, 'there is no serious injury, but these two front teeth are quite loose now. You will need to be careful with them and hope that they will settle back into the gums. But they may not. You may need to lose them.'

Pneumaticus groaned at this and said something which sounded like, 'But what about my luck with the ladies?' which would have been typical of him as he was very popular with ladies of a certain kind. But neither Magnus nor Graecus could be sure what he had said as his mouth was so swollen that his speech was unintelligible.

Magnus called to the two men who were passing to help him and Graecus get Pneumaticus to their tent where they laid him on his bed and Magnus gave him a tiny amount of the diluted magic mushroom to ensure that the pain of his fall would not be felt.

Outside the tent, Graecus said, 'Please make sure that the other men know that Pneumaticus's fall was a pure accident caused by some idiot leaving a hammer in the way and that his injuries are not to be regarded as an omen.'

'Yes, Domine.'

Graecus now went back to his desk and tried to concentrate on the major problems and the decisions which must be made.

He knew that there was no real alternative to their having to leave Dubris without any fresh orders and that, in the circumstances, they would just have to do their best to find Suetonius and his legions. Granted, they would glean intelligence from forts and other garrisons on the way and there were plenty of good Roman roads and not-so-good drovers' roads to guide them, but the fact of the matter was that they were only two centuries of light infantry who would need to make their way across hundreds of miles of unfamiliar territory surrounded by people who could, by now, be their sworn enemies.

This did not cause Graecus the sort of fear which may be imagined. Graecus was not afraid of dying – that was something he had lived with every day of his life for the last twenty years – no, what really frightened him was that Germanicus would be killed, he would be left alone and then the light would go from his life and he would cease to want to live.

Graecus considered this for a few minutes and thought of all the joy his son had brought him and all the many ways in which he delighted him. These thoughts cheered him and he made himself think of what life could be like when he had retired from the army with his money and his plot of land and how proud he would be if Germanicus became a high-ranking officer.

But then he realised that there was another concern bubbling under the surface of his mind – the worry that they would be ambushed and massacred before they even reached Suetonius, and how the honour of his century would be stained and how his name would be spoken with contempt rather than with pride.

This was equally troubling.

Graecus had made himself miserable with these thoughts so it was time to go and find Acerbus who, now it was drawing towards sunset, would be thinking about his belly and how to fill it.

True to form, he found Acerbus hanging over Felix's pot of stew, sniffing the fragrant air above it, saying, 'I think I detect some bay leaves, and is there not some rosemary in there?'

'Yes, there is, but you're not getting any of it till it's ready and that won't be for another half hour.'

Acerbus knew that although it had been delivered in a jocular tone, Felix meant what he said so he turned gratefully to Graecus, looking for a distraction until dinnertime.

'My friend! What ails you? You look so sad and so thoughtful. Come, let us walk a little.'

'Well, I am a little sad but I am giving much thought to our predicament.'

'Which particular aspect of our predicament is causing you most concern?'

'The fact that we may be ambushed by insurgents before we meet up with Suetonius and then no one will know what happened to us and we shall have died without glory.'

'Ah, so you wish to die with glory? You are thinking of honours for your century.'

'I am not *planning* on dying, I do not seek death, but if it is the gods' will, I would prefer that it were an honourable death.'

'So would we all, my boy, so would we all. But it is not ours to choose. Just think of those honourable soldiers, the legionaries who retired to Camoludunum after their years in the Army. Just think of how they had earned a peaceful retirement, and then what happened? The way that they would look at it is that some uppity British queen took it amiss that Nero questioned her husband's will and so she attacked the town killing everybody and burning it to the ground. Where is the honour in that?'

'Yes, I see your point, but you cannot say that I am wrong in wanting not to spill my blood in vain.'

'No, my dear boy, I cannot say that you are wrong, but you must accept that if your blood is spilled in vain it will not be the first time that has happened, nor will it be the last.'

'You are correct as always, my wise friend.'

'Good. Now let us have our supper and make merry while we

33

are here in the safety of Dubris, for I fear that we must leave tomorrow.'

'Yes, we must, and we must make all haste to find Suetonius.'

'I have had some thoughts about that. I found some good maps in the Commander's room. They will help us. You and I had better have a good look at them in the morning and get some advice from Afranius – presumably he knows the present state of this country better than we do.'

'I suppose he must. But then, we have brought local knowledge with us – we have Britons in our centuries. We may need to ask them for assistance with our journey.'

'Yes, we may need to do that.'

The two Centurions then returned to their colleagues and sat at one of several trestle tables which were now covered in bowls and spoons and bread and pots full of hot stew.

Graecus and Acerbus sat together opposite Germanicus, whose bright hair shone in the light of the burning rushes placed around the edge of the dining area. Germanicus was spooning stew very quickly into his mouth as if he were very hungry, but next to him was Pneumaticus who was using the back of his spoon to crush pieces of carrot, leek and turnip into the hot liquid in an attempt to puree his food so that he could eat it with least discomfort.

There was the usual chatter about the army, there were the usual complaints about the uselessness of their equipment and the awfulness of the place where they were stationed, but underlying all of the banter was the knowledge that in the morning they would be marching across enemy territory with no certainty of where they would meet their colleagues.

Acerbus sensed this feeling among the men and called for more wine. Then, when they were feeling mellow, he said, 'Graecus, sing one of your favourite songs for us,' and Graecus, ever happy to oblige, treated them to a wonderful refrain about a mermaid who fell in love with a sailor and wanted to be a beautiful young woman but the spirit of the bay in which she swam was jealous and although it granted her wish to be human, it condemned her to a life as an ugly old crone.

This song, plaintive though it was, sparked some less worthy thoughts among the men, and soon they were singing the bawdiest songs they knew and this put them all in a better, braver frame of mind so that they went to bed feeling more confident about the morning and the part they were about to play in the history of the Roman Empire.

CHAPTER THREE

Graecus woke early with a thick head. It was not merely that he had had too much wine; it was also that he had been disturbed in his slumbers with Pneumaticus's dreadful snoring in the contubernium tent which they shared. It was true that this was an old problem, indeed, Pneumaticus's colleagues had, some years before, threatened murder if the problem had not been resolved but Incitatus, clever, resourceful Incitatus, had come up with the solution – a wooden bobbin on a leather string which Pneumaticus wore round his neck with the bobbin at the back so that, if he lay on his back, the bobbin would wake him up before he snored. This had been so successful that Graecus could now hardly remember the last time Pneumaticus had snored, but this last night, presumably because of the nasty injury he had received, the old soldier had decided not to wear the bobbin, and because he did not wish to trouble him more than necessary, Graecus had not disturbed Pneumaticus's sleep to order him to don the device.

Now, in the stark light of the new day, Graecus was not feeling so charitable and made a mental note that he would, this night, tell Pneumaticus to wear the bobbin so that they could all get some sleep.

That thought out of the way, Graecus turned his mind to the pressing issues of the day: firstly there was the matter of the regulations and how could their chosen course of action be made to fit into the rules? And then there was the problem of the route they would take to find Paulinus. He thought a little more and decided that as far as the rules were concerned, he would give the matter over to Incitatus who could be relied on to find some interpretation, however strained, which would cloak their actions with legitimacy. And then, as far as the route march was concerned, he and Acerbus would need to look at the maps and discuss with Miseryguts where they could expect to find Suetonius and where they could safely stop for rest and re-provisioning.

Swinging his legs from his truckle bed, Graecus felt better that he now had a plan and quickly performed his morning toilette of splashing his face and body with cold water before brushing at his teeth with a twig covered in the dentifrice which Magnus made for the century. Graecus was rather proud of his teeth and looked after them as best he could in the hope that his men would do the same – a soldier with toothache cannot truly have his mind on the job in hand.

Graecus then tied a cloth around his middle and under his crotch to protect his manhood and threw his tunic over his head before donning the figured leather breastplate and sectioned leather girdle which would protect him from the attentions of opportunistic arrows while he was seated on his horse. Next, having put on his boots, he strapped on his greaves, the thick leather coverings which protected his shins and called for Germanicus to help him put on the leather cuffs which strengthened his wrists – it was impossible to put these on by oneself, and over the years, Graecus had taught Germanicus how to lace them up with the minimum of fuss.

Germanicus bowed his head over his father's wrist, concentrating on the fiddly task of putting the leather laces into the alternate holes in the opposing edges of the cuff. He was smiling as he did this and Graecus asked, 'What is it that you find amusing this morning my son?'

'Oh, it isn't that I find anything particularly amusing father, it's just that I am excited because it seems to me that you and the other men in the century have taught me so much over the past years and now I may be able to put in into practice. I have worked hard at my weapon training father and I know that I am fit and strong and I am looking forward to meeting our enemies so that I may do my best for Rome... I want you to be proud of me father.'

'Germanicus, I am as proud of you now, at this moment, as I could be if you had won a thousand honours in battle. You make me proud of you every day simply by your goodness and your thoughts for everyone in our century.'

'I know that, father, and I learned from you that we only survive in this army life by considering the man next to us and you
have taught me the value of comradeship and unity but I also
want glory.'

'My boy, I cannot tell you that that is a vain hope: I would
imagine that there is not one soldier in our century, nor in
Acerbus's, who would sensibly wish anything other than glory,
nor do I wish to curb your enthusiasm. But I would caution you
to bear in mind that fighting, no matter how illustrious the army,
is not always glorious – there are times when it is more searing
than we might wish, and please consider this carefully, there are
times when it is downright cruel and we are asked, ordered, to do
things which we do not wish to do.'

'I do know that father. I know that you have been ordered to do
things you did not wish to do but is it not all for the glory of Rome?'

'We fight for the Pax Romana which civilises barbarians and
brings them the inestimable advantages of being part of the
greatest empire the world has ever known but I wish you to bear
in mind that glory is not always present in the minds of those
who lead us – some of them are moved by greed and selfishness.
Now, my son that is enough philosophy for this morning, please
go and see to it that Perdix has been fed and watered and make
sure that you have a good breakfast – we shall need to make
swift progress today.'

Acerbus appeared in the opening of Graecus's tent. His voice
was brisk and business-like when he said, 'I am ready and my
men are just finishing their breakfast. Shall we go and speak to
Afranius now?'

'Yes, that is a good idea,' said Graecus and, snatching a large
piece of bread and bacon from Felix's hand as he passed, and
shouting to Incitatus that he was looking to him for a favourable
interpretation of the Army regulations, he quickly followed
Acerbus, cramming the food in his mouth as they went.

Miseryguts was in his office speaking to the young man they
had met when they arrived. As the auxiliary Centurions entered,
he said to the young soldier, 'How many died in the night?'

'Nine, sir, mostly those of whom we had little hope but the Commander's wife whom we had thought would recover was reunited with her husband in the early hours of the morning.'

'This sickness is very powerful. I cannot understand what it is we can have done to cause the gods to punish us in this dreadful way.'

'It is not the gods who have chosen to punish you. It was your habit of eating raw oysters which gave you the bloody flux,' said Graecus and now taking a step forward to emphasise his point, he said, 'Our medical man and our cook confirmed that raw shellfish can be fatal in this way and you would be wise to keep that in mind in the future. You cannot be too careful with shellfish.'

'I had not thought that oysters could be so poisonous,' said Miseryguts, looking thoughtful.

'When they are uncooked they can be fatal,' said Graecus. 'But we must be on our way today. We hope that we have been useful to you in your plight while we have been here, brother, but we must now move on and we require your help in making our way to find Suetonius and the legions. We have these maps and it seems that the best course would be to take these ridge way roads to the Icknield Way and then march north until we find them.'

'Yes, that is probably the best route open to you,' said Miseryguts. 'And it has the advantage of there being various forts and fortlets along the way where you will find better protection for your men at night than camping in the open. The main problem though is that we have no real idea where Suetonius and his men are at the moment. I mean, we know he must be marching south east from Mona but we do not know which route he is taking – we can only guess. You may need to march further eastwards to the Fosse Way to meet up with them, I just do not know, but you will probably find better information along the way. We would, naturally, have had more information if the semaphore signalling system was still working but Boudicca was wise enough to destroy enough of the wayside stations to put paid to that.'

'This is a difficult time for us all when we can no longer rely on much which we took for granted', said Acerbus, 'And we would have asked you for some mounted infantry to help us but we know that you cannot spare anyone because of the sickness so we shall just have to make the best of it,' he continued, looking determined.

'I would willingly have given you whatever support we had but there is no one who can now be spared – we need all the men we have here.'

'Thank you, brother. It will be sufficient for our purposes if we can take the maps.'

'By all means and may the gods give you speed and protection in your journey.'

The three Centurions clasped hands in farewell and Graecus and Acerbus left Afranius to his sad duties.

When they returned to their own men, the tents and all the equipment had been packed away on the carts, the mules were in position, the horses saddled and the men were lining up. Germanicus put on his helmet then the wolfskin, shaking his head from side to side to ensure that his cumbersome headgear would remain in place once the march had begun. Zig was looking on while all this activity was taking place, his eyes bright with excitement.

Graecus and Acerbus mounted their horses and their men fell in behind them with Germanicus and Solitarius in their wolfskins, Germanicus carrying the standard and Solitarius carrying the horn, and their counterparts from Acerbus's century immediately behind the Centurions and the rest of the men in two sets of two following behind.

The Centurions set a smart pace knowing that the men were capable of marching twenty five miles in a day and that these were exactly the circumstances in which a forced march was appropriate.

It was still early in the morning of a fine clear day, the men had been rested after their Ocean crossing and they had been well-fed.

Morale was good as the two centuries marched uphill leaving Dubris behind them. Then they took one of the ridge ways –

roads built by the Britons along ridges going over hilltops – going north-eastwards.

This was not a surfaced road, as a Roman road would be, but it provided good views of the surrounding countryside and, it was to be hoped, minimised the possibility of ambush. The men made steady progress and had left the coast far behind them by mid-day when the Centurions gave the signal to halt and rest.

Graecus and Acerbus dismounted and joined their men who were milling about. On a forced march it was not usual to eat at mid-day as it made the men sluggish in the afternoon but this rest-break gave them the opportunity to slake their thirst and to relieve their bladders so there was the general sound of men noisily swallowing water from leather pouches or gourds and men competing with each other as to the highest arc which could be achieved while holding onto one's member.

Pneumaticus was not joining any of this high spirited behaviour and was sitting on a rock looking very unhappy as Magnus tended to his swollen face. Graecus saw this and went over to the rock.

'How are you faring, Pneumaticus?'

'Well, I shall live but my face is such a mess that I do not think that I shall be enjoying the attentions of any ladies for some time.'

His face was indeed a mess – bruised from above his right eyebrow all the way down his right cheek to his chin and the whole of his mouth so swollen that his voice was thick and his words slurred.

Magnus asked Pneumaticus to open his mouth and gently probed his top two front teeth. There was too much movement in the teeth and Magnus was able to rock them back and forth.

'Hmm,' he said, 'I'm not too happy with these. They do not seem to be settling back into the gums.'

'Well, whatever you say, those teeth are staying put. I'm not going to be one of those grinning idiots with no teeth,' said Pneumaticus with as much vehemence as he could muster but the effort made him choke and he set himself off on a violent coughing fit for several minutes while Magnus slapped his back.

The men had made themselves more comfortable, and Acerbus having given the order to fall in line, the column set off again marching with the sun overhead and then, as the hours went by, with the sun behind them.

As the shadows lengthened, Acerbus and Graecus urged their horses on to speed up the pace of the men behind – they had calculated that they would reach the first Roman fort before nightfall.

Just as Graecus was beginning to think that they had miscalculated and that they would soon need to make camp, there it was ahead of them to the left of the ridge way. A cheer went up from behind the Centurions and they urged their horses on even more, knowing that the men would be as keen as were they to feel the walls of the fort around them now that night was falling.

As the sun set, the column drew up outside the gatehouse of the fort. Graecus and Acerbus dismounted and called 'Hail' in the direction of the guards standing on the wall above the gate.

'Hail,' came the reply, 'who goes there?'

'Marcus Caelius Caldus and his century and my colleague and his century. We have come from Lower Germania to reinforce Suetonius Paulinus in the fight against Boudicca.'

'Open the gate! Let these good men in.'

Graecus and Acerbus remounted and led their men into the fort, all of them feeling relieved to see the gate close behind them.

The fort was small, housing only a manipula, two centuries, from another auxiliary cohort. There was insufficient indoor accommodation for another two centuries but there was plenty of space within its ramparts for the visitors to pitch their tents. The Commander, a weathered man in his fifties, was welcoming and invited Graecus and Acerbus to dine with him in his quarters. They could not, of course, refuse, but each of them secretly thought that whatever would be put on the table, it would not be the equal of Felix's cooking.

And these misgivings were borne out by the facts. Neither Graecus nor Acerbus knew what were the problems of securing supplies in this place but it appeared that they were acute because what they were served was dull fare, badly cooked – a tasteless green soup which lacked seasoning and whose flavour could not be assigned to any particular vegetable, then a stew which was certainly hearty in that it had many large pieces of meat floating in it but they were grey and stringy and similarly unidentifiable.

But the commander was hospitable, filling their wine cups as soon as they were emptied (which was often, given the mediocrity of the food) and he was forthcoming about the present problems.

Pushing himself back from the table in an expansive gesture as if he had eaten sumptuously, the commander said, 'Gentlemen, while I am glad that you have come all this way to help us deal with this threat, I do not envy you your battle against this woman. She is clever, gentlemen, as clever as a cage full of monkeys and she is fighting for her honour and the honour of her daughters.'

'Why is that? What has Boudicca's honour and that of her daughters got to do with it?' said Graecus.

'Do you not know what that fool of a Procurator, Catus Decianus, did?'

'No. We heard that he was incensed about her husband's will but that was all.'

'Well, he had Boudicca flogged and her daughters raped.'

Both Graecus and Acerbus inhaled sharply and sucked their teeth at this and were silent for a few moments before Acerbus said, 'What did he think he would gain by that?'

'I know not, he was not given to discussing his thoughts with the likes of me and now he's buggered off to Gaul. But I suppose he thought that Prasutagus had insulted Rome by leaving only half his estate to Nero and perhaps Nero was breathing down his neck about it but his retaliation to the so-called insult was out of proportion, and to add to it, the tribes were strapped for cash and he demanded repayment of the loans Claudius had made to them.'

'Was the money due?' asked Acerbus.

'Well, it depends what you mean. You see, you have to remember that these people are barbarians and do not understand our ways – to them, if someone gives you money, even if it is a

43

large sum, then they have no concept of its being a loan – it is a gift and to be made to repay a gift is unknown to them and it is a dishonour.'

'I begin to see why they are so incensed,' said Graecus.

'Yes,' said the Commander, 'but they must learn to understand the ways of the civilised world.'

At this moment, Graecus was thinking that there could be more honour in giving people money than in lending it to them and was having a philosophical argument with himself as to why it might be regarded as civilised to flog a widowed queen and rape her daughters but Acerbus and the commander had moved on in their discussion to the fighting methods of the British warriors.

'Well,' said the commander, 'they are fearless, that is certain. Many of them refuse to wear armour and they are excellent horsemen – their little chariots are very manoeuvrable and they are able in battle to run along the traces causing mayhem with their swords and javelins. Yes, their warriors are formidable fighters but they have no army as such, the rest of them are just farmers or peasants and they are neither armed nor disciplined.'

'But they managed to dispose of 1500 of Cerialis's men. I mean, is it not the case that they massacred several legionary cohorts on their way to reinforce Suetonius?'

'Yes, they did, by employing tactics which favour the Iceni sort of warfare. They are good at short, sharp, surprise attacks and ambush works very well for them because they know the landscape and can strike from seemingly nowhere then disappear back into the woods and marshes.'

'Then Suetonius needs to chose the battle site to favour our sort of warfare,' said Acerbus and the other Centurions nodded, each of them hoping that the Fates would actually allow Suetonius a choice.

The visitors withdrew to their respective tents shortly after this, Graecus to a night of tossing and turning in his bed, partly on account of having eaten badly but mostly on account of his internal discussion concerning the meaning of civilisation. He wrestled with this for some time before he came to the conclusion that the answer must be that the Pax Romana brought such wonderful benefits to people that the ends justified the means. This was doubtless the political explanation but it did not really cure Graecus's queasy feelings about the way Boudicca and her daughters had been manhandled by the Procurator. He considered this for a while before deciding it was all too complicated for him and fell into an uneasy sleep.

The next day was very similar to the previous one and progress was sufficient to ensure that they reached the Icknield Way. This Roman road went from the hills above Dubris across country all the way up to Iceni territory and was well-built in the way of all Roman roads so the men were able to march all the more quickly, their boots making a satisfying, rhythmic noise on the hard surface.

They had their rest period at mid-day and set off again, in the usual formation, four abreast with the Centurions on their horses at the front and Zig trotting happily at Germanicus's side. The trees had been cleared from the sides of the road, as was the Roman practice giving good visibility of the road ahead and the contours of the surrounding landscape.

Graecus was humming to himself as he trotted along on Perdix. He was humming the century's favourite marching song but he was humming it quietly because he had earlier forbidden Germanicus from singing it on account of the fact that if the men all joined in with the rousing chorus of 'We fight for ROME and the EMPEROR', this would not merely advertise their presence more than necessary but could be irritating to any native listener.

The beat of the marching song's tune mimicked the beat of the men's feet on the road and it was difficult, now that Graecus had the tune in his head, to dislodge it.

They had just descended an incline and were entering a little valley which gave way to another, steeper, incline opposite over which the road curved slightly to the left showing cleanly between banks of scrubby trees which, those nearer to the road having been cleared by the road-builders, were set well back.

Thump, thump, thump went the tune in Graecus's head.

Thump, thump, thump – it was becoming really quite irritating but then Graecus's attention was rudely snatched from this percussive reverie by the sound of Zig barking.

Graecus and all the century knew that this meant trouble – the little animal was normally silent but if he perceived a threat to his beloved master, then he was the best early warning system in the Empire.

Graecus was just trying to work out what was the source of the perceived threat – Zig may have picked up the scent of a wolf – when another sound caught his ear.

It was a rumbling and it was getting louder.

Graecus looked in the direction of the rumbling and saw a large cart hurtling towards them from the hill ahead of them. There was no mule pulling the cart and there was no one in the cart – it was a runaway cart and it spelled danger.

Graecus and Acerbus exchanged a quick worried glance. Graecus's mind was working frantically – obviously this was an ambush – the cart was there to bring the column to a halt and to trap them in this little valley so that they would be a sitting target for whatever insurgent force wished to kill them.

But where were the attackers?

These thoughts passed through Graecus's mind at breakneck speed and he came to the conclusion that they must be hidden on the left hand side of the road as that was the direction in which Zig was barking – the dog was now pointing his head to the trees on that side of the road, and in any event, now that he looked more closely, he saw a little stream back from the road on the right hand side which meant they would not be attacking from that side.

'Get off the road!' Graecus shouted, indicating with his arm that the men should get on to the right hand verge in front of the stream. But this was more easily said than done as a column of marching men has its own momentum and the men at the back could not see the cart, nor would they have been expecting to break their step in this place, and there was a general confusion as men further down the column bumped into the men at the front who were attempting either to obey their Centurion's order or simply to remove themselves from the path of the cart.

Graecus turned in his saddle and again shouted, 'Get off the road! Get onto this side of the road!' Acerbus now saw what was in Graecus's mind and shouted, 'Weapons out! Shields out! Testudo!'

Now that it was clear to all of them what was happening, the men began to obey and as the runaway cart reached the bottom of the valley, the last soldier was scrambling off the road onto the verge drawing his gladius and putting up his shield as he did so.

So far, so good – the column had survived the runaway cart and the men were busy putting in place the protective 'tortoise' formation.

But Graecus and Acerbus, on horseback, were very exposed and Zig, who had warned of the danger, was similarly vulnerable – standing a little way apart from the melee.

Whilst Graecus had no wish to die or be injured in this skirmish, neither did he wish to lose his horse and he imagined that Acerbus would be thinking similar thoughts so, scooping Zig up and holding him on his lap, he wheeled Perdix round and walked her to his century's baggage wagon where, having unceremoniously dumped Zig in the back of the wagon, he quickly dismounted and tethered her.

Perdix, being a Centurion's horse, was accustomed to being at the front of the column, and being a proud filly, so disliked this new placement to the rear of the mules that she snorted and whinnied but Graecus had no time to comfort her as groups of armed men were now coming out of the trees.

Acerbus tethered his horse to his baggage wagon and stood by Graecus's side, gladius in hand.

Their men were all now formed into ten testudoes of sixteen men each –two contubernia. The contubernium, a group of eight men, was the basic unit of the Roman Army where the men's loyalty to each other and their ability to act as a team was fostered by their sharing every aspect of their everyday lives; these men who lived together were more inclined to die together in pursuit of glory than to betray their comrades in cowardice or their oath of loyalty in mutiny.

But there was no such protection for Graecus and Acerbus – it was their job to observe the enemy and to give orders to their men based on those observations; one of the purposes of the testudo was to provoke the enemy into fruitlessly letting go of its long-distance weapons – arrows, javelins and spears, while the Romans still had theirs and it was the Centurions who made the decision when their men would loose their weapons and when they would engage in hand to hand combat. This process was repeated throughout the Roman army and ensured that Centurion casualties were higher than those of any other rank.

Given that they would be obvious targets for enemy fire on this exposed turf, Graecus and Acerbus positioned themselves just behind Graecus's century's baggage wagon, nearest the road and observed from there.

The enemy's progress across the open land had halted now that it had become clear to them that their plan to cause havoc with the cart had failed. Graecus had good eyesight and he was observing their faces, and insofar as it was possible to tell with people whose culture was very different from his, he would have said that they did not now know what to do; there were about 300 of them and they must have thought that confusion and superior numbers would bring them an easy victory but Zig's alertness had foiled their plan.

Graecus saw that there was a leader in their midst – a very tall, red-headed man with a red moustache and beard – a striking looking man, standing in the middle of the others and seeming to harangue them. Graecus had no knowledge of the local tongue but the expressions on the faces of the protagonists seemed to show indecision.

'Seems as if they've got cold feet,' said Acerbus.

'Perhaps they're thinking of sending for reinforcements.'

'Well we can't afford to wait around for that, we're much more exposed here than they are and we are still miles from the nearest fort.'

'We need to get this attack over and done with, otherwise we will end up in a much worse situation,' said Graecus.

'Well, while they're having this strategic discussion, why don't we just loose a few spears at them to provoke a response – they're hardly going to ignore us then, are they?' said Acerbus.

'They are too far away from us for any of our spears to find their mark, but we're vulnerable to their arrows.'

'But time is on their side, it is not on ours,' said Acerbus.

At that moment a crow flew noisily overhead and both Graecus and Acerbus looked up to see it.

What they did not see was the archer nocking an arrow into his bow and letting it loose.

The bellowing from Acerbus's horse was therefore a surprise to the Centurions whose eyes were quickly distracted from the crow, but at first, they did not know what was the cause of the horse's distress as the arrow was not visible to them but then they could see a puddle of blood forming underneath the horse's far flank.

'Ye gods, they've wounded my horse. I love that horse! What a bloody cheek!'

Graecus turned to face his friend and said, 'Well, it seems they mean to pick us off little by little. We cannot hope for help from anywhere so I suppose that we have no option but to try to provoke them.'

Graecus turned to look at the enemy again and gave a small sigh of satisfaction as this latest development seemed to have galvanised them into action – they were now slowly making their way towards the Romans, some of them holding their bows with arrows nocked ready to be loosed.

'Hold steady men, hold steady' Graecus shouted while Acerbus told his men to,' Wait for it, just wait for it' and the two centuries, most of them experienced soldiers and drilled in the ways of the Roman army, did just that. They waited under their shields calmly and quietly while arrows flew all around them, over their heads, behind them and fell like rain in front of them – they just waited.

One of the enemy archers was successful – Graecus and

Acerbus heard a muffled scream of pain from under one of the testudoes; even this most protective of formations was not impregnable and the odd arrow was capable of penetrating the banks of shields but the Centurions knew that, even if there had been a fatality, the other soldiers would not allow this to challenge their resolve to wait for their leader's order.

Graecus and Acerbus took swift glances from behind the wagon, observing the enemy's progress towards the testudoes, judging the best moment for the destructive power of the Roman spears to be unleashed.

The hail of arrows was abating, and judging by the silence coming from the Romans, they had not done much harm.

'Spears at the ready!' 'Spears at the ready!' the Centurions called and the testudo formations were swiftly put aside as the soldiers readied themselves.

'First Spears GO!'

'First Spears GO!'

Graecus and Acerbus shouted this command simultaneously and a forest of spears flew over the road at the enemy.

Twenty or so Britons hit the ground while the Romans reformed the testudo.

'Second Spears GO!'

'Second Spears GO!'

Again the orders were simultaneous and this time about thirty tribesmen fell to the ground.

The Britons were on the road. It was time to engage with the enemy and Graecus and Acerbus both shouted, 'ENGAGE!' while running from behind the baggage wagons to the small arena on the road and grass verge in front of the stream where this minor battle was beginning in earnest.

Graecus was aware that something other than Acerbus was running beside him and glancing quickly downwards, he saw Zig.

His heart fell for he knew that he did not now have the time to put the animal back in the wagon and he also knew that, if the little dog thought that Germanicus was in danger, then it would do its best to protect him, but if that meant that the dog was killed, then Germanicus would be heartbroken.

'Dog, dog, dog,' he muttered to himself, 'what am I going to do with you?'

But it was too late to be able to do anything and Zig would just have to take his chances like the rest of them – he was a member of the Roman army, after all.

The soldiers were busy now – gladius in one hand and shield in the other. The gladius was quite a short sword and was better at sticking than at slicing so the easiest way to dispatch your opponent was to stick your gladius in his guts, and if he looked as if he was about to cut you first, then, as he leaned into the thrust, you shoved your shield in his face and the pointed metal work on it distracted him enough for you to be able to stab him with your gladius while he was still reeling with surprise.

Graecus looked for Germanicus in the crowd of fighting men, and seeing he was in the thick of it, made to go to stand next to him but there was a huge Briton blocking his path, snorting like a stuck pig. His nose was running and there was spittle drooling from the corners of his mouth. He stank worse than an animal and Graecus wrinkled his nose in disgust. The giant said something in a guttural language which meant nothing to Graecus but he knew it was not friendly, and as he said it, he raised his arm and made to bring an axe down on Graecus's head.

Graecus had his gladius at the ready and was about to stick it in the giant's belly when, all of a sudden, the giant pitched forward and fell straight onto Graecus's drawn sword, impaling himself on the blade.

Graecus did not know what had caused the giant to fall, and in the heat of battle, did not have the leisure to enquire, but as he pushed the man backwards, with some effort as he was such a big man, to try to retrieve his sword from the man's belly, he saw Zig ahead of him, busily biting into the back of the ankle of a Briton who was skilfully parrying the blows from Germanicus's sword.

As he withdrew his sword, warm and glistening with stomach juices and blood, Graecus saw that Zig was now attacking Germanicus's opponent's other ankle and then, just as had happened with the giant, the man fell forward face down, this time onto the ground where Germanicus quickly pierced him in the back of the neck.

This was a new phenomenon and Graecus was amazed at the dog's skill, but to the Roman army, a battlefield was not normally the place for a dog, nor was it the place to let your concentration wander into thoughts other than killing the enemy without getting yourself killed so he postponed his thoughts until a more convenient moment.

Graecus could now stand next to his son. He knew that Germanicus would feel boosted by his father's presence and he, too, wished to be next to his beloved boy while they put their lives in the balance.

And they were attuned to each other as warriors – each instinctively knew how the other would react to the fighting styles of their enemies and they fought more as one unit than as two men; the rhythms of their thrusting and parrying blows became synchronised in an elegant dance of death. As they fought, shoulder to shoulder, the continued cut, bash, thrust, cut, bash, thrust made Graecus think of the rhythm of another of their songs and he began to sing:

'Let me die a young man's death
While I am in my prime,
Let me die while strong of breath
While I am in my prime,
Let me die while my sword arm's strong
While I am in my prime,
And though death's coming be short or long
Let THIS day NOT be my time.'

Graecus heard Germanicus laugh when he began the song and then he joined in. Felix, fighting on Germanicus's far side, also began to sing and Magnus and then all the others as they fought their way to victory in the heat of the afternoon.

But Pneumaticus was not singing – from his current standpoint, retrieving his sword from yet another Briton's belly, Graecus could see that his face was contorted with what appeared to be pain and he was concerned that his century's longest serving soldier had been severely wounded but then, above all the groaning and grunting of the battle field and his men's singing, he heard a sound he had not heard for a very long time – the music of Pneumaticus farting.

Pneumaticus had been a farter of great repute and effect, indeed he had been given his nickname on account of his talent in this respect, but many years ago, his farts had become so unpleasant that Magnus had had to take strong measures to render their colleague fit to enter their contubernium tent. This treatment had worked so well that Graecus had forgotten the poisonous qualities of Pneumaticus's farts but now, the combination of a wounded face, the magic mushrooms and fighting for his life seemed to have caused a return of this trouble, but looking at the expression on the face of the Briton standing down-wind of Pneumaticus and his loss of concentration which allowed Acerbus to stick him with his gladius, it occurred to Graecus that Pneumaticus's wind was one of Rome's secret weapons and he hoped it might continue throughout the battle as long as it discontinued while he was in their tent.

The battle was all but over – the Britons had fought bravely but they were no match for the Romans' tactics and better weapons. There were a few of the enemy still standing but they made no move to seek to surrender and Graecus was relieved by this as, if they had had to take prisoners with them, even if only to the next fort, it would further slow their progress and they were already way behind schedule in their journey that day.

The enemy were all down now and the soldiers systematically went over the fallen picking up their dead and injured and finishing off the enemy wounded. The enemy dead would be left for the crows but the soldiers began putting the Roman dead in one of the baggage wagons and the three badly wounded in the other.

Happily there were few dead– only two from Graecus's century and one from Acerbus's.

But Acerbus's horse was in a bad way. The arrow had pierced its flank, and while the battle had been going on, the animal had gone into shock and its back legs had all but buckled under it. It was clear that there was no possibility of its walking all the way to the next fort and it could not be left to a slow, lonely death.

'Would you like me to put the animal out of its misery, my friend?' Graecus said to Acerbus.

'No, I shall do it myself. It's the least I can do for this creature which has patiently borne me all these years,' said Acerbus as, swallowing hard, he took his dagger and cut the horse's throat.

This produced a huge torrent of blood and Acerbus, not having stepped back from the flow in time, was splattered from head to foot in it

'Serves me right for being bloody stupid!' he said. 'I'd better go and rinse off in that stream or the flies will make my life a misery for the rest of the day.'

Several other soldiers were rinsing themselves in the stream and the men's bodies and voices were beginning to relax after the strain of battle – there was even some relieved splashing in the stream with two of the young soldiers from Graecus's century throwing water at Acerbus's men when a scream went up from that direction followed by Zig's barking and a cacophony of shouting.

Graecus stopped looking at a wound on Impedimentus's leg and looked past the back of the baggage wagon to the stream.

Zig was standing stock-still, barking his head off with an arrow protruding from his left shoulder, Acerbus was lying on the bank of the stream with an arrow in his leg and there were two soldiers lying in the stream with arrows in their chests, dead.

But they had just killed all the insurgents, had they not?

No, that was not true. The two Centurions had not seen from which direction the arrow which had wounded Acerbus's horse had come – they had assumed that it had come from the archers on the left hand side of the road but it had hit the horse's far flank and that would more easily be achieved had it come from the opposite side of the road.

Now he thought about it, it would have been very stupid of

the Britons not to have had men positioned on each side of the road – they would be needed to pick off the Roman stragglers who, after the massacre they had envisaged, might have been tempted to cross the stream and make for the woods.

Germanicus was now running towards Zig.

'Germanicus! Stop! There are archers in those trees! Stop! I order you to stop! GERMANICUS! HALT!'

Germanicus halted but that was worse as he had merely turned himself from a moving target into a stationary one.

'In the names of all the gods, drop down, you young fool!'

Germanicus dropped to the ground and lay there trying not to listen to Zig's pain.

'Testudo' called Graecus. 'Testudo of 1st and 2nd contubernia!'

The men who had been thinking that that afternoon's drama was over had to drag their minds from a hot bath and a good supper at the next fort, now had to pick up their shields yet again and form themselves into the tortoise.

Graecus put himself on the outside front of the tortoise and ordered the men to move forward –towards Germanicus.

The tortoise edged forward and eventually the formation was over Germanicus who stood up, and protected by the shields of his colleagues, was taken back to the relative safety of the baggage wagons.

'Now we will get the others,' said Graecus and the operation was repeated, firstly for Acerbus and then for Zig.

The arrow wound in Acerbus's leg was not as deep as it might be but it would require careful surgery. He lay in the wagon cursing his stupidity and lamenting the loss of his horse but Zig was silent although he was panting and his front legs were twitching with pain.

Graecus had to consider whether it would be worthwhile sending some men into the trees to see if they could apprehend the archers but he decided against it; if they were still there he would undoubtedly lose more men but there was also the possibility that if they just tried to march away, more men would be picked off.

No, it was better to make as much haste as was possible to the next fort, but to make it as difficult as possible for any remaining archers to find their mark, Graecus ordered the men and the wagons off the road and onto the far verge so that they would be as much out of range as possible.

The soldiers made the best column they could, bloody, bruised and battered as they were, and at the back, the badly wounded in the wagons.

Graecus was at the front, alone again, on Perdix. He felt very solitary indeed – not afraid, just solitary.

'Column forward, quick march!' he called and hoped that the tired men behind him would find the energy to follow his order. He thought that there were about three more marching hours ahead before the fort would come into view but he did not know and he certainly did not tell the men that it was so far away.

Once Graecus felt sure that they were well away from sniping archers, he ordered the men back onto the road and quickened the pace.

As the sun began to fall away in the west, Graecus was aware of the exhaustion behind him; he sensed that the men were dragging their feet and he could hear the odd sigh followed by a sharp intake of breath as the perpetrator of the sigh realised that it was bad form to let one's physical failings become so evident.

The sun was getting perilously low and there was still no sign of the fort. Graecus had to make the decision whether to make camp now, while it was still light enough or whether to hope that they would get to the fort before sundown. He really did not know how far they were from the fort but the thought of cleaning himself all over with oil and steaming in the *caldarium* was wonderfully attractive – he, in common with the rest of the men who had not gone to the stream, was covered in blood, spittle and other bodily fluids. He knew that his boots and feet were covered with the fluids which had spilled from the Britons' guts and now dried into a horrible crust and would soon begin to stink unbearably. Graecus knew that his discomfort was no worse than that suffered by any of his men but that did not lessen his desire for the reviving effects of olive oil and hot water and he was very tempted to push on in the direction of the fort which, as far as he could tell from the map, looked large and was likely to be well-appointed.

On the other hand, if they did not find the fort very soon, they would be forced to try to make camp in the dark and it would be more difficult to find a suitable place to spend the night.

Much as he wanted to find the fort, the only decision in the circumstances was to make camp now, in the most convenient place.

Graecus put up his arm to signal to the column to halt.

'Men, we will not now be able to reach the fort before night-fall and we must make camp in the next half hour. Take ten minutes now to refresh yourselves and then we shall look out for a convenient camp-site.'

There was an audible groan of disappointment but the men then busied themselves drinking water, eating the small pieces of bread and bacon they had with them and emptying their bladders. Graecus poured some cold water over his head and rubbed at his wet face with his neckerchief to remove whatever had dried onto his skin. Having then poured some water over his booted feet and down his throat he felt a little better.

Walking back down the line of men, he reached the baggage wagons where Magnus was tending to the wounded.

One of the severely injured men from Graecus's century had died since they left the skirmish and another man seemed to be in his final hours. Acerbus, however, was in reasonable spirits, and reclining backwards onto a sack, was cradling Zig in his arms, each of them being careful not to nudge against the arrow in the other.

Germanicus had also come to see how the injured were faring, and being pleased to see his dog quietly resting in Acerbus's arms, he gently stroked him behind the ears and whispered to him that he would soon be chasing rabbits again.

When he heard this, Graecus fearing that the dog may not recover, looked at Magnus while Germanicus was tickling the animal's ears, and raised an eyebrow.

Magnus made a non-committal gesture but indicated that the sooner Zig could be operated on, the better.

Graecus was not sure how this could be achieved but felt that they should make camp as soon as possible, and going back to the front of the line he shouted, 'Back in line, men and MARCH!'

On they went, tramp, tramp, tramp with Graecus at the front of the column on Perdix keeping his eyes peeled for a suitable camp-site.

CHAPTER FOUR

He found it soon enough. A large mound set back from the road with a flattish top and the little stream still flowing at the side of the road so they could replenish their water supplies.

'Column HALT! We shall make our camp on top of that mound.'

The men halted and most of them knew that it was now his job to co-operate with his colleagues to dig the trench and make the rampart which would protect them from their enemies during the night.

Magnus and Impedimentus made themselves busy with their jobs: Magnus, assisted by the medical orderly from Acerbus's century, deciding how best he would deal with the wounded and Impedimentus, despite his wound, supervising the unloading of the wagons and unpacking the supplies. Felix, too, was busy.

His immediate task was to light the first of several fires and put on a large pot of water. This would be used to provide hot water for the soldiers to clean themselves of the dirt of battle. Then he found his knives and began chopping onions and garlic as the basis for the stew which would put fresh life into the men. Felix did all of this as quickly as possible as he knew that, as soon as the men had clean hands and faces and could smell the aroma of fried onions, their spirits would rise and their disappointment at not reaching the fort would be forgotten.

The ditch and the rampart were finished and hot water was now being ladled into mess bowls for the men's ablutions. Torches were being lit in the centre of the camp and the smells from Felix's bubbling pots were wafting on the air as the sun finally went down.

Having seen that all was in order, Graecus went to see Magnus in the tent which was serving as a makeshift infirmary.

Here all was calm. In the light from the oil-lamps, Graecus could see that there were about ten wounded men... and Zig.

'What is the status of our patients?' asked Graecus.

'Well, we have two serious stomach wounds and I have done

my best for them but they are notoriously difficult to treat and if they last the night they will best be left at the next fort. The other wounded, apart from Acerbus and Zig, have superficial cuts to arms and legs and I have every confidence that they will recover quite quickly.'

'What about Acerbus and Zig?'

'Well, arrow wounds are more complicated because of the problem of retrieving the arrow head from the body without doing more damage to the patient but we have been lucky because Acerbus's wound is to the outer thigh where it should be easy to remove the arrowhead from the muscle. I intend to operate on him here tonight. Because of the risk of infection, I cannot leave it till we reach the fort.'

'And Zig'

'The arrow is in his shoulder and has not pierced him deeply – his shoulder is so muscular and the arrow was loosed from so far away that I feel it will not be too difficult to restore him to his usual self.'

'When will you begin the operations and do you require any more men to assist you?'

'I shall begin very soon, when I am sure that the magic mushroom I gave to Acerbus has had full effect.'

'What about Zig? Will you give him some of the mushroom?'

'I really cannot make up my mind about that – we have no idea of the effect it would have on an animal and I am conscious of the fact that it would be so easy to give him too much – he is only quite a small dog after all.'

'Well, perhaps the best thing is if Germanicus holds his head while you are taking the arrow out.'

'That would help, I'm sure.'

The medical orderly from Acerbus's century was scrubbing a large table in preparation for the operations and Magnus now began to unpack his knives. Taking out a piece of stone, he sharpened them before wiping them on a clean cloth soaked in olive oil. Then he placed them in the bowl of water which was boiling over the fire, and having dried them with another clean cloth, he laid them carefully in ascending order of size on the small table next to the operating table.

Magnus seemed to be in a kind of trance as he did these jobs and Graecus, having seen him do this many times before, knew that he was communing with himself and preparing for the task ahead, asking the gods for their help.

Graecus went over to where Acerbus was lying on his back on a trestle table, the arrow clearly protruding from his upper leg. His eyes were closed and his face looked drawn and pale but his breathing was steady and a small smile played around his lips. It seemed that the mushrooms were working their usual magic.

Graecus then turned his attention to Zig.

The little dog was curled up on Germanicus's wolfskin, lying in a basket. When Graecus leaned over him, Zig opened the eye which was pointing in Graecus's direction.

'Well now, old chap, and how are you?' said Graecus, stroking the dog's soft velvet ear. Zig regarded Graecus without fear with the one open eye and the Centurion marvelled at the dog's calm demeanour despite the fact that the arrow was sticking out of his shoulder and there was dried blood on his coat and around his mouth.

Then Graecus remembered Zig's contribution to the battle in biting into the enemy's ankles and causing them to fall forward just as they were trying to kill the Romans and he realised that the blood round his mouth was not his own.

'Well, Zig,' he said, 'you truly are a member of the Roman army now. You will have battle scars just like the rest of us.'

Magnus was calling for two men to help him lift Acerbus onto the operating table and Graecus turned to leave as he did not wish to be a gratuitous spectator and he had every confidence in Magnus's ability.

Outside the tent, Germanicus was standing moving nervously from one foot to the other. 'Father, how is Zig, will he live, is he in pain, can I see him, will he hunt again?' he said.

'Magnus is operating on Acerbus at the moment but then he

will remove the arrow from Zig's shoulder and he is a very good surgeon as you know but he and I think it will be best if you hold onto Zig's head when Magnus performs the operation.'

'I will do that gladly.'

'I know you will, my son, but now we should have something to eat as Magnus will be busy with Acerbus for a while.'

The Centurion and his son went to join their colleagues whose immediate concern was the welfare of the injured, including Zig, and Graecus tried to allay their fears by saying that he and Magnus hoped that all of them would pull through.

A little while later, Magnus appeared at the table saying to Graecus that Acerbus's operation had been successful but that he was still under the influence of the mushroom so it was not possible to speak sensibly to him.

Germanicus stood and said, 'Is it now time to remove the arrow from Zig?'

'Yes, my son, it is. Shall I come also – I may be able to hold Zig's legs steady.'

'Yes, father, I wish you to be there to help comfort him.'

The three men went back to the hospital tent where Germanicus gently lifted his dog onto the freshly scrubbed operating table and Magnus called to the medical orderly to put more oil in the lamps as they were burning too low for him to be able to see properly.

Magnus now looked closely at the arrow and carefully explored the region around the entry wound, pressing it softly with his fingers.

'Hmm,' he said 'there has not been much internal bleeding. That is good. And he is a strong, brave animal. I propose to dig the arrow out by cutting round it and then sewing up the muscle and the skin.'

Germanicus, who had single-handedly (but with a sword in either hand)) killed two grown men when he was about ten years old, looked pale at this but went to stand at Zig's head and cradled it tenderly, whispering softly in the animal's ear.

While Graecus held Zig's front legs steady, Magnus took a

thin knife with a long point and began to open up a cut around the arrow head, enlarging the entry wound so that he could put his fingers into it and ascertain the depth and angle of the intruder. He followed the grain of the muscle with his fingers and cut a little more and felt again while Zig whimpered but did not struggle.

Magnus now took a smaller knife and cut again and inserted his fingers into the cut yet again but this time, when he removed his fingers, he brought the arrow head and the arrow in them.

A small cheer came from the open tent flap and Graecus and Germanicus, turning in surprise to look at what had caused this, saw a huddle of concerned faces staring into the tent.

'Will he recover?' said Felix.

'Yes,' said Magnus throwing the enemy arrow dismissively to the floor.

'We shall have some wine now, I think,' said Felix as he, Pneumaticus and Incitatus turned to rejoin their colleagues.

Magnus was now closing the wound with a needle threaded with gut and still the dog did not move.

The stitching was over quite quickly and then Germanicus was allowed to pick up his dog and put him back onto the wolf-skin in the basket where he made himself comfortable and fell asleep.

'The best patient I ever had,' said Magnus. 'If only they were all so calm and trusting.'

Germanicus ruffled Zig's ears and bent to kiss the top of his head. Then he said, 'Thank you, my friend, I am very grateful that you have saved my dog's life.'

'Well, I think that we in the century are all grateful to Zig for his having saved our lives.'

Graecus and Germanicus left to join their colleagues in drinking their wine while Magnus boiled his knives and the orderly scrubbed the table again.

After an hour, Germanicus looked less strained and the other men were feeling restored after their long and challenging day but Graecus needed to take a walk to soothe his nerves.

He grabbed a handful of burning rushes and began to patrol

the perimeter of their camp, looking at the beauty of the night-sky as he walked and noticing that the moon had nearly waned. He was just thinking of all the night skies he had admired while they had lived at their fort in Lower Germania when he almost tripped up over Magnus who was kneeling on the chalky earth, peering closely at the ground.

'Magnus! What are you doing? What in the name of Jupiter are you looking for?'

'Snails, Domine, I am looking for snails.'

Graecus's expression of incredulity was lost in the dark but his tone gave away his feelings. 'You're looking for *WHAT*?' he said.

'Snails, Domine, I should be able to find quite a few in this chalky soil as they come out at night at this time of year to mate.'

'And why are you interested in the mating habits of snails?' Graecus asked with a hint of desperation in his voice.

'Because, Domine, their slime has certain healing properties and is helpful against infection. I want to find enough to be able to treat the stomach wounds, Impedimentus's leg and Acerbus and Zig.'

Graecus knew, from many years' experience, that when Magnus called him 'Domine' in this formal manner, it meant that he was tired and running out of patience so Graecus did what any sensible Centurion would do in the circumstances and dropped to his knees to help Magnus find the biggest snails.

Being large and slow moving they were quite easy to find and soon the two men had put about a dozen in the basket Magnus had brought, and as he stood up and straightened his back, he said, 'That should be enough. I'll look after these and they can be used for treatment for as long as necessary – they're quite long lived and may outlast some of the patients.'

Graecus clasped his colleague by the shoulder and said, 'I know that you have done your best for all the patients today and you have done it in very difficult conditions. If some of the wounded die, then it is because the gods will it, not because there has been any lack of care on your part. You are tired now, go and make your patients comfortable for the night and get some sleep yourself. We'll reach the fort in the morning and you will be able to hand over some of the wounded to the infirmary there.'

'Yes, you're right. I'll go to bed as soon as I can. Goodnight, Domine.'

'Goodnight, my friend.'

Graecus went to make sure that all was sound in the marching camp, satisfying himself that the guards were alert, and then he rounded up any men who seemed tempted to sit too long around the embers of the fire, and went to bed.

Graecus lay on his camp bed, trying to work out just how they could be sure that they would find Suetonius but he was too tired and fell asleep almost straightaway into a deep, dreamless slumber.

* * *

The next day was dull, misty and overcast and the greyness of the weather affected the men's mood – there seemed to be a grumpy tetchiness affecting many of the company that morning; as Graecus walked round the camp, he heard men cursing their blisters, swearing at their equipment and blaming their lack of humour on the bland diet they had had to endure since they had come to this accursed island.

Walking back now to the centre of the camp, he was surprised to see Felix, normally the most cheerful of men, grimly stirring a big pot of porridge, and sitting nearby, on a stool with his head in his hands, was Pneumaticus – looking glum.

By this time, having had to endure looking at so many sour faces and having listened to so many half-hearted responses to his greeting, Graecus felt that whatever it was which had affected both his men and Acerbus's was contagious because his own humour, which had been cheerful enough at dawn, was now being replaced by the black clouds he saw over every one else's head.

Graecus was just pondering this phenomenon that a camp-ful of men in one mood could retire for the night and be replaced in the morning by a camp-ful of men in the opposite mood and resigning himself to spending the day in the company of misery when he saw Germanicus's bright head emerge from the hospital tent.

His son was grinning broadly.

'Father,' he said, 'Zig is awake. He has had some breakfast and he can walk unaided. Is it not a miracle!'

Graecus's spirits lifted instantly at the sight of Germanicus's unaffected joy. 'That is wonderful news,' he said. 'And how is Acerbus?'

'He too is awake and has eaten very heartily.'

'That is the best sign possible with him. When he stops thinking of his belly – that is the time to worry.'

Graecus entered the hospital tent and went to speak to his friend who was propped up into a sitting position. There was a gobbet of porridge drying on his stubbly chin and he was picking at his teeth with a bit of twig.

'Hail! You had us all worried yesterday but the gods spared you so that we can enjoy our victory over Boudicca together.'

'Yes. And just so that I *can* enjoy our victory over Boudicca, you must promise me that you will not, however much anyone tries to persuade you to the contrary, leave me in the infirmarium at the next fort. I'm perfectly able to travel – all I need is a new horse. I'm not going to miss the showdown with Boudicca on account of a little arrow wound.'

'I promise you that you will be with us when we leave the fort as long as they have a fresh horse for you. Now, tell me, how was the operation? Did the magic mushroom work?'

'Did it work? In all truth, I cannot tell you. All I know is that I spent the latter part of yesterday and all last night, at the best banquet I've ever been to and it was attended by hundreds of beautiful, willing virgins.'

'I am glad, my friend, that your dreams were so much to your taste. Now, tell me, how fared the men with the stomach wounds during the night?'

'One of them died but the other is stronger this morning.'

Graecus made a mental note that he must inform Incitatus of this latest casualty so that the appropriate letters could be written to the man's family and the century's records kept up to date. He hoped there would not be any further skirmishes before they rendezvoused with Suetonius as the centuries were daily losing good men.

Graecus now clasped his friend's arm and said, 'We shall be moving on shortly, would you like to take Perdix until we get to the next fort? I am happy to walk.'

'Happy to walk? And turn up at this fort on foot, and you a Centurion? No, I shall not take Perdix, I shall lie in the back of the wagon as I did yesterday with Zig for company. You need the horse to be able to see what is going on at the side of the road and you need it to be able to impress the legionaries with your rank.'

'I will ask Magnus if he has any more of the mushroom for you, to ease your journey.'

'That's a much better offer!'

Graecus left the tent, asked Magnus to spare a little of the mushroom drug for Acerbus, and then went to find Impedimentus to ensure that all the baggage was loaded. Then he mounted Perdix and called to the men to form the column and they were off, Graecus in a more buoyant mood now that he knew that Acerbus was recovering but the majority of the men behind were still sullen.

The sun broke through the clouds about two hours after they began the march and Graecus could feel that this had lifted the men's mood. He gave the order to halt for water about an hour later and then, after they had crossed a wide plain, and Graecus on Perdix had reached the top of an incline, he saw the fort on top of a hill about two miles away from them.

It was large and imposing and there was a huge cloud of black smoke rising from its centre – a huge cloud of black smoke which should not be there.

Graecus's heart sank as the prospect of spending a few reviving hours in the safety and comfort of the fort rapidly receded.

The smoke could only be bad news.

The smoke could only mean that the fort was under attack and decisions would need to be made about what his and Acerbus's centuries must do in this situation.

Breathing deeply to calm himself, and keeping well back from the top of the incline so as to be out of sight from the fort, Graecus gave the order to halt and turning to the men behind him, called to Magnus and Germanicus to fetch Acerbus from the wagon and carry him to the front of the column. In answer to the soldiers' questioning look, he pointed to the distant pall of black smoke.

While he was waiting for Acerbus to appear, Graecus turned over several possibilities in his mind. If the fort were under attack, then the insurgents must have succeeded so far as to breach its defences and set fire to some of the buildings, and if they had managed to achieve this much success, then there must be many thousands of them and would it be best to carry on to find Suetonius or to risk more casualties in a desperate attempt to regain control of the fort? Graecus was agonising over this when the soldiers brought Acerbus to the front of the column and sat him on a nearby rock.

'What's the matter?' he said, looking pale but alert.

'Look over there. That smoke should not be there. It looks to me as if the fort over there is under attack.'

'Well, if it is, then we have a difficult choice and I am not sure that I know the answer.'

'Well, you could say that it would be more efficient if we were to find Suetonius because that way we shall at least be sure of meeting Boudicca in battle and that is what we were ordered here to do.'

'What makes you so sure that she's not attacking the fort? It might be part of her plan now to start picking off the isolated forts.'

'Yes, it could be, but if it is her, then she must have thousands of men with her and it seems very quiet. I mean, there doesn't seem to be much evidence of movement, does there?'

'Perhaps the attack is over, perhaps it happened two days ago and they're all dead.'

The two Centurions paused to consider this unthinkable thought and then Incitatus who had been listening to the Centurions spoke.

'Domine,' he said, 'I can see the smoke, there is obviously something amiss in the fort. It would be very easy for me to run along this line of trees here and get as close as possible in the hope that I might be able to see or hear what is happening.'

'Yes, that is an excellent idea but take the greatest care to keep under cover.'

Incitatus set off sprinting at his superhuman speed running towards the fort but hidden by the trees set back from the road.

The soldiers waited in silence, each looking at the smoke casting a black cloud over the horizon and thinking that all bets about this expedition could be off and that they would now be meeting Boudicca and her hordes here in this isolated place, without Suetonius and the legions.

Incitatus was as swift as the wind but it seemed to Graecus that he had been gone for a long time as he sat on Perdix, straining to see any sign of the young man's return.

Then the wind must have changed for Graecus's nostrils suddenly detected a rather unusual smell.

He was not sure at first that he had smelled anything so he sniffed hard and then he decided that there was definitely something in the air.

It was a burning smell and it smelled a little like burned bread but it was stronger and more acrid than that and a cheerful thought had just occurred to him when he saw Incitatus reappear from the line of trees.

'Well done,' said Graecus, 'you have returned unharmed! What did you see?'

'As far as I could tell, everything seems normal. There is no evidence of an attack. I couldn't see or hear anything to indicate that the fort was under siege nor that it had fallen into enemy hands but there is a very odd smell.'

'Yes, that smell has carried here on the wind. I think that the smoke is coming from the granary and the smell is burning grain,' said Graecus.

'Yes, that's it!' said Acerbus, 'I knew it from somewhere. The granary's on fire. It's nothing worse than that.'

'Thank Jupiter, we shall be able to refresh ourselves there and obtain supplies,' said Graecus, 'and maybe we shall learn more of Suetonius's whereabouts.'

Acerbus was lifted back into the wagon and the two columns set off at a rapid pace for the fort.

Graecus was humming to himself with relief as they passed through the gate and he gave the signal to halt.

There was some commotion due to the fire, but that aside, an air of normality prevailed.

Graecus dismounted and looked about him.

To his right was a large stone built construction which must be the *praetorium*, the administrative headquarters of the fort – and the most likely place that he would find the duty officer.

Feeling his lack of pedigree yet again, but most of all the lack of Acerbus at his side, Graecus entered the building, and shuddering at another large bust of Claudius in the centre of the hallway, was made most welcome by the legionary officer who took him to a barrack block where his century could be housed next to Acerbus's men while Acerbus was taken to the *infirmarium*.

Graecus was allocated two rooms to himself because he was a Centurion, and at first, he marvelled at the separate washroom and lavatory, complete with running water, and revelled in the degree of comfort this afforded him but then he reflected that this was the first time in weeks that he had been separated from the men in his contubernium and, although rank had its privileges, loneliness was its price.

Even so, it was with gratitude that Graecus sank onto his bed and fell into a deep sleep although it was only mid-day.

He woke, refreshed, about three hours later and took himself to the bath-house where he oiled and steamed himself in the *caldarium* then cooled himself in the *tepidarium* and the *frigidarium* and emerged two hours later ready for his meeting with the most senior officer present at the fort, the *praefectus*, who, he hoped, would have some idea of where they might find Suetonius.

The *praefectus* was a weary looking, light-haired man with yellow eyes. He was called Marcus and was an auxiliary like

Graecus and, like Graecus, was not a Roman, but unlike Graecus, he was clearly a man of great means. He told Graecus to sit down without raising his eyes from the papers on his desk and continued to read them for several minutes. Graecus thought this was rude but it gave him an opportunity to look around the spacious room with its painted walls and elegant furniture. He was unused to such magnificence and openly stared at the rich hangings and opulent ornaments.

Marcus now looked up from his papers and caught Graecus staring at a particularly lurid mural of the rape of the Sabine women.

'Yes,' he said, 'it's ghastly, isn't it? But my wife's brother thinks he's an artist so we have to indulge him.' Marcus passed a weary hand over his brow as if his wife's brother's artistic ambitions were his greatest problem but maybe he was thinking of something else for now he said, 'Well, Centurion, you and your men have come to us all the way from Lower Germania. You are either very skilful or very lucky to have made it thus far. I do not make any judgement as to which of these applies but we must now seek to ensure that you find our General and his troops as soon as possible.'

'Do you know where they are at present, sir?'

'Yes, we do. They are just over twenty miles west of here.'

'I do not understand. Why are they there? Are they not in pursuit of Boudicca and her tribesmen?'

'Yes, but Boudicca has turned south.'

'South?'

'Yes, we do not know why exactly but she has entered the territory of the Belgi and is resting there with her many followers and allies.'

'And where is Suetonius in relation to Boudicca?'

'About twenty five miles north of her in a position where our army can most easily be supplied while keeping its enemies under scrutiny.'

'Does Suetonius know what she is plotting with the Belgi?'

'I do not know but it is very difficult to guess what will happen as many of the supposedly loyal tribes have begun to favour

71

Boudicca and are turning against Rome… frankly, we have no idea what will happen next.'

'Our orders are to join up with Suetonius and the legions and I feel that is what we must try to do even if Boudicca and her people stand in the way.'

'Happily, they do not. Happily, all that stands between you and Suetonius is twenty odd miles of possibly hostile territory.'

'My men and I are accustomed to operating in hostile territory.'

'That may well be true but you do not know Britannia – you do not know the dreadful surprises of which this land is capable – the marshes, the bogs, the rain, the forests, the sudden fogs – I tell you it is a truly terrible place.'

'But I must take my men and find Suetonius.'

'Yes, you must and in order to help you to find him, I have orders to give you ten cavalrymen to escort you.'

'That is most gracious sir, and my men and I are most grateful.'

'Do not be too grateful Centurion, they are Batavians and very independent of mind. I cannot guarantee that they will deliver you and your men safely to Suetonius but they are all I can spare at the moment.'

'Well, sir, we need supplies and a new mount for my colleague – his horse was struck by an arrow in a skirmish on our way here.'

'As was he, by all accounts but he is healing well, I hear.'

'Yes, he is and he is keen to be back in the saddle and on his way to meet this Boudicca woman who has caused so much trouble.'

'Well, I guarantee that whenever and wherever you meet her, you will never forget it, Centurion, believe me. But yes, of course we shall provide you with all the supplies you need, including a new horse for your colleague. Now, I must tell you that when you arrive at our General's camp you should report to Senior Centurion Norbanus – he will tell you what to do. Hmmm, I think that is all I need to say to you, other than to wish you success in your endeavours and that the gods should look favourably on you.'

'Thank you, sir. Farewell.'

'Farewell, Centurion.'

Graecus saluted to Marcus and marched out of the room.

They were due to leave at sunrise the following day as it was important that they would reach Suetonius's camp before nightfall so Graecus tried to ensure that his men did not avail themselves too much of the wine which seemed abundantly available at this fort. He also made sure, before he retired to his solitary bed, that he told Felix that he thought that, despite the better facilities here, the cook was rubbish and could not hold a candle to him

The next morning was bright and sunny with a clear cloudless sky. The men lined up in front of the gate waiting for the cavalry in the still chilly morning air.

After a while, they could hear the sound of the horses' hooves coming in their direction and then, coming round the corner, were the magnificently caparisoned horses and their riders.

The early morning sun glittered from their silver helmets, glistened from their scale armour shirts and dripped from the long swords hanging by their sides, their bright shields and the javelins they carried but the shining men were almost eclipsed by their stunning horses whose leather chamfrons and harnesses were heavily decorated with bronze. Had these men not been armed, thought Graecus, you would have thought that their job was to dazzle the enemy to death.

The standard bearer was leading the troupe and brought them to a halt facing Graecus and Acerbus who were sitting on their horses which were fine animals but now looked drab and meagre next to their cavalry counterparts.

Graecus, always a little proud of his good looks, straightened himself in his saddle and squared his shoulders as the Batavian standard bearer saluted them and Acerbus who was sitting a little stiffly in his saddle due (he being utterly devoid of vanity) to the arrow wound in his thigh, looked down his crooked Roman nose at him.

The Batavian addressed them in Latin but with a heavy, harsh accent. 'Hail, comrades. We are come to escort you to our

General's camp. Fall in behind me, gentlemen, and my colleagues will distribute themselves around your men. We must set a sharp pace so take your time from me.'

Acerbus seemed not to be impressed by the Batavians' splendour for, in a rather sharp tone, he said, 'We are experienced infantrymen and well accustomed to a forced march. Our men can adjust to any pace you wish to set. We are ready when you are.'

'Then let us proceed,' said the standard bearer, and prevented any reply by pulling down from under the front rim of his helmet a fitted silver mask which covered his whole face but had strategically placed holes large enough to allow him to see and to breathe. Face mask in place, he wheeled his horse round and set off at a brisk walk out of the camp followed firstly by Graecus and Acerbus then by the army standard bearers and horn-blowers and then the rest of the soldiers with the other masked cavalrymen placed at intervals along the column.

To any bystander, this was surely a most amazing sight with the sun bouncing off all the burnished metal, the spectacle of the colour parties' animal skins, the scarlet of the Centurions' cloaks and the sound of the horses' hooves mingling with the music of the men's feet on the hard road.

Graecus sat upright in his saddle and felt a rush of pride throughout his body – a feeling of joy that he was a member of such an august organisation.

CHAPTER FIVE

They had been under way for several hours without incident or mishap; there was just the clop-clop of the horses' hooves and the tramp, tramp of the men's boots as they marched in perfect time along the road. Once or twice, Graecus thought he heard something like a groan coming from behind him and, in thinking that he recognised Pneumaticus's voice, he was concerned as he knew that his two front teeth had begun to turn black and they would be troubling him. But the old soldier was still too stubborn to allow Magnus to pull them. Acerbus was not in a talkative mood and Graecus thought that he must be concentrating on sitting properly in the saddle so as not to aggravate the wound in his thigh.

On and on they went, horses and men, through the middle of this strange land. The sun was high in the sky now and Graecus was beginning to wish he had arranged some sort of 'halt' signal with the Batavian in front of him as he was increasingly in need of emptying his bladder and felt that he could not be alone in this.

On and on they went through woods and vales and villages where the people came out of their funny little round houses to stare at this spectacular caravan but Graecus's concentration was waning with the increasing pressure in his bladder.

They had just passed by a small settlement and had seen that there was now a stream next to the road when the Batavian put up his right arm to signal 'halt.'

Turning in his saddle, he said, 'We shall stop here for a quarter of an hour,' and the men behind gratefully ran to the trees and relieved themselves before drinking from their water pouches and refilling them in the stream.

Graecus and Acerbus dismounted and led their horses to the stream where they drank deeply. Then Graecus strode quickly to the trees to relieve himself against a large oak tree.

He had just finished and was adjusting his undergarment when he heard a scream, a female scream, followed by muffled male laughter from somewhere ahead of him.

75

Graecus's ears twitched at this. It could just be some locals larking about innocently in the woods but he thought he had heard genuine fear in the scream. Then again, if it were locals, even if they were up to no good, as long as it was nothing to do with the Roman Army maybe they were best left to themselves.

Graecus straightened his tunic and rearranged his breastplate to make it more comfortable and was just about to go back to his men when he heard another noise, and this time it was a definite sob, the sob of a very young girl.

Graecus now felt that he could not let this, whatever it was, pass and looked carefully into the trees to see if there were any clues as to what was happening.

What he saw made him very angry – very angry indeed.

He saw the flash of metal glinting as whoever was wearing it was scrabbling around on the ground trying to hold onto something. Then he saw it again from another slightly different direction and realised that there were two of them.

Two of those flashy Batavians. The bloody fools.

Drawing his sword, Graecus turned to look down the hill and whistled and waved to Germanicus and Magnus who were nearby, to follow him before starting up the incline towards the laughing Batavians. He hoped to be able to take them by surprise.

It took him only half a minute to reach them.

They were in a little clearing, each of them almost prone on the ground trying to hold onto the thrashing legs of a young girl in a coarse brown dress. One of the Batavians had his big red hand over her mouth to stop her screaming and the other seemed to be trying to remove her underclothing.

The girl, who had mid brown hair and very white skin, could not have been more than twelve years of age and she was sobbing even though the Batavian's hand was clamped hard over her mouth.

'Let her go!' shouted Graecus. 'What do you think you're doing?'

The Batavians looked round and gave Graecus an insolent stare as if he had no authority to interrupt them. Graecus saw that they had unbuckled their long cavalry swords which were lying on the ground some feet away but they were still in their scaly metal tunics and it was these he had seen glinting close to the ground, through the trees.

'Stand up when I speak to you, you miserable scum!'

The Batavians turned their attention from the girl and sullenly raised themselves to their knees but they did not stand.

'What's it to do with you?' said the one with the big red hands.

Germanicus and Magnus had now appeared and drew their swords when they saw the sobbing child lying on the ground, her eyes still closed in fear.

'By your animal behaviour, you have put me, my men, my colleague and his men and your own colleagues all in great danger. Do you not see what you have done? You have given the village people every reason to want to attack us or betray us all.'

'We don't give a toss what you think,' said the other Batavian, who, Graecus now noticed, had very bad teeth.

'Well, you'd better, because my father is in command here, and you'd better do as he says,' said Germanicus.

'Ooooh, lithen to the pretty boy,' said Bad Teeth, trying to mimic Germanicus's slight lisp. 'We're really thcared, aren't we?'

'I don't think so,' said Big Red Hands, 'he's only a pipsqueak. We were killing people for Rome long before he was born.'

This was galling for Germanicus whose valour had been proved beyond doubt when he was only ten years old but he fought the urge to stick his gladius in the Batavian's guts and said, 'It's a shame that you're so stupid. Killing you would be just too easy.'

Graecus realised that he needed this stand-off to be brought swiftly to an end and that they should get away from this place as quickly as possible, before the villagers came looking for the girl.

'Tie their hands behind their backs and get them to their feet,' he said and Germanicus and Magnus did this while Graecus stood over the Batavians with his sword at the ready. 'Now, Magnus, take them down the hill to the men and hold them there till I come.'

Magnus turned the Batavians round using the point of his

gladius to encourage them in the required direction, and to help them on their way down the hill, Germanicus gave Big Red Hands a smart kick up the arse.

The girl was still lying on the ground, eyes tight shut, frozen to the spot with fright, mumbling repetitive rhythmic sounds which might have been prayers to her gods.

Graecus did not wish to leave her there as she could come to more harm but he knew it would be difficult to communicate with her without alarming her further. He thought about this for a moment and then said, 'Germanicus, I need you to try to speak to the girl and let her know that she can go but you must try not to frighten her. You are nearer her age than I am and you may be able to reassure her.'

Germanicus nodded to his father, thought for a few moments, and then took off his wolfskin and his helmet and unbuckled his sword. His blonde hair shone in the dappled light and he shook his head a few times to loosen it so that it was falling softly about his face. Then he looked around him at the ground for a few moments and went over to the edge of the little clearing and bent down and picked a small yellow flower which was growing there.

'Father,' he whispered, 'I see that there is an upturned basket behind you. The girl was gathering nuts and berries which have spilled on the ground. It would be helpful if you could refill the basket and hold it so that she can see it when she opens her eyes.'

Germanicus now knelt beside the girl and, speaking very slowly to her, he told her that he wanted her to open her eyes. It was unlikely that she understood what he said but his tone was gentle, and as he spoke he slowly and tenderly stroked the flower across her eyelids.

Graecus, holding the basket into which he had replaced the nuts and the berries the girl had gathered, watched as Germanicus's soft words and the motion of the flower over her eyelids changed her.

At first she seemed puzzled – he could see her eyes moving from left to right and back again under her closed lids – then her tensed body began to relax and her clenched face took on a hopeful, questioning look. Then, some moments later, the girl opened her eyes, which Graecus saw were light green, and looked straight into Germanicus's bright blue eyes.

She stared at Germanicus who, without his helmet and sword and with his beautiful hair almost touching hers, looked more like a romantic suitor than a soldier and she smiled shyly at her rescuer who continued to speak softly to her.

Germanicus smiled at the girl who kept her eyes on him and she then allowed this wondrous being to take her hand and raise her to her feet.

She took the basket from Graecus who bowed to her and then she smiled broadly at Germanicus before walking steadily away from them in the direction of the little village. The soldiers' eyes followed her steps as she gathered momentum and skipped away out of their sight.

'My son, you are a genius. The child will think she was rescued by the god of love.'

'She was rescued by my father. A man of principle.'

Graecus embraced his son and said, 'Thank you – it is ever our desire to uphold the standard. Now let's go and deal with those stupid Batavians.'

Father and son walked down the hill to where Magnus was waiting with the errant Batavians and their standard bearer.

'Your men have brought disgrace upon us,' said Graecus, 'and they have put us all into unnecessary danger. It was only because my son here acted wisely that disaster has been avoided. How do you propose to punish these men?'

'Well, I think that their conduct was not as bad as you are trying to make out. After all, we are more or less at war and men will be men... at least, my men will.'

'You must be as stupid as they are then,' said Graecus. 'Do you not understand that they could have brought about an attack on us by these villagers? And that they had unbuckled their swords and put them on the ground up there? Their swords are still up there in the woods. How can you excuse such conduct?'

This last piece of information seemed to move the standard

bearer more than the plight of the girl for he now pursed his lips and looked thoughtful.

'Yes, I see,' he said, 'I shall recommend to our senior officer that they be given twenty lashes and lose three months' pay. Does that satisfy you?'

'Yes. Now can we get moving? We've wasted too much time in this place already.'

Graecus and Acerbus mounted and the men formed themselves back into their column with the Batavians evenly distributed along the length of it as before except that Big Red Hands and Bad Teeth still had their hands tied behind them. Graecus knew that they would be able to hold on with their thighs and, of course, their four cornered saddles would hold them, but it was still a long way to the camp and even for a very experienced horseman, this would be an uncomfortable way to travel.

When they had been under way for about ten minutes, Acerbus said in a low voice to Graecus, 'They need watching those Batavians – they're very unreliable – far too independent of mind to be good soldiers. They're as courageous as the next man but they don't like taking orders.'

This was the second time in less than twenty four hours that he had been warned about troublesome Batavians so Graecus said, 'Thank you, my friend, for the warning. I shall be on my guard.'

The column proceeded without further incident through more countryside and across a range of hills then down along the side of a big river. They rested for a further quarter of an hour at about two hours after mid-day, and Graecus having asked the Batavian standard bearer if he knew when they would reach Suetonius's camp, was told that they would reach it in about two hours.

Graecus remounted his horse and contemplated this.

He could hardly believe that they were now just a short way from reaching their goal.

They had set out from their sleepy little fort in Lower Germania many weeks before and so many things had happened on their journey that it was difficult to recall them all. He looked across at Acerbus sitting stiffly on his horse and smiled at his friend, feeling great relief that they would soon be with the Legions.

* * *

It was at about four hours past the mid-day when, from the vantage point of a hilltop, they saw Suetonius's camp below them and Graecus's eyes were transfixed.

Spread across the expanse of a large valley with gently sloping sides, it was vast and hugely impressive. Graecus quickly took in the scale of the camp and calculated that there must be the best part of two legions there, almost ten thousand men. And he could see cavalry, possibly two *alae* of cavalry – about a thousand horsemen. Plus several cohorts of auxiliaries. It was the largest marching camp he had ever seen, and looking at the huge numbers of men scurrying about, he did not know why he and his men had been called all the way from Lower Germania.

'It's quite something, isn't it,' said Acerbus. 'I wonder where this Senior Centurion Norbanus is among that lot. It's funny that I can't recall his name from among my acquaintance – I mean I know, or know of, nearly everyone of importance in the European Legions and I cannot bring him to mind. I hope he's not one of those ill-tempered bastards.'

'I was just having the same thought,' said Graecus.

The column set off down the hill towards one of the camp's main gates – in common with all large marching camps, it had four gates but only two led to the *Via Principalis*, the camp's main road.

Now they halted at the gate and stated their business to the guards on duty and were given the all clear to enter the camp.

At this point, the Batavian standard bearer and his men just rode off, presumably in the direction of their quarters, without any farewells or backward glances save that Big Red Hands and Bad Teeth glared at Graecus and Germanicus as they trotted by, looking murderous with their hands still tied behind their backs.

Graecus and Acerbus did not know where they would find Norbanus but they halted the two centuries in front of the large *praetorium* tent, dismounted and went in.

Inside, there were many desks and many clerks scribbling away in ledgers, and although they looked busy, the atmosphere was calm and ordered. No one looked up at the two Centurions as they stood in the open entrance to the tent.

Graecus felt rather stupid just standing there so, after a few moments of trying to decide whom to address, he went to the nearest desk and spoke to the young scribbling clerk.

'Hail, I seek Senior Centurion Norbanus – my colleague and I and our men have come from Lower Germania.'

The clerk was unimpressed by this and, without lifting his eyes from his ledger he said, 'You'll find him with the other auxiliaries. He's trying to knock them into shape. They're just behind us.'

Smarting at this jibe from a callow youth who had probably never even held a sword, Graecus turned on his heel and he and Acerbus stomped off to find Norbanus behind the *praetorium* tent.

The auxiliaries were camped next to the *Porta Praetoria* and there were at least two cohorts of them in tents set out in long straight rows, a tent for each contubernium.

Graecus and Acerbus walked as quickly up and down the rows of tents as Acerbus's injured leg would allow, looking for anyone who resembled a Legionary Senior Centurion, but although they saw many in auxiliary uniform, they did not see any legionaries.

Graecus was just beginning to wonder if they had been misinformed as to Norbanus's whereabouts when he and Acerbus came to the end of the rows of tents and there was the *intervallum*, the large gap in all camps between the ramparts and the tents left there to ensure that the tents were out of range from the weapons of any enemy scaling the ramparts.

And here in the *intervallum* was a group of about a dozen auxiliaries engaged in weapon and combat training. They were big men, more Batavians by the look of it, and some of them were well over six feet. They were using their swords and both Graecus and Acerbus were content to watch this for a while as it was always interesting to observe other men's skills with the gladius. Then in the midst of these giants they saw a much smaller man, about Acerbus's height, who was wearing the uniform of a Legionary Senior Centurion.

Graecus glanced at Acerbus, wanting to signal to him that they should make themselves known to the Legionary Centurion, but he saw that Acerbus was looking very puzzled.

In fact, he was scratching his head and looking pleased at the same time.

'What is it my friend? What is puzzling you?'

'Well, if that is Senior Centurion Norbanus then there's something fishy going on. When I knew him last, he was called Caecilius and we were in some tight corners together.'

'You know him then?'

'Oh yes, I know him well....' At this point, Acerbus burst into laughter, his own very special laughter which was more of a series of snorts leading to several barking noises, and from long experience, Graecus knew to stand well away, so that he would avoid the necessity of wiping Acerbus's spittle from his face.

Acerbus was now well into one of his paroxysms of mirth and was snorting and barking very loudly while Graecus wondered what it was that was causing him so much amusement when the crowd of giants parted and there standing in front of them was the Legionary Centurion.

He was older than Graecus but younger than Acerbus, probably in his early forties, olive-skinned and with rather lank-looking black hair. Obviously a Roman. But the most striking thing about him was his eyes – coal black, glittering eyes – so black that you could not see where the irises ended and the pupils began and you could not see what was behind them. Graecus found this unsettling. But that was not all – encircling his right eye was an unusual scar – it did not seem to have been caused by a weapon, nor did it appear that it had been caused by a burn. In fact, Graecus could not work out what could have caused such a scar and he was busy staring at the Legionary and concerning himself with whether he was, indeed, one of the ill-tempered bastard Centurions when the man came forward and threw himself at Acerbus, grabbing his arm in greeting, exclaiming, 'Brother! Friend! You have arrived at last. I have been most concerned. I heard that you had been sent for but we expected you four days ago.'

Acerbus grinned eagerly at the Legionary and in his most warm but teasing voice said, 'Well, I didn't know it was you or we'd have been here earlier! Why have you changed your name, you scoundrel? What was wrong with the name you had – it was a perfectly respectable name. Indeed, I was rather fond of it.'

'Yes, it was,' said the Legionary laughing. 'And you honour me in saying that you were fond of it – but my uncle on my mother's side left his huge estate in Puglia to me on condition that I changed my name and my father was dead by then, so it seemed impolite to refuse.'

At this, both Acerbus and the Legionary exploded into uncontrolled laughter at what appeared to be a private joke and Graecus and the Batavians had to stand and wait until they subsided.

At first Graecus did not mind this at all – it augured well for the Legionary's being a reasonable man and, he thought to himself, any man who so obviously appreciated Acerbus's excellent qualities, would be someone he would be able both to like and respect. But then, unannounced and unwanted, a cold feeling snaked into his heart – something which was new to him.

Now the two Centurions had stopped laughing and Acerbus turned to Graecus and said, 'Allow me to introduce you to one of the bravest but also one of the craziest men in the Roman Army. And Norbanus, you must meet my great friend and esteemed colleague, Graecus.'

Graecus and Norbanus clasped their forearms and said, 'Hail!' in greeting and Graecus looked straight into Norbanus's eyes and saw that, although his eyes were impenetrable, there were deep laughter lines around them and, for a moment, he felt cheered by this.

But on reflection, if he were honest with himself - and he usually was – he must give a name to the cold feeling and he realised that he was envious that Acerbus, whom he regarded as his friend and mentor, would now need to be shared with someone else. He thought about this again and tried to feel differently but there was still a cold spot somewhere in his heart and a worm wriggling in his belly that the comfortable settled structure of the relationships in his life, unchanged since Acerbus's arrival in Lower Germania many years before, and which had given him more happiness and confidence than he had ever know before, would be changed.

He hated himself for thinking this and tried to dislodge the feeling but it stuck fast in his heart and his belly.

But all around him was now activity and bustle as they were shown where to pitch their tents and then the wagons were unloaded and the men and the animals were fed and wounds were tended and water was fetched and wine was drunk and Graecus saw his men throw off the dust and fatigue of their journey and begin to settle into this enormous gathering of men who were, in many senses, their kinsmen.

As the sun began to go down, Felix went looking for his counterparts in other centuries – those men who knew where and how to obtain supplies; years of experience had taught him how to recognise them and how to trade with them to their mutual advantage. When he saw Felix set off on this quest, Graecus smiled approvingly at his friend's disappearing back as he knew that what Felix had in mind was that the century was bored with the bland food they had had since landing in Britannia and, now that they were in the midst of a huge camp, there would be opportunities for barter and the likelihood of more flavoursome fare for his men in the days to come.

Graecus was not avoiding Acerbus but it was still late that night before he had the opportunity to speak to him again, and even then it was only to say 'Goodnight'; so as far as he was concerned, there was still an uncomfortable question mark hanging over Norbanus and, as he went into his tent, he realised it would have to wait until the morning.

Once inside the tent, Graecus went to prepare for slumber but saw Germanicus sitting on his bed in a deep reverie with tears falling softly down his face. This was unheard of – Germanicus was a stoic young man. Graecus was very concerned and immediately went to sit next to him.

'What is it Germanicus? What is wrong my son? Is it Zig? Has he taken a turn for the worse?'

'No father. It's what happened earlier today with the girl. It has stirred memories for me….things I had forgotten until now.'

Graecus looked into his son's eyes and said, 'Do you wish to tell me what it is you have remembered?'

'Yes, father, I will tell you. I have remembered my mother… and my little sister…. and how they died.'

'You remembered your mother and your little sister? But what is that to do with the girl today? How did the episode with the girl make you remember?'

'Well, when I stroked the flower across the girl's face, I knew that that was the right thing to do because Aoif used to wake me like that when we were slaves together. You know how Aoif used to look after me and she was the only one who could wake me because, if anyone else tried to, I would open my eyes and punch them in the face and spit and knee them in the groin because of what happened to my family. Aoif understood this because she herself had been cruelly treated even though she was so beautiful.'

'Yes, she was and we must hope that she has made a good life for herself in Rome. I will always be grateful to her for looking after the dirty little boy that you were before the slave master gave you to me and I shall always be pleased that I was able to buy her freedom and that of her unborn child.'

Graecus knew that Germanicus was struggling with himself and this tender reminiscence of the beautiful Aoif, the pregnant girl from Ierne whom he had bought from the same slave-master who had given him the wild urchin, gave Germanicus time to try to control his feelings.

While Germanicus blinked back his tears, Graecus recalled to himself how he had left the pregnant girl with the lady innkeeper in the small town so that she and her child would have a roof over their heads, but when he had passed by some months later to enquire after them, the innkeeper had told him that Aoif had gone to Rome with a rich man who had been taken by her looks.

Germanicus was still struggling and not ready to speak so Graecus's mind wandered back to the small town and the handsome lady innkeeper, Arminia, whom he had pleasured several times and he was thinking fondly of the soft spot on her neck which smelled of lavender when his son said, 'Father, they were murdered by raiders. My mother and my little sister.'

'Did you see this?'

'No! I would have defended them! No, it happened while I was out taking the pigs to another field, quite a way from the village but, when I came back, the village was in flames and my mother and my sister were lying in our hut with their throats cut. They had both been raped. My little sister was five years old.'

'That must have been terrible for you. What did you do, my son?'

'I buried them as best I could and I said the words over their grave. I couldn't remember all the words but I said the ones I could remember.'

'Was there no one else from your village?'

'No, I was the only one away from the village when the raiders came and they had gone by the time I got back.'

'What happened after that?'

'I stayed just outside the ruins of the village. I don't know how long I was there. I lived off nuts and berries and roots but I did not live there through the next winter – the other people came before that and they captured me and made me into a slave.'

Graecus moved nearer to his son, put his arm around the young man's shoulder and said, 'That was how I found you. That was how I came to have the best son a man could wish for. What happened to your mother and your sister was dreadful and I wish in all my heart that it had not happened and that you had not seen it but the gods are merciful sometimes and out of that dreadful thing came something wonderful.'

'Yes Father, I see that and I sometimes wonder whether I

shall one day have a family of my own. I mean, I sometimes wonder whether I might marry someone as lovely as Aoif and have children. I dream about her on many nights. She was as gentle as she was beautiful and would be a perfect wife for any man.'

Graecus looked at the wistful expression on his son's face and saw something different, something which should not have surprised him, but it did. He saw that his son was experiencing the awakening of love.

Graecus saw that this young man, the trained and skilled warrior but still innocent in some of the ways of the world, was struggling with the competing emotions of these newly recalled memories and the sweet agonies of first love and he was over-come with compassion for his son.

And Graecus felt chastened. He felt chastened that he had allowed himself to feel envious of Acerbus's friendship with Norbanus when his son was enduring such torment.

'Germanicus, you shame me,' he said. 'I have had my head filled with all sorts of nonsense today and you have reminded me of what is truly important. You are truly a good man and any woman would be fortunate indeed to have you as her husband.'

'Thank you, father. I often wonder if I will ever see Aoif again.'

'Who knows, my son, if the gods wish it then it will happen,' said Graecus, but as he said these words he fervently hoped that it would not come to pass – that would mean that Germanicus would be in Rome and he wished to keep his boy as far away from the Eternal City as possible. But wanting to comfort him, he said, 'Shall I go and see if Zig is well enough now to be brought back to the tent? Would you like him here with you tonight?'

'Oh yes, father, please fetch him.'

Graecus went to the tent where the wounded were and saw that Zig was quite ready to be restored to his usual place with the contubernium, so he picked him and his wolfskin up and carried them back to the tent.

Germanicus was now lying on his side on his bed with his eyes closed, his bright blonde hair falling to his neck, and Graecus, not wishing to disturb him, put the dog on his wolfskin on the bed next to his son. The dog carefully eased his way into the hollow between Germanicus's folded arms and legs and then the young man put his arms around his dog and gave a sigh of relief.

Graecus watched until he was sure that Germanicus was deeply asleep and then went to his own bed but lay there awake until the rest of the men returned. His final thought before he fell asleep was that it would not be long before Germanicus would be seeking the comfort of something less bony than Zig.

CHAPTER SIX

The next day was miserable. The British rain of which Graecus had been warned by Marcus the *Praefectus* which had, so far, been blessedly absent, arrived with a vengeance.

It came heavily down in straight lines – great, grey globs of water – soaking everything it touched, turning the manicured order of the camp into a sodden mess of muddy tracks and grumpy men over which hung the smell of leather whose dampness revived the stench of the tanneries from which it had come.

Graecus was up early wanting to know what was expected of them in this regime and, leaving his tent in search of Felix and breakfast, he almost ran into Acerbus who was coming the other way.

'Oh there you are,' he said, 'I was coming to find you. Feeling better now, are you?'

'Um, I am not sure that I know what you mean.'

'Well, my friend, I know you very well, I know you better than you know yourself sometimes, and there was definitely something wrong with you yesterday. I know there's something wrong when you look down your long nose at people.'

'Was I looking down my nose?'

'Yes, you were, you looked down your nose at Norbanus. I could see that you did not like him, even though you were smiling at him.'

'Well, it was not that I did not like him, I do not know him and it seemed odd to me that he had changed his name but I see now that he is a great friend of yours and that is a sufficient recommendation for any man – if you trust him then that is good enough for me.'

'Thank you for that, anyway. I do trust him, I trust him as much as I trust you and I tell you this – we are very fortunate to have been given him as our immediate commander – he is straight and honest and puts his men before himself, not like some we could mention. He will be fair with us, and in this situation there is a lot to be said for that – there are many men in this sort of caper who would be looking after number one and nobody else – they would be interested in plunder and booty and glory and would not care whom they sacrificed in order to get it.'

Graecus nodded in agreement to this and then Acerbus went on to say, 'While we're on the subject of self-seeking good-for-nothings, that reminds me, have you seen the letter we've had from Verus?'

'No, I have not. Did he address it to us both?'

'Yes, he did.' Here Acerbus's tone took on a sarcastic note. 'And he enquires tenderly after our health and wishes us and our men the protection of the gods in this campaign and exhorts us to earn many honours for the cohort.'

'Oh yes, while he stays as far away as possible from any actual fighting or danger....it is beyond satire that he's our commanding officer.'

'I agree with you but would you rather that he were here, getting in our way and making a fool of himself?'

'No! I would not. The further away he is from me and my son, the more I like it.'

It was unfortunate for Graecus and Acerbus, professional soldiers, that they had Verus as their cohort commander as he was one of the *equites*, that breed of ambitious Romans who must have experience as army officers but who were more interested in politics than soldiering. It was even more unfortunate for Graecus that some years before, when Germanicus was just a boy, he had discovered Verus attempting to importune the child and had threatened to take his head off if he tried that again. And as if that were not bad enough, there had immediately followed the dreadful events of the night-time attack by insurgent tribesmen when Verus had been caught unawares, and taunted by some of the insurgents, had to be rescued by Germanicus who killed two of the men himself.

Graecus despised Verus as both a pederast and a coward and had been aghast when he had been made their cohort commander but their General, Flavius, who was as revered as Verus was hated, had been as good as his word and had kept them apart –

Verus being busy improving his acquaintance with Nero's inner circle while his Centurions policed the Empire's borders.

Verus had, however, been dutiful enough recently to appoint the new horn-blower to the century even though the post had been vacant for some time. Graecus and his century had no choice but to accept the new man into their camp but Graecus refused to have him in his contubernium and his sullen, watchful nature ensured that he became no one's friend thus earning his nickname of Solitarius.

Graecus knew he was Verus's spy and that he did not have the century's welfare uppermost in his thoughts, and this, coupled with the man's unfortunate looks (thin sandy hair, white eyebrows and lashes, sweaty looking skin, yellow teeth and red rimmed pale blue watery eyes) meant that it was difficult for Graecus to conceal his dislike of the man even though, on the face of it, he was a model soldier.

Uncomfortable thoughts concerning the contents of Solitarius's reports back to Verus coursed through Graecus's mind while Acerbus said, 'Well, you'd better have a look at the letter in case you can see something in it which I have missed... it may not be what it seems to be. Verus is as trustworthy as a whore's protestations of love.'

Graecus went with Acerbus to his tent where he gave him the letter. It was not a long letter, but to the naked eye it conveyed all the correct sentiments that a commanding officer would wish to his junior officers who were about to place themselves in great danger – a danger which he would not himself be sharing. Graecus snorted derisively when he read it, feeling that it was just another of Verus's political ploys and then he snorted again when he saw the signature – for Gnaeus Claudius Verus had signed his name with his usual flourish and an extra stroke to the bottom of the final 's' which made it look like a cross – an entirely useless piece of ostentation which Graecus, proud of his own clear, bold hand – felt accurately summed up the man himself.

'We should be grateful that conditions here are so awful that he'll keep well away.'

'Indeed, now let's go and find out what's happening. I want to know what's going on.'

The two Centurions left the tent and went to find Norbanus, Graecus feeling relieved to discover that the cold feeling and the worm of envy had gone from his body even though he had not yet had his breakfast.

Norbanus was busy in his tent writing up reports when they found him.

'Hail, brothers!' he said. 'Have you and your men settled in?'

'Yes,' said Acerbus, 'but we are anxious to know when we shall be on the move again. When are we going to have our battle with Boudicca?'

'When Suetonius is good and ready, and not before. So much depends on this battle that we need to be very careful. Suetonius does not want to have to report to Nero that he is the man who lost Britannia for the Empire.'

'Where is Suetonius now? Is he here?' said Graecus.

'No, he's taken a small number of infantry cavalry and they've gone on reconnaissance to try to find out what she's up to. We don't know what her plan is or if she even has one. She seems to make decisions on the spur of the moment.'

'Do we know where she is now, and how many men she has?' said Acerbus.

'Well, we think she is still in the territory of the Belgi. They've been neutral so far, and we think she will be trying to persuade them to take up arms against Rome.'

'Will she be successful in that?' said Graecus.

'Who knows? Her successes so far have been very impressive and the more successful she is, the more successful she will be as more tribes will wish to join her banners so that they will not have to face her wrath if we are driven out. But all is not lost –Suetonius is no fool and he is as cunning as she is.'

'How many men does she have?' said Acerbus.

'We think she has about two hundred thousand.'

Acerbus gave out a low whistle and said, 'And we have about ten thousand, give or take a few cohorts or *alae*.'

'That's about the size of it, yes.'

'How can we hope to win against those odds?' said Graecus as Acerbus looked grim at the thought of being outnumbered twenty to one.

'Well, as I said, Suetonius is no fool and he will want to ensure that the battle ground favours us. He is a keen follower of military history and he has been studying the battle of Thermopylae.'

'Thermopylae? Ah, I begin to see...' said Acerbus and Graecus nodded his head and stroked his chin as he thought how the strategies of the legendary Spartans in their battle against the might of the Persian Empire could be used to good effect to help the Romans.

'Mmm. So what we need is a narrow sort of bottleneck with enough room for us behind it and something which prevents them from attacking us from the rear. Something like a hill per-haps, and that way, only a few of our men would be exposed to them at a time,' said Acerbus.

'That, as I understand it, is pretty much what happened at Thermopylae and it is what Suetonius is hoping for here. It is our only chance – if the Britons are given enough room to use their chariots and their horses to full effect, then we will fail and Nero will lose Britannia.'

'Which does not bear thinking about but what are we to do in the meantime?' said Graecus.

'Wait. We must wait until Suetonius gets back with the results of his reconnaissance. But it would not be good to let your men sit around. The best thing is to keep them occupied – they can busy themselves with combat training and they must ensure that their weapons are ready for battle, but we need to pray that this rain will stop – it is bad for morale – our men do not like the slap of wet leather on the back of their necks and when it stops we all need to practise our marching and our responses to the battle horns –I'm not having any mistakes made by the men under me.'

'When do we expect Suetonius to return?' said Graecus.'

'Soon. Within the next few days.'

Graecus and Acerbus saluted their colleague and went back to their tents and their men to tell them that they would need to wait yet longer before the battle they had come so far to join. This was bad news for some of the men who were impatient for blood and glory but, after some grumbling, they accepted it and went about their business.

Graecus eventually had his breakfast and settled down to do some paperwork with Incitatus. And this was how the day passed, listening to the sound of heavy rain drumming onto the leather roof of the tent and getting up to date with the century's records while the men cleaned their weapons and their kit and gossiped about army life.

In the evening, proof of the success of Felix's rendezvous with other talented procurers was put on the table and the men fell greedily on to the hare stew flavoured with garum, leeks and garlic and their tempers improved.

After the evening meal, the men sat around drinking and talking but Incitatus was working on something new; Graecus noticed that he was busy measuring a new leather hide and marking it off. Then he would measure Zig and mark another area of the hide, backwards and forwards from hide to dog and back again until he had marked out the area he needed on the hide and then he cut out a shape in leather which was an oblong with four slight protuberances, two on either side. Graecus had no idea what he was doing but Incitatus was concentrating very hard, and whatever it was, was taxing his ingenuity.

Then he seemed to have finished with the oblong piece and started on a new shape which involved measuring Zig's head and marking the leather and backwards and forwards many times until he was satisfied and cut out another piece, a strange shape which looked, for all the world, as if Incitatus were making a bonnet for the little dog. Graecus's curiosity was reaching fever pitch – *what could he be doing?* Then Germanicus came into the tent and said to Incitatus, 'Oh good, you've begun to work on Zig's armour. How is the work progressing?'

So *that* was it. He was making armour for the dog. 'Ye gods!' thought Graecus. 'What is the world coming to?' How would he live this down with other centuries, and in particular, the Batavians, if they came to know about it? The possibilities for ridicule were legion. He could just imagine the Batavian catcalls and insults which would be levelled at him, at the century and at Germanicus in particular – his boyish good looks had already singled him out for their attention and it would not be wise gratuitously to attract further derision.

Graecus made up his mind that he must forbid Incitatus from making this armour and tell Germanicus that, for his own good, he must not insist on it, and having made up his mind, he turned his gaze back in the direction of Incitatus and his son who were engrossed in a discussion as to how much scale armour could be put on the leather jacket so as to protect Zig's back without restricting his movement and being too heavy for him.

Listening to this, and looking at Germanicus's soft blonde hair curving over the back of his neck (he had refused to let Felix cut it any shorter on the pretext that, being longer, it stuck out less but it was more likely that this was a hint of youthful rebellion) he felt that he must stop this there and then so he went over to where Incitatus was working.

'You are making armour for Zig?'

'Oh yes, father, is it not wonderful that when next he goes into battle at my side he will have his own armour and I shall not need to worry about him.'

'Germanicus, I do not think that this is a good idea. A dog in armour is unheard of and I do not think that he will be at your side in battle either. This idea could make us a laughing stock, especially with those brassy Batavians. I have no alternative but to forbid it.'

Germanicus's face crumpled. He looked as if Graecus had slapped him very hard. The hurt in his eyes was terrible to behold. Graecus could not believe that anything he had just said could have given his son cause for such grief.

'What is it? Why are you so sad? What have I done?'

'Oh father, Zig was such a help when we were attacked on the way here. You saw him biting the enemies' ankles and biting through the tendons so that they could not stand up. And you know that he has saved our lives more than once just by his sense of smell or because he is aware of things that humans cannot know. He is as much a part of this century as I am and he is more useful than some men I could mention.'

Bearing in mind the conversation he had had earlier that day with Acerbus about the serious shortcomings of Verus, Graecus could not argue with this observation and was thinking about this when Germanicus went on, 'And he was wounded, just like a proper soldier.'

'But if we kept him away from the battlefield, then he would not be in any danger.'

'And just how are we to do that father? When even the Ocean was not enough to keep him away from me and the century.'

Germanicus's voice had had an edge of steel to it when he said this and it cut Graecus to the quick, partly because it was the first time ever that his son had spoken harshly to him or challenged him and partly because he was referring to the recent incident when they had tried to leave Zig with a tavern owner in Gesoriacum but he had jumped into the sea and followed Nauplius and, to Graecus's despair, Germanicus had swum a long way back landwards to rescue him and bring him to the ship.

Germanicus sensed his father's hurt and said, more gently, 'And when Jejunus wanted to kill him because he said it was bad luck to have a dog onboard, *you* told him that he was a member of the century.'

Zig knew that this discussion was about him and his sensitivity to the moods of these two men was so finely tuned that he knew they were both deeply distressed by it. Zig thought that he was the cause of the disagreement between father and son and, sitting on his haunches in the floor-space between them, he was the picture of misery – his ears were pinned to the back of his head, his eyes were dull and he was shaking with fear.

This was not the bright, bold, confident dog who was normally not afraid of anything and Graecus, glancing down at him, could not bear it.

He swept the dog into his arms, and nuzzling his ear, he said, 'And when you rescued him from the sea, I told you that your heart was greater than my head….and so it proves again; this brave and trusted warrior, this Zig of the Roman Army, shall have his armour so that, when he fights with us, he is our equal!'

'Oh, thank you father. Thank you! I know you were only trying to protect us from the Batavians' taunts but they would have been nothing compared with the thought of losing Zig.'

'Yes, Germanicus, I see that you are right. But there is one thing on which I shall insist.'

'What is that father?'

'That Incitatus will also make a chamfron for Perdix – Zig cannot be allowed to be the only caparisoned animal in the century!'

At this, both Germanicus and Incitatus laughed and Germanicus embraced his father who was still holding the dog but Zig, seeing that all was now well, pricked up his ears and licked his young master's face.

Graecus now put the dog down and, as Incitatus, watched by Germanicus, resumed measuring, he went for a walk.

The next thirty six hours were uneventful except that the weather improved and, with the coming of the sunshine, they were all engaged in hours of drill under the watchful gaze of Norbanus who ensured that they all knew what the horns' sounds meant and that they would respond automatically even in battle. This exercise was welcome and the men relaxed and gained strength and confidence after the privations of their long journey.

In the evenings, Incitatus worked continuously on Zig's armour and Graecus watched with amazement as he sculpted the larger piece of leather to fit the animal's body and sewed straps on it so that it could be anchored in place under his chest and around the tops of his legs. Then he sewed pieces of scale armour onto the leather in several lines down the middle of the coat so that Zig's spine would be protected.

When he was satisfied that the leather body armour was

perfect, he made a padded undercoat for extra protection. This was made from the same material as the garment the men wore under their scale shirts when they were dressed for battle and was somewhat bulky for a dog so Incitatus cut it carefully with a bevelled edge to fit easily under the leather top coat to ensure maximum freedom of movement.

Then he began work on the helmet –shaping and measuring and shaping and trimming and shaping and sewing. At first, the helmet just looked like an unremarkable piece of leather, but once Incitatus had cut the holes for Zig's ears, eyes and nostrils and had edged them in brass (Felix had made friends with a smith from the Legions who was now enjoying one of the cook's celebrated hare and apple pies), it began to take on a life of its own. Then he added 'eyelids' of perforated brass which started higher than Zig's own eyes but came down in a languid way and this, coupled with the exaggerated flare of the brass nostrils, gave the helmet its own facial expression of haughty disdain.

Germanicus loved it and so did Zig – the little animal paraded up and down in his new armour, sometimes turning around several times to see if the armour impeded him then stretching towards the ground, putting his front legs as parallel to the floor as possible, trying to make the armour fit perfectly to his body.

Graecus had to admit that Zig looked magnificent in his armour and went out of his way to say this to both Germanicus and Incitatus and he looked forward to Perdix's chamfron being ready but then the peaceful atmosphere they had all enjoyed over the last few days evaporated and was replaced by a ripple of excited unease as the news spread quickly along the lines that Suetonius had returned.

The news came at about two hours past the mid-day and Graecus immediately went to look for Acerbus whom he found sitting in his tent at a table which was covered in maps.

'Hail, brother! I expect you come to give us the news of Suetonius's return?' he said.

'Yes, brother, and to tell you that, by all accounts, he is in no mood for pleasantries of any sort – according to the guards on the gate, his face was as cold as marble and the expression on it would have turned lesser men to stone,' said Graecus.

'Nothing's changed then. He was a hard bastard years ago when we were here with Claudius and normally age does nothing to soften those who've risen in status since they were ambitious young men,' said Acerbus.

Graecus did not like to hear this and said, 'You make it sound as if we have a monster for a commander.'

'You know I am candid to a fault and why would I lie to you? I tell you this, if we fail in this enterprise, if this woman succeeds in driving Rome from this island, then Suetonius will see to it that he isn't the only one to fall on his sword – our lives will be less than worthless.'

'But we are outnumbered twenty to one.'

'All the more glory for Suetonius when he succeeds. Put yourself in his place, either you win a dramatic and glorious victory against tremendous odds or you lose Britannia for Nero – which would you prefer?'

'I see,' said Graecus. 'Thank you for explaining it to me. We shall need to ensure that we play our part in an exemplary way.'

'We shall do our best as we always do and I know that you will never fail me in the same way that you know I shall never fail you.'

Graecus and Acerbus clasped hands and forearms and said, 'Brother!' each to the other in affirmation of the great bond between them. Then Graecus said, 'I do not know what I would do without your wise counsel. You have so much experience of a world which is strange to me.'

'Your heart is good and that is more important than being worldly-wise.'

'But you combine each of these qualities.'

'That is my genius!' said Acerbus, laughing. 'Now let us go and see if Norbanus knows any more about what is happening than we do.'

Norbanus was standing outside his tent having a loud discussion with three other officers when Graecus and Acerbus arrived,

Acerbus still limping due to the wound in his thigh.

'Hail!' he said. 'You two are just the men I need. This lot can go – I've told them all I'm going to tell them and now I need to speak to you two – sharpish. Come into my tent.'

The three Centurions went into Norbanus's tent which was larger than theirs and had better furniture but then he was a Senior Centurion – one of the most important officers within a Legion.

Norbanus sat at his desk, leaned forward towards his fellow officers and said, 'Now, you each of you have men in your century who are true born Britons, that is correct, is it not?'

'Yes,' said Graecus and Acerbus at the same time, each of them somewhat mystified by the question.

'Do you happen to know if you have anyone from the land of the Belgi, either of you?'

Graecus and Acerbus thought about this for a moment, Acerbus scratching his head as he did so and then Graecus said, 'Yes, one of my senior men, Pneumaticus, is from Venta Belgarum, but it is many years since he left. Why do you ask?'

'Because Suetonius wants to speak to him, that's why.'

'But why would he want to speak to Pneumaticus?'

'At the moment, I have no idea – he does not share his most intimate thoughts with me. If he tells me that he wants to speak to a native from that tribe then that is good enough for me and I must find him one. Happily, we do not need to look very far. Go and fetch the man immediately and report to Suetonius. Acerbus, I need detain you no longer, you may go about your business.'

Acerbus was as surprised as Graecus by this as they could see no reason why Suetonius would want to speak to Pneumaticus and they both left the Senior Centurion's tent in silence, each lost in his thoughts.

'It must be some idea he's got. Something to do with the Belgi – that's why he needs a native speaker,' said Acerbus as they walked slowly back to their lines, Graecus adapting his usual swift pace to his limping colleague.

'But Pneumaticus has not been anywhere near his native land

in thirty years,' said Graecus, feeling apprehensive on behalf of one of his most trusted men (and for his own part as the summons to Suetonius did not include Acerbus and he would be facing this most awesome of men without his mentor).

'Well, I have no inkling as to what this is about,, but in asking for a native of the Belgi, Suetonius must know very well that any man he might have found in either of our centuries would be a stranger to their homeland by now.'

'Yes, I suppose so.'

They had arrived back at their tents and Acerbus went to step into his saying, 'Well, I wish Pneumaticus the assistance of all the gods, whatever it is that Suetonius wants of him.'

With a feeling of foreboding, Graecus went to find Pneumaticus.

He was sitting with Felix, peeling carrots, and despite Felix's brisk good company, he looked glum and very down in the mouth.

'My friend,' said Graecus, 'I need you to come with me immediately. Suetonius has asked to speak to you, and as your officer, I am commanded to accompany you.'

'What? Suetonius wants to meet me? Why would he want to do that? Is he so concerned about the welfare of his troops that he wants to enquire about my aching face?'

'As far as I am aware, he knows nothing of your face ache but he has asked to meet a native of the Belgi tribe and you answer that description. Now, stand up straight and brush yourself down, we cannot meet our new Commander looking sloppy.'

Pneumaticus stood as straight as he could, even though it hurt his face to keep his head up and marched smartly beside his Centurion to the large tent in the centre of the camp where Graecus explained to yet another whey-faced youth who appeared never to have seen daylight that they were expected by Suetonius.

'Wait here,' the young man said, and looked pityingly on the auxiliaries who could not be expected to know of Suetonius's moods.

The youth disappeared into the interior of the large tent and left Graecus and Pneumaticus to stand waiting and he had been gone for about five minutes when they heard shouting and terrible oaths coming from that direction.

'Get me the right maps you fool! Can I not rely on you to get anything right? Do I have to do everything myself? Is there no one in this fucking Army with any fucking sense?' And as these words were being bellowed so that all could hear, there was the noise of many large documents hitting the floor as if they had been swept from a table in a fit of rage.

'I hope that is not Suetonius,' said Pneumaticus under his breath to Graecus, but as he said it, they both knew that it was unlikely that anyone else would dare to have such a fit of pique while the man himself was in earshot and each of them felt a knot of apprehension in his stomach – just the way it felt before going into battle – but worse, as this time, neither of them knew what to expect.

The young man reappeared looking shaken and even paler than before. 'He will see you now,' he said, and in a lower voice, 'May the gods be with you.'

The young man gestured in the direction of the centre of the tent and Graecus and Pneumaticus stepped in that direction.

Suetonius had a tent within the tent, the door-flap to which was open.

The Governor of Britannia was sitting behind an enormous desk which was empty of clutter – because it was all in a heap on the floor beside him. There was a ray of sunlight coming through a flap in the roof and motes of dust moved in it, still dancing from the disturbance of the maps' flight to the floor.

He did not look happy.

The two auxiliaries stood in the open flap staring stupidly at the patrician Roman who had the power of life and death over them.

He was looking into the middle distance – looking in their direction but not seeing them. Graecus did not know whether they should come forward or stay where they were and this uncertainty was one of his nightmares – involving delicate questions of protocol of which he had no knowledge and the knot in his stomach tightened but then Pneumaticus, his nose, no doubt, tickled by the dust, sneezed loudly and broke Suetonius's reverie.

'Humph,' he said, 'I suppose you are the native of the Belgi tribe and you must be his Centurion.'

Graecus said, 'Yes, my lord,' and Pneumaticus said, 'Yes, sir.'

'Well, come forward, then! I cannot see you standing there in the shade, step forward and be smart about it!' Suetonius growled at them.

They came forward – completely in step, as luck would have it – and stood in front of Suetonius's empty desk.

Humph!' he said again, looking very carefully at Pneumaticus.

'What is wrong with your face, auxiliary?'

'I had an argument with a plank, my lord, and the plank won.'

'I see. Does it hurt? Hmmm?'

'Yes, my lord, it does.'

'Humph.'

Suetonius now settled back into his reverie, leaving Graecus and Pneumaticus shifting nervously on the balls of their feet.

'How long is it since you last visited your homeland?'

'About thirty years, my lord.'

'And you still speak the language?'

'I do, my lord, but I have been speaking Latin for so long that I fear my accent may sound odd now to another native speaker.'

'Humph. And you, Centurion –what I want to know is, can this man be trusted? Hmmm?'

'My lord, he is the longest serving soldier in my century and I trust him with my life – he has saved it many times in combat.'

'Can he be trusted to do Rome's work without you standing over him with the vine staff in your hand?'

'Yes, my lord, he can, I would stake my life on it.'

'If he fails, or he betrays us, you will have to!' growled Suetonius, but then, pointing at Pneumaticus, he said, 'I need you to go behind enemy lines to find out what's going on,' and as both Graecus's and Pneumaticus's eyes widened, he went on, 'Yes, that's what I said – I need you to go to Boudicca's camp, disguised in some way, and find out what her plan is because, so

far, the workings of her mind are a mystery to me,' and in saying this, he passed a weary hand over his brow and Graecus
realised that this man must have spent the best part of the last
three months in the saddle; he looked exhausted and drained and
at the end of his tether and this was before meeting Boudicca on
the battle-field.

Suetonius looked into the middle-distance again, as if he
were seeking inspiration, but then he appeared to recollect himself and he beckoned Graecus and Pneumaticus to sit on the two
stools in front of his desk.

This gave the soldiers the opportunity to study the great man
at close quarters.

Although he was sitting down, it was possible to discern that
he was quite short – about half a head shorter than Graecus and
he had light brown eyes but they were watery and bloodshot. It
was not possible to say what colour his hair had been as there
was only a little of it left – a rim skirting his ears – and what was
left was white. His skin was dreadful – red with bluish blotches
and scaly patches, peeling from his head. He did not look well.

'You see,' he said, 'there's not that much time left. The fighting season in this dreadful land is more than half over and we
need to put down this rebellion this year or it gives her too much
time to make more allies. She's with the Belgi elders now trying
to persuade them to join her, I imagine, but I need a battle soon
and I need it on my terms. D'you understand me, hmm?'

'Yes, my lord,' said Graecus and Pneumaticus in unison,
feeling like children sitting in front of their schoolmaster.

Graecus felt that he should try to give some sort of impression of having a brain and summoned up the courage to say,
'What are your terms, my lord?'

At this moment there was a rush of perfume on the air and a
very pretty young woman, obviously Roman and of high birth,
came into the tent within a tent and gave Suetonius a silver wine
cup, smiling sweetly at the crusty man and then at the two auxiliaries before she withdrew.

'And you can put your eyes back in their sockets you two,

she is my daughter,' he said and then went on, 'My terms are that we must have a pitched battle – we cannot allow them to pick us off in ambushes – we have lost too many good men that way already. Hmmm?'

Each time he ended his speech in this way, the great man leaned forward and raised an interrogatory eyebrow at his audience as if they were exceptionally stupid. It was very irritating but Graecus and Pneumaticus nodded, again in unison.

Suetonius took a deep gulp from the wine cup and wiped his mouth with the back of his, none too clean, hand.

'And we need to have it in a funnel – I mean that we need to make sure that there is only a very narrow front to the battle, so that their superior numbers count for very little as they cannot engage them all at once.'

'As happened at Thermopylae, my lord?' said Graecus, relieved that he already knew from Norbanus that this was, indeed, what was in Suetonius's mind.

'Yes, by Jupiter! You have put your finger on it exactly!' said the great man and smiled for the first time since the beginning of the auxiliaries' audience with him.

'Good, good,' he said, 'I see that at least one person round here understands tactics! And knows a bit of history, hmmm?'

At this, Graecus shifted uncomfortably on his seat, as he had been given this nugget of inside information but he felt it would not be appropriate to say so and spoil Suetonius's delight in encountering at least one other military genius in his camp. Graecus would swear that Pneumaticus knew nothing about the battle of Thermopylae but he, too, rose to the occasion by nodding sagely in the great man's direction.

This thawing of the atmosphere gave Pneumaticus the courage to say, 'My lord, what is it exactly that you want me to do?'

'I want you to go to Boudicca's camp, which is this side of Venta Belgarum and go among the people gathered there and find out what she is up to. Find out what the gossip at the campfireside is all about. I want to know if she has any plans, and if so, what they are – I want to know how I can make her dance to my tune. You will need to disguise yourself. Have you a trade? Can you play an instrument, hmmm?'

'No, my lord, nor do I have any trade other than that of soldier.'

At this point, Graecus had a flash of brilliance and said, 'My lord, may I make a suggestion?'

'Yes, yes, make a suggestion, if you must.'

'My lord, Pneumaticus is suffering greatly with his two front teeth which were damaged when he fell on the plank. If he were to have them removed, then he could pass himself off as a beggar – a former flute player but whose livelihood has been ruined by the loss of his front teeth. This would also change his voice so that his odd accent would be seen to have been caused by the loss of his teeth.'

While Graecus was saying this, the great man was drinking his wine and belching in between the large gulps.

He then leant forward with a large gesture as if he were about to say something very important, but whatever it was, was left unsaid as, when he opened his mouth, he brought up all the wine he had drunk and a great deal of blood besides, splattering it all over his desk in an ever widening pool and then he fell face forward into the bloody mess. Unconscious.

CHAPTER SEVEN

This was terrible. Awful. The great man, their commanding officer, Rome's representative in this benighted place, had fainted in front of them – two auxiliaries from a tiny camp in the middle of nowhere. Graecus and Pneumaticus stared at each other in horror. What should they do? There was nothing in their Army Standing Orders which gave any clue as to the correct course of action in a situation like this.

Then Graecus took hold of himself and realised that the man, great man though he was, was only human and he was quite clearly very ill – but the fewer people who knew about it, the better.

Graecus got up, and breathing deeply to calm himself, went to the tent flap, and looking out, saw the whey-faced youth passing by.

'Suetonius wishes to speak urgently to his daughter – please fetch her immediately,' he said.

Graecus closed the flap of the tent within a tent behind him and stationed himself in front of it, earning a few startled glances from other pasty looking young men scurrying to and fro but then Whey Face returned with the pretty girl who was smiling at Graecus in a questioning way.

As they approached, Graecus drew himself up to his full height, and looking down on Whey Face, he said, 'Thank you, you may go.'

Then, bending down to the young woman's ear, he whispered, 'My lady, your father has been taken ill. He has collapsed and he needs medical attention but this must be kept very quiet – it would be very bad for his command and for morale in the camp if it were known that he is so sick.'

The young woman put her hand to her mouth in shock and made a faint moaning noise. Seeking to reassure her, Graecus said, 'My lady, I did not wish to upset you, I merely wished to prepare you. We shall go in now and see your father.'

They entered the tent within a tent where Pneumaticus had

lifted Suetonius back from his desk-top and he was sitting in his chair, comatose, with his head lolling to one side.

The young woman inhaled sharply, said, 'Father!' in a stricken voice and rushed to cradle the great man's head in her arms. Graecus put his finger to his lips to indicate that she must be circumspect and then he went to her and whispered, 'My lady, I do not know if your father has his own doctor here, but if he does not, it will be quickest to send for my century's medical man, Magnus, he is a very experienced and gifted healer. Your father will receive excellent treatment from him and he is utterly discreet.'

She was very distressed and all she could say was, 'Yes, do it,' while trying not to sob out loud and Graecus sent Pneumaticus off to find Magnus.

While they were waiting for the big man to appear, Graecus tried to distract her by speaking softly to her, 'My lady, my name is Graecus, please tell me your name.'

'My name is Aurora and my father is all I have.'

'Is your mother not here with you?'

'No, she died when I was born. My father loved her very much and it broke his heart but he has devoted himself to me ever since.'

'Has your father been ill for some time?'

'It is difficult to tell – he has been away for weeks and he works so hard. He has had hardly any rest since we came to this dreadful island.'

'It must be very worrying for you,' Graecus said softly.

'Yes, it is,' she said. 'Sometimes, I just do not know what to do for the best.'

She was very young, about seventeen, and she was sobbing quietly when Magnus and Pneumaticus came into the tent.

Pneumaticus had told him what had happened and he quickly went to Suetonius's desk and put a finger into the pool of bloody wine lying there and then sniffed his finger... then he grimaced and said, 'Acid – far, far too acid.'

Now he looked at the great man, whose colour was still bad

and, gently dislodging Aurora's hands from his head, he looked in his commander's eyes and into his mouth.

'What is wrong with him?' said Aurora.

'He has excess stomach acid and it is eating into his gullet. He has been bleeding internally.'

'Oh, no!' said Aurora. 'Will he die?'

'One day, my lady, undoubtedly, but I hope that we will be able to make him fit to deal with Boudicca.'

'What do you require?'

'I need a cold poultice for his head to bring him round and a hot poultice for his stomach to warm it. Also, I need to mix a special paste for him to take and you must help me with his diet. Has he been eating many pickled foods?'

'Why, yes, they are his favourites and when they are away from home, spending all day in the saddle, the pickles are easy to carry.'

'Well, he cannot have them any more, they will kill him. He needs bland foods, no spices, no garum, no heavy fatty things – nothing which will irritate his stomach.'

'But those are all the foods which he likes!'

'My lady, if you wish to keep your father alive, then you must persuade him that a more delicate diet is necessary for his health.'

'I will try. I will tell his cook.'

'Now, I must mix the paste and I would be grateful if you could prepare the poultices,' said Magnus and he and Aurora almost fell over each other as they left the tent.

Graecus could not bear to look at the bloody pool on the desk any longer and, taking off his neckerchief, he told Pneumaticus to remove his, and then he used them both to wipe the red mess onto the dirt floor where it sank into the ground.

Graecus had just finished this task and had resumed his seat next to Pneumaticus, the better to think about this situation, when Suetonius began to come round: the great man's head rolled forward and then he opened his eyes, starting as he did so.

'Oh yes' he said. 'Where was I?'

This posed Graecus and Pneumaticus another delicate question – should they tell the great man that he had just spewed his guts up and fainted in front of them or not? Graecus thought about it for a split second and decided against it: better let the great man continue with the discussion they had been having as if nothing had happened.

'You were considering my suggestion that Pneumaticus's two front teeth should be removed. I suggested this as they are going bad anyway and it would provide a convenient excuse for his odd accent,' he said feeling Pneumaticus stiffen with repressed rage at his side.

'Good idea, very good idea!' said the great man, 'And the sooner the better. See to it this very day as you need to be on your way tomorrow. Now leave me and ask that pasty faced wretch at the desk outside to come in here.'

'Yes, my lord,' said Graecus, and he and Pneumaticus left the tent within a tent. Graecus breathed a sigh of relief that they had escaped relatively unscathed and was about to voice this opinion to Pneumaticus but thought the better of it as, at the very least, the old soldier was about to lose his front teeth, and at the very worst, could be unmasked as a traitor by his own people with predictably ghastly results.

So, instead, Graecus said, 'I am sorry that it will be necessary to lose your teeth but you will be stronger after they are out – they have been giving you pain for some time.'

'It's easy for you to say that, they're not your teeth that are coming out today,' said Pneumaticus looking very downcast.

Graecus changed the subject and said, 'I know that I probably need not say this to you, you who are such an experienced and fine soldier, but in order to be very sure, I am saying it: we must keep all of this day's events to ourselves. I mean, that we need to keep not merely your mission secret but also what happened with Suetonius – it would be very bad for his reputation if it were known that he collapsed today and it would not be helpful to our army if Boudicca were to find out.'

'Yes, I understand that, I really do. Now, I suppose I'd better

111

get it over with but I want as much of that magic mushroom stuff as Magnus will give me.'

'I'm sure he will be as generous with it as is possible without doing you any harm.'

They found Magnus in their tent, mixing a potion with a pestle and mortar.

'How is Suetonius now?' he said.

'Well, it was rather odd,' said Graecus. 'He came round shortly after you left, and because I had just swept all that stinking stuff off his desk onto the floor, he did not know what had happened and he carried on just as though he'd nodded off for a few seconds. He carried on with our discussion and then dismissed us.'

'But what am I to do with this mixture then? I can hardly barge in there with it and tell him to take it! Men have been flogged for less than that!' said Magnus.

'No, you cannot do that. What you must do is to ask his daughter to get him to take the mixture.'

'But how am I to do that? How do I get to speak to his daughter without incurring camp gossip and his wrath?' said Magnus.

'By turning round and speaking to me now,' said Aurora who had, quietly and unobserved, come to stand behind Magnus, and from the half-smile playing on her face, was somewhat amused by his predicament.

'My lady,' said Magnus, 'I meant no disrespect to either you or your father! I meant only to ensure that your father would receive his medicine with the minimum of fuss.'

'That is why I have come here. I told my father what happened and he is grateful for your discretion. I also told him that I would fetch the medicine on the pretext of seeing you on behalf of my native serving girl who has the colic. That way, we hope that my father's illness will be kept quiet.'

When Aurora finished speaking, both Graecus and Magnus bowed to her and said, 'My lady,' in acquiescence of her plan, and Pneumaticus said, rather dramatically,

'My lips are sealed.'

Magnus went back to his mortar for a few moments working the pestle to finish grinding the chalky ingredients to a fine paste. Then he added more oil of peppermint to the mixture and put the medicine into a glass phial saying, 'Make sure that your father takes a sip of this before every meal and that he sticks to the diet I gave you.'

'Yes, I will tell him. He is so dear to me that I cannot bear the thought of losing him.' Tears filled Aurora's eyes and she turned to leave the tent.

Just as Germanicus was coming in.

Just as Germanicus was coming in, fresh from his physical training, sweaty and a little muddy, stripped to the waist revealing strong arms and a muscled torso, with a towel round his middle, his bright hair falling onto his face.

'Father, I need to speak...' he said, obviously meaning to address Graecus but then he saw Aurora and words failed him.

Having lived in camp with the century for all his formative years, Germanicus was not accustomed to the company of young women and his gaze greedily drank in her soft black hair, her flawless pale olive skin, her startlingly violet eyes and her slender but definitely female figure.

Germanicus stood stupefied by this vision, who as far as he knew, could have been Venus personified.

Graecus could not help but notice the effect Aurora had had on Germanicus and looked searchingly at the young woman to see if she, too, had noticed how his son had been mesmerised by her. He looked at her and saw that she was looking at Germanicus with the same awed loss of self-control and good manners. Indeed, she was as stricken as was Germanicus.

Observing this age old phenomenon of the stirrings of mutual attraction, Graecus was at first filled with fatherly pride that a patrician lady should be so drawn to his son but then he felt that this was merely a reflection of the lady's good taste as Germanicus was undoubtedly a fine specimen. Then Graecus felt amused by the silken madness which had enveloped them both and he smiled indulgently at them, each staring at the other as if wishing to remember the glorious vision for ever.

Then Graecus had another thought and he, at least, regained his senses. Ye gods! What had he been thinking of? He had been thinking that someone like Aurora – beautiful, gentle, kind and… well, patrician, would make a perfect wife for his boy if Germanicus were to do well in the Army or if… if he could safely make his way along the rocky path that was his natural heritage but that was so dangerous a thought as not to be entertained.

No, the best thing, the safest thing, the kindest thing, would be to nip this in the bud now and, as Germanicus's commanding officer, Graecus knew that it would be folly of the most extreme nature if he, a lowly auxiliary, were even to contemplate pursuing a girl so far above him in the social order as Aurora… especially with the inquisitive Solitarius watching their every move.

Graecus was about to open his mouth to say something, perhaps a little caustic, to bring the two star-crossed lovers back to earth with a bump and then he had another thought, but this time it was more of a feeling than a thought and it came from his heart where he was more of a father and less of a Centurion, and the thought was that Germanicus should be allowed to dream – the young man should be allowed his innocent dreams and that it was not part of Graecus's job as a father to trample all over his son's tender aspirations. But then again, it was a father's job to keep his son out of harm's way and Graecus thought that he should try to steer a middle path.

So Graecus, instead of a withering comment, said, 'Ah, Germanicus, my son, allow me to introduce you to Aurora, our Commander in Chief's daughter – she is here collecting some medicine for her native slave girl who has the colic.'

On learning that the beautiful vision on whom he had been so greedily feasting his eyes was their Commander's daughter, Germanicus managed both to blush and grow pale at the same time.

He bowed, holding the towel closely around his middle and stuttered, 'Mmy… mmy… my lady, I must apologise for my lack of formal dress,' while she smiled very prettily and said,

'I am sure, soldier, that I could not have enjoyed meeting you more had you been clad in cloth of gold from head to foot.' Then she turned coquettishly on her heel and left.

'Hmmm,' said Graecus to himself, 'The minx! Perhaps not as innocent as I thought!' And then, turning to Germanicus, he said, 'My boy, I think that you need to clean yourself up now and I recommend that you use cold water – the colder the better.'

'Yes father, but why cold water?'

'Because that young woman has so heated your blood that it could be bad for your health!'

'She is very beautiful, is she not?'

'Yes, she is and she seems devoted to her father.'

'Do you think that she liked me, father?'

'Who could not like you, my son, you are a good man and a fine soldier.'

'Thank you, father, I try to follow you in those respects... do you think that Aurora will need to visit us again for more medicine?'

'I do not know but I doubt it – she is probably very busy with her other household duties and looking after her father.'

'That is a great shame... I would have liked to have spoken more with her'

'That would not necessarily have been a good thing, my son!' Graecus said, more sharply than he intended.

Germanicus looked puzzled then said, 'Well, I had better go and get clean now,' and left the tent.

'Well, Aurora certainly made an impression on Germanicus and he on her!' said Magnus. 'You could have tethered an ox with the rope binding her gaze to his. I do not think I have ever seen two young people more attracted to each other.'

'That, I think, is the nature of young love,' said Graecus. 'It arises suddenly out of nowhere, rendering its subjects mad with sweet thoughts and then, as often as not, it is all over within the month. And that is what I hope will happen here – Aurora is not the right girl for my son – she is a patrician and her father would have him whipped to within a inch of his life if he thought that Germanicus harboured any thoughts about his daughter.'

'I am sure that you are right but you will find it difficult to convince Germanicus of that.'

'Indeed, so the less they see of each other the better – let us hope that we shall all be too busy getting ready for the big battle for them to cross paths again.'

'Yes, that would be the best thing.'

'Well, I think they made a very handsome couple,' said Pneumaticus. 'And if I'd been ten years younger, I would have been competing with Germanicus for her attentions. She is a *very* pretty girl – a bit thin and a bit too pale for my taste but very pretty nevertheless, and even though I say it myself, I was always popular with the ladies.'

Graecus felt rather irritated by the fact that Aurora had reduced his closest colleagues, strong fighting men, to gibbering idiots and he wanted to bring their minds back to the matter in hand so he said, 'We know all about your reputation with the ladies and how much trouble it causes from time to time and I do not want my son repeating your mistakes. Now, Magnus, we need to press on with the extraction of Pneumaticus's front teeth. Do you have the correct instruments to hand?'

'Yes, Domine, but I need to give him a little of the magic mushroom first and wait until it takes effect. It will be better for him that way.'

'Please proceed immediately.'

'I am not looking forward to this,' said Pneumaticus.

'You will not feel a thing, the teeth are loose anyway and you will be having wonderful dreams – probably about those ladies you keep mentioning,' said Magnus.

It was not necessary that Graecus was present for the operation so he left the tent and went to look for Acerbus, rehearsing in his head what, if anything, he would be able to tell his friend about the strange events he had so recently experienced. He thought about this as he walked along and decided that he would be able to say very little.

He found Acerbus in his tent working on some plans at his desk, and when Graecus entered, his friend and mentor raised first his head and then a questioning eyebrow.

'So?' he said

'So, there is a secret mission and I cannot tell you the details, only that Pneumaticus will be away for some days, and if it all fails, I may as well be a dead man because Suetonius will need someone to blame.'

'Like that is it? Well, you should never underestimate Suetonius so you can take comfort from the thought that he will have worked it out that he can trust you and you will just have to hope that this mission, whatever it is, is successful.'

'I could not have put it better myself. Tell me, did you know that Suetonius has a daughter?'

'I have heard of her, naturally, but I have not met her.'

'She is here, in camp, looking after her father. She is very pretty. Pretty in a natural sort of way – not like those haughty painted creatures one often associates with high born young women.'

'Well, that's encouraging. Something for us to look at if she ventures out from her tent.'

'She has ventured out already. She met Germanicus. They could not tear their eyes from one another.'

Acerbus gave a low whistle through his teeth and stood up to stretch his legs. Then he said, 'I hope that Germanicus is not foolish enough to have hopes in that direction. It could be very dangerous for him.'

'Precisely my thoughts so I intend to keep him busy to take his mind from it.'

Graecus then left his friend to his work and, feeling a little better now that he had told Acerbus at least something of what had happened and that Acerbus had concurred with him about Aurora, he went to make sure that Germanicus was kept very busy.

The day wore on. Pneumaticus lost his teeth and lay on his bed with a gummy grin on his face as the mushroom made him insensible to his pain and what was going on around him. Graecus gave Germanicus one task after another and did not let him rest for a moment – fetching and carrying and helping Felix and seeing to the horses and making sure that Impedimentus knew what supplies they needed. Then it was time for the evening meal and Pneumaticus, regaining his grasp of normality, was able to eat sitting at the table with the rest of the men. Incitatus was next to him and, having mashed up some vegetables, gently fed them to the older man with a spoon while the other men looked on sympathetically.

Then it began to rain – not the heavy rain they had experienced days before but heavy enough to drive them back into their tents and Graecus sat at his desk reading while Incitatus lit several oil lamps and sat staring at two objects lying in the palm of his hand.

They were small black things and, if Graecus did not know any better, he would have said that they were teeth. They looked for all the world like two blackened front teeth. Human teeth. But what would Incitatus be doing with two front teeth?

Incitatus was now turning them over and over in his palm and studying them intently.

Graecus could not contain his curiosity any longer.

'What is it you have in your hand, Incitatus?'

'Pneumaticus's teeth, Domine. I asked Magnus to keep them for me.'

Graecus felt queasy for a moment as he allowed this statement to sink in. Incitatus had asked for Pneumaticus's teeth. Incitatus had asked for Pneumaticus's teeth? What in Jupiter's name could he be doing with his colleagues teeth? Was this some obscure Spartan ritual?

Incitatus was still busy studying the loose teeth and had not seen his Centurion's bafflement. Now he said, 'Yes, I asked him to keep them because I thought that I may be able to make some false ones for Pneumaticus if I could replicate the shape of his real teeth and it will make him happy again.'

'Incitatus you are a man of great talents! And you are a kind colleague to want to restore Pneumaticus's smile to his many female admirers. Does he know of your plan?'

'No, I want it to be a surprise for him. I had a good look in his mouth when he was unconscious after the operation and I have an idea how I could fix the teeth into his mouth.'

'But from what will you make the teeth?'

'Well, if I could get some ivory that might work or I could try carving some cow bone – that might work. I think that ivory would be best but I don't know how to get hold of it.'

'Well, the one person who could get it is Felix and I shall ask him immediately to try.'

'And I need some gold wire too, so that I can make a sort of cage to fix the ivory teeth to Pneumaticus's other teeth.'

'Well, that is beginning to sound like a tall order but if anyone can get such things in this outlandish place, then it is Felix.'

Graecus left the tent and went to find Felix who was discussing recipes with someone from Acerbus's century and signalled to him that he wanted urgently to speak to him.

Felix told the man that he would not give him the secret, the mixture of spices which made it so delicious, of his hare and apple pie and then came to stand next to his Centurion.

'Felix, I need your help. Incitatus wants to make some new front teeth for Pneumaticus and he needs some ivory – he thinks that ivory would be best. Will you try to get some for him? And he needs some gold wire. He will not need much but you are the only person who can get it for us, no one else has your contacts.'

'Oh what a good idea. The new teeth I mean. I am thinking of who could help us....' Felix stroked his chin as he thought, and then he rubbed it a little and said, 'Well, now that I think about it, some of the legionaries here have served in Africa and their Centurion will have had more money to spend so he may have something and I've heard that he has a good appetite so I may be able to twist his arm. Leave it to me.'

'Can you find him now?'

'Yes, I can. But I cannot at the moment think of who would have gold wire'

'Well, whoever it is will more readily part with it for money so please take this,' said Graecus emptying a month's wages from his purse and giving it to Felix.

119

Felix set off on his quest for the treasures of the orient and Graecus smiled at the resolute set of his friend's back, knowing that, as he walked, Felix was thinking of how to strike the best bargain.

Graecus went back to the tent and spent a few hours reading and waiting in happy anticipation of Felix's return with the ivory and he was so pleased at the thought that Pneumaticus might have new teeth that he did not notice until it was well after dark that Germanicus was not there. And neither was Zig.

Once he realised this, and that his son had not told him of his intention to be absent, nor told him why, he had a horrible sinking feeling in his belly and he heard the blood rushing in his ears.

Felix returned, triumphant, with a promise of ivory and gold wire to be delivered in two days' time and Graecus struggled to muster up the required enthusiasm for this feat of procurement.

Now, around him there were the usual sounds of men getting ready to retire to bed, their long familiar voices echoing in his head while his mind went into a state of exaggerated alertness and thoughts tumbled over each other as he tried to work out where his son might be.

He dared not ask anyone if they knew where Germanicus had gone as this would draw attention to his absence and the fact that Graecus did not know where he was and, if they went looking for him, who knows what they would find? And what would Solitarius put in his next report to Verus?

But one word – one name – kept coming back into Graecus's mind – one name which would not, much as he wished it, go away: Aurora.

Aurora. She would be a good explanation for why his son, who had hitherto been the most truthful and forthright and open young man imaginable, had suddenly become secretive.

But how could she have communicated with him?

Where could they be?

What, in the names of all the gods were they *doing?*

Graecus sat down heavily on his bed, his head in his hands and let out a small groan.

It would be the most natural thing in the world. People had been doing *it* since time began. He very much enjoyed doing *it* himself. But he hoped, hope against hope, that Germanicus had more sense than to have been doing *it* with Aurora.

But what had sense to do with it? Graecus smiled ruefully – he well knew that when a man's passions are inflamed, and there could be no doubt about the fact that Germanicus's passions were ablaze, then sense flies out of the window. And Aurora had been so coquettish with Germanicus that it was possible that she was no virgin.

This was dreadful. How could Germanicus be so thoughtless as to put himself in danger just so that he could pleasure himself with Aurora?

Graecus groaned again and covered his eyes with his hand. He sat in despair, he did not know for how long.

'Father?'

It was Germanicus standing in front of him. Germanicus looking enquiringly at him as the other men slept soundly in their beds.

'Father? Are you ill?'

'No, my son, but I have a bad headache.'

'Shall I ask Magnus to get you a tincture for it?'

'No, thank you, I feel it is getting a little better. Where have you been my boy?'

Much as he did not want to do so, as it implied that he did not trust his son, Graecus felt that he had to ask this question and he also had to observe Germanicus closely as he gave his answer.

Germanicus shifted from foot to foot and looked at the ground a little while before saying, in a voice which was, to Graecus's ear, unnaturally high, 'Zig and I have been for a walk, father.'

'It must have been quite a long walk – you have been gone for some time.'

'Yes, it was a long walk.'

'And you saw fit to put on your new tunic for this long walk in the rain?'

'Yes, I did, father,' sounding bolder now, and a little defiant.

Graecus's heart was in his mouth. He felt that his son, his

beloved boy, the most precious person to him, was lying to him. He could have wept. The sacred bond between him and his boy was being stretched by the young man's raging passions.

Graecus did not know at this moment whether he was a father or a commanding officer but, even if he could decide which role to play, it would not help him as he did not feel competent in either respect in this very tricky, delicate situation.

His heart spoke first and, without his thinking about the words, without his having the opportunity to censor them, he heard himself say, 'I hope you are being truthful with me, my son.'

'I hope I am always truthful with you, father. I *have* been for a walk.'

'Then I must trust that you *are* telling me the truth.'

Graecus saw Germanicus swallow uncomfortably. 'Yes, father,' he said.

Graecus would have given much, given everything he had, for Germanicus to have said something to have broken this evil spell which had grown up between them in such a short space of time. He would have given anything for his son to tell him openly and honestly where and with whom he had been. Each of them knew that Germanicus was not telling the whole truth and each knew that the other knew but neither of them could break this spell.

Graecus's heart was breaking. He wanted to tell his son that he loved him and to warn him of the terrible dangers inherent in what he was doing but he could not – he was powerless to stop him – indeed, he knew that Germanicus's nature was such that, if he forbade him to see Aurora again then that would only spur him on to see her more and to descend deeper into desperate actions and deceit. His only hope was that this madness would run its course quickly and without disastrous consequences.

But, for now, all he could do was sigh deeply and say to his boy, 'It would be wise to go to bed immediately and get out of that wet tunic before you catch cold in this infernal land,' and be grateful when Germanicus did as he was told.

Graecus prepared for bed but before he retired he looked at

his son as he lay on his back in his bed, his soft hair playing about his face (it really was too long but now was not the time to tell the boy to get it cut) and his heart cried out for help.

What could he do? He could not ask any of the men in his century who were themselves fathers of sons for help as their merely knowing what had happened would put them all in danger, nor could he draw on the experience of his relationship with his own father for he had no knowledge of it and he felt entirely bereft. He could not even ask Acerbus for advice as that would endanger him also.

Graecus felt that this was the worst situation he had ever encountered as it touched him in the deepest most tender part of himself – that part of him which loved his boy so much that he would gladly give his life for him a thousand times and, as he lay in his bed listening to the steady rhythms of sleeping men breathing all around him, he envied them their rest.

His soul was in torment. He felt that he had lost his son and that wonderful closeness they had had all these years – that closeness which had nourished Graecus and had made his life worth something – that closeness which had been a part of his every waking thought and many of his dreams now felt as if it had been shattered as easily as a glass goblet on a stone floor, and worse, as carelessly.

Where had his beautiful, bright sunny boy gone? How could it have happened in an instant that he had been replaced by a deceitful young man?

Tears slid hotly down Graecus's cheeks as he lay on his back and it irritated him that they ran into his ears. He took off his neckerchief and wiped his eyes and nose and resolved that he would, after all, discuss this disaster with Acerbus – it was too awful to keep to himself.

Then he fell asleep.

CHAPTER EIGHT

The next day was dull and overcast but it was not raining and Graecus was comforted that Pneumaticus would not be going on his dangerous journey with a sore mouth in wet weather.

Graecus washed and dressed quickly and asked Germanicus to help him with his leather cuffs. The boy came over and, through long practice, expertly began threading the laces through the holes but there was none of the usual light-hearted banter between them, nor the animated talk of what the day would bring. There was only a deep, frightening silence and Germanicus's failure to meet his father's gaze.

Graecus's heart was in his mouth and his belly was somersaulting, churning over and over as he tried to think of something to say – something which would restore them to their previous happy state of loving father and son but nothing would come and all he could say when the job was finished was, 'Thank you my boy. Now you had better go and get your breakfast,' while Germanicus mumbled something unintelligible and sped off, away from his father, as soon as he could.

If he had had the time and if he could have allowed himself to indulge his turbulent emotions, Graecus would have vomited – so violent was the disturbance in his heart.

But then that would have meant explanations – and more lies – and he did not want that. Nor did he want to disturb the rest of his men when they were all so close to a decisive battle against a multitudinous enemy.

Graecus breathed very deeply several times and squared his shoulders. He might be feeling as weak as a kitten in the face of this cold war with his son but he *was the commander and he did have the other men to consider* and he found somewhere very deep inside himself that there was a ball of iron resolve.

So, Graecus determined that Germanicus must learn that actions have consequences and that the boy's failure to uphold the standard would have the result that his Centurion would keep him very busy and that his father would distance himself from him.

But how would he put this into practice without alerting the other men to the filial discord?

Graecus thought for a moment and then concluded that his best ally in this would be Impedimentus as he was the least likely of their group to notice that anything was amiss, and in any event, there was always much work to be done in his area of responsibility.

Graecus left the tent and went to have his breakfast with the rest of his men and hoped that he was putting on a convincing performance of the resolute officer but even Felix's cooking did not stir his appetite and all he could stomach was a small bowl of honeyed porridge which then stuck to his ribs. Germanicus was nowhere to be seen.

Pneumaticus, encouraged by Magnus, was eating a big bowl of porridge and looking brighter than for some time.

'You seem to be in good spirits this morning, my old friend,' said Graecus.

'Well, much as I do not wish to admit it, I feel a great deal better for losing those black teeth,' said Pneumaticus through a mouthful of porridge. 'And I look forward to a celebration when I get back from my travels.'

As Pneumaticus was speaking with his mouth full, Graecus could not tell whether the loss of his teeth had affected his voice and was about to ask him to say a few words with an empty mouth when a young legionary appeared telling Graecus that his presence and that of the Belgi native were required in Suetonius's tent.

Pneumaticus swallowed his porridge so quickly at this that he began a coughing fit and needed to be slapped on the back several times before he and his Centurion were able to follow the legionary.

Neither of them spoke a word on the walk to their leader's tent and each of them was deep in thought.

They were ushered into the presence of the great man immediately.

He looked in rather better health than the last time they had met – brighter of eye and with a more healthy colour.

They did not dare to hope that he might be in a better temper but he smiled when he saw them and beckoned them forward to stand in front of his desk and then he motioned them to sit.

'Ah, gentlemen,' he said, 'Today is an important day in the history of the Roman occupation of this terrible island! Today is the day when our gallant friend here' – pointing to Pneumaticus – 'Will take his life in his hands and go back among his own people as our spy. And as a result of his spying I shall at last find out what that infernal woman is up to! Hmmm?'

'Yes, my lord,' chorused the auxiliaries.

'How is your mouth, soldier? How is your voice this morning?'

'My lord,' lisped Pneumaticus, spitting slightly as he spoke, 'I find my voice ish mush altered and I am having difficulty pronouncing shome of my words at all.'

'Good, good. That is all to the good. Now, we must see to it that you have suitable clothing – one of the staff tribunes has been looking into that and has the garments ready for you so that you will pass freely among the tribes gathered around Boudicca's campfires. Now, keep in mind that I want to know what her battle-plans are, if she has any, but I also want you to do something else, hmmm?

'Yesh, my lord?' lisped Pneumaticus.

'Yes, as you are making your journey to her camp and back, I want you to look out for a valley such as this,' and Suetonius produced a drawing of a valley with a wide, open neck but which narrowed and ended with a steep escarpment at its bottom.

'Ish there sush a plashe?' asked Pneumaticus but had difficulty pronouncing all the 's's' and the 'ch' in the sentence so that Graecus, who had learned to dodge Acerbus's spray when he laughed, made a mental note to stand clear of Pneumaticus – or at least until he was wearing his new teeth.

Suetonius snorted at this question and then he said, 'There had better be, because if there is not, we stand no chance of defeating this woman.'

'I will look very carefully my lord.'

'Yes, you had better and you had better be back here within

five days or your Centurion here will be answering for your absence, understand me, hmmm?

Graecus was just wondering quite what this meant when a rush of familiar perfume came into the room heralding Aurora's appearance.

She was carrying a silver goblet and decorously put it on her father's desk saying in a soft, almost girlish voice, 'Here is your medicine, father, please take it. You know it is doing you good.' Then she turned and Graecus saw that her violet eyes were glittering like jewels and there were pink spots of high colour on her cheeks. She was radiant. She was glowing.

And, as she smiled at Graecus, she was triumphant.

Up until this moment, Graecus had tried to give Aurora the benefit of the doubt. He had tried to think of her as an innocent young girl catapulted into an ill-judged affair by the overwhelming passion she felt for the upright, wholesome, handsome young man who was his son. Thinking in this way had made it easier for Graecus to bear the unbearable but now, seeing the victorious, lascivious smile on Aurora's face, he knew this was not so.

He knew that she had been the instigator and he knew that she was not an innocent. He knew that she was sexually experienced and that she had seduced his boy.

This strengthened his resolve but it made it no easier to deal with the problem. How, for instance, would he explain what had happened if the liaison were disclosed to Suetonius by the ever-vigilant Solitarius? Would Graecus be able to absolve Germanicus from blame by telling Suetonius that his daughter was a trollop?

Hardly.

Would Graecus be able to ensure that there was no further contact between the lovers by telling Germanicus that this lovely young woman was a harlot?

Hardly.

Would Graecus be able to dissuade Aurora from further contact with Germanicus by telling her that he knew what she was up to and he would reveal her secrets to her father?

Hardly.

So, what could he do?

Now he realised that Suetonius was speaking to him because the great man had just leaned forward in his direction and said, 'Hmmm?'

Aurora had seen that Graecus had not heard her father and Graecus would have placed a year's pay on the wager that she knew precisely what her lover's father had been thinking.

She smiled very prettily at the Centurion and said in a sweetly condescending voice, 'My father asked you, soldier, if you had anything to add to the orders he has given to your man?'

'Indeed, my lady, I was just considering the question and I find that I have nothing to add as your father has so succinctly given my colleague all the information he needs,' said Graecus giving Aurora one of his most winning smiles exposing his excellent teeth.

Each of these protagonists knew exactly what the other was thinking and each knew it was war between them.

War for the love of Germanicus.

Graecus knew that he really loved Germanicus because he always wanted what was best for his boy and he knew that, despite her very obvious attractions, Aurora was not good for his son and that, once she had lured him into her passionate web and made him fall desperately in love with her, she would tire of him and dispense with him on a caprice.

And then Graecus and Felix and Magnus and Pneumaticus and Incitatus and all his other real friends would need to pick up the pieces of his broken heart.

Graecus knew that this was just a game for Aurora, one in which she was very skilled but he also knew, because he knew his son, that Germanicus would give his heart freely and without reservation.

Graecus groaned silently and resolved to put this whole sorry mess before Acerbus who was more worldly wise.

Suetonius was speaking again, this time to Pneumaticus, 'You will leave as soon as you have changed your clothes. We will provide you with an escort for the first five miles – you will appear to be our prisoner – then you will make your own way for the rest of the journey on the back of the mule we will give you.'

Graecus saw Pneumaticus's shoulders sag a little at this as he knew that his old colleague was no great lover of quadrupeds but he could see that a mule would be a fitting beast for the part Pneumaticus was about to play.

'Now, there will be more field exercises this afternoon, but until then, you and your men may be at your ease,' said Suetonius, beaming indulgently at his lovely daughter.

'Thank you, my lord,' said the auxiliaries and left the tent.

The staff tribune was waiting outside the tent within a tent and he had several coarse woollen garments over his arm.

'Come with me,' he said to Pneumaticus.

'Farewell my old friend,' said Graecus. 'May the gods smile on you in this enterprise.'

'Thank you,' said Pneumaticus. 'The worsht part will be the bloody mule. I hate thoshe shtubborn four-legged bashtardsh!'

And then he walked away with the tribune leaving Graecus feeling cold and empty with a sick feeling that so much hinged on what Pneumaticus would achieve and how the situation between Germanicus and Aurora was a dry tinder box under a hot sun.

The only thing he could do now was to find Acerbus and unburden himself to his oracle.

Graecus went immediately to Acerbus's tent and was relieved to find him there, sitting on his bed with a big bowl in his lap, spooning its contents quickly into his mouth.

'Oh, there you are,' he mumbled through porridge-filled teeth, 'I hear that Suetonius has graciously given us the morning off. How about a bit of hunting? I'm sick of bread and bacon.'

'That is a good idea,' said Graecus but there are a few matters I need to discuss with you urgently.'

'I thought you were wearing your serious face this morning. What is it? Is it that business with Germanicus and the great man's delicious daughter?'

'Why, yes it is,' said Graecus going pale at the thought that the story of their coupling had gone all over the camp and was inches away from Suetonius's ears by now. 'How did you know?'

'I didn't, I just guessed. I guessed because you do look so very serious that it could only be about Germanicus – nothing else matters to you quite as much as that.'

'You are correct, as always, and the nub of the matter is that I suspect, no, I am sure, that they are having a full-blown liaison and he is lying to me about where he is going.'

'Let us be quite clear here. Are you saying that Germanicus is actually shafting our Commander's daughter?'

'Short of finding them in the act, I could not be more sure.'

Acerbus whistled the long low whistle he used when he was foxed.

'Well, you can hardly blame him. I mean, she is v-e-r-y tasty – as tasty a morsel as I've ever seen.'

'While I am glad that you approve my son's taste in women, I am very concerned about it all. When did you meet her?'

'I didn't meet her exactly but she walked past here yesterday afternoon with her native slave girl, they were carrying baskets of fruit and bread for the wounded in the hospital tent and Aurora had a smile for everyone.'

'Did she indeed? Well, that is part of the cause of my discomfort.'

'Why, I mean, why shouldn't a pretty girl smile at an old soldier?'

'When she is supposed to be a demure young girl. When she is supposed to be in love with my son. When she is supposed to behave with decorum.'

'Oh, I see, you think that she is a little too forward.'

'That is a gross understatement. I think she is a cunning, conniving, sly minx who has bewitched my boy and no good will come of it. She was not chaste when she met him and she has used her wiles to ensnare him.'

'Are you not being a little harsh on the girl? Is it not possible that she *has* fallen in love with him?'

Graecus was becoming very frustrated that his mentor, his guide in all worldly affairs was being so obtuse in this most important of matters. Why could he not see that this was a desperate situation?

Graecus banged on the desk at Acerbus's bedside and said, 'She is a trollop. I am convinced of it. I saw her this morning in Suetonius's tent and she smiled *triumphantly* at me. She gave me the smile the lion gives to the antelope just before killing it and she smiled at me in that way because she knows that we are battling, she and I, for Germanicus's heart.' Then, as he finished speaking, he was so overcome with emotion that he fell onto the chair next to the desk and slumped forward with his head in his hands, trying to disguise the fact that he was crying.

'Oh, my dear boy, I am sorry that I did not understand. I am so sorry that I did not appreciate the gravity of what has been happening. I see now, I see that you are ill with worry. I will get you some honey water from Felix, and then, when you are feeling a little more composed, we shall discuss this and see what we must do.'

'Thank you,' said Graecus from under his hands and then, when Acerbus had left the tent, he gave full vent to his feelings, sobbing as he had never sobbed before, his tears falling freely onto the desk, his tense shoulders heaving with pain.

Then he realised that he had a snotty nose and that it was a cold unpleasant feeling so he took off his neckerchief, blew his nose with one corner and wiped his eyes with the other.

He pushed back the lock of hair from his forehead and breathed slowly and deeply to prepare himself for Acerbus's return. His nose was running again and his neckerchief was wet so he wiped his nose unceremoniously on the back of his hand.

Now he heard Acerbus's feet behind him and he turned his grief stricken face towards his friend and stretched out his hand to take the cup of hot honey water from him.

He took a gulp of the comforting liquid and smiled wanly at Acerbus.

'Now then,' said the older man softly, 'what has been happening?'

'Well, Germanicus went out last night in the rain supposedly for a walk with Zig but he did not tell me before he went and he was wearing his new tunic and he was lying to me when he said he had only been for a walk. I knew he was lying and there is a terrible atmosphere between us now – a horrible coldness which I cannot bear.'

'Has he said anything to show what he is thinking or feeling?'

'No, he could hardly wait to get out of my sight this morning.'

'He is behaving very stupidly. This could turn nasty for him.'

'And for the rest of us. But there is one thing I really do not understand.'

'What is that, my boy?'

'Well, I do not understand how someone like Aurora, a girl from a very good patrician family could behave in such a way. I mean, it is quite clear to me from her knowing looks that she is sexually experienced and I cannot fathom why she should wish to ape the actions of a trollop and how she gets away with it. How does her father not come to hear of it?'

Acerbus thought for a while, sucked his teeth and then said, 'Well, consider that she has been brought up without a mother. She has been brought up in a series of postings in various parts of the empire and, without a mother to guide her, she probably spent much of her time with the household staff and listened from an early age to kitchen talk.'

'Kitchen talk?'

'Oh, you know what that is – the sort of things that people prattle about when they are chopping vegetables – you know, who is pregnant and how the child cannot have been fathered by the lady's husband as he was away on military exercises when it would have been conceived? And then the speaker would go on to speculate who was the real father and then go on to gossip about whose boots she saw in the lady's chamber, et cetera, et cetera.'

'Yes, I see what you mean. You think that a girl could be corrupted by this talk.'

'Yes, she could, especially if she heard it all the time and had no mother to correct such influences and if her father were away for long periods.'

'But how does he not see what I see?'

'Because he is not looking for it – she is probably demure when she is with him and it would not occur to him that she is anything other than a sweet, innocent young girl –and, I dare say, he has hopes of her marrying well.'

'But what am I to do? How can I protect my son from both Aurora and her father?'

'I was thinking about this when I went to get the honey water and I reluctantly conclude that there is nothing you can do without making it worse or without drawing unwelcome attention to what is happening. You must let it run its course and hope that she is a flibbertigibbet who likes a frequent change of lover.'

'But what about Germanicus? He will be heartbroken.'

'He will be heartbroken but he will recover. First love is always painful but rarely fatal.'

'I would wish to spare him the pain.'

'Yes, you would because you are a loving father but you cannot protect Germanicus from all the ills of this wicked world and, when all is said and done, he must learn by his own mistakes. That is a lesson you must also learn.'

'I do not follow you. What are you telling me?'

'I am telling you that a truly loving father allows his son to make mistakes so that he can learn from them.'

'I had not thought of it that way before. Those are very wise words.'

'Yes, they are and I knew that when my own father spoke them to me many years ago and left me to my own devices in a most unsuitable affair which ended, as he knew it would, badly, but I had learned a great lesson.'

'Thank you for your counsel, my friend. In these delicate matters I am sometimes at a loss as I had not the benefit of my own father's wisdom and, at times, I keenly feel the lack of it.'

'You honour me, my boy, in allowing me to be a poor substitute.'

'Poor substitute! You are no such thing! I would have been proud to have been your son.'

'Oh, my boy, what a wonderful thought. But hold fast now – we are getting a little too sentimental. As there is nothing you can do to help Germanicus in his doomed love affair, and as you cannot tell me any more about Pneumaticus's mission, then we must turn our minds to other things. For example, you could tell me about Gideon. Was that not the name of the young oarsman whom Jejunus flogged to within an inch of his life?'

'Yes, it was and it was only because of Magnus's efforts that he survived.'

'Did you speak to him?'

'Yes, I had some very strange talks with him. He is a Christian.'

'Ye gods. Then you wasted Magnus's time in saving his life – Nero is blaming them for all that's wrong with Rome and seems likely to use them as fodder for the animals in the Circus.'

'Funnily enough, I did ask him about that – I did ask Gideon why Nero is so against his people when Rome usually embraces the gods of conquered nations and makes them its own.'

'What did he say?'

'He said that his God is the one and only God and that Nero persecutes the Christians because, if they are correct, then he cannot himself be a god.'

'Yes, that is a good answer but it also makes sense for Nero to have someone else to blame for the lack of bread and the poor housing in the city even though much of this is due to his extravagance and that of some of his predecessors.'

'Well, Gideon would forgive him for that, just as he would forgive Jejunus even though he took all the skin and most of the flesh from his back.'

'Why in the names of all the gods would he forgive him for that?

'Because, according to Gideon and the Christians, the answer to everything is love.'

'Hunh?' said Acerbus, a sound which was new to Graecus, but as it was accompanied by a shrug of incomprehension, he took it to mean that Acerbus was mystified by what he had said.

'Well, I do not know that I understand it any better than you but what he seemed to mean is that you must love people even though they harm you. You must love them so that they can learn to love themselves and then they will stop doing harm because they too will then realise that love is the answer to everything.'

Graecus finished speaking and expected that Acerbus with his quick mind would immediately respond to what he had just said but his sharp-witted colleague was silent and Graecus could see that he was deep in thought and that this novel idea was taxing him.

Acerbus shifted his position on his bed, crossed his legs and then uncrossed them and then ruffled his hair in what looked like exasperation before saying, 'But if Gideon's God is the one God, does that mean that he is my God also? That would be the logical conclusion, would it not?'

'Yes, it would and that is exactly what Gideon said to me, he said that his God is our God even though we are unaware of him.'

'Well, that is a comforting thought.'

'Only up to a point! I gave the matter much thought after I spoke to Gideon and I must admit that I found the idea of a God of universal love very attractive but I decided that if I had Gideon's beliefs then it could make it difficult to be a soldier.'

'In what way, precisely?

'In the way that it could mean that I would sometimes find it distasteful to carry out my orders.'

'I am sure that you are not alone in that. We have all been ordered to do things which we did not want to do but we did them all the same.'

'Yes, I know that but there are times when I wonder whether the much vaunted *Pax Romana* is worth all the blood shed in its maintenance. I mean, I well remember your telling me that Rome is much more than a city, much more than an empire even – that it is now an ideal to which most of the world aspires – and I see that it is an amazing phenomenon but I worry that Rome and many of its representatives are corrupt, selfish and vicious and I just thought that if I paid heed to this Christian teaching about love then I would have to put down my gladius.'

'And where would you be then?'

'Precisely. So Christianity, as explained to me by Gideon, is a luxury I cannot afford.'

'That is a very interesting thought, but following on from it, my studies of philosophy and logic dictate that I must ask you this question – if this Christian God knows you and you have now heard of Him – are you able to ignore Him?'

'I swear that I know not. I swear that my thoughts are in turmoil. I swear that I have hardly had a moment's peace since we landed on this terrible island.'

'Oh, my boy, I had hoped to distract you by asking about Gideon but it seems that I chose the wrong subject. Tell me, what is it you would wish to talk about – something which will not distress you?'

Graecus's mind was full of dark thoughts and he wished to think of brighter things so his reply to Acerbus was in relation to something odd which had been niggling at the back of his mind for some time – 'When you introduced me to Norbanus, you told me that he is one of the craziest men in the Roman army – what did you mean by that? In what way is he crazy – he seems to have been quite normal so far.'

Acerbus began one of his snorting laughing fits and Graecus was pleased that he was out of range.

'Oh my dear boy, you have not yet seen him drunk. He is quite different then! He loses all his pretensions to being the important officer and becomes quite the reckless young man I knew twenty years ago.'

Here Acerbus gave himself up to mirth and sat snorting and spitting for a few moments before leaning forward and saying in a conspiratorial manner, 'It's how he got that peculiar scar, you know.'

'What is?'

'His party trick. That's how he got the scar'

'The scar over his eye? The one that looks like a burn but not quite like a burn?'

'Yes, that's how he got it.'

'Very well, but how did he get it? Are you going to tell me or not?'

'Well, his trick, which he uses to great effect when he is trying to entertain his men is that he sets fire to his farts. What he does is make sure that he has had a lot of leeks and onions and

136

beer then he uses a torch to set fire to the gas from his rear end and this usually causes great amusement but one night, and I should not laugh at this. The trick,' and here Acerbus rolled about on his bed with laughter at his own play on words, 'Backfired… and a freak gust of wind blew the flame around and burned him on the eyebrow.'

Graecus was not sure what to make of this as it seemed to him to have been a very stupid thing to do but it did at least show that Norbanus was a human being and not just a war machine as was the case with some legionaries, especially the senior ones.

'Thank you for telling me,' he said, 'I will view him in a new light from now on.'

'Well, my boy, we have had a good long talk and I hope you feel a little better for it but shall we now go and do that bit of hunting?'

Graecus felt as if Acerbus were now speaking to him as if he were a child, but instead of feeling resentful of this, he felt comforted – the rawness of his earlier emotions was less keen and he could allow himself to leave his troubles behind for a few hours in pursuit of game for the pot.

'Yes,' he said, 'that is a good idea. I shall quickly get my bow and meet you at the gate in a few moments.'

Acerbus nodded in agreement and Graecus left his tent and walked swiftly back to his contubernium's tent where he tried to find his bow and the new arrows he had acquired from Impedimentus just a few days before.

Then he remembered that Germanicus had borrowed his bow and thought that perhaps the boy had forgotten to return it so he went over to Germanicus's bed and started to look underneath it.

It was dark under the bed so he felt around with his hand and the first thing which he brought to light was a wooden case: the type of wooden case which housed the wax tablets on which people wrote notes or aides memoires with a stylus.

Graecus smiled at this as he knew that Germanicus liked to practise his lettering in pursuit of an elegant hand and his mind wandered fondly to the times when his boy would sit furrowing his brow in concentration, trying to perfect his writing.

He opened the case wanting to view this proof of happier times, when his son was an uncomplicated young man, but what met his eye was not the proof he sought.

The lettering was untidy and childish, varying in size and orientation and it certainly was not Germanicus's writing.

What was this?

Then he began to read the sense of what was written and his stomach turned over.

It was a letter from Aurora.

It was a 'love' letter.

Graecus's eyes quickly scanned the tablet and he made out the first purple phrase: *'I love the way your soft hair curls sleapily into your neck',* then: *'I love your warme kisses and the way you stick your hard tounge into my mowth.'*

Really her spelling was atrocious.

Then: *'I wish we can run away together.'*

'Tut tut!' he thought, 'She has not mastered even the rudiments of the use of the subjunctive.'

Then: *'But the best thing, the most wunderfull thing imiganable, is the moment when you put your hard...'*

Ye gods, what was he doing, complaining to himself about this girl's grammar and spelling when, here in his hand, was the proof of Germanicus's stupidity for anyone to read?

Well, at least the 'letter' was not actually addressed to Germanicus by name, it merely said 'My love', but it was under his bed.

And Graecus must put it back there so that Germanicus would not know he had read it – for, if this terrible situation came to a good end and peace was restored between them, he had no wish to be thought of as an inquisitive father.

Graecus put the letter carefully back under Germanicus's bed and, as he did so, he considered its contents.

It was as he had thought.

The letter did not disclose the workings of the heart of a young girl in love for the first time. No, it disclosed the workings of a young woman skilled in the arts of seduction.

Poor Germanicus, he did not stand a chance against this woman with her beauty and her superior knowledge of the act of love.

But Graecus could do nothing, except try to keep the boy busy and hope this passion would soon burn itself out.

He could not find his bow but, as he had decided earlier that morning, he must tell Impedimentus to take an inventory of their equipment and use Germanicus to help him.

Graecus stood up and turned to leave the tent but saw someone standing in the open flap and was shocked to see it was Solitarius. How long had he been there? How much had he seen? How much did he know about Germanicus's liaison?

All colour left Graecus's face as these thoughts raced through his mind and he silently thanked the gods, including Gideon's God, that he was standing in the shadows and Solitarius could see neither his expression nor his wan complexion.

Pretending to brush himself down but giving himself time to compose his feelings, Graecus took a while to stretch his back and to adjust his clothing before saying to his horn blower, in what he hoped was a cool voice but which, to his own ears, sounded like a bat squeak: 'Ah, Solitarius, what is it you want? Are you looking for me?'

'No, sir, I am looking for Germanicus, there was a servant girl, from Suetonius's household, I believe, who wanted to give him this.'

Solitarius had another of the wooden writing cases in his hand and held it out towards Graecus.

Graecus could see that the case bore initials on its face, and although Solitarius's thumb was obscuring some of them, he could make out the letter 'A.'

'A' for 'Aurora.'

Graecus's bowels turned to water at the same moment as his throat turned as dry as the desert and he had to blink very rapidly as he thought he was going to scream with anger and frustration at the insanely reckless way in which these two young people were behaving.

He was still in the shadows of the tent and prayed that Solitarius had seen nothing of this; it was too much to hope that Solitarius had not opened the letter but he did not want Verus's spy to know that he knew of the affair.

Swallowing hard, he said, 'He is not here at the moment. Give it to me and I will see to it that he gets it later in the day. I take it that it is not urgent, whatever it is?'

But Solitarius was not fooled by this and said with a negligent shrug of the shoulder, 'I know not sir. The girl did not tell me what the letter contains.'

'Thank you, Solitarius, you may go now.'

The horn blower smiled, showing his yellow teeth and turned on his heel and left.

Graecus sat, or rather fell, onto his bed, his stomach turning somersaults.

He must read the letter, even though it made him feel unclean to be snooping on his son. He must read it so that he would know what that serpent Solitarius already knew.

He picked up the wooden case and opened it.

'My darling, I miss your touch. Meat me at the usuall place at the evening hour. I will pine for you untill then.'

It could hardly be more clear. The Serpent must know everything and Germanicus was in great danger as Verus would be sure to use this tasty morsel of knowledge against the boy to his own greatest advantage when the opportunity presented itself.

Graecus closed the case and looked at the cover.

But what was this?

The writing on the cover was not what he had expected to see. He had expected to see Aurora's initials; indeed the writing began with an 'A' but what it said was, *'Absque Amore Nihil'*.

Graecus pondered this for a moment, thinking that it was an odd motto for Suetonius's family – 'Without Passion There is Nothing' – although it seemed that Aurora was doing *her* best to live up to it – and then he had the cheering thought that there was nothing, nothing, nothing, on the face of this letter to link it to Aurora herself.

140

Indeed, now that he looked at it in that light, the crude hand-writing, the slipshod spelling and the disregard for the rules of grammar, made it unlikely on the face of it, that it could have been written by the demure, patrician daughter of their commanding officer.

Graecus's mind now slipped into its most analytical mode and he pictured himself arguing the case for the letter's having been written by Aurora's slave girl and he came to the conclusion that he could, with the slave girl's acquiescence if it came to that, argue that Germanicus's liaison was with the servant rather than the mistress.

Firstly, the letter was not signed. Secondly, it was more likely that the young auxiliary soldier would be conducting an affair with the slave and thirdly who would believe that Aurora could be so ill-educated and lacking in modesty as to express herself in such a manner?

Feeling cheered by this, Graecus then thought that there was one flaw in this hypothesis – the wooden case itself. Why would a servant girl be writing to her lover on one of her mistress's household tablets?

Why not? The case looked rather old and battered and was this not the sort of thing that girls gave to their slaves where there was perhaps too much of an intimate relationship between them?

Graecus felt relief course through his body. All was not lost. It was possible, likely, even, that the Serpent did not have conclusive incriminating evidence against Germanicus and it was doubtful that the servant girl had unburdened herself to Solitarius – after all, thought Graecus with a smile, it was not that he could have charmed her with his looks, was it?

Graecus decided that it was now time to take some control over this situation and went to find Germanicus.

Happily, his son was in conversation with Impedimentus and this enabled their Centurion to give them their orders but Graecus ensured that he sent Impedimentus away first so that he was alone with Germanicus.

He held out the letter to his son and said, 'This is for you. A servant girl from Suetonius's household came looking for you, and not being able to find you, left it with Solitarius. I hope it is not too important or urgent, we cannot be sure that he left it unread – you know how curious he is concerning all our business.'

The poor boy's face was a picture of embarrassment, fear and eagerness. Embarrassment because he knew from whom the letter had come (and he knew that his father knew), fear that Solitarius also knew and eagerness because he wanted to read his lover's soft words.

As he looked at his boy's face and his struggle to appear nonchalant, Graecus had recourse to the ball of iron at his core – this was not the moment for him to feel any sympathy with Germanicus's plight. This was the moment to remember Acerbus's words about letting the boy learn from his mistakes and for resolution and for leadership on his own part so Graecus swallowed the words of comfort which were swelling in his breast and said, 'I am going hunting with Acerbus, I will be back by the afternoon,' and left.

CHAPTER NINE

Hunting with Acerbus was exhilarating as the older man was fearless, and wounded leg notwithstanding, wonderfully athletic for his age; he and Graecus crossed across fields and plains in pursuit of birds large and small and after a few hours they had a good bag of feathered creatures and a small deer which Graecus carried back to the camp slung over his shoulders.

The exercise, the fresh air and Acerbus's company had cleared his mind and refreshed his body and it was a calmer Centurion who gave the deer to Felix with strict instructions to let it hang for a few days before preparing it for the pot.

At their mid-day meal, Graecus made sure that he sat next to Felix and Magnus so that he could not speak to Germanicus although he noticed that the boy was quiet and seemingly withdrawn into his own thoughts and Graecus ached to go to his son and try to talk to him but he knew it was the best thing to leave him alone.

The afternoon was interesting. Suetonius, ably assisted by Norbanus, ensured that they all – all the legionaries, all the auxiliaries and all the cavalry – practised battle stations and responded to the different notes of the horns which corresponded to different signals and they did this again and again and again until it was all perfect and each man, listening to the sound of his century's horn, and the legionary horns knew exactly what was required of him at any moment.

Graecus had not experienced these manoeuvres with such a large body of troops for many years and he found it thrilling how, over the space of four or five hours, this huge number of men and horses, could meld together and behave as if they were of one heart and one mind and how they became by a seemingly alchemical process an Army.

Graecus noted how Germanicus played his part and saw that he did it with aplomb but it must have cost the boy dear to be standing next to Solitarius when he did not know whether the horn-blower was planning to betray him.

Once the exercises had been completed successfully, the men were stood down and returned to their lines.

Felix went to his pots and pans and began cooking something which smelled delicious. Incitatus was waiting for the ivory and the gold wire for Pneumaticus's teeth so took up a piece of leather and began to make the chamfron for Perdix. Magnus was grinding some herbs in a bowl with a pestle and Impedimentus was working on lists of equipment, sometimes holding the stylus between his teeth as he tried to get the lists to tally.

Graecus looked at them all and felt that they were his family. His heart swelled with a warm feeling and he knew that he would have been blissful in this moment had Germanicus been there.

But he was not, and nor was Zig.

Blessedly, no one remarked on Germanicus's absence and the men ate their supper but they had to eat it in their tent as the rain returned – the British rain which made everything grey and sodden and lowered everyone's spirits.

Graecus sat at his desk, trying to concentrate on the book before him and its account of the battle of Thermopylae but all he could think of was to hope that, wherever Germanicus and Aurora were holding their tryst, it was under cover and dry.

He bent his head over the book, trying to rid his mind of thoughts of Aurora and his boy lying on wet grass together made oblivious to the elements by their raging passion but to no avail.

And there was something else which was disturbing him. He could not place it at first but then he realised.

It was the disgusting smell of the herbs Magnus was pounding.

'What *is* that smell?'

'Henbane; I am making a decoction but I need to pound the mixture first.'

'Is it a new thing? I cannot recall having smelled any herb quite so awful ever before.'

'No, it is not new, it is an old cure but I have not used it much before.'

'And who is to be the beneficiary of this cure?'

'Aurora.'

'Aurora?'

'Yes, it is to help with the cough she has. Her slave girl asked me to make it for her, she has had it before and found it beneficial. It is an anti-spasmodic.'

'Ye gods, she will need all the perfumes of the orient to disguise the smell if she rubs that on her chest.'

'Do not be so sure, it is rumoured to have aphrodisiac properties.'

'Then Cupid has a great sense of humour and no sense of smell.'

'As you say, Domine.'

Magnus continued pounding the herbs and Graecus tried to return to the Battle of Thermopylae but he could not concentrate. Now, all he could think of was that Aurora had feigned a cough so that she could acquire this evil-smelling aphrodisiac to drive his son even more mad with desire.

It was unbearable.

The evening wore on and the men began to get ready for bed and then, just before Graecus himself retired, Germanicus returned.

He was trying to be as quiet as possible but Zig was wet and shook himself noisily once he was within the tent making a thunderclap sound with his flapping ears and Graecus was obliged to notice their return.

But he was not obliged to be helpful to his son in this mad enterprise so he merely said, 'I see you and Zig have been for a walk,' and received the curt answer, 'Yes, father, we have been walking,' which each of them knew was both the truth and a lie and that was that.

Graecus went to bed and lay with his eyes open for some time turning this situation over and over in his mind.

He was at his wits' end. He needed help. Divine help. He tried to think of which god would be most helpful to him, which god would be appropriate? It was a problem concerning romantic love so it should be Cupid. But Cupid must be a fool if that foul henbane were regarded as an aphrodisiac. He needed to do something different.

He decided he would pray to Gideon's God.

It was a peculiar experience. He did not pray often– usually only in extreme circumstances and then it was to Jupiter or Mithras – but if Gideon were correct, then that was a waste of time and only this one true God could help him.

But how to address this God in a formal prayer? What was His name? Was He, indeed, a God not a Goddess? It was all so confusing but he decided that the best thing would be to address this God simply as 'God.'

So he prayed and poured out his heart to this God saying, 'Most powerful and only God, please keep my son safe. Please let him emerge from this danger unharmed.'

And then he could do no more and he went to sleep.

* * *

The rain continued unabated throughout the next day and the sodden ground could absorb no more so the camp's walkways became slippery and unpleasant. Walking from one place to another was difficult, sitting in the contubernium tent was impossible as the noise of the rain drumming on the leather was deafening and even Felix, whose culinary capabilities withstood most challenges, was struggling to cook on fires where there was more smoke than flame. In this wet, clingy atmosphere there was a tension hanging over everything which made the men, bored by inaction, jumpy and tetchy with one another and there were sporadic exchanges of insults and harsh words during the course of the day but there was nothing Graecus could do to alleviate the gloom, especially as it so perfectly matched his own mood.

Germanicus spent the morning sharpening his gladius and his dagger, communicating in grunts or monosyllables when anyone spoke to him. Graecus struggled to preserve an air of indifference and to prevent himself from desperately trying to make conversation with his son. He tried to remember what he had been like as a young man and how he had felt when love first presented itself to him but his experiences with local girls in the nearby town when he was being trained by a strict Centurion in a barracks in Caesarea were so long before and were so different that they could not help him understand his son's behaviour and, in any case, he had not had a father against whom to rebel.

Graecus hated the close confinement of the tent and the stiflingly humid air but he hated the coldness of his son more and he dreaded the coming of the evening as he feared that Germanicus would again leave for one of his 'walks.'

Darkness approached and Germanicus, having cleaned himself, put on a dry tunic and whistled for Zig.

Graecus did not know what to say as his son openly performed his toilette, and if, indeed, he should say anything.

Germanicus put on his belt with its sheath for his dagger and then made to leave the tent but it was raining very hard outside and he was going out in the rain bareheaded.

Graecus could not let this go unremarked and said, 'If you must go for a walk in this heavy rain, at least take your cloak with you.'

But Germanicus merely mumbled something about 'Not going very far' and left, unprotected from the weather.

It was madness. It was madness for him to think that anything could come of his relationship with Aurora and it was madness for him to be going out night after night for his 'secret' trysts with her and to think that they would not be attracting the attention of those who would use this passionate affair against them.

Graecus groaned at the stupidity of it all and then remembered Acerbus's wise words – he must leave the boy to make his own mistakes.

So Graecus busied himself with his studies of the Battle of Thermopylae and tried to convince himself that, with the right choice of battlefield, the Romans could beat their vastly superior number of foes.

Looking at the narrow gorge in which the Spartans – a brave 300 warriors, and their 700 Thespian allies – kept the might of Xerxes' Persian army at bay, Graecus did see that, given the right kind of valley, the Romans did have some chance but then he asked himself whether such a place existed in this region of

Britannia and how would Suetonius ensure that the battle took place there and not elsewhere?

Well, Norbanus had said that Suetonius was wily and should not be underestimated, had he not? And Pneumaticus, good old reliable Pneumaticus, had been sent to find out what were the Warrior Queen's plans and to find the magic place where the Romans could win.

Given all of that, what could Graecus do? Nothing. He could do nothing other than wait for Pneumaticus's return just as this very evening he could do nothing other than wait for Germanicus's return.

He felt tired and old and impotent, and in a strange way, pointless.

What was the value of his life? For most of his life he had thought that his service of Rome was point enough but he had been having misgivings about that for some time.

Then again, ever since he had taken responsibility for Germanicus, he would have said that the boy gave his life purpose but now, now that his golden boy had become a sulky young man, was that still true?

He knew that he loved Germanicus, he loved him more than life itself, but he had to admit that, at the moment, he really did not *like* the stubborn, selfish, uncommunicative boor he had become since meeting Aurora.

The other men began to make preparations to retire to bed and Graecus himself was cleaning his teeth when a very wet Germanicus and a dripping dog returned to the tent.

Zig shook himself violently and showered Felix with water.

'Germanicus, what is going on, why in the names of all the gods do you want to go out in this terrible rain?' said Felix in an exasperated voice.

'Because, I want to, that's all,' replied Germanicus who did not see the look of hurt surprise on Felix's face but it was plainly visible to Graecus who was concerned that Germanicus was in danger of alienating all his friends in addition to his father so he said, 'Germanicus seems to need a great deal of time alone at the

148

moment,' in the hope that this would satisfy their closest colleagues who might imagine that his behaviour could be explained by the turbulence of youth.

Germanicus made no further comment and there was an unusual silence while the men prepared for bed.

Graecus merely said a general 'Goodnight' to all and did not single his son out for a personal valediction, but before the Centurion went to sleep, he repeated his prayer to Gideon's God: 'Most powerful and only God, please keep my son safe. Please let him emerge from this danger unharmed.'

Then he went to sleep.

* * *

The rain the following day was even worse and tempers were even more frayed and Germanicus was even more sullen and withdrawn but still he went out for his evening 'walk' with Zig although Graecus was pleased to see that, this time, he did at least wear his cloak.

Graecus did not want another confrontation when his son returned so he made sure that he was in bed and appeared to be asleep when he returned.

But, before he really did go to sleep, he repeated his prayer to Gideon's God: 'Most powerful and only God, please keep my son safe. Please let him emerge from this danger unharmed.' And so ended another intolerable day.

* * *

The following day was dry, the sun appeared and the camp began to dry out – much to Graecus's relief as the men's mood and morale rose with the sun.

In the early part of the morning, Graecus spent time with Impedimentus ensuring that their century could quickly be ready to move with the rest of the camp when Suetonius's plans became clear and then he went to find Incitatus to enquire whether the century's records were up to date.

He found the scribe sitting at his campaign desk working on a pile of documents and was asking him if he had informed the lost soldiers' families of their deaths when a young native slave girl came up to them, and recognising Graecus as a Centurion, said, 'Oh, sir, please help me!'

'I will try to help you, what is it you want?'

'Oh sir, I need to find Magnus. It's very urgent. My mistress, Aurora, is very sick. She began a fever in the night and she can hardly breathe this morning.'

Graecus wondered whether this was another of Aurora's ploys for procuring more of the evil-smelling henbane but then he looked closely at the slave girl and saw that she was distraught – in fact, she had tears in her eyes. Graecus then wondered if the tears were for her mistress or what would become of her in the highly unlikely event that her mistress perished but the girl began to sob out loud and Graecus was obliged to give her his neckerchief so that she could blow her nose and dry her eyes.

Then he said to her, 'Come, let us go and find Magnus; he has wonderful healing powers.'

They found Magnus in their tent, and after hearing from the slave girl what were Aurora's symptoms, he went with her to see their commander's sick daughter without delay.

Graecus had no idea whether Aurora was really sick or not – perhaps the slave girl was being hysterical in the manner of slave girls – and having decided that he would keep the news of Aurora's illness to himself, he went about his business for the next couple of hours.

But then Magnus returned.

An ashen faced Magnus.

A stunned, ashen-faced Magnus who threw himself onto a stool and sat with his head in his hands, groaning.

'Magnus! Magnus, what is it? What is wrong?'

'Aurora.'

'Is she very sick?'

'No, she is not.'

'What is it then, why are you so distressed?'

'She is dead, Domine. She died about half an hour ago. I could not save her. It was too late.'

'Dead? But she was a healthy young girl!'

'She was a young girl but I do not think that she was robust. She was very slender and I do not think that she had a strong constitution.'

'What was it that killed her?'

'A congestion of the lungs. I knew she had had a cough, but according to her slave girl, it became much worse in the middle of the night and, by the time I saw her, it was too late – she had a very high fever and her lungs were filled with water. It was terrible to see – she drowned in her own fluid.'

Graecus could not take any of this news in; he could not get it into his head that Aurora had died. It was incredible that she could have perished so suddenly.

Then he remembered his prayer to Gideon's God – 'Please keep my son safe. Please let him emerge from this danger unharmed.'

Then he realised that it must be his task to tell his son that Aurora had died.

And he must undertake that task knowing that it was his fault for making that prayer to Gideon's God and knowing that the news would break his boy's heart. And he also knew that it would be no consolation to Germanicus to tell him that he had merely been one among many and had not been the love of Aurora's life.

Then another matter came into his mind.

'Does Suetonius know yet?'

'No. He is out with the Batavian cavalry scouts. He will not be back until dusk.'

'Who will tell him? He will not be able to bear it. He was devoted to her.'

'I suppose it will have to be his steward but I do not envy him the task and I expect that I shall be summoned to account for my actions in failing to save her.'

'But you did all you could. You always do all you can. Sometimes, the gods do not hear our entreaties, they do their own will,' said Graecus and wished he had not said it as he was convinced that it had been his prayer to Gideon's God which had killed Aurora.

'That will not be sufficient explanation for Suetonius, I fear.'

'Then I shall accompany you and explain that you did all that was possible.'

'I would welcome your company in such a situation but I do not know that you can tell him any more than I am able to say.'

Graecus's stomach turned over at these words – they were very far from the truth. Of course Graecus could say a great deal more – he could, for example, tell Suetonius about the potency of his prayers for Germanicus's safety or, then again, he could tell the grieving father about Germanicus's night-time adventures with his daughter in the pouring rain, which, now he came to think about it, could have been as much a contributory cause to her premature death as his own intervention.

Ye gods! or was it, God!? (whichever deity was appropriate in these circumstances) what a mess he, Germanicus and Magnus were in. How could he protect his son and his close colleague without himself incurring Suetonius's wrath?

For the moment, he did not know. For the moment, the important thing was that he must immediately take Germanicus to one side and tell him of Aurora's death and, given the current coldness between father and son and the strength of the young man's attachment to his first love, that was a difficult enough job on its own. Once he had delivered this terrible piece of news, then he could concentrate on what needed to be said to Suetonius, or, more importantly, what needed to be kept from him.

Graecus put his hand on Magnus's shoulder and said, 'Magnus, we have faced many dangers together and this will be just one more. As your commanding officer, I am able to speak of your abilities and, as your friend, I wish to do so. But now, I have another urgent task to perform and you must excuse me.'

Graecus left the tent and went searching for Germanicus.

He found him in the *intervallum* in the middle of a bout of swordplay with Acerbus – each of them thrusting fiercely and parrying skilfully with their gladiuses while a group of auxiliaries looked on, cheering the better moves.

This was not where Graecus had wanted to find his boy; it would be difficult to gain sufficient privacy for this most delicate of conversations and there was a danger that the news of Aurora's death would spread so quickly through the camp that it could reach this group of men before Graecus could tell Germanicus himself.

But now Acerbus laughingly put down his sword and said to Germanicus, 'Well, my boy, these days you have the advantage of youth over me but I see that the skills I taught you have been employed to good purpose. I have had enough for this morning.'

Acerbus nodded to Graecus and walked away from the group of men, limping slightly, while Graecus went over to Germanicus who was oiling his gladius, bending slightly forwards as he did so.

Graecus leaned over his son's ear and quietly said, 'Germanicus, I have something very important to say to you. I know we have not been on the best of terms these last few days but this is a piece of news which must come to you from me, your father.'

While he was speaking, Graecus could feel the unyielding, resentful stiffness of his son's back, but when he gently added the words, 'What I must tell you concerns Aurora,' Germanicus dropped his gladius and turned swiftly to face him with an expression of questioning wonderment which broke Graecus's heart.

'My son,' he said, 'it would be better if we were to walk away from our colleagues. This is news you need to receive in private,' as he took hold of Germanicus's elbow and guided him towards that part of the *intervallum* which was nearest the rampart and furthest away from prying eyes and ears.

'What is it, father? What is this news?'

Graecus allowed himself a moment's rejoicing that Germanicus had called him 'Father' but then he needed to steel himself to say, 'My boy, you must brace yourself for some

153

difficult news. I have the unfortunate duty to tell you that Aurora is dead.'

Germanicus looked as if he had been slapped across the face with a whip.

'I do not believe you. It is a wicked lie. You are trying to keep me from her!' he hissed.

'No, my son, it is the truth. I have never lied to you. Magnus was with her when she died. He tried to save her but he could not. The news of her death will shortly be common knowledge around this camp but I wished to tell you myself so that you would have the opportunity to deal privately with your grief.'

Germanicus stared insolently at his father as if he were trying to decide whether his words were true and this scrutiny seemed to Graecus to last for a very long time – he saw many thoughts pass through his son's mind and he felt as if he were being judged, as if his actions and his motives were being called into question. It was excruciating to be subjected to this process by the person for whom you would die a thousand deaths and, just as Germanicus's expression darkened and he drew in a big breath preparatory to the next barrage of insults, Graecus's patience snapped.

Acting purely by instinct and without thinking, he took his hand and slapped Germanicus as hard as he could across the young man's face and said,

'That is enough. That is enough of your disrespectful behaviour. I have always treated you with honour and, as your father, I require you to treat me in the same way, and as your Centurion, I insist that you respect my rank. Now, you will pull yourself together and you will go about your business in a manner befitting the standard bearer of my century. When you have found the correct words of apology, then you may approach me with them, but until then, I wish to hear nothing from you, I have other men to think of.'

Then Graecus turned on his heel and walked away with his heart in his mouth, his stomach churning and his bowels threatening to burst. He walked steadily away from his son– the light of his life – and the temptation to turn round and go back, to try to patch up this dreadful mess, was overwhelming but Acerbus's words kept running through his mind and he kept on walking, leaving Germanicus to contemplate the harshness of life.

Graecus walked swiftly to the latrines.

The benches over the ditch provided many holes for back-sides and he knew that here he could not only empty his boiling bowels but also be undisturbed as it was an unwritten rule of Roman society that, if you sat as far away as possible from other users, then they knew you wanted solitude and left you alone.

So he sat on the bench and enjoyed those moments of sweet release while blanking his mind.

When he had finished, he felt so comfortable and so safe that he stayed in that position for some time, relishing the peace and emptiness.

Then his ears picked up the fragments of a conversation between two legionaries six or seven seats away from him.

'He will be inconsolable…'

'I hear there were goings on… creeping out at night…'

'In all that rain…? Young love…'

'Young lust more like, but she never looked strong… too scraggy for my taste…'

'…well she certainly made the most of her life among all these lusty man but you always preferred your women with more meat on them…'

Graecus pretended not to be listening and busied himself with the sponge on a stick then washed his hands and left. He had heard enough. He now knew what he must do and he thanked the gods (God?) for the opportunity to be able to do so before Suetonius returned.

What he planned to do was against his principles but he need-ed to protect Germanicus and the end therefore justified the means.

He needed to speak to Aurora's slave girl and he needed a seemingly legitimate reason to approach the household.

Wracking his brains as he walked, he avoided the gaze of anyone coming the other way – he had no wish to engage in camp gossip and speculation as to Suetonius's reaction to his daughter's sudden and unexpected death.

He now approached Suetonius's private quarters – a series of large tents around which milled scores of people – both military and civilians, slaves, citizens and freedmen – but Aurora's slave girl was not in sight.

Then he saw Norbanus who hailed him from across the roadway separating Suetonius's quarters from the rest of the camp.

Graecus walked over to the Senior Centurion who said, 'I suppose you've heard the news.'

'Of Aurora's death?'

'Yes. It is dreadful beyond words and it will affect us all.'

'Because of how it will affect Suetonius?' asked Graecus

'Yes, he will be demented. I fear for his sanity when he finds out and *that* will have terrible repercussions for the rest of us. I mean, he went mad when his wife died and it was months before he returned to normal – normal for him, that is.'

'This could hardly come at a worse time, could it? Just when we're facing a fearsome number of enemy tribesmen.'

'You are correct. If only we could find a way of calming him, of deadening his pain, so that the rest of us can get on with our jobs.'

Graecus thought for a moment as an idea gradually formed in his mind and then said, 'Do you and I agree that it would be best for all concerned if Suetonius were, in effect, to be kept from the sharp edge of his grief, at least until we have defeated Boudicca?'

'Most certainly,' said Norbanus.

'Then I wish to suggest that we ask Magnus to prepare a soothing mixture for him which I am sure he will be happy to do as he does not wish to face Suetonius's wrath for failing to save his daughter.'

'But how would we make sure that he takes it?'

'His household steward will probably be pleased to see to it that he gets it – after all the steward will otherwise be on the receiving end of Suetonius's fabled temper,' said Graecus.

'That sounds like a very good plan. Let us put it into action. If Suetonius is calmer then we have a chance of winning against

Boudicca– we are all good soldiers, we all know what we need to do, we just need a sane commander. Please ask Magnus to make up a sedative mixture and I will tell the steward that he is to administer it to his master, by stealth if necessary,' said Norbanus.

'I will do that but first I need to speak to Aurora's slave girl – she has been seeing one of my men and I wish to put a stop to it – it is interfering with his concentration. Do you know where I will find the girl?'

This was not completely a lie and Graecus comforted himself with this thought.

'She is probably in the female slaves' tent, over there, crying her eyes out – life will be tough for her now that Aurora is not here.'

'I will speak to her now and afterwards I will tell Magnus to prepare the mixture. Farewell.'

'Very good. Farewell.'

Graecus walked over to the large tent which Norbanus had indicated and looked in.

There were about fifteen women present but no one was speaking, there was silence except for the sound of weeping. How was he to find Aurora's slave girl among these keening women? He hardly dared enter the tent – it was no place for a soldier and he did not relish having to speak to the girl in these circumstances.

Graecus cleared his throat to try to attract someone's attention. No one noticed. He tried again but more loudly this time and still no one noticed – they were all lost in their sorrow. This time he decided to speak and said, 'Hail, I am looking for Aurora's slave girl.'

A woman who appeared to be in her thirties, with a face swollen from crying, lifted her head from the couch on which she had been lying prostrate just long enough to point to a dark haired girl who was sitting on a stool with her face buried in a pillow, sobbing quietly.

Graecus's courage nearly failed him. He felt so totally out of place, surrounded by grieving female slaves.

But he had come to do a job and he must do it now or it would be too late so he strode purposefully over to the dark-haired girl and said to the top of her head. 'Miss, I regret that I must speak to you privately and urgently. Please come outside.'

The girl looked at him with alarm and put her hand to her mouth, trying to stifle a gasp. Then she looked as if she might scream and this was the last thing Graecus wanted so he said to her in his softest voice, 'Miss, I am not here to arrest you or to harm you. I wish merely to speak to you about a matter of great importance. Please follow me outside.'

He then turned and walked out of the tent, relishing the sun on his face after the oppressive atmosphere of all that female emotion and he waited outside the tent, affecting a casual pose for any passer-by who might wonder why an officer would be loitering next to the female slaves' tent.

He waited for what seemed like minutes and was attempting to decide what he must do if the girl did not appear when she came out of the tent and approached him. She had washed her face and combed her hair. Graecus took this as a good sign.

'Miss,' he said, 'I need to speak to you about a matter which concerns us both but it is very private and it would be best if we were to stand away from this tent. Let us go and walk in the *intervallum*.' The girl nodded her head and they walked away.

Once they found a suitably empty part of the walk-way, the girl said to Graecus, 'What is this about?'

'It is about the young man, Germanicus. He is the standard bearer for my century and I know that he was conducting a liaison with Aurora. I also know that you played a part in their meetings – you were carrying messages to and fro between them.' Graecus paused to let his words sink in and the girl, her shoulders sagging, put her hand to her mouth. 'I also know that if Suetonius found out about this liaison he would have my standard bearer whipped to within an inch of his life and he would punish you severely also.' The girl nodded. 'I am aware that Germanicus's affair with Aurora was not her first taste of love, but sadly for us all, it was her last.' The girl nodded again.

'What I wish to say to you is that we are taking steps to ensure that the repercussions of Aurora's death are not as dreadful as may be feared insofar as Suetonius's grief is concerned, and I want to assure you that I shall not tell him any of what I know about the affair, including your collusion with the lovers, but you must also keep the secret. Do you understand me?'

'I think I do but I do not see why your colleagues would wish to shield Suetonius from feeling his grief.'

'That is because you are not a soldier. Feeling his grief would unsettle his mind and it is vital to us to have a commander who is not driven mad by his loss. We are so outnumbered by Boudicca's hordes that we cannot afford to have a mad commander.'

At this, the girl stood up straight and looked Graecus in the eye. She had green eyes and very white skin which glowed with a bluish tinge like milk against her long black hair. She was a striking creature but now, in place of the sorrow she had earlier displayed, there was defiance in her gaze.

A smile began to play around her lips and her nostrils flared. Her face became contemptuous and she said, 'Some of those hordes you mention are my people – the people who will teach you arrogant Roman bastards a lesson and I, for one, will not be sorry if every last man of you perishes under Boudicca's chariot for, when you are gone from my land, I shall be free.'

Graecus now knew that the girl's earlier misery was not genuine grief at Aurora's death but uncertainty as to what was to happen to her as a result of it and he knew what to say to her.

'You are a very silly little girl if you think that a victory for Boudicca would mean freedom for you. No, it is more likely that Suetonius would have you put to the sword first so that you did not have to suffer the indignities which would be visited upon you by your own people for having collaborated for so long with Rome.'

The girl gasped as she saw that Graecus was speaking the truth and, feeling that he had made his point, he continued, 'And even that might be better than what Suetonius would do to you if he thought that you had been instrumental in his beloved daughter's death. I am sure you know that Roman law prescribes the death penalty for a slave who has killed her mistress and I am sure you know, if Suetonius decided to have you put to death, he would go to great ends to see to it that you suffered for a long time first.'

Graecus said these words as calmly as he could but he hated having to say them to an unarmed girl, even if she wanted to annihilate him and all his kind.

The girl dropped her gaze and started to cry again. Graecus did not give her his neckerchief this time and just waited for her to stop.

When she saw that her tears were having no effect, the girl wiped her eyes and nose on the back of her hand, looked up and said, 'So, what is it you want me to do, Centurion?'

'I want you to burn anything of Aurora's which is evidence of the affair and to keep your mouth firmly shut – if we all keep quiet, this storm may pass. If it does not, then I and my men and all our colleagues will die on the battlefield but that will be infinitely preferable to what will happen to you. Do you understand me?'

The girl looked very pale now and she shuddered as she said, 'Yes, I do. I will go and burn the letters now.'

Graecus nearly fainted at the thought that Germanicus had sent letters to Aurora – it had not occurred to him that his son would have been quite so stupid but the girl had said she would burn them and he knew that his words had pierced her like an arrow.

'Go then, and remember – when you are praying to your gods – it is a Roman victory you seek.'

'Yes, Centurion.'

Graecus turned on his heel, and when he knew that he was out of the slave girl's sight, he sprinted towards the latrines, gaining access to the hole in the bench just in time.

It had been quite a morning.

CHAPTER TEN

Graecus sat on the bench for a little while, breathing deeply, experiencing the emptiness in his belly and relief at the thought that disaster might be averted. He was relieved now, both physically and emotionally but his legs felt like jelly and he realised he was hungry and it felt good as his appetite had been poor for the last few days.

Graecus cleaned himself and, walking carefully on his wobbly legs, he left the latrines on his way to find Magnus.

Solitarius was standing outside, waiting, it seemed, for him.

'Oh, Domine, I am glad to have run into you. I hear there has been some bad news. I hear that Suetonius's daughter died this morning. I wondered if there was anything we needed to do….if we could… help… in any way?'

'And why would Suetonius's loss be anything to do with us, Solitarius? Surely our Commander has the right to endure his grief in private?'

'Oh, yes, I agree but it was just that, you know, with Germanicus being… close, as we might say, to… the household… I just thought, maybe there was something…'

'Well, if I were you I would stop thinking about matters which are none of your business and I would stop hanging about the latrines hoping to pick up titbits of gossip and I would stop poking my nose in places where it does not belong. Such activities are not popular. Do you understand me, Solitarius?'

'Oh yes, Domine, you have made yourself perfectly clear,' said the horn-blower, smiling his oily ingratiating smile showing his horrid yellow, snaggly teeth.

'Well, I am sure that you have work to do, horn-blower – work for the good of the century, that is – so off you go and get on with it.'

Graecus now turned his back on Solitarius and went in search of Magnus reviewing this exchange with Verus's placeman as he walked. It was clear to him that each of them now knew the other's situation – Solitarius knew that Graecus knew he was Verus's spy and Solitarius knew that Germanicus had had a liaison with Aurora and that Graecus also knew it. But what Graecus did not know was how much, if any, actual evidence the hornblower had.

Much would turn on what the slave girl could say although his recent conversation with her would ensure that she feared Suetonius's punishment much more than any harm which might come to her from another source. But there was also the matter of the messages in the wax tablets. Solitarius had seen at least one of these but it had not been signed and, as Graecus had reasoned before, it could easily have come from the slave girl herself. Graecus presumed that Germanicus still had the tablets and would probably want to keep them as a memento of his love but it was too dangerous to leave them lying around; the less evidence there was the better and no evidence at all would be best.

Graecus went straight to his contubernium's tent and was pleased to see that Germanicus was not there but Impedimentus was and this was good as it meant that nosy Solitarius probably would not have had any luck in finding the tablets before Graecus could retrieve them. He then went onto his knees and felt under Germanicus's bed, telling Impedimentus that he was looking for his bow.

He felt all the way under the bed but apart from an apple core and a dirty neckerchief with some interesting stains on it (really Germanicus was quite untidy!) there was nothing. Surely Solitarius could not have been here already and taken the tablets?

Graecus then rummaged through Germanicus's few belongings in his leather satchel and found nothing of interest. There was no other way forward – he would need to ask Germanicus where the tablets were.

But Magnus was coming into the tent now. Good. This was the perfect opportunity to ask him to make the potion.

'Impedimentus, I wish to have a private word with Magnus concerning one of his patients, please leave us alone for five minutes.'

'Yes, I am happy to do that as I would like some fresh air but I need to be able to resume my task soon,' said the fussy Roman.

'Indeed, but I asked for only five minutes, so we can all accommodate one another can we not?' said Graecus with a sharp edge to his voice as Impedimentus left the tent.

'Now, we have not much time, so listen very carefully to me, Magnus.'

'Yes, I am listening.'

'I have been speaking to Norbanus and he and I agree that it will be disastrous for us all if Suetonius is allowed to give full rein to his grief. It will send him mad.'

'Well, it is a well-known side-effect of extreme grief and I see that a lunatic leader is the last thing we need at the moment. But what is to be done about it, I mean, we can hardly keep her death from him, can we?'

'No, we cannot but the answer is in your hands, or in your head, anyway. Or both, perhaps.'

'I do not follow you.'

'Well, if Suetonius were to be given something strongly sedative and calming, something which really blunted the edge of his perceptions but left him conscious, then we could all get on with our jobs – we already know what the battle plan is – and we would all be spared his recriminations.'

'Y-e-e-s, I begin to see what you mean.'

'Well, what would you give a man in these circumstances? What mixture would be best?'

'Hmm. I am thinking. Well, the first thing would be quite a dose of poppy extract, then I think I would add a little hypericum and a little heart's ease – I have seen it growing nearby – and for good measure, a very small amount of our favourite mushroom, just to keep his dreams sweet.'

'Do you have all those ingredients?'

'Yes, save that I will need to pick the heart's ease from the meadows outside the camp. But how will we get him to take it?'

'Norbanus will get his steward to give it to him, by stealth if necessary.'

'Well, I suppose I could put it into the mixture I make for his acid stomach – the peppermint oil will disguise the taste.'

'Excellent! Please make up a draught as soon as you can and give it to Norbanus – he is expecting to receive it.'

Graecus grasped his friend's arm and said, 'With your help, it is possible that we will surmount this unfortunate hurdle and be in a good position to defeat our enemies. This is probably the most important mixture you will ever make as the lives of all of us here may depend on its efficacy.'

'I will ask the gods for help.'

'Then you should include a prayer to Gideon's God, for good measure.'

'Yes, Domine, I will do so. I was impressed by Gideon and it cannot hurt to have the help of his God also.'

'Good, now I must find Germanicus. Have you seen him?'

'Well, not recently but I did see him about an hour ago, walking out of the camp.'

'Did he have Zig with him?'

'Yes, I suppose they were going hunting. He did not speak to me.'

'Thank you, I will see if I can find him out and about.'

Graecus now left the tent and went to find Felix. He had no idea where Germanicus would have gone, but if he could find Zig, then he would find his son and there was an easy way to find Zig.

Felix was busy skinning a couple of hare and was concentrating on holding his knife at the correct angle so did not hear Graecus approach him.

'Hail,' said Graecus to his old friend quite close to his ear and in quite a loud voice and this gave Felix such a jolt that he slipped with the knife and gouged himself at the base of his thumb producing a gout of blood which spurted over the partially skinned animal.

Felix turned to see who had greeted him so loudly, and on seeing that it was Graecus, in a mock challenging tone, said, 'Why did you have to do that? Could you not see that I was just doing the fiddly bit, trying to get the fur from this little bugger's head? I think it's ruined now, it's got more of my blood on it than its own.'

'Well, in a strange kind of way, that is more to my purpose than I could have wished.'

'How very helpful of me. But please, dear leader, tell me why you require my blood?'

'Because I need to find Germanicus and I think he has gone hunting with Zig and if I find the dog, then I find the man. And to help me find the dog, I need something which will attract his nose.'

'All very logical I'm sure, but what I want to know is what is the matter with Germanicus? Why is he mooning about the place behaving like a spoiled baby and why are you the picture of misery?'

'Has it been so noticeable?'

'Well, I know you as well as I know the back of my own hand and I have been a part of the boy's life for many years. Yes, I have noticed and I am not the only one. Whatever it is between you, will you please sort it out as it is unsettling the rest of us.'

'I am doing my best but I find it difficult to deal with the irrationality of youth's all-knowing inexperience.'

'I think it has always been the case that only a wise man knows he knows nothing.'

'How very true. Now, give me that creature – I need to find my son.'

Felix put the hare into a small leather bag, already fragrantly bloodstained and gave it to Graecus who smiled at his old friend as he remembered happier times when they would sit around the camp fire in their little fort in Lower Germania, drinking red wine and singing songs. Life seemed uncomplicated then.

These thoughts ran through his mind as he walked swiftly out of the camp trying to work out in which direction Germanicus would have gone.

Had he gone hunting or had he, perhaps, gone to revisit the scene of his meetings with Aurora? Probably the latter. Where would two young people go (in the rain) to commune with nature? To a cave, perhaps? Maybe, but there were no caves in the vicinity – Suetonius would have made sure of that – too handy for Boudicca's scouts. To a copse? To one side of the valley was a fine stand of trees which would offer both concealment and shelter. That would be the best direction to try.

Graecus set off in the direction of the copse, holding the bloody bag aloft, gauging the direction of the wind and changing the bag's position so as to ensure that its heady scent would carry to Zig's nose. It occurred to him that he was using the bag as a kind of divining rod and he smiled at the thought and he began to enjoy the walk.

It was invigorating after all those days in the claustrophobic atmosphere of wet leather and grumpy men to be out in the open in the sunshine and he filled his lungs with fresh air (avoiding the aroma of the bag) and shook the tension from his arms and legs. He remembered his earlier feelings of hunger which had now grown and he felt almost light-headed.

Graecus strode on towards the trees, wondering if his beloved boy would be there, thinking what he would have to say to his son.

The sun was high in the sky, beating down on the top of his head and Graecus began to feel hot. Then he noticed the crows, wheeling overhead.

Crows – death's noisy, greedy companions.

Graecus stopped in his tracks and felt his heart pounding so hard that he thought his chest would burst. He had been in this position before, when two of his best men had gone missing after the night-time attack in Lower Germania; Verus's cowardice had ensured that his men had endured a dreadful death and Graecus had, with the crows' help, found their mutilated bodies. But he had had Pneumaticus with him then and they had faced the carnage together. What if Germanicus had, in an agony of grief and disappointment killed himself?

Should he go back and get Felix?

Surely Germanicus could not have thought so little of all Graecus's years of love and care as to want to put an end to himself because of Aurora, but if he had, then it was a father's task to make sure that the boy's honour was saved if at all possible. So he must face this alone.

The crows were calling to each other over his head, mocking him, chattering loudly and excitedly to each other in anticipation of their bloody banquet.

It was torture to think what he might find in the copse. How would he bear it?

Then he realised that the crows were calling over his head and not over the copse.

Had he, perhaps, died without knowing it? How would he know? How could he be sure?

Then he realised that the crows were swooping over the bloody bag which he was stupidly holding up in the air – luring them with its pungency.

Graecus snorted at his own foolishness and threw the bag as far away from him as he could – the idea that he could be food for the crows was too close to what might happen to him if Pneumaticus failed to return from his mission or what would happen to the old soldier if his own kinsmen recognised him as Suetonius's spy. Graecus shuddered at each of these thoughts.

Then he started off again in the direction of the copse which was further away from the camp than it looked.

The sun beat down on his bare head and Graecus was both hungry and thirsty. He had hardly eaten for the last four or five days and the lack of nourishment was beginning to take its toll on him.

Would he actually find Germanicus in the copse? And if he was not there, then where was he? And where was Zig?

Soft grasses tickled at his legs and an insect bit his arm as he walked, almost in a trance, towards the copse, his heart hardly daring to hope that all could be well. But now, it leapt with relief as he saw a grey streak, running low across the long, wild-flower filled grass, coming towards him from the copse.

Then Zig was at his side and he bent to ruffle the dog's ears and say to him, 'I have never been more glad to see you, my little friend. Where is your master?'

At this question, clever Zig turned in the direction of the copse and the Centurion and the dog set off towards it. Then, as they approached the stand of trees, there looking out towards them was Germanicus, his hair sticking out in all directions from his head, his eyes and nose red-rimmed.

'Father!' was all he said, and Graecus caught him as he fell, weeping, into his arms.

Graecus held his boy close and patted the back of his heaving shoulders while Germanicus wept, his tears streaming down his face and falling like big raindrops onto the dry earth of the copse. Graecus hated it that his boy should be feeling so much grief and wished with all his heart that he could bear some of it – all of it – for him but the gods (God, even) did not allow this – all a father could do was to keep on holding his boy until the storm passed.

Eventually, Germanicus's tears ceased and Graecus gave him a clean neckerchief from his belt pocket to dry his eyes.

Germanicus blew his nose and hiccoughed a few times before saying, 'Father, I have been selfish, I know, and I have put my own happiness before the century's safety and your own and I apologise for that… but she was so beautiful and so lovely and I could not help myself. Please forgive me father.'

'I forgive you, my son, from the bottom of my heart. You are a young man and it is nature's way for young people to feel the madness of passion but I am heartily glad that we are now able to talk of that – you were so distant that I could not approach you.'

'Yes, father, I see that now.'

'And Felix noticed your sullenness – he remarked upon it to me.'

'Then I am doubly ashamed to have injured my best friend.'

'He will forgive you, my son, as I have.'

Germanicus now sat on a fallen tree trunk and ran his fingers through his long unruly hair and Graecus, welcoming the opportunity to rest for a while, sat next to him.

For a few minutes, neither of them spoke although Germanicus sighed deeply several times as recovered his composure. A blackbird sang sweetly in the tree above them and it was soothing to Graecus's frayed nerves.

'Father, I have been thinking about recent events and turning them over in my mind with what I remembered about my early childhood and there is something which I do not understand,' Germanicus now said.

'And what is that, my son?'

'Well, father, all the women I have loved – my mother, my sister (well, she was a little girl) and now Aurora – they have all been taken from me. Is it a curse? What have I done to bring this punishment down on my head? Why do the gods hate me so?'

This was a very complex question for Graecus, not least because it involved 'the gods' (and the coming into his own life of Gideon's God was not something he had discussed with Germanicus) then the delicate matter of Germanicus's blood heritage added to the complexity, and in any event, he did not know the answer.

Graecus scratched his head for a few moments, dislodging the lock of dark hair onto his brow, and thought very carefully before he said, 'Germanicus, I am a humble soldier and the gods do not include me in their schemes but what I do know is that you are by nature a good man and that is the path you must follow. I have no notion of what the gods may have in store for you but my advice to you is to retain your good nature – whatever provocation the gods may throw at you, do not let it compromise your loving heart.'

'Father, I have no wish to be anyone other than myself but these sudden losses of the women I have loved have made me think that I should never give my heart again.'

'There is just one thing wrong with that, Germanicus.'

'What father?'

'Well, what I am saying to you is that when you next meet a woman you could love, it will not be your head which is doing the thinking – it will be your heart and I am relieved that it will be so – it is your heart which is pure and loving.'

'I am still not sure that I understand what you have said father but I will think about it.'

'Good, now we must turn back and see what our colleagues are doing. I hope that Felix has supper ready for us – I am famished.'

Graecus put his arm round his son and they walked back to the camp together with Zig running beside them. As they walked, Graecus pondered that they had done this many times – father, son and dog, out walking together in Lower Germania when Germanicus was growing up and the worst worry then was attack from insurgents and life was simple and sweet.

Now, there were so many things complicating everything and Graecus had not yet broached the subject of the wax tablets.

So, as they walked, he said gently, 'My boy, there is another matter which I need to ask you – it is for your own safety. Where are the wax tablets you received from Aurora? It would be best if they were kept out of harm's way.'

'I burned them father, on Felix's cooking fire. I could see no point in keeping them as a reminder of my sorrow.'

Graecus did not know what to say to this. On the one hand he was greatly relieved that there was now no physical evidence of the affair, but on the other, he was amazed that the boy, who had so recently been driven to madness by his passion for Aurora, could be so down to earth about the aftermath.

Graecus's mind raced with all sorts of questions but he decided that it was best just to nod and say, 'That was the wisest thing, in all the circumstances.'

They re-entered the camp and Graecus immediately went to find Felix as he was so hungry.

Felix gave him a bowl of leek and turnip soup with a big piece of bread and some slices of roast boar which he washed down with several mug-fuls of red wine and then he wiped his lips very appreciatively saying to his old friend and colleague, 'By Jupiter, you are the most wonderful cook in the whole of the Empire. I cannot believe that anyone eats better than we do.'

Graecus sat in the late afternoon sunshine, resting for a while after the day's strange events and closed his eyes for a few moments, feeling relief that imminent disaster had been averted.

He enjoyed this relief for some minutes but then he saw that the sun was beginning to fall towards the horizon and he began to wonder what would happen when Suetonius came back and learned the terrible news.

Would they hear his cries of anguish all across the camp? Would he seek revenge on all those who had been close to Aurora? Would heads roll?

These were very uncomfortable thoughts and Graecus felt it would be wise not to meet trouble halfway by continuing to have them so he decided to drive them from his head by discussing the battle of Thermopylae with Incitatus whose ancestors had become the byword for valour and whose strategy in holding the narrow pass had been pivotal in driving the Persians from Greece.

Incitatus was both knowledgeable and enthusiastic. He told Graecus that the Greeks had made the Persians' task of taking the pass even more difficult by leaving the bodies of the dead where they had fallen so that there was, in effect a wall of corpses between the opposing forces and, when the Persians attempted to clear the bodies, they made themselves an easy target for Greek arrows and javelins. This had proved increasingly successful as the more the wall of corpses became more of a barrier the more the Persians tried to clear it away and made themselves easy targets for the Greeks. After two days in the sun, the smell was terrible, of course, but this was a cheap price for the strategic benefit gained and it was only when a Spartan traitor led the Persians up a secret path which brought them down into the pass behind the Greek warriors, that the Spartans and the Thespians were defeated.

There was nothing about this wall of bodies in Graecus's book on the subject and he was greatly excited and impressed by Incitatus's knowledge and said, 'My friend, how do you come by these facts? How do you know that this is the way it happened? This is not in the histories I have read. This tactic could be useful in our battle with Boudicca.'

'It is simple – my grandfather told me and his grandfather told him and so on, all the way back along our family tree to the time of the battle. It was one of the proudest moments in our history that we saved Greece by keeping the Persians at bay long enough for the Athenians to gather their forces.'

'I see that and I see it may come to be used to good effect again. Your knowledge of what really happened at Thermopylae may be what turns the battle in our favour.'

'That would be a most marvellous outcome for me. I would be as proud for us as my forefathers were for their forefathers,' said Incitatus.

'I will ensure, then, that Norbanus gets to know about this as he may wish to pass the knowledge on to Suetonius but I will also ensure that he knows that it came from you, a native Spartan.'

'Ah yes, Suetonius. I am sure that we are all dreading his learning of his daughter's death. Grief will not improve his temper.'

'No, it will not,' said Graecus. 'But now I must go and find Norbanus to tell him of your ancestors' clever stratagem.'

Graecus left the tent and went straight to Norbanus's quarters thinking as he strode purposefully along the lines of tents that this nugget of golden information from Incitatus was just the excuse he needed to speak to the Senior Centurion (hopefully before Suetonius's return) to be sure that their plan for the administration of balm to their commander's soon-to-be-broken heart was all in place.

Luckily, Norbanus was at his desk in his tent and looked up with relief when he saw that it was Graecus standing at the open flap which passed for a doorway.

'Ah,' he said, 'I suppose you have come to ask if everything's ready?'

'Yes, I have but I have also come to tell you something which could be really important.'

'Well, before we speak of whatever that is, just allow me to tell you that Magnus made the potion and I have given it to Suetonius's steward who was most co-operative and deeply grateful. He will give it to Suetonius before he tells him the terrible news and I'm sure we all hope that Magnus's mixture will work quickly and effectively.'

'Indeed – much depends on it. But I must tell you of what I have just learned from Incitatus my scribe who is a Spartan by birth.'

'The skinny one? He does not look much like a Spartan to me.'

'Well, his family were lawyers not warriors but he is clever and resourceful and he told me of a tactic which they used which was instrumental in holding the Persians at bay but which is not, to my knowledge anyway, in the accounts of the battle in our history books. Did you know that they used the dead as a wall to keep the Persians away?'

'No, I did not.'

'Well, they did and the Persians had to climb over it to get to the Greeks which made it easy to pick them off and it was only when they were betrayed by one of their own people giving the Persians a way to get behind the Greeks that they were defeated.'

'But how does that help us?'

'Because if we were to forego our usual practice of clearing the dead from the battlefront then the enemy will have to climb over them to get to us – if we can find the narrowing valley which allows us to recreate Thermopylae, that is.'

'Yes, I can see it now in my mind's eye. I can see that it could be a good tactic to keep the fighting front to a very narrow point, and if we have a hill behind us, to make the enemy very vulnerable in trying to engage us. Hmm. Yes, I can see that there is something useful here and I shall bear it in mind, but for now, we need to survive the next few hours – to see what is going to happen when Suetonius learns of Aurora's death and, as Pneumaticus has not yet returned from wherever he's been sent, I suggest that the best thing you can do is to make yourself scarce.'

'That is good counsel and I will take it immediately. Farewell.'

'Farewell, I hope when we meet again our fates are more certain.'

Graecus went back to his tent and spent the rest of the evening waiting.

Waiting for the dreadful backlash of Suetonius's grief.

Everyone was on edge but nothing happened that evening. Perhaps their leader had been delayed. If so, the best thing would be to go to bed and face whatever consequences there would be the following day.

As Graecus took off his clothes, he looked at his son, lying on his bed next to Zig, seeking comfort in the animal's soft neck, and wished that his first journey into love had been less traumatic.

As he got into his bed he thought about what the following day might bring and none of it was comforting and, wondering whether his dreams would be bad, he fell deeply asleep.

He need not have worried as he dreamed that they were all back in Lower Germania but, in the way in which dreams differ from memories, Arminia was at the fort, running a tavern there and Graecus could visit her as often as he wished. This was as close to a perfect life for Graecus as he could possibly imagine and he woke with a smile the following day.

CHAPTER ELEVEN

It was a bright clear day – not too hot and not too humid – and in the normal course of things, Graecus would have been feeling invigorated by his good night's sleep but he desperately needed to know what had happened with Suetonius without making it appear that he had any reason to be more interested than the next man.

He thought about this while he was having his breakfast and decided that the best place to go for information would be the latrines so, after finishing the bread and olive oil which accompanied the hot porridge, he took himself to the wooden planks and, this time, did not distance himself from other users.

There was a legionary sitting to his right.

'Hail!' said Graecus. 'What a gift of a morning.'

'Hail!' said the legionary. 'Yes, we can put this weather to good use by practising our battle stations if Suetonius gives us the order, but from what I hear, he's taken to his bed.'

'His bed?' said Graecus incredulously.

'Yes, the news of Aurora's death has quite unmanned him – apparently, he took it very quietly and said that he wanted to go to bed.'

'But where does that leave us? Who will lead us against Boudicca?' said Graecus, wishing to know what the legionaries thought of this.

'Who indeed? But you must remember that we need to meet the woman first, and so far, there's no sign of that. My brothers and I are sick of waiting – all this hanging about is bad for morale. My legion just wants to get stuck in and get it over with.'

'I am sure you speak for us all when you say that but we need to chose a place and time which favours our troops.'

'Agreed, but only Jupiter knows how that is to be achieved,' said the legionary with a sigh.

Graecus thought that he would know more of how it could be achieved if only Pneumaticus were to return to camp but, even if he brought good news, they still needed Suetonius as their General, sitting on his horse, looking as if he knew what he was doing.

Graecus kept these thoughts to himself and merely nodded his agreement to the legionary at which the conversation ended.

Leaving the latrines, Graecus decided that he would return to his tent via Solitarius's contubernium tent just to see what kind of mood Verus's spy was in now and, as he approached the tent, he saw his quarry sitting outside on a low stool, polishing his horn with a soft cloth.

As Solitarius was looking down, Graecus could not yet see his face but, just as he drew level with the horn-blower, Graecus saw that he was wearing a pained, puzzled expression and this so pleased him that he was whistling cheerfully as he walked on towards his own tent but, several yards before he reached it, he ran into Norbanus.

'Just the man I'm looking for,' said the Senior Centurion. 'We need to discuss battle lines and where your century would best be deployed so let us walk in the *intervallum* while we talk.'

Graecus allowed Norbanus to steer him by the elbow away from the lines of tents and then, when they reached the *intervallum*, Norbanus said, 'I don't really want to talk about that just yet, it's too soon – I just said it to deflect Solitarius's attention. What I really want is to talk about Germanicus.'

Graecus's heart sank. What interest could Norbanus have in Germanicus which could not, on the face of it, be discussed in even Solitarius's presence?

Graecus could not fathom this so he felt the best thing was just to say, non-committally, 'Germanicus?'

'Yes, Germanicus, your son. I haven't much time and, given the difficult situation we're in, I haven't too much patience either, so you'll just have to listen and stop playing the innocent with me. I don't know what it is about the boy that makes him so interesting but you need to know that Solitarius has been writing to Gnaeus Claudius Verus and sending him juicy gossip about Aurora and your son and saying that it could be useful information in the future.'

'But he had NO PROOF!' said Graecus with a knot tightening

in his stomach.

'Oh, so it is true that he was tupping her then?' said Norbanus with a raised eyebrow.

'Yes, it is true, although I never caught them at it,' said Graecus miserably – ashamed that his surprise at Norbanus's words had elicited such a revealing response.

'Well, he wasn't the first and he wouldn't have been the last – it's just unfortunate that he was her lover at the time of her death and Suetonius could never forgive him for that, could he?'

'No, he could not and that is why I have taken steps to destroy all the evidence.'

'All the evidence except Solitarius's little notes to Verus,' said Norbanus

'But how do you know about them?'

'Because I make it my business to know. I make it my business to know what creepy crawlies like Solitarius are up to and to know what nastiness useless pieces of shit like Verus are planning.'

Graecus did not know what to make of this. On the one hand, he desperately wanted to believe that Norbanus was as good a man as he seemed and that he shared at least some of his own thoughts about the decadence of the imperial regime, but on the other hand, what if this was a double bluff and he was being tricked into disclosing information which could harm his beloved boy.

So he said, 'You will readily imagine my reluctance to tell you anything about my son which could harm him but you already know that he has excited the interest of Verus, and I might add, his cousin, Vulponia, the priestess if Isis – she wanted Germanicus for her sect but I refused her and she flew at me in a terrible rage.'

'That Gorgon! Ye gods, she is a vicious woman and a very dangerous enemy. They are a cold and calculating pair and will step on anyone to get what they want.'

In terms of Norbanus's loyalties, this was encouraging so Graecus said, 'You have no sympathy then with the ambitions of some of Rome's rising stars?'

Norbanus spat plentifully on the ground at this and with a disgusted expression said, 'I would not give them the drippings from my nose – they are vile and I despise everything they stand for.'

'But what would you have in their place?' said Graecus.

'The same as many other honest men would have in their place – government by a Senate of good men chosen by the people on account of their desire to serve Rome.'

'I applaud those sentiments but Verus told me that, these days, he and his kind *are* Rome – that the Republic and its ways are gone forever.'

'He thinks that because it allows him to believe he's important and it gives him an excuse for his disgusting behaviour.'

'His liking for boys you mean?' said Graecus bridling at the memory of Verus's attempted assault on Germanicus.

'Yes, and his treatment of his wife.'

'Julia?'

'Yes, do you know her?' asked Norbanus

'No, I do not but I know that she is Flavius's niece and I know how distressed he was when Nero decided to marry her off to a known pederast.'

'Ah yes, Flavius, now there is a man who embodies the virtues which Rome needs!' said Norbanus and it was at this sincere and enthusiastic mention of his cohort's founder's name that Graecus decided that he could trust this man who was not only recommended by Acerbus but also a Flavian acolyte.

Graecus felt the knot in his belly unravel and he looked very carefully at Norbanus taking in the black eyes, the oily, wavy black hair and the deep olive skin –all the marks of a true Roman but then there was that other thing – the scar over his eye – the scar which demonstrated that he was a human being and Graecus felt very grateful that he could trust this man to uphold the values which he held dear but which had fallen out of fashion in Nero's Rome.

'I think that the Rome you and I serve is one and the same city,' said Graecus.

'Yes, I think it is and it is that city which Acerbus also serves,' said Norbanus smiling.

The two Centurions grasped forearms in a gesture of solidarity before Norbanus continued, 'And you will be happy to know that there are others like us, some of them in politics, some of them patricians, some are even equites, who want a more efficient, less corrupt form of government.'

'It gives me great heart to think so,' said Graecus. 'Now, tell me, what has happened to Solitarius's letters to Verus? Have they been sent to him?'

'No, certainly not – I did not want Verus to have evidence against Germanicus because, whatever it is that makes him interested in the boy, makes me want to protect him. So, I had the letters destroyed and that accounts for the puzzled look on Solitarius's face because we have had the diplomatic bag today and he would have expected a congratulatory message from Verus but none was forthcoming. There *was* a message for him from Verus berating him for not keeping him informed but I had that destroyed also.'

'Poor Solitarius – it must be difficult to be so despised and not even have the satisfaction of knowing why you deserve it,' said Graecus.

'Save your tears,' said Norbanus, 'he is as slippery as his master.'

'I am more grateful than I can say for your words and I feel I can now concentrate on the coming battle.'

'Indeed'! said Norbanus. 'That is one of the reasons why we shall need to speak, for we shall require your help and that of your Spartan when Pneumaticus returns from his visit to the Belgi.'

'Oh, so you know all about Pneumaticus's mission also?'

'My spies are very thorough,' said Norbanus in a mock-conspiratorial voice, 'but, so far, we have no news of your man's whereabouts.

'Yes, I must own that I had hoped he would be back by now – every day which goes by strengthens Boudicca's reputation and brings us nearer to defeat,' said Graecus.

'There is that, but there is also the point that, had Suetonius not taken to his bed – becalmed by Magnus's magic potions – then you could by now have been looking out over this valley through sightless eyes from the vantage point of a cross. As it is, Suetonius is not thinking about Pneumaticus and whether he has betrayed us, he's not thinking about anything, so it's my view that we should continue to keep him quiet until Pneumaticus gets back,' said Norbanus.

'And if he does not return?'

'Well, sooner or later the Legionary Legates will take control and *they* will have you crucified, we will probably lose to Boudicca and Rome will be evicted from these islands.'

'The Legionary Legates are not good fighting men, then?'

'No – you know as well as I do that they command their legions only for a few years as a stepping stone to political advancement and they are no match for a man like Suetonius who, albeit very strict, is a good soldier and shrewd strategist. But if Pneumaticus does not return soon, the legates will be looking for an explanation for the delay in exacting Rome's revenge and they will be seeking a scapegoat who will, more than likely, be you.'

'I hear what you say and I have no fear for myself but if the legates do execute me, I would like to have your assurance that you will do all in your power to look after Germanicus.'

'I give you my word and I accept that you do not wish to tell me what it is about the boy which makes him special.'

'I cannot tell you as it could be dangerous for both of you but what I can say is that, if you knew, you would be very keen to protect him against all harm and that, if I do perish and you need to know the full facts, then Acerbus can tell you.'

'Ah, Acerbus, as honest and as decent a man as I ever met!'

'Yes, I have been fortunate beyond measure to have had him as my colleague and friend these many years,' said Graecus. 'But I see that you are a man of similar integrity and I am grateful that our paths have crossed.'

Norbanus now offered his forearm again to Graecus and said, 'Brother!' and Graecus grasped the Senior Centurion's arm and repeated the word, which created a bond of loyalty between them: 'Brother!'

'We have been absent long enough,' said Norbanus. 'Let us rejoin our colleagues,' and the two men walked back to the busy lines of men, parting company with a simple 'Farewell' at the point where the auxiliaries' tents abutted those of the legions and leaving Graecus to walk back to his tent in a very mixed frame of mind.

On the one hand he was joyful, exhilarated even, to have had such an uplifting conversation with Norbanus and to feel that his own humble views were shared with someone of great pedigree and standing and, even better, that the man was willing to put himself in harm's way to serve the principles he espoused. Here was a man he could really admire! Here was a man as admirable as Acerbus and Flavius and, to Graecus's astonishment, they all seemed to value him and his good opinion.

This was truly uplifting and made him think that, maybe, there was hope for Rome and her people. Maybe, a way could be found to give the Eternal City the honest government which would enable her to be as good as she was great. Maybe Rome could have an Emperor who was honourable, just and fair and had been brought up in the best traditions of the Army – not some spoilt brat made rotten by the excesses of the Imperial Court. Maybe. And maybe Graecus had a part to play in that...

This was all very exciting but very dangerous and the hairs on the back of Graecus's neck stood on end as he thought of these amazing possibilities.

But then there was the small matter of Pneumaticus's failure to return. He had been expected back within five days and was now several days overdue. Graecus began to calculate how long the old soldier had been gone but soon abandoned this, deciding it was best not to dwell on it.

How long would the legates wait? How long would they allow Suetonius the luxury of lying in his bed, crazed (as they thought) with grief?

And if Pneumaticus did not return soon, how long did Graecus himself have to live?

Graecus was now at his tent, and ducking his head under the door flap, went in.

Germanicus was sitting on his bed oiling his gladius, Zig at his side, while Impedimentus appeared to be writing a letter and Felix was shredding some herbs by hand, sniffing avidly at his fingers as he did so, thinking which dish they would best complement. In the opposite corner sat Incitatus putting the finishing touched to Perdix's chamfron.

Graecus smiled at this picture of calm normality in the middle of the turmoil which was his life.

How easy it would be to lessen the burden of knowledge by sharing it! How easy and how pleasant to unburden himself and let others know of the currents and eddies of political and personal intrigue which were playing under their noses and in which he was himself perilously involved.

How easy and pleasant and how dangerous! No, he could not unburden himself and put them, any of them, even Felix who had shared the secrets of his heart for many years, in danger. No, he must just do his best to appear normal and get on with life in this terrible time of waiting.

Waiting for Pneumaticus, waiting for the Legionary Legates, waiting for Boudicca, waiting for death, waiting for victory. Waiting, waiting, waiting. How many times in combat had he told his men to 'Wait, just wait' when they were desperate to engage the enemy and get the dreadful waiting over? How many times had he stood there outside the testudo and envied them its safety when his men, far less able than him to see what was happening on the field, just had to wait?

And now he was the one who was just waiting and he had no idea what he was waiting for. Which would come first? Pneumaticus or his own death? Ignominy or glory?

Whichever of these it might be, for the moment, he must keep his thoughts to himself – this was the burden of rank and loneliness was the price.

Two more days passed. Two more agonising days while Graecus was on edge waiting for the sound of a detachment of booted feet come to arrest him and arraign him before the tender mercies of the legates.

And on the afternoon of the third day, he, sitting alone, dejectedly on his bed, picking distractedly at his teeth with a soggy bit of twig, heard such a sound.

Graecus's mouth went very dry as the noise of the feet came nearer and nearer to his tent. Tramp, tramp, tramp, tramp, tramp. It sounded as if there were about six men marching together. Tramp, tramp, tramp. And then it stopped.

Outside Graecus's tent.

The tent-flap opened and in came a legionary Centurion whom Graecus did not know.

'Centurion Graecus?' he said.

'Yes,' said Graecus.

'Accompany me, please, we have orders to take you to the legates.'

Graecus hoped he could pass the coming ordeal with courage and grace and that there would be a future for Germanicus by being under the protection of Acerbus, Norbanus and Flavius but who would love his son as he had?

Felix loved him, yes, that was a comfort for Graecus but the thought that his boy would now need to mourn him on top of his other grief was almost too much to bear and he had to bite his lip to stop himself from crying out as he stood to face the Centurion.

'Am I to know why?' he asked.

'I don't know exactly,' said the Legionary, 'but you are not to speak to anyone on the way. Now, line up with the men and let's be off.'

So Graecus left the tent and was escorted away with the legionaries past many questioning and some pitying glances.

The *praetorium* tent was not far away but the walk seemed to take forever and Graecus's mind was doing somersaults – hoping that Norbanus would be able to explain to Germanicus that his father had been executed for political reasons and that he had not dishonoured the century and that Verus would not be able to blacken his name for his own selfish ends.

Now they were at the *praetorium* and the Centurion took Graecus into the big tent where the pale-faced scribblers were hard at work.

'The legates wanted to see this man,' said the officer to one of the scribblers.

'Oh, yes,' he replied, very casually, as if it were a matter of little import.

How lightly they regard another man's life, thought Graecus, and how little do they know what torture is in this for me, knowing that I must leave my son behind.

'Come with me,' said the scribbler and led Graecus into another of the tents within a tent similar to the one used by Suetonius but smaller.

Facing him as he entered the inner tent were three desks at each of which was seated a legate.

They were a grim looking trio.

He could expect no quarter from these men. They would think nothing of sacrificing an auxiliary Centurion of no known parentage to further their careers.

'Bring the other man in,' said the one in the middle.

Other man? What other man? Who else were they going to crucify?

No one said anything while they were waiting for the other man to appear. No one looked at Graecus and he felt almost cheated that his death would be just a matter of routine for these ambitious Romans.

Then there were footsteps behind him and a familiar-sounding voice said, 'Hello chief! I'm mightily glad to see you.'

Graecus spun round in the direction of the voice and was astonished to see Pneumaticus, still dressed in the coarse woollen garments he had been wearing when he left oh-so-long-ago, coming across the dirt floor to stand next to him. Norbanus was behind him.

Graecus did not know whether to weep with relief or to batter Pneumaticus to death for having put him through such torment but he saw that the legates were talking to each other and ignoring the auxiliaries and managed to hiss at him, 'Where have you been, you swine? You were meant to be back days ago! What took you so long?'

'I'd have been here four days ago had it not been for that sodding mule. Stubborn isn't the word for that beast! It fought me every step of the way. I practically had to carry that animal back here.'

'Why did you bring it back then? Could you not have left it somewhere and made your way back in time?' hissed Graecus.

'What – and been put on a charge for losing valuable army property?' said Pneumaticus, wrinkling his face into a mask of incredulity.

Graecus was dumbstruck by this – shocked into silence by Pneumaticus's rationale which could have ensured a long and painful death for him all on account of a mule.

And to add insult to injury, when the old soldier said 'property' his missing front teeth ensured that he showered Graecus with spittle.

'Did you forget that Suetonius said that I would have to answer for you if you did not return in five days?'

'Well, I'm sure you would have thought of something to say, I mean, it wouldn't have been your fault would it?'

'No, it would not but that wouldn't have stopped him from executing me! But we can discuss that another time. You need to know that Aurora died several days ago and Suetonius took to his bed – that's why he isn't here. That's why we're talking to the legates.'

'Oh no!' said Pneumaticus. 'She was so young and so beautiful, what a tragedy…'

'When you have finished…' said the middle legate in a loud, testy voice to attract the auxiliaries' attention, '…when you have finished your private conversation, perhaps we can get on with the business in hand.'

Graecus and Pneumaticus stood to attention, staring straight ahead and Graecus felt Norbanus, at their backs, similarly straighten his posture.

'Now, you with the missing teeth, tell us what you learned from Boudicca's camp.'

'Sir,' spluttered Pneumaticus, 'there is unrest in her camp.'

'Explain,' said the middle legate.

'Sir, there are many tribes gathered there and their leaders are keen to strike at us while they feel they have the advantage.'

'Explain,' said the middle legate again.

'Well, sir, it's like this – there is not all that much time left of this year's fighting season and the other tribes need to get back to their own lands to harvest their crops so they are saying that they need to have the decisive battle with us soon, while there are so many troops mustered and then, having defeated us, they can return victorious to their homes.'

'So why has Boudicca delayed?'

'Well, sir, I did not, of course, speak to her myself on this matter but the talk at the camp-fire was that she wants Suetonius to come to her – she says that she will not come to him.'

'Explain,' said the middle legate. He was about thirty and had close cropped black hair which exaggerated the shape of his square head and his bull neck. His voice was Roman in the extreme – a lazy drawl with the hint of an affected lisp. Graecus disliked him as soon as he opened his mouth and was beginning to find this monosyllabic interrogation very irritating.

'Well, sir,' said Pneumaticus with admirable patience, 'what she is rumoured to have said is – "I'm not running after a man – he must run after me." '

This time, the middle legate did not say, 'Explain,' he said, 'And what did you understand by that?'

Graecus thought it was clear enough but Pneumaticus, calmly and steadily but sibilantly, said, 'Well, sir, I understood that what she meant was that the battle would be on her terms...' Here he paused to allow himself time to swallow, but then, anticipating another request for clarification, he went on, '...by which, I mean, on her terms as far as when and where are concerned.' Graecus had never heard Pneumaticus express himself so eloquently before.

'I see,' said the middle legate, but looked mystified.

'My lord,' said Graecus taking his courage in both hands, 'may I ask a question, the answer to which could help you in deciding what is our best strategy in these circumstances?'

'I suppose so, if you think it would help,' said the middle legate in a bored voice.

'My lord, we know that our leader was hoping to use some of the Spartan tactics from Thermopylae in the forthcoming battle and he asked my colleague here to look for a very specific type of valley somewhere close to Boudicca's camp. What we need to know is, did he find it?'

'Yes, yes, of course, that was to be my next question, said the middle legate, whose lack of military expertise was so damning, that in Graecus's mind, he was now named 'Clueless'.

'So, soldier, tell us, did you find the valley that Suetonius is looking for?' drawled Clueless.

'Yes, my lord, I did,' said Pneumaticus, pausing to let this fact sink in before continuing, 'It is about eighteen miles south of here and it is in the same shape as the drawing which our leader gave to me except that the narrow part of it is longer than shown here,' at which he unfolded the scroll he had taken from being tucked into his belt and pointed to it in illustration of his words.

Graecus was very impressed by this. He was impressed by Pneumaticus's attention to detail and by the calm, measured way in which he was dealing with Clueless. All Graecus's anger at Pneumaticus's thoughtlessness over the mule drained away and he was proud of the old soldier from his century who had done a very good job in dangerous circumstances.

'Hmm,' said Clueless. 'So we need to have the battle in that valley?'

'Yes, my lord, that is what Suetonius was seeking,' said Pneumaticus.

'But she said she will engage only on her terms,' said Clueless almost petulantly.

The other legates looked glum.

'My lord,' said a voice, 'may I make a suggestion?' and Graecus was both surprised and horrified to learn that it was he who had spoken.

'It would seem that you are determined to be *excessively* helpful today Centurion, so please do not let me stand in your way,' said Clueless in his bored way.

'Well, my lord, we have heard that Boudicca is under pressure from the other chiefs to have a battle soon so to that extent she has no more latitude than do we. If we were to send a message to her saying that Rome's army will meet hers at this place (taking the scroll from Pneumaticus and indicating the valley) at a given date, then surely the other tribal chiefs will prevail on her to take up the challenge as it is in accordance with their wishes.'

'I was thinking that myself,' said Clueless, after which there was an uncomfortable silence.

'My lord, permission to speak?' said Norbanus, coming round from behind to stand next to Graecus.

'Yes, Senior Centurion?'

'My lord, I think that is an excellent suggestion, and all the better for chiming with your own views but it is also the case that these Britons will not, as a matter of their own honour, resist the challenge. And because they feel absolutely assured of victory due to their superior numbers, they will not question our choice of battleground.'

'Yes, I see that,' said Clueless.

'Well, my lord, the sooner we send the message the better,' said Norbanus, who, Graecus now decided, was not merely a good man but also a brave one and skilled in dealing with these ambitious politicians who only played at being soldiers.

'Indeed,' said Clueless testily. 'Now you may leave us – my fellow legates and I will discuss what we have heard and will decide on our course of action.'

'My lords,' said Graecus, Norbanus and Pneumaticus simultaneously as they bowed and, turning, gratefully left the room.

'Phew,' said Norbanus when they were out of earshot, 'Sometimes it's like drawing teeth!' And then, realising to whom he had made this unfortunate allusion, he turned to Pneumaticus and said, 'My apologies – I meant no offence!'

Pneumaticus laughed but Graecus did not remove himself from spraying distance in time.

'Will they do as we suggested? After all it is our only hope of winning,' said Graecus wiping his face with his neckerchief.

'I agree but that does not guarantee that they will decide to do it. No, what we must do now is to ensure that Suetonius leaves his bed and rejoins the fray and I leave that little detail up to you,' said Norbanus, winking at Graecus.

'Understood. I will see to it,' said Graecus and he and Pneumaticus went back to their contubernium tent.

CHAPTER TWELVE

Pneumaticus was overjoyed to be back with his brothers and, although they knew they could not question him about his mission, they did make a great fuss of him and he revelled in the attention.

Incitatus was not present in the tent when Pneumaticus returned so Graecus could not just then present him with his new teeth but, in the early evening, their scribe returned and took the little wooden box he had made for the teeth from under his bed and silently handed it to Graecus.

Graecus stood and cleared his throat, signalling that he wanted the men's attention and their silence.

All eyes were on the Centurion who, turning to face Pneumaticus said, 'Brother, friend, colleague – we are all greatly pleased and relieved by your safe return but we have been aggrieved by the loss of your teeth. We have on so many occasions listened with astonishment and rapture to the stories of your adventures with women and we would be desolate indeed if there were no more. So, dear friend, we have organised these for you,' at which he opened the little box and took out the teeth which, deprived of any context, looked like some sort of barbarian tribal necklace then he gave them to Pneumaticus.

Pneumaticus had clearly not seen false teeth before and, mystified, turned them over in his hand several times before it dawned on him that he should put them in his mouth in place of his lost teeth and, as he realised this, his honest, weather-beaten face broke into such a wide gummy grin of total happiness that Graecus had a lump in his throat.

'Here,' said Incitatus, 'let me help you put them in. It is quite easy, and once I have shown you a few times, you will be able to do it yourself.'

Incitatus then slipped the gold wires over Pneumaticus's remaining top teeth and adjusted the ivory ones so that they fitted snugly in the gum and asked Pneumaticus to smile.

All the men nodded their approval and Pneumaticus said,

'Thank you, thank you, thank you, I cannot tell you how much this means to me. I can be happy again.'

'Well,' said Graecus, 'you need to thank Incitatus who made them for you and Felix who managed to get ivory and gold in this barren land.'

'And you need to thank Graecus because he paid for the ivory and gold,' said Felix firmly.

'Brothers,' said Pneumaticus, 'I can only thank the gods for giving me such generous colleagues and say that I hope it will not be too soon before I have interesting romantic tales to tell you.'

'Romantic is not necessarily the word I would chose to describe your stories,' said Graecus laughing.

Magnus now entered the tent and, having admired Pneumaticus's dazzling new smile, followed Graecus to the far corner where the Centurion whispered to him, 'We need Suetonius back on his feet. The legates have taken charge, but having met them this afternoon, I would say that is very dangerous for us all – they are woefully inexperienced in warfare, so Suetonius will have to get out of his bed.'

'Well, I can give him a lower dosage and that will probably bring him back to the world but I cannot guarantee his temperament.'

'What will happen if you give him less narcotic but more of the heartsease and a little more of the mushroom, perhaps?'

'I cannot give him more of the mushroom, it would be too risky, but I could give him more of the heartsease and a larger dose of the hypericum – that raises the spirits.'

'Well, we have no choice – the lives of 10,000 men depend on Suetonius's at least appearing to be in charge.'

'I will see to it. I will adjust the night-time dose now in the hope that he may get out of bed and return to his duties in the morning.'

'Excellent. Having suffered an audience with the legates, I will welcome the sight of Suetonius back at his desk – he is a soldier to his fingertips.'

Magnus then began mixing Suetonius's medicine as the rest of the men engaged in banter with Pneumaticus who could not stop admiring his shiny new teeth in one of the polished silver mirrors they used when they shaved.

And, Graecus was pleased to note, Pneumaticus's new teeth being in place stopped him from spitting so that it was now possible to have a face-to-face conversation with him and remain dry.

The evening passed in pleasantries and Graecus felt the stress of the last few weeks fall away from him as he enjoyed the company and comradeship of these men who, technically, were his colleagues but who were really his family.

Magnus slipped away to deliver Suetonius's new medicine to the steward of his household, and when he returned, the men began to retire for the night and Graecus, putting his head on his pillow, felt so happy and so relieved that all the imminent dangers to his loved ones had been removed, that he offered a silent prayer to Gideon's God – 'All powerful and only God, I thank you for granting my requests and for keeping my son and my friends safe. I also thank you for sparing my life. I know nothing of your cult and do not know how to worship you but I like your idea that love conquers all and I give you my heartfelt thanks for your help and hope that will suffice.'

He felt lighter after the prayer, cleansed somehow, and was just about to drop off to sleep when he had the most disturbing thought. Could he be turning into a Christian?

No, THAT REALLY WOULD BE TOO TERRIBLE TO CONTEMPLATE.

A Christian Centurion? It did not bear thinking about.

Then he fell asleep.

* * *

Events moved swiftly the following day. Rumours swept the camp that Suetonius was back in charge and had told the legates that the battle would be in the valley near Boudicca's camp. Then it was rumoured that a cavalry scout had been dispatched with a message for the Warrior Queen that the Roman Army would meet her and her allies ten days' hence.

Then the orders came that they would strike camp in three days' time and that there would be intensive drilling and battle station practice in the meantime.

It was wonderful, after all that waiting about, just to be outside being busy, getting hot, dusty and tired, wheeling and turning, listening to the clear sounds of the horns and memorising what the different notes meant so that each man's reactions were automatic.

Graecus enjoyed all of this and, sitting on Perdix, he several times caught Acerbus's eye and each smiled at the other knowing that the purpose of their long journey from Lower Germania was soon to be fulfilled.

Then began the march to the new camp. It was about sixteen miles away and was to take just one day but because there were so many men, horses, wagons and baggage, they needed to start at dawn.

There were those who said that this was a dangerous move in that it made the Romans vulnerable to attack en route but Graecus agreed with the other school of thought (led by Suetonius) that Boudicca would not have time to mobilise enough men and supplies to make a meaningful attack before her opponents were safely ensconced in their new camp and, anyway, someone had to make a move or they would be stuck in this impasse for ever and Nero would run out of patience.

As it happened, the march was uneventful except for the usual twisted ankles, lame horses and strained calves which were inevitable when so many men and animals embarked upon a long march.

Being auxiliaries, and therefore more disposable, Graecus and his century and Acerbus and his men were at the rear of the long column and arrived at the site of the new camp just before dark and, by then, much of the site, in a valley close to the chosen battle site, had been laid out in the familiar lines and cooking fires were burning. The Centurions soon found the places allotted to them in the lines (too near to the troublesome Batavians for Graecus's liking) and then supervised the men erecting their tents, checking their equipment, watering their animals and generally settling in to this new camp which was to be their home for… no one knew how long.

But, as he walked around, seeing that everything was in order, Graecus noted that the mood in the camp was good – the men were in high spirits knowing they were soon to fight the woman who had caused all this trouble and relishing the prospect of honours for their centuries, *alae* and cohorts.

Felix had cleverly saved some prized top quality *garum*, the pungent fish-sauce which the men so loved, and made a wonderful leek and mushroom soup which had them smacking their lips in appreciation and, after enjoying wine and some rousing songs, they all went to their beds.

Graecus put his head down and felt grateful that they had all arrived safely and his family were all in good spirits and he made a short prayer to Gideon's God – 'God of love, thank you for keeping those I love safe.'

Surely a short prayer, without mentioning any names, could not be harmful, could it?

Then he fell asleep.

* * *

The next day was bright and sunny and the men were up and about early so as to be ready for whatever orders came.

Just after the fourth hour of the morning, Norbanus appeared and told Graecus that he, Pneumaticus and Incitatus were needed in Suetonius's tent and the three men set off to meet their leader.

As they walked briskly to the big tent, Graecus thought how different was this from that dreadful time so recently when he had been summoned by the legates and why, given that they had not actually wanted to arrest him and have him crucified, had they not foreseen that it would appear to any who saw him being frogmarched to their tent, that Centurion Graecus was in deep trouble? Why did they not see that it was humiliating for him?

Why? Because they were rich, ambitious, men – intent on increasing their personal power within the most powerful empire the world had ever known and they gave no thought to the feelings of men like him, men who were easily replaced and who counted for nothing in their gilded world. They behaved in this way simply because they could and no one would call them to account for it.

Now they were at the *praetorium* tent and, on entering, Graecus noticed that the whey faced clerks looked up when they saw the auxiliaries and the most senior of them even stood and said, 'Gentlemen, you are expected. Please wait here, I will announce you.'

When he returned, the clerk said, 'Follow me, please,' and led them into the large tent within a tent which was Suetonius's workplace.

He was sitting behind his desk, upright and alert, pink of cheek and with a glint in his eye.

The Legionary Legates were ranged on either side of him with Clueless to his right and the other two to his left.

It was a formidable panel of high born Romans and Graecus felt his lack of pedigree until he noticed Norbanus coming in to sit next to Clueless and the pounding in his chest subsided.

'Gentlemen,' said Suetonius, 'You may know that we dispatched a note to Boudicca telling her that we will be at battle stations here (pointing at a map of the valley found by Pneumaticus) waiting for her in just a few days' time. We have not yet had a reply but we must assume that she will meet us – as our Belgi friend here (nodding at Pneumaticus) made clear, she will find it hard to resist an open challenge and the other tribal leaders wish to return to their crops, hmmm?'

The auxiliaries all nodded in unison while the legates stared at them.

'Now, I hear that you are from Sparta?' Suetonius said to Incitatus.

'Yes, my lord, I was born and brought up there till my fourteenth year.'

'Humph. You don't look much like a Spartan to me.'

'My family were lawyers, my lord, but in any event, the

splendid musculature sported by my ancestors in the well-known ancient sculptures is a little... *exaggerated,* shall we say?'

Incitatus said these last words in a mocking, half-conspiratorial tone in such perfect Latin and with such confidence that Graecus was very proud of him and the legates looked at him with some interest while Suetonius laughed.

Actually laughed. And said, 'Oh, so the famed Spartan physiques were not as fine as portrayed? Ha ha ha! That makes the rest of us feel more secure in our manhood then! Ha ha ha!'

The legates also laughed while Suetonius gestured to a young man standing at the door-flap to bring forward stools for the auxiliaries.

They sat in unison – all that drilling had ensured that when they moved, they moved as one man.

'Now, Spartan, I hear that you have an interesting piece of information for us, about a wall of death at Thermopylae?'

'Yes, my lord, in defending the pass against the much larger Persian forces, my ancestors found it helpful not to clear away the bodies of the fallen as they formed a deadly barrier over which the enemy had to climb in order to engage with the Greek troops. This made it very easy to pick off the advancing Persians and, as the battle continued, the wall became ever deeper and more difficult to overcome.'

'Hmmm,' said Suetonius, 'I see that was a shrewd move in those circumstances, but the Greek forces were defending their own land and they had space behind them into which to retreat.'

'Yes, my lord, but we shall have the hill behind us to protect us and I know that not one of our soldiers ranged against Boudicca will contemplate retreat.'

'Spoken like a Spartan, albeit a skinny one!' said Suetonius, laughing again, at his own joke this time, and this time, the legates guffawed.

Suetonius now picked up a large piece of parchment on which was drawn a diagram of the funnel-shaped valley and some differently coloured blocks which, Graecus having seen battle plans before, knew represented the legionary infantry, the auxiliaries and the cavalry. Suetonius laid the parchment on the big table so that everyone could see it.

Graecus saw that Suetonius's chosen formation with the legions in the middle, the auxiliaries on either side of them and the cavalry at the extreme ends of the infantry was a classic lay-out and noted with approval that their General had set out his army at the bottom of the funnel facing the enemy and with their backs to the wooded escarpment.

'Gentlemen,' said Suetonius, 'this is my desired formation for our battle. Now, the point is, how, if at all, does this idea of the wall of death help us?'

'Permission to speak, my lord?' said Pneumaticus.

'Go ahead.'

'Well, my lord, it may be useful in coming to a decision, for you to know that the Britons will not be able to attack us from the rear, the hill behind us will protect us totally.'

'Explain,' drawled Clueless.

'Because, my lord, the hill is sacred as it is covered in oak trees, and even though their best fighters, the charioteers might possibly be able to negotiate the slope they will not do battle there.'

'Ye-e-e-s,' said Suetonius. 'So we are able to assume that the Britons will not in any circumstances seek to go behind our backs?'

'That is correct, my lord, they are deeply religious people and oak groves are sacred to their gods. In fact, they will likely feel that their victory is even more certain because their gods will be insult-ed by our abuse of their groves,' explained Pneumaticus.

'Yes, I see that,' said Suetonius. 'So if we engage them at the bottom of the funnel and allow the dead to pile up, then the Britons will be forced to climb over them to continue the engagement but if they saw that they were being slaughtered would they not with-draw?' – raising a questioning eyebrow at Pneumaticus.

'My lord, I do not think withdrawal will enter their minds. They are drunk on victory and Boudicca cannot allow her judge-ment to be seen to be flawed… at the moment, she is the goddess of freedom for these people and she relishes that position so she cannot be seen to fail.'

'I will allow you that this battle is as decisive for her as it is for us so a tactical withdrawal on her part is very unlikely. But we need to consider how we ourselves can advance if the wall of death is in our way.'

'My lord,' said Graecus, 'is it not the case that our cavalry are able easily to melt into the trees?'

'Yes, it is – they are unencumbered by those old-fashioned chariots which the Britons seem to prize so much.'

'Well, my lord, may I suggest that, at your signal, our cavalry pull back into the trees behind us and then the infantry can move forward round the wall of bodies but in such a way that they can easily attack the vulnerable wings of the Britons who will be unable to retreat? That way we could advance with minimum risk to our men.'

'Hmm,' said Suetonius, stroking his chin slowly and thoughtfully. 'Hmmm, hmmm. Ye-e-e-s. I begin to see how that could work. And the cavalry can be deployed wherever they will be able to pick off the most Britons? It's unorthodox, it's very unorthodox but these are very unorthodox circumstances and this idea has the element of surprise about it. I like that!'

Graecus squirmed on his stool as he felt the cold eyes of the legates upon him while Suetonius sat and beamed, positively beamed, in his direction.

But then, 'Ha!' bellowed Suetonius, his face changing from benevolence into stone in a split second. 'Now I see what it is you are up to!' pointing angrily at Graecus whose bewildered face expressed what most of the others in the room were feeling.

'Now, I see that what you want are honours for your century! You want to advance from the wings because your auxiliaries will be there and you want them to have the battle honours – not my legions!' said the General banging his fist so hard on the table that it made everyone, even the legates, jump.

This was grossly unfair – it was the last thing in Graecus's mind – all he really cared about was that his son and his comrades would be unharmed but, thanks to his having had to sail with mad bad captain Jejunus, he had some experience of dealing with lunatics and, after looking Suetonius straight in the eye for several seconds, he said,

'My lord, I have been a soldier in the greatest army the world has ever known for as long as I can remember. Rome's army has given me a purpose and a family and I am greatly in its debt for its having given me so much. But I have served Rome well and I take pride in the fact that my century has acquitted itself with valour wherever it has fought. I seek to protect Rome's interests and to promote the Emperor's rule wherever I draw my sword. And if my century wins honours in the coming battle then I shall rejoice, but it is not for that reason that I draw my sword. No, the reason I draw my sword is for the honour of the whole army and to protect the brothers standing next to me.'

Graecus had the absolute attention of every man in the room while he was delivering this oration in a calm, measured tone, and, as he spoke, Suetonius's face lost its harsh expression and softened into what was, at first, sympathy, but then, to the discomfort of all who could see him, deep distress.

Graecus finished and sat bolt upright waiting for a reply. All anger had left Suetonius. He was leaning forward, slumped almost, onto his desk.

The silence in the room was deafening. Graecus could feel Pneumaticus and Incitatus on either side of him, their backs stiffened in apprehension, each of them hardly daring to breathe.

Now Suetonius looked up and looked straight at Graecus whose grey eyes were fixed on his General who, in a soft voice, said, 'I understand what you have just said, Centurion and I commend you for your sentiments. Those of us who have recently been bereaved know how grievously the loss of a loved one affects us mortals. I do not wish to traduce your wish to keep your comrades safe nor do I wish to cheapen your natural desire for honours.'

Now he took his eyes from Graecus and, looking around the room at the rest of the soldiers, he said, 'That is all for now. I am satisfied that we have a workable plan for the battle – all we need is good weather and the knowledge that she will meet us on the appointed day. Gentlemen you may go.'

Graecus was just standing up and feeling very relieved to be on his way out of range of Suetonius's changeable temperament when the General's voice boomed out, 'Yes, you may go, all of you, except you, Centurion Graecus – I want you to remain behind.'

Graecus sat down again on the stool and waited until the others left the room, his anxiety mounting with the departure of every man. Norbanus was the last to leave and, as he passed Graecus's stool, he managed to give his junior colleague a sympathetic smile but this did nothing to lessen Graecus's discomfort.

Here he was, the man who hated his lack of ancestry almost as much as he hated politics – here he was alone with an extremely high-born, powerful Roman and that was bad enough, but worst of all, here he was with the man whose daughter had, to some extent at least, perished because his son, his beloved boy, had insisted on making love to her in the pouring rain (well, maybe it had been the other way round but that would make no difference to a grieving father).

Norbanus had left the tent within a tent and the door-flap had been closed.

Suetonius was signing a document and Graecus watched him, noting the casual way in which he added his Great Seal – the important man who had been important for a very long time and no longer noticed the trappings of power.

Now the great man had finished and he looked up at Graecus but he did not speak and Graecus did not know what to do. Should he speak? Should he smile encouragingly? Should he be impassive?

Suetonius cleared his throat in a hesitant manner and then Graecus understood – he is finding this (whatever it is) as difficult as me, he thought.

Suetonius now opened his mouth to speak and in a very low voice said, 'You may wonder why I spoke very harshly to you just now?'

Ye gods! What was the answer to that? How did you answer an unstable mad man who asked you if you were wondering why he was behaving in an insane fashion? Graecus had no idea and was opening and closing his mouth like a fish but no sound was coming forth.

'You have no idea?' said Suetonius.

'No, my lord,' said Graecus truthfully.

'I sought to make an example of you in front of the legates because, otherwise, they will make your life hell,' said Suetonius. 'They saw how much you and your men had to contribute to the battle plan and that demonstrated how little they know of strategy, so, they would not wish to be bested by a mere auxiliary, even if he is a Centurion with many years' service – that was why I had to shout at you.'

'I see, my lord. Thank you,' said Graecus.

'But you mentioned brotherhood in your reply and it unsettled me somewhat. And that is the other matter – I wished to speak to you about my dear daughter, my darling girl who has gone to join her mother and the ancestors.'

Suetonius paused to wipe the back of his hand across his eyes before continuing, 'My steward and Aurora's slave girl have told me how helpful you and your medicine man were and how much he tried to save her life and I am most grateful to you both. It was a difficult life for my daughter among all these men and I wish with all my heart that I had been here when the gods took her but I take some comfort knowing that she was properly cared for in her final hours.'

Graecus was so surprised by Suetonius's gentle words that, again, he did not know what to say.

But then he thought of the great man as just another father – a father who had lost the child who was dearest to him in all the world and then the words came easily to him.

'My lord,' he said, 'I cannot begin to know your grief but I know that there are many who could not bear it with such fortitude and grace and I am deeply honoured that my century was of assistance to your daughter.'

'Thank you, Centurion,' said Suetonius wiping his nose. 'Now, we must see to it that your century is at the front line – we don't want you missing out on those battle honours, do we?' he said clapping Graecus on the back as he ushered him from the room.

Graecus left the *praetorium* tent even more confused than before. Now it seemed to him that he had been transformed from an auxiliary sacrifice into Suetonius's new best friend and confidant all within the space of less than a week. And all without his having done anything.

Of course, it was deeply flattering that he and his men had played such a large part in this rehearsal for the *consilium* – the strategic discussions which took place between the officers on the eve of a battle – but he seemed to have made enemies once more – of the legates– again without his having done anything.

All this politicking was so alien to Graecus's nature. He had been raised in the army tradition of the strong arm and the quiet conscience – the knowledge that you fought for the *Pax Romana* but now it was all so different – with all these factions vying for power and control and very few of the people involved being at all interested in what was best for everybody.

Indeed, the characteristics which were present in all the people Graecus now found himself up against was that they were all, to a man, selfish and often casually cruel.

Graecus turned this over in his mind as he walked back to his contubernium tent and he wracked his brains to find a way through the maze of conflicting thoughts. Then he had an idea which instantly made him feel more peaceful – he would pray to Gideon's God – because Gideon's God was a God of love and surely what was most lacking in this situation was love.

So as he walked back to his tent, he prayed, 'God of love, please bring love to this place and please help me keep my son and my men safe. Oh, and please keep me safe so that I can continue to keep them safe.'

These thoughts and this prayer kept him occupied until he reached his contubernium where he was surprised to see Acerbus in deep conversation with Impedimentus.

'Hail,' he said to them, 'what news is there today?'

'Well, the news, hot from the mouth of the man who saw the

cavalry scout's return, is that Boudicca has agreed to meet us in battle but that she sent the message written, in good Latin, in his hand, in his severed hand – the poor bastard had to ride back here with one hand keeping his other, bleeding hand wrapped in a piece of sky blue Iceni cloth on his lap,' said Acerbus.

'Ye gods these people are barbarians,' said Graecus.

'Well, she probably needed to demonstrate her strength and her resolve to the other tribal chiefs so the loss of a cavalry hand was a good way to do it, was it not?'

'I suppose so,' said Graecus 'but it will only make us all the more determined to beat her. Will she meet us at the appointed place?

'As I understand it, yes,' said Acerbus. 'The Britons have not seen how the valley will work to our advantage.'

'And do we know when the battle will take place?' said Impedimentus. 'Because if it is to be soon, then I have much work to do.'

'My informant said that Boudicca had written that she will meet us the day after tomorrow but it's not official yet – the maimed cavalry scout passed out as soon as he got to the medical post so Suetonius has not had the chance to speak to him yet and we won't know definitely until then,' said Acerbus.

'All this waiting!' said Graecus. 'It is so hard just to wait when there is so much to be done and when every man here is itching to have his chance to avenge Rome.'

'I agree,' said Acerbus. 'But when those British chariots are coming towards you with their naked warriors covered in blue paint and screaming their heads off, you might wish for a quieter life.'

'The sooner this is all over, the better I will like it!' said Graecus.

'Well, there is still a great deal to do before we are ready to meet that woman,' said Impedimentus. 'We need to move our medical equipment and food and water supplies and have them in place in good time. I think I had better go and have a chat with Norbanus's baggage master and see what he wants us to do. I mean, I am assuming that we will move to the battlefield from here and leave our tents here – we will not be moving the whole camp again, will we?'

'That would make no sense to me,' said Acerbus. 'It would be better if we left our tents and belongings here and marched to the battlefield early in the morning on the appointed day.'

Just then a young legionary ran up to the Centurions and told them that they should muster their men and report to Norbanus in the *intervallum* and Graecus and Acerbus nodded to each other in recognition of an urgent order as each of them set off in search of his men.

The Centurions responded as quickly as they could and within a half hour the two centuries, other auxiliaries and assorted cavalry, including the Batavians, were all standing to attention waiting to hear what Norbanus had to say.

Norbanus was not a tall man but he had presence and when he opened his mouth to speak, there was instant silence among the men.

'You will have heard rumours,' he said. 'Now I am going to tell you what is really happening. The cavalry scout Suetonius sent to Boudicca with a personal message, leader to leader, written in his own hand brought back a message written by her in the scout's own hand – his own *severed* hand.' Norbanus paused here to allow the men to vent their anger at this by muttering and growling, then he said, 'Her message said that she agrees to meet us at our chosen site in battle the day after tomorrow. The battle will start at about the fourth hour so we shall leave here just after dawn.' Norbanus paused again to let the rousing cheer from some of the men die down.

'This is where we are to be positioned,' he continued, holding up a large copy of the battle plan showing the placements of the auxiliaries and the cavalry just as they had been positioned in the plan Graecus had seen earlier and he was encouraged to hear a grunt of approval from Acerbus standing next to him.

'Now listen carefully,' said Norbanus. 'We all know that Boudicca has numbers on her side and the odds are heavily against us BUT we do have a chance to win this battle if we all act our parts and follow our orders to the letter; our General has a very specific strategy here and we will use the Britons' numbers *against* them.'

This brought the sound of many sharp intakes of breath from the listening soldiers and Norbanus paused again to let what he had just said sink in.

'As you will see, our troops are positioned at the bottom of this funnel-shaped valley so, in order for the Britons to engage us, they will have to come forward down to the bottom of the valley, but because it is narrow with steep sides, they can advance only in small numbers at one time. Now, who is clever enough here to tell me what that means?'

There was a general shuffling of feet and some sheepish looks for several long seconds before Germanicus's voice rang out clearly saying, 'Sir, it means that we shall all the more easily be able to pick them off – one by one almost.'

Graecus was proud of his son's acuity in divining Suetonius's strategy but had the fleeting thought that Germanicus's slight lisp, which he had had ever since his encounter with the wild boar, made him sound like a high born Roman – just like one of the legates, in fact.

'Well done!' said Norbanus. 'Now, what will happen when there is a build up of fallen Britons – some of whom will be in their chariots?'

Again there was a shuffling of feet. Maybe these men were not accustomed to thinking for themselves, thought Graecus, and then he could see why Norbanus was asking them to think through the rationale for the strategy – that way they would remember it and there was less chance of a mistake which could be very expensive in terms of Roman lives.

'Come on now, somebody must have a brain that's working today? What will happen when there is a build up of British bodies?'

'Well, we usually clear the dead away if they are in the way of our advance,' said a tall legionary who looked as if he had seen many years' service.

'Good answer!' said Norbanus. 'Good answer; but in this case, it's not the right answer.'

There was more foot shuffling and there was beginning to be a feeling of slight unrest among the men when Norbanus said,

'Oh, all right then, I see that I will have to tell you. The answer is that nothing will happen.'

Norbanus paused again to let this sink in before saying, 'Nothing will happen until a special order to the cavalry on the wings here (pointing to the plan) when they will withdraw into the trees behind us as quickly as they can and then, at the next blow of the trumpets, you auxiliaries from either end of our lines will advance round the columns of the dead so that you are going forward into the enemy lines in a pincer movement, followed in due course by the legionaries and then, once the infantry have advanced into the enemy lines, Suetonius will decide what the cavalry will be doing.'

Norbanus paused again and looked closely at the assembled soldiers to see if they had understood.

Some of them still looked mystified so the Senior Centurion repeated his explanation of Suetonius's strategy again and again until he was satisfied that every man knew exactly what was expected of him. Then he asked if there were any questions and one of the tall Batavian cavalry said, 'I see that this is a good plan but how steep is the foot of this valley? I mean, how do we know that we can withdraw quickly?'

'Because several of your legionary brothers have already tried it on a similar slope some miles from here (we don't want Boudicca's spies to know what we're planning, do we?) and have been successful in a swift manoeuvre. The trick is to be ready for the special command and then to do it an orderly fashion which you will be practising this afternoon.'

'But what if the Britons try to move into the space we have vacated?' said the Batavian.

'They will find it difficult because we have the element of surprise and their chariots are less manoeuvrable than our men, if they have any chariots left by then, that is.'

There were no more questions and Norbanus then gave out smaller copies of the battle plan to each unit commander present with orders to familiarise themselves with it and that all the infantry were to muster at the seventh hour, outside the

Praetorian gate for more battle station practice.

The group of men began to break up to go back to their units, but as he turned on his heel to walk away, Graecus saw Big Red Hands and Bad Teeth staring in Germanicus's direction and making faces at him – trying to ape his open countenance and making lisping noises.

Graecus made sure that his boy saw none of this by taking his elbow and drawing him away from the prankish Batavians, but as they walked, father and son, back to their contubernium, Graecus pondered that it was all too easy to make enemies in the Roman army.

CHAPTER THIRTEEN

The rest of the day passed quickly in a flurry of making arrangements, battle station drilling, receiving and giving orders and making as sure as was possible that nothing was left to chance. Of course, one of the most important of all matters would be left to chance as there was nothing the Romans could do about it – the weather.

Graecus knew that Suetonius would want a dry day with firm ground as these were the conditions which most favoured the Romans' reliance on infantry and their highly disciplined tight battle formations – in the dry they were formidable opponents, but their job became more and more difficult the wetter and slippier the ground became. Graecus had never met the Britons in battle before so he did not know by experience, but he surmised that they would be favoured by wet conditions – firstly, because they were more accustomed to them in this damp, dark land and secondly, because their light chariots would be reasonably stable on soft going albeit useless on really muddy ground.

It was infuriating really that the outcome of a hugely important battle could turn on something so chaotic as the exact amount of rain falling on the battlefield but that was exactly the way it was – battles had turned on matters more esoteric than that.

Graecus had fought enough times to know that there was often an indefinable something which pitched a battle in favour of the one side and not the other; obviously, superior numbers and well-designed weapons counted a great deal, as did discipline which turned a rabble into an army but belief in the cause for which one was fighting and confidence in one's comrades counted as much, if not more. As he turned this over in his mind, Graecus was satisfied that his century would be properly motivated in these respects and, now that his beloved son had been restored to him, he felt calm and almost content about the imminent conflict. Perhaps it would turn out well after all and he allowed himself a few moments' daydreaming of a wonderful future when Germanicus was a high ranking army officer with a loving wife and family and he a kindly grandfather laughingly hoisting his grandson on his shoulder after teaching the boy how to hold his wooden sword. The thought that this was all a possibility warmed his heart and made him feel that there was a purpose in his life.

Another beguiling thought occurred to him. Maybe *he* would find a wife. Maybe at some stage his life would be stable enough and he would not be too old to marry. What would she be like? Then his thoughts turned to the woman who had meant most to him in the last few years – Arminia –and he thought of her lovely blue eyes and the smell of chamomile in her dark blonde hair and he thought of other, more secret, parts of her and he felt a stirring in his manhood, rare in recent times, but pleasant as it undoubtedly was, he did not at the moment have time for *those* kinds of thoughts and put them reluctantly to the back of his mind.

The day wore on in preparations for this decisive battle but when evening came the frantic activity of the day quietened, weapons and armour were unbuckled, the horns were silenced, the torches and the fires were lit and cooking smells – some more appetising than others – filled the still air.

The smells coming from Felix's pots were especially tempting and Graecus was looking forward to his supper, trying to work out from the aroma what it was that Felix was cooking when he felt a slight stabbing pain in his belly – nothing terrible, just a short sharp stab in the gizzards which he put down to nerves and went back to checking his official orders which had come, several sheet of them, sealed, from the legates' office earlier that afternoon but he did have cause to wipe his brow once or twice and with the corner of his neckerchief.

It was soon supper-time and Felix had surpassed himself in producing a venison stew flavoured with rowan berries and sage, served with hot bread and a side dish of buttered onions and carrots.

Graecus's men were delighted by this and ate greedily and appreciative noises filled the night air but, even though Graecus had been looking forward to his supper, when his steaming portion was handed to him, he suddenly felt nauseous and, unceremoniously pushing the bowl away from Felix's out-stretched hand, had to get up and go behind the tent to be sick.

Having brought up an amount of clear fluid streaked with yellow bile, Graecus stood, holding his belly, gasping for air. He knew that all colour had left his face and that his eyes were watering but then, raising his head to try to help his breathing, he realised that someone was taking a hammer to the inside of his skull.

Graecus was horrified. He could not afford to be sick. Whatever was wrong with him could hardly have come at a worse time – just when he needed to be at his most effective, here he was spewing up his guts with his brain feeling like porridge and his lungs like a soggy piece of sponge. Just when his leadership of his century was to be tested in a battle of great importance for the Roman Empire, here he was with boiling bowels and shaking hands. Ye gods, his hands *had* begun to shake! And his knees were knocking.

And he was shivering all over his body.

But he must keep calm and get a grip on himself. It would be very bad for his men's morale if they were to see him like this. And he could not bear to think that anyone might consider him lacking in courage – what if creepy-crawly Solitarius reported to Verus that Graecus had been shaking with fear before the battle (Norbanus's spies may not be entirely effective in intercepting all communications between Verus and his placeman)? What if the brassy Batavians thought that he was trying to avoid fighting in the front line? What if Suetonius decided that he was not only *not* his new best friend but also a coward?

He must stand straight and walk steadily back to the tent and find a way of attracting Magnus's attention without anyone else noticing that something was wrong. Yes, that was what he must do.

That was what his mind told his body to do – put one leg in front of the other, and repeat this – come on you can do it – you've been walking for many years now – why are you finding it so difficult? Why can you not do this simple thing? Why is the ground moving? Where is that strange 'whooshing' noise in your ears coming from? Why is everything so blurred? Why, all of a sudden, are you lying on the ground looking at the stars? Why is breathing so difficult? Who told you to lie down?

Then a face appeared between him and the stars. It looked familiar but he could not quite place it, then a familiar but not quite identifiable voice said, 'What's the matter, is there something wrong with my stew?' And then on peering more closely, the voice said, 'Oh shit! Shit. Shit. Shit!' before disappearing and leaving Graecus to appreciate the brightness of the stars once more. But then he realised they were hurting his eyes so he closed them and lay flat on his back. But that made him dizzy and he wanted to be sick again so he turned on his side and managed to bring up a little more clear fluid while wondering how he would ever be able to stand up.

'Turn him over very gently,' said another voice, and then someone was prising open his eyes, feeling his forehead and saying, 'He's burning. He seemed in good health earlier today. Has he eaten the same food as the rest of us?' And another voice said, 'What in the name of all the gods is wrong with him? Is he going to die? Is my father going to die?'

Germanicus! Was Germanicus there? Thank Jupiter! Or was it, thank God? Graecus felt so ill that he really did not care which god was on duty that evening and just wished, as he now felt so profoundly cold, that he was in his bed tucked under three blankets.

Now someone had put a cold cloth over his eyes and strong hands were under him lifting him and carrying him. He wanted to speak, he wanted to say that he was in control and would be back at his post early in the morning but he could not form the words and felt so tired, so very tired that all he could do was gratefully close his eyes and lie still like a stone on the bed upon which they had placed him. He slept for what seemed like hours but it may only have been seconds – he did not know.

He dreamed of being back on board 'Nauplius' lying on the deck yawing from side to side but, when he woke, he was surprised to find himself in bed and there were voices murmuring around the bed. Worried voices. Someone was poking long, stiff fingers into his belly – probing and palpating – it was horrible and made him want to be sick and his brow broke out in a sweat. Someone prised open his eyes again and shone a light into them.

One of the voices, the one who seemed to be in charge, now said, 'I cannot be sure, it is difficult without speaking to him but he is delirious and I cannot get any sense out of him, I cannot be sure but I think he has been poisoned.'

'Poisoned?' a chorus of incredulous voices said.

'Yes, the symptoms are pointing that way, but if I am correct, then we must be very circumspect about it – if he has enemies, we must try to keep him from them.'

'Enemies?' sobbed a young man. 'Why would he have enemies? My father is a good soldier and a good man!' And Graecus thought how pleasing it was to hear a youth speak so warmly of his father in these modern times when the young no longer respected their elders.

'Exactly,' said another, much older voice with a pure Roman accent, 'and that is why he may need to be protected from people with strong personal ambitions.'

Now this other, older Roman person seemed to be in charge and said to the one who had formerly been in charge, 'If he has been poisoned, what can be done?' while the young man started to sob and took hold of his hand, squeezing it hard while saying, 'Don't die, don't die, don't die!'

Mr–Formerly-in-Charge seemed a very long way off and sounded as if he were speaking from the bottom of a deep well when he said, 'Not knowing what the poison is, I cannot give an antidote but the best thing, the only thing we can do is to purge him and try to rid his system of it – whatever it is.'

'Well, you had better start now, I think,' said Mr Now-in-Charge, while the young man kept on squeezing his hand and repeating his incantation: 'Don't die, don't die, don't die.'

They made him sit up. The effort brought on such a sweat that it ran into his closed eyes and stung them but this was nothing compared with the paroxysms which contorted his whole body and caused the young man to speed up his prayer while squeezing his hand with ever more force.

Now someone was prising open his lips and saying, 'Drink this, drink this – it will do you good.' He took the liquid into his mouth and swallowed it but it made him gasp – it was so very bitter. Then they wanted to give him more of it but he did not want to take it.

Then he could smell honey. He loved honey and, even in his fractured state, he wanted it, so he opened his mouth for the spoon and felt betrayed when, instead of the promised sweetness, he was fed more of the bitter liquid.

Mr Now-in-Charge said, 'Will that be sufficient?' and Mr Formerly-in-Charge said, 'I think so. He is not a large man and he normally has a good digestion so I have dosed him accordingly. It should begin to work within the next half hour.'

He burned, he sweated, he shivered and all the while the young man held onto his hand and said, 'Don't die, don't die, don't die!'

Then something stirred in his stomach – a wave of nausea unlike anything he had ever felt before and a vile tasting vomit rose in his throat.

He tried to say something but the bilious brew was coming down his nose and he was choking on it when the young man pulled him up into a sitting position and said, 'Here, spit it out into this bowl.'

He spat gratefully. Then more and more of the dreadful stuff came up from his stomach, and just when he felt as if there could be nothing left inside him, he knew he had to empty his bowels and he tried to rise to go to the latrines but his legs would not work and he collapsed back in the bed.

Mr Formerly-in-Charge said, 'Quick! Get that bucket, it's working at the other end now!' and Graecus felt himself being lowered onto a wooden pail whose rough edges felt prickly against the naked skin of his backside but he was deeply grateful for it as the bitter purging medicine continued to do its work.

Just as he had earlier thought he had brought up everything he had inside him, now he thought that he was voiding himself of anything he had ever eaten but, curiously, as he did so, whoever it was who was hammering inside his head became tired and stopped and he felt less shivery and there was less pain in his guts.

Now, after what seemed like forever, he felt he could leave the pail and someone lifted him back into bed and pulled the blankets over him. Someone also washed his face and hands with a wet cloth and gave him a drink of honey water and then, utterly drained and exhausted, he fell asleep.

He dreamed again. He dreamed of being knifed in the stomach by someone whose face he could not see but then, when he looked more closely, he saw it was one of the legates – the one whom he had nicknamed 'Clueless.' This made no sense to him and he was trying to find Acerbus in order to ask for his opinion on the matter when he was woken by something licking his hand.

He raised his head from his pillow and opened his eyes to see Zig sitting at his right hand, his velvet head cocked quizzically on one side.

'Zig,' he said, 'Zig of the Roman Army,' and fell back on his pillow but, in doing so, he saw an array of faces staring curiously at him.

It was most strange – at the foot of his bed were Germanicus, Felix, Acerbus, Magnus, Pneumaticus, Incitatus and Impedimentus – all standing there staring at him.

'Father,' said Germanicus, 'you have come back to us!'

'Come back to you? Where have I been? Have I been away?'

'You have been very ill,' said Acerbus, 'but Magnus gave you the correct medicine to help you.'

'We're all very grateful to him,' said Felix. 'We could not contemplate life without you.'

And all the others, even Impedimentus, nodded their heads and said 'Aye, aye, you are our chief.'

Then Acerbus said 'Brothers, I wish to speak privately with our friend here, will you now leave us? All except Magnus, that is.'

'Must I go?' asked Germanicus.

'Yes, you must go, I need to get to the bottom of what has happened here and I do not wish to make life more difficult for you,' said Acerbus. 'You must trust me to have your father's best interests at heart.'

And Germanicus smiled and said, 'I trust you with both my life and with his,' and went outside.

The others left the tent and Magnus and Acerbus sat on the bottom of Graecus's bed.

'We think you have been poisoned,' said Acerbus, and Magnus nodded before saying,

'Did you eat anything unusual yesterday? Did you eat anything given to you by anyone other than Felix? Did you eat berries from anywhere?'

Graecus shook his head and said, 'No, I did not, but do you mean that I have been poisoned *by someone? Deliberately?*' and Acerbus answered,

'We think it is a possibility. Is there anything you can think of which was different about yesterday? Did anything unusual happen? When did you first feel ill?'

Graecus was still feeling light-headed and weak but he tried to review the events of the previous day, 'Well, I first began to feel strange just before supper, when I was reading the official orders I got – you know, yours will have been the same – the ones which came late in the afternoon, sealed by that useless legate, the one I call Clueless.'

'Well, that is interesting,' said Acerbus. 'My orders came from Suetonius and they were not sealed, but surely, although we do not always welcome our orders, they are not poisonous!'

'They can be,' said Magnus in a low, serious voice. 'They can be if the poisoner puts the poison onto the parchment knowing that the reader will be turning the pages over, handling them, touching them and then, perhaps, wiping his hand across his mouth or licking his fingers and then touching the pages. This is an acknowledged method of poisoning and is very effective with certain substances which are very potent.'

'But how would the poisoner put the poison onto the parchment?' said Acerbus.

'Well, I do not know for certain, but if he were using aconite,

215

for example, which the Greeks called the Queen of Poisons on account of its being very toxic, he would need to transfer only a very small amount and it could be done by carefully rubbing the parchment with a piece of the plant's root or even one of its leaves. He would need to wear gloves, of course, because the poison can even penetrate the skin.'

'Phew,' whistled Acerbus through his teeth, 'that sounds like a real possibility. But why would Clueless, in particular, want you out of the way?'

'It makes no sense to me but Suetonius listened to what I said about the battle strategy and then he warned me that the legates did not take kindly to having their lack of military skills demonstrated by a mere auxiliary.'

'And Clueless *is* ambitious, apparently,' said Acerbus. 'From what I hear of him, he has done well politically in Rome and has the ear of some important people but he does not shine in these circumstances and would not wish to be compared unfavourably with one who did.'

'Ye gods,' said Magnus, 'so he just decided, just like that, that Graecus was expendable?'

'Yes.' said Acerbus. 'You must always remember that other people's lives are of no interest to these young men who will dispose of anyone who threatens their advancement.'

'I had not realised that it is so corrupt,' said Magnus with a sad shrug of his broad shoulders.

'Oh yes, it is corrupt. Much of the government at the heart of the empire is corrupt,' said Acerbus. 'You must recall that Nero poisoned Claudius's son, Britannicus and that his mother, Agrippina, had Claudius poisoned but then, when she had outgrown her usefulness, Nero had her murdered so, you see, the example is set at the very highest levels of Roman society.'

'Then I wish to stay as far away from Rome as I can,' said Magnus.

'It is not always possible to do that,' said Acerbus. 'Sometimes, Rome comes to you.'

'Well, I shall do my best to keep my head down and try to be invisible to these people,' said Magnus.

'It is not that I have tried to attract attention,' said Graecus in a wry voice, 'but, without my even thinking of it, I seem to have made enemies in several directions – from the legates to the Batavians.'

'What a potent mix of mischief makers that is!' said Acerbus. 'Let us hope that in wanting to do you harm, they cancel each other out! But first and foremost, we need to get you back to good health. Could you manage a small bowl of honeyed porridge – just to see if you can keep it down?'

Graecus said that he felt that he could eat a little and Felix brought him a bowl of porridge – with just the right amount of sweetness for Graecus's palate – then he was dispatched for more and then Graecus ate a little bread and bacon and drank a small amount of spiced wine.

'I feel much stronger now,' he said and put his head back on his pillow, thinking that he would just close his eyes for a few moments before getting up and getting on with the day's business. He could hear Acerbus speaking in a low voice to Magnus and this made him feel safe, even though Clueless had just tried to poison him and he smiled as he rested... just for a few moments.

CHAPTER FOURTEEN

When he woke it was dusk. He had slept all day and his mouth was dry. His tongue was furry and his teeth felt coated. There was no one in the tent so he put his feet gingerly on the floor and tried to stand.

Yes, he could stand. Good.

He found a pitcher of water and drank some of it eagerly. Then he used the rest to rinse his mouth after he had cleaned his teeth with one of the pieces of twig cut by Magnus and some of the special dentifrice he made for the men.

Then he rubbed the lower part of his face with olive oil and shaved with a cut-throat razor.

Feeling a little better, he combed his hair with the bone comb which Arminia had given him many years before then put on a clean tunic and sword belt and, wanting fresh air and company, went outside.

There was no one to be seen.

Graecus went back into the tent and went to put on his boots. This was very strange. Where was everyone? How could it be so deserted in a camp of 10,000 men? He must have missed something very important.

What had happened? Where was Germanicus? Where were the rest of his men? Where was Acerbus? Where, for that matter, was Zig?

As he laced his boots, these thoughts raced through his mind and made his fingers clumsy; he felt something was urgent and that he needed to find someone and it seemed to take forever to get the laces done but, eventually, he was able to step out from the tent and listen to the air to find out if there were any clues as to what was the cause of this deserted camp.

He listened very carefully and, after about a minute, he thought he heard a noise coming from where the Batavians were camped.

He cocked his ears in that direction and heard it again – it was a sort of muffled shout followed by laughter.

Graecus did not know what could be the cause of this but he knew that he must find out and his instincts told him that it would be a good idea to get both his dagger and the other sword someone had left in the tent before he went in search of the source of the noise.

Stepping out again from the tent, he heard the noise again and this time it was louder – whatever was happening seemed to be increasing in intensity and Graecus quickened his pace as he approached the Batavian lines.

The evening air was clear and the moon was beginning to rise as Graecus turned the corner from the infantry lines into the *intervallum*.

The moonlight showed the profiles of soldiers watching something in the middle of the circle that the braying onlookers made. There was an atmosphere of excitement but it was a suppressed excitement as if they were a little ashamed to be watching whatever was going on.

Then Graecus saw the two men contained within the circle of onlookers.

Graecus took in the scene and wondered why colleagues would want to fight each other on the eve of an important battle but then one of the combatants swerved his head to avoid a blow from the other's sword and he realised with horror that it was Germanicus, his long blonde hair glinting like silver under the moonlight.

The other combatant was Big Red Hands who was stalking round the crude arena with his long cavalry sword in his hand while Germanicus appeared to be unarmed.

As the Batavians taunted Germanicus, poking fun at his youth and his 'girlish hair,' Graecus quickly scanned the spectators to see if any of his own men were there and had just concluded that the answer was 'no' when he spotted Solitarius's unwelcome face made all the more ugly by its leering expression and his cold-fish eyes glittering in the white light of the moon.

Graecus had no time to consider why or how Germanicus had been inveigled into an uneven battle nor to enquire of Verus's spy what he was doing here, allowing an empty handed colleague to fight off an armed Batavian – no, all he could do was to make his way through the throng of spectators and try to help his son.

As Graecus elbowed his way through the gaggle of tall Batavians, there were more taunts in guttural Latin addressed to the young infantryman – poking fun at his lisp – and while they were thus occupied, Graecus was able to step quietly into the circle making sure that he entered Germanicus's line of sight as he did so.

Germanicus again avoided Big Red Hands' long cavalry sword which, thankfully, was more difficult to manoeuvre when the holder was not mounted and the nimble young man was able to jump out of the Batavian's way with some ease but then, having seen his father and having instantly seen that he had a sword for him, he leapt further away from his attacker and caught by its pommel the sword which Graecus threw to him.

Big Red Hands was distracted by this unforeseen event and let his attention wander sufficiently for Germanicus to tighten his grip on the gladius and position himself on the balls of his feet.

The victim was now the stalker as Germanicus, more accustomed to fighting on the ground than the Batavian, circled him and said, 'It's not so easy is it now, you ugly bully?'

Graecus now saw that Bad Teeth was standing at the front of the crowd opposite him, urging his colleague to 'Give the interfering little bastard what he deserves. My back and my pocket are still suffering because of him and his nosy father.'

But Big Red Hands was tiring now, his sword was heavy, much heavier than Germanicus's gladius and he was having difficulty is keeping ahead of the fit young man but it was only when his helpful colleague again distracted him by shouting, 'Come ON, show that meddling cunt who's boss!' that Germanicus was able to get under his opponent's cumbersome weapon and point his gladius straight at the Batavian's guts.

'Shall we drop our weapons?' Germanicus said dropping his sword. 'Yours seems to be a bit heavy for you, old man, and besides, I'll enjoy beating the daylights out of you.'

Big Red Hands dropped his sword with, what appeared to Graecus, to be a look of relief but then he took a wide swing at

Germanicus with his great clunking fist.

He missed his target by a long way and Germanicus was on the balls of his feet dancing around the heavy man saying, 'Come on big fella, come and get me, come and show me who's boss!'

'I'll show you, pretty boy. Who the fuck d'you think you are with yer airs and graces and yer clever ideas?' said Big Red Hands in his broken Latin, taking another swing at Germanicus and again missing as his quarry effortlessly jumped out of the way.

Now the Batavian was very angry and had a big red face to match his Big Red Hands but anger did not improve his combative skills and he blundered about the ring running after Germanicus who evaded him with all the ease and grace of a dancer.

The spectators were laughing again now. Laughing at Big Red Hands as he lumbered around like a big bear after a gazelle.

Now Germanicus stopped dead and turned to his opponent with a different look on his face, a killer's look, and with his hands ready to strike said, 'Do you really want to fight me old man?' But Big Red Hands could not back down in front of his friends and took another swing at Germanicus, who used the opportunity of the Batavian's opening his guard to come in close and punch him very hard on his nose which, with a sickening splattering noise, spread a long way over his face as the bully fell to his knees in the dust.

Germanicus now hauled him to his feet and taking hold of his tunic to keep him on his feet, used his other fist to batter him again and again about the face whilst bawling at him, 'Now how does it feel? How do you like it? And where is my dog?'

Now Graecus understood at least something of this situation. Now he understood that they had used Zig to lure Germanicus here to this trap.

Germanicus was still pummelling at Big Red Hands's face which was a bloody, pulpy mess and Graecus felt that Germanicus was in danger of killing him. This would have terrible consequences for the boy so he stepped forward, and with all the strength he could muster, tried to stop his son from murdering a fellow Roman soldier.

Eventually, Germanicus ceased using Big Red Hands's head as a punch-bag, and pausing for breath, allowed Graecus to step between him and his prey and let go of Big Red Hands's tunic.

Germanicus's fists had done a great deal of harm and Big Red Hands again sank to his knees while there was silence from all around. Graecus looked at his son and saw cold fury in his eyes – an icy anger which transformed the sunny, golden boy into a killing machine and it unsettled him.

Big Red Hands was trying to stand but Germanicus had not had an answer to his question. 'Now, you bastard, tell me where my dog is, or I'll hit you again!' he hissed as he leant over Big Red Hands his fist at the ready.

Big Red Hands spat out several large clots of blood and then said, 'He's in the grove staked out as wolf bait.'

When he heard this Germanicus leaned over the kneeling man and said, 'If he's dead, then so are you! You had better pray very hard to your gods that my dog is unharmed or you'll pay for it with your life – and THAT is a PROMISE.' Then he went to pick up his sword, but as he bent to do so, Bad Teeth said in a sarcastically silky voice, 'Quite the gladiator, aren't you? And you were quite the lover, weren't you?'

Germanicus again straightened his back but did not pick up his sword. Instead, he launched himself at Bad Teeth and punched him hard in the mouth splitting his lip and connecting forcefully with his front teeth.

As the Batavian reeled from the blow, Germanicus said, 'I'd spit those rotten teeth out if I were you, they weren't doing you any good anyway, you ugly git. Now, if you'll excuse me, I need to take my dog for a walk.'

And, with this, Germanicus picked up his sword and went to join his father, but seeing Solitarius slinking away, he ran after him and, catching him by the elbow, said something to him which Graecus did not hear but now that the Serpent had gone Graecus could speak to his son.

'Thank Jupiter you are safe! What was Solitarius doing here? Where are your brothers?'

'Father, father, please compose yourself. Firstly, *I* am grateful for *your* safety – I really thought last night that you were dying and I could not bear to think of life without you.'

'Thank you, my son, your concern for me and the concern of our other brothers has been very humbling. But tell me, where are they? Where is everyone?'

'They have gone to the religious service for the reading of the auspices.'

'Of course! Why did I not think of that? But how did the Batavians manage to separate you from your brothers?'

'That swine, that serpent, that snake Solitarius knew that I could not find Zig,' spat Germanicus. 'And he told me that one of the Batavians had said he had seen a stray dog so would I care to walk with him to the Batavian lines and he would point the man out to me.'

'He is the spawn of the lowest of the low, that man. I detest him and all he stands for,' said Graecus. 'But where is Zig? We must find him immediately.'

'We have been walking in the direction he indicated father, the grove he mentioned is about a quarter of a mile from here. I just hope that we get there before the wolves do.'

When he said these last words, Germanicus's voice lost its harsh tone and he sounded like the young man who, only hours before, had pleaded with his father to hold onto life.

Graecus's heart was again in his mouth as he knew that the loss of Zig would be as bad for Germanicus as the loss of himself and he could not bear to think of the Batavian method of staking an animal as wolf bait.

At that moment, he wished he did not know that they tied the animal to a stake in the ground, preferably in the forest, and placed at the head of the stake a piece of well-hung raw meat to attract the wolves' attention.

He wished he did not have the thought in his head of brave Zig, who had saved their lives three times, being faced with a pack of slavering hungry wolves and not being able to fight back; brave Zig, of the Roman Army being torn to pieces all on account of the petty jealousy of the brassy Batavians.

Germanicus was stepping out determinedly, his booted feet making little clouds of dust in the moonlit night and Graecus, still weak from his recent poisoning, struggled to keep up with his son.

'It's not far now, father,' said Germanicus as he strode up a slight incline spotted with trees, 'it's just over the brow of this hill.'

But his words were not the only noise to be heard in the still night air – from a short distance away could be heard the sound of wolves. It was unmistakeable. They both knew the sound very well – they had heard it many times in Lower Germania – they had heard it in the winter when the wolves were hungry and they had heard it in the summer when there was a full moon.

It was not winter so Graecus instinctively looked up at the sky and squinted at the moon.

It was full – as full as could be.

Perhaps the wolves were baying at the full moon.

Germanicus sprinted to the top of the incline and looked over.

'Zig!' he shouted, 'Zig, Zig, Zig – hold on! I'm coming to untie you!'

Graecus reached the top of the incline and, looking over, saw Germanicus running down the other side of it towards Zig.

The dog was lying motionless in front of a tree trunk, his little grey body shining in a shaft of moonlight and, in front of him was a wooden stake bearing a dark stain at its top. Graecus could not tell from this distance whether the animal was alive or dead.

He ran as fast as he could down the hill but Germanicus was way ahead of him. A cloud passed over the moon temporarily dimming its bright light and, even though he was nearer now, Graecus still could not tell whether Zig had survived.

But then he heard Germanicus's voice and it told everything he needed to know.

'Thank Jupiter! Thank Jupiter that you are safe!' said Germanicus.

Now Graecus arrived at the clearing and was overjoyed to see Germanicus's smiling face as he bent to ruffle his Zig's ears and stroke his back as the little dog stretched his legs and shook himself to clear the cramp from his body.

'Oh father, I am so relieved. I did not think that I could go into battle tomorrow without Zig. But he is safe and he will be there in his armour – as befits a Roman soldier.'

'Yes, my son, he will be there. And his calm way of dealing with this affront is a credit to him –there are not many dogs who would have just sat here, patiently waiting – knowing that the wolves were about.'

'No, and look here, father, see here where they left the meat as a lure for the wolves?' said Germanicus indicating the dark, bloody stain at the top of the stake. 'Clever Zig managed to eat it himself so that they did not get the scent of it!'

'He is truly a marvel,' said Graecus clapping Germanicus on the back as his son finished checking Zig for injuries before they all set off back to the camp.

* * *

When Graecus, Germanicus and Zig reached their tent, their colleagues had returned from the ceremony and were sitting on their beds looking miserable.

'Where have you *been*?' they all shouted when they saw their officer and his companions.

'We thought we'd lost our chief last night when you were so ill and then we thought we'd lost the three of you tonight. In the names of all the gods, will you all stay in good health and within my sight for a while so that my nerves can recover?' said Felix sounding as much like a mother and a scolding wife as a veteran soldier is able.

'I will tell you everything you want to know when you have given me my supper,' said Graecus, 'I'm famished.'

'Well, that's very encouraging' said Felix and bustled out of the tent returning a few minutes later with steaming bowls of bean and bacon soup and bread for Graecus and Germanicus and a meaty bone for Zig.

Once they had had their soup and while Zig was enjoying his bone, Graecus and Germanicus told their brothers of the trap set by Big Red Hands and Bad Teeth and there was much tutting and sharp intakes of breath as they spoke of the part played by Solitarius in the deceit but then, in his inimitable fashion, Pneumaticus made them all laugh by saying that, now Germanicus had relieved Bad Teeth of his dental problems, his new nickname should be 'No Teeth' and this was all the funnier coming from Pneumaticus whose new smile was dazzling.

Graecus joined in the laughter and felt relieved that the battle they had come so far to fight would be joined the following day – the waiting had been intolerable in this dreadful land aggravated by all the self-serving intrigues and shenanigans of the camp – whatever happened on the morrow would, at least, be something with which they were familiar and for which they were trained.

Graecus's head was filled with these thoughts and he suddenly felt that the tent was hot and stuffy and he wanted to go for a walk. He had slept most of the day and needed some fresh air.

He stood up and said to Germanicus who was running his fingers through his hair in a thoughtful way that he was going for a stroll to clear his head.

Graecus left the tent and walked steadily down the auxiliary lines, nodding to the various men he saw on the way.

The moon was high in the night sky and Graecus thought of the line from Caesar's Gallic Wars, '*Eadem nocte, accidit ut esset luna plena*', as he looked at the silhouettes of the trees along the horizon and the rows and rows of tents making up this enormous camp.

The Britons were not far away and their camp must be huge. They all knew that these tribesmen had travelled with their wives, children and animals and Graecus's mind boggled at the thought of the amount of food needed by Boudicca's army and retinue.

He was trying to work it all out in his mind as he walked along – if there were, say, 100,000 men and, say, 60,000 women and, say, 80,000 children then that would be 240,000 human mouths to feed each day and there would need to be foraging for their horses and their pack animals. They would also need to carry heavy equipment for mending their weapons, some kind of shelter for bad weather, which he thought ruefully, could be guaranteed in this inhospitable land.

Graecus walked and walked, enjoying these calculations in his head, thinking how, if he were Boudicca, he would have organised it all and thinking that she must be quite a clever woman to have managed to unite the previously disparate and warring tribes in this bloody insurrection.

But if she were so clever, why had she not seen that Suetonius's choice of battleground would work to her disadvantage? Perhaps she had been urged to accept Suetonius's challenge by the other leaders. Or had she just been grateful that battle would at last be joined?

Graecus walked and walked as his mind ran on with all these thoughts and then it occurred to him that he felt cold. He had come out without his cloak and, although it was a summer's night, it was almost cloudless and there was bite to the clear air.

Graecus stopped walking, shivered and decided to retrace his steps.

It was then that he noticed where he was.

He was nowhere. He was in the middle of nowhere.

He had been walking and thinking about things with such concentration, without paying any attention to where he was going, that he had no idea where he was, nor in which direction his camp lay.

Graecus stood and scratched his head and thought that it was quite a feat to lose a camp of 10,000 men and assorted animals. How long had he been walking?

He looked at the moon's position and decided that he had probably been walking steadily for an hour but he had not been walking particularly quickly so he could have covered about three miles.

Could he remember anything about the walk? From which direction had he come to the spot on which he now stood?

He thought he had come via the stand of trees on a hillock over to his left and set off in that direction.

He reached the trees and then, thinking that he recognised the valley below, he descended into it and again considered his position.

But this time he had no idea of how he had come to the place. He stood still for some time, turning the situation over in his mind and was hoping that inspiration would strike when he heard the most unlikely sound.

No, it couldn't be. No, he had not heard that.

But there it was again – the sound of a baby crying.

What in Jupiter's name could be the explanation for that?

Well, obviously, if he could hear a baby crying, then there had to be a baby in the vicinity. That much was clear, but what about its mother? Was she there or had it been abandoned? Was she present but in some kind of danger?

Graecus's thoughts now went back to the disgraceful behaviour of Big Red Hands and Bad Teeth (no, now it was 'No Teeth'), with the young British girl and he did not need to think about it too long before he decided that it would be best to see if he could find the baby as it was all too possible that the Batavians had kidnapped a local woman for sport.

The sound seemed to be coming from a large boulder about a hundred feet to his right.

Cautiously drawing his sword, therefore, he tiptoed towards the source of the sound.

The boulder was in front of him, casting shadows in the moonlight, but there was no sign of a baby, nor of its mother.

Graecus let out a sigh of frustration and was about to turn back the way he had come when he heard another sound.

It was a gurgling noise. Followed by a loud sucking sound.

Graecus was again puzzled but he must now go round the boulder, into the moonlight, to investigate.

Cautiously again, he edged his way round the boulder and peered ahead.

The first thing which caught his eye was a naked breast, its extreme whiteness highlighted by the moon.

Graecus was so startled by this that he did not at first see the baby attached to its mother's teat.

But then the surprisingly loud sucking noise began again and there was no doubt that the woman, whose pale blond hair was also glinting in the moonlight, was feeding her baby.

Her hair was long and hung in braids down the back of her light blue cloak.

Light blue; a striking colour. Light blue, the colour of the Iceni.

Ye gods he had stumbled upon an Iceni woman. Where were the rest of her tribe?

It was clear from the peaceful scene of the woman nursing her child that she was not in danger and, as there were no Batavians in sight, Graecus decided that he would withdraw discreetly from the situation by stepping backwards and slowly, silently making his way round the boulder.

Unfortunately, in taking the first step backwards he trod on a twig which snapped under his weight and the noise sounded like the crack of lightning in the still night air.

In a split second and with an economy of effort and agility he could only admire, the woman was on her feet, one hand supporting the baby still at her breast but the other hand holding a dagger close to Graecus's throat.

Now that they were very close to one another, Graecus could see in the light of the full moon that she was tall and her eyes matched her cloak and that her features were dainty and even. He imagined that he must have a surprised expression on his face for the woman took a small step back from him in order to take a better look at the man whose throat she could cut at any moment.

Graecus could see that the woman was trying to decide who he could be; he was not wearing his full uniform and he did not, at that moment, necessarily look like a Roman soldier.

She stared at him for some moments and then said something in a language Graecus did not understand but, whatever it was she said, it sounded like a question.

Graecus needed to make a decision very swiftly – should he pretend to be dumb or that he was simple-minded or should he answer her in Latin?

She took a step nearer now, her eyes glinting in the moon-light, the dagger poised to regain its position at Graecus's throat.

He decided that he must say something.

Trying to make his voice comforting, he said, 'My lady, for-give my intrusion. I wish neither you nor your baby any harm. I am lost. I wandered too far from my companions.'

The woman thought for a second and then said, in correct but slightly quaint Latin and with a soft foreign accent, 'You say that you wish me no harm tonight but surely you and your compan-ions will wish me and all my kind great harm tomorrow.'

This was a tricky question for Graecus and he did not know how to answer her as, now that he had made the woman's acquaintance, and he had as good an eye for a lovely woman as any man, he wished her no harm at any time but she misinter-preted his silence and said, 'Ah, you are surprised that I know your language. You have been told that we are all savages and that we sacrifice our young to our gods.'

Graecus now found his tongue and said, 'My lady, I am not surprised that you, a gentlewoman, are able to speak my lan-guage and it is quite clear that you do not eat your young. It is clear that you care for them as tenderly as any mother any-where.'

'But you have been told that we are barbarians.'

'It would be dishonest of me to deny that.'

'Are you an honest man?'

'I try to be.'

'Then why do you serve Rome – the great deceiver.'

This was another delicate question as, if he gave a reason why he served Rome, then it would be implied that he had accepted that Rome was deceitful which would then make him either a fool or a man of no principle, but if he were to enquire in what way was Rome the great deceiver, then he would look uninformed or, at the least, gullible.

The woman again misinterpreted Graecus's silence and said, 'You cannot deny that you are a Roman.'

'I must deny it, my lady, I am a man of no known origins – I knew neither my mother nor my father and I do not know where I was born. All I know is that the Roman army took me in and brought me up and that is why I serve Rome. I am a humble auxiliary, not a legionary, not a Roman citizen.'

Graecus had surprised himself with this long explanation to a woman he had only just met but she *was* holding a dagger to his throat and it seemed to him that she deserved the full story.

The baby began to cry again and the woman gazed lovingly at it as she reattached it to her breast.

Graecus could, of course, have run her through her while she was preoccupied in this way and when she again gave him her attention she said, 'You could have killed me just now. Why did you not?'

'Because I said that I wish you no harm and I am a truthful man.'

'I will accept that you are truthful but those you serve are not.'

Graecus realised that he would need to make his lack of knowledge plain and said, 'My lady, it is often the case that circumstances force our rulers to be less honest in their statesmanship than they would wish, but tell me, please, what particular piece of dishonesty is it of which you complain?'

'The dishonesty that has been visited upon my people. The dishonesty that reduced a proud independent people into Rome's slaves.'

'But how did that happen, my lady, surely your king agreed to Rome's terms?'

'Yes, he did, he agreed to pay taxes, he agreed to send corn and the bravest of our young men to fight Rome's wars but he did not agree to the rest.'

'The rest?'

'The taking of our weapons, the theft of our lands and the demand for repayment of the money we were given.'

Graecus did not feel that it would be prudent to explain to the woman at this point the difference between a gift and a loan, so he said, 'But did you not have years of peace as a result?'

It was as if he had struck her.

She spat on the ground. 'Peace? Is that what you call it when you oppress people – when you make them do things your way? When you destroy their way of life, crush their spirit and impose your way upon them? Is that what you call peace?'

The woman's anger had disturbed the baby and it started to cry again, its sobs shattering the clear air.

The woman held it nearer to her face and made soothing noises to it before putting it back to her breast.

'But many of the tribes in this land have benefited from Rome. They have enjoyed the wine, the spices, the silks and the trade that we bring,' said Graecus.

'I do not doubt it,' said the woman. 'But that is of no consequence to the poor peasants whose sons have been forfeit to Rome and whose lands bear the burden of her taxes.'

'But have they not benefited from the civilization brought by Rome?' said Graecus.

This time he thought the woman really would cut his throat.

'Civilization?' she said witheringly. 'You call it civilized to flog a queen and rape her virgin daughters? We may be barbarians in your eyes but we would not have done that.'

'Catus Decianus should never have allowed that to happen,' said Graecus. 'But is there no benefit to your people from its contact with Rome? Is there nothing good about Rome?' said Graecus, despairing of his ability to fight Rome's corner as he had silently agreed with most of what the woman had said.

'There could be benefit. There could be benefits for both sides. We could send our horses and our hunting dogs, we could send our tin and our silver, our corn and timber – all of which Rome wants and needs and we would welcome the wine and the fine things in return but what I do not understand is Rome's desire to subjugate every man, woman and child to its will. Why must Rome rule those with whom it trades? Why does Rome steal people's freedom? Why can Rome not allow them to rule themselves?'

'I am but a soldier, my lady, I am not an emperor. I do not know the answer to your questions but I do know that they are good questions and I am honoured to have spent time with you. I hope we do not meet tomorrow and I hope that, whatever happens, you and your child will be safe.'

'Prettily spoken, soldier, but that is not the Roman way.'

'As I said, I am not a Roman.'

'Why are you so far from your camp?'

'I was lost in my thoughts as I went for a walk and then I was just… lost,' said Graecus.

'You will find your colleagues in that direction,' said the woman, pointing to the right with the hand still holding her dagger. 'And I too wish that we shall not meet tomorrow – I would not like to kill you – it is easier to kill strangers – those whose faces are not known to you.'

'I agree, my lady. Thank you for your directions. Farewell.'

'Farewell, soldier.'

Graecus turned on his heel and walked briskly in the direction indicated by the woman.

It took him nearly an hour to regain his camp and while he walked he pondered what the woman had said. Why did Rome find it necessary to oppress most of the known world? Why could it not just trade with people and leave them to govern themselves? He was not sure but he felt that it must be connected with Rome's opulent extravagance and the need to keep her citizens well supplied with corn, slaves and wild animals for the circus.

But he could not convince himself that this was a good reason.

Eventually he reached the camp gate and gave the password to the sentries.

He felt tired now – the discussion with the woman had given him too much to question and he needed his bed.

He reached his tent and stepped quietly inside.

They were all waiting for him and there was a sigh of relief when they saw him.

But when he saw Germanicus, he gasped in surprise.

'What have you done to your hair?' he said taking in the new shape of Germanicus's head as revealed from under his formerly flowing locks. Now his hair was cropped and the difference was very marked. Before he had looked like a romantic young man. Now he looked like a soldier.

'Felix cut it for me,' said Germanicus. 'I did not want the Batavians mocking me any more. I have had enough of their stupid comments about my hair.'

'That was your own decision my son and whilst I regret that you chose to cut your hair for that reason, I do see that you are now the image of a fighting man.'

'Thank you, father. I am sure that we all hope that we will acquit ourselves honourably tomorrow,' said Germanicus.

'I have no doubt about it,' said Graecus. 'But tell me, what were the auspices? What did the priests say?'

'They said they were very good. Excellent, in fact but there was some funny thing with one of the entrails – a dark blot, I think someone said, and they did not know how to interpret it,' said Felix.

'Well, whatever it was, I do not think that it will prevent Suetonius from having his battle tomorrow,' said Graecus.

Then they extinguished the lamps and got into their beds.

From his pillow, Graecus could see the top of Germanicus's head. It was astonishing how different he looked – it was still clear that his hair was blond and it still shone but the boy – his boy – had gone and now his son was a man.

CHAPTER FIFTEEN

It was dry the next day and Felix was up at first light – making a fire and getting the porridge and bread ready for the men and all over the camp similar fires were being lit in braziers to make the breakfast for these thousands of soldiers; everyone knew it was vital to eat well now. After all, who could say when the next meal would be?

Graecus woke to the smell of warming bread and quickly washed, shaved and put on his tunic while the others in his con-tubernium were sitting up, rubbing their eyes and scratching themselves around their middles in the way men do first thing in the morning.

All was calm. Everything was orderly. No one would see from their behaviour that this would be the last day on earth for some of these men and that their death would come painfully and possibly slowly. The only hint of the importance of this day was that every-one in the camp was acting strictly in accordance with a ritual.

Impedimentus was marching up and down Graecus's century's lines checking everyone's equipment while Magnus carefully ticked off his emergency medical supplies, Germanicus polished their standard and Pneumaticus put in his new teeth while Incitatus made sure that the century's records were in a safe place and Zig watched them all in a proprietorial manner.

Graecus walked up and down the lines, speaking to his men, wishing them good luck. He knew that he could rely on them and he spoke from his heart when he wished them safety and glory but when he came to Solitarius his words, even to his own ears, sounded hollow – as did the horn-blower's reply.

Then they all began to dress themselves in their armour and help one another with those items which were fiddly –like the lacings on the cuffs and Graecus needed help with the stiff buck-les on his greaves – the pads which protected his shins.

It was not warm so far and Graecus silently gave thanks for this as the padding they wore under their armour was thick and, in the heat of a summer's day, would be stifling.

Then came the difficult business of putting on the scale armour shirts. These were heavy and it was best if another man put it over your head for you.

As the Centurion, Graecus did not wear the scale shirt – he had a metal cuirass which fitted over his chest and his back and buckled at the sides but he did not need to concern himself with harnessing Perdix as today he would be on foot – there was no place for Perdix in this battle.

Then they buckled on their belts and sheathed their gladiuses. Then they put on their helmets with the heavy cheek-pieces and the neck guards and Graecus's helmet had a magnificent red plume marking him out as an officer.

Germanicus had been busy putting on Zig's armour and was the last man in their tent to put on his helmet but it sat oddly on his head and Graecus went to adjust it for him.

He fiddled with the chin strap and wriggled the helmet about on his son's head trying to seat it better over Germanicus's cranium but there was still too much movement of the helmet over his head. It seemed too big but that was impossible.

'It is very odd, my son, but all of a sudden, this helmet of yours seems too big!' he said, struggling again with the chinstrap.

'Well, he has had his hair cut, hasn't he?' said Felix, neatly making the very obvious point which Graecus had missed.

'By Jupiter, you are right!' he said. 'And I think that this setting of the strap is as good as we can manage until your hair grows back,' he added, nodding to Germanicus, who put the wolfskin, the sign of his rank as the standard bearer, over his helmet and then they were all ready to go.

They left their tent and began to muster with their century which joined with Acerbus and his men and together the two centuries went to the auxiliaries' mustering point.

Graecus and Acerbus were next to each other and, although they were standing to attention, Graecus managed to say to his colleague, 'May the good wishes of all the gods be with you today my friend.'

'And with you. May we be celebrating a great victory tonight, drinking to our gallant brothers and looking forward to honours for our centuries.'

Norbanus appeared.

'Men, I will be brief. We all know that this battle is not merely against Boudicca and her allies, it is THE battle for this island. If we fail today then Nero can kiss goodbye to Britannia and we shall all be lucky to escape with our lives. You have had the battle plan, you have practised the battle positions, you know the notes of the horns and what they mean. Now all you need to do is to follow your orders. TO THE LETTER. FOLLOW YOUR ORDERS TO THE LETTER. And don't let me down.'

The mustered men gave Norbanus a loud cheer and he smiled at them as if they were his children and they had just pleased him enormously.

Norbanus gave the order to move off and the auxiliaries set out behind the columns of the legionaries with Graecus and Acerbus leading their men in twos behind them.

The noise of the Roman columns stirred Graecus's blood.

There was the sound of all those feet pounding the ground and the sound of their metal armour chinking and the sound of leather fastenings creaking against the distant sound of the cavalry's hooves, the rumbling of carts and sometimes the plaintive call of a horn telling them to change direction.

Then someone began to sing, and many voices joined the refrain. This time Graecus did not try to stop his son.

'Tramp, tramp, tramp,
Forward we go,
Tramp, tramp, tramp,
On to meet our foe,
Who is it we defend?
What is it we're for?
We fight for ROME,
AND THE EMPEROR!'

By the time that thousands of men were singing this song in unison the noise was deafening and Graecus hoped that the Britons could hear them approaching but deep down inside himself he hoped that the lovely Iceni woman would not be among them.

They marched for about an hour and then they saw the valley which was to be their home for the day.

It had a narrow opening and lightly wooded sides, opening slightly towards the bottom and ending in a steep, more densely wooded escarpment.

They marched in their ranks into the valley and down to the bottom where the legates positioned everyone in accordance with the battle plan – cavalry on the extreme outer wings left and right, auxiliary light infantry next to the cavalry and the legionary infantry – by far the largest in numbers, in the middle.

Graecus and his men and Acerbus and his men were on the left wing of this formation and, true to his word, Suetonius had put them in the front with a mounted legate at the back of their ranks.

Suetonius appeared, splendid in his purple cloak and helmet with large matching plume dancing in the breeze, as he moved about on his big grey horse.

Graecus felt strangely comforted by his presence.

They were all in position. Their general was there.

The horns sounded the note that told them that Suetonius was going to address them. He rode round to the front of his forces and positioned himself in the middle of the legionaries, facing them and those flanking them. Sitting perfectly still on his horse, he spoke to them.

Although he was some way off, Graecus could hear exactly what he said,

'Gentlemen, it is early in the day. We are here, mustered, ready for battle. You, soldiers of the Roman Army, the greatest army the world has ever known, are all poised to play your part in what will be a great victory. You are armed to the teeth, you are disciplined, you know exactly what your role is today. Now, gentlemen, I ask you – where is the enemy? You have marched here in plenty of time to meet your enemies but (here Suetonius paused to make a wide gesture with his left arm) I ask you – where are they? Where is Boudicca's rabble? Where are her screaming blue tribesmen? Well, I can only conclude that they have taken fright or they are still… in bed!'

The men roared with laughter at this and Suetonius waited until their laughter had abated before continuing, 'So, soldiers of the Roman army, while we wait, if you feel peckish, please eat a hunk of bread or bacon, if you want to take a leak, please feel free, but if you feel in any way cowardly, if you feel that you have not the stomach for our work this day, remember that you answer to ME. Stand easy.'

Graecus could hardly believe it, here they were on the day of the battle, the day on which Boudicca had agreed to meet them, and as she was nowhere in sight – they must just wait for her.

So they stood in the early morning air, drawn up in their ranks, their standards glinting in the pale sun and the plumes in the officers' helmets bending with the breeze. They stood and Suetonius and the legates and the cavalry sat on their horses. Occasionally, a horse whinnied, Zig swatted flies with his tail, or someone would leave the ranks to relieve himself, but for the most part, they just stood motionlessly and in silence.

Graecus could feel the muscles in his legs beginning to go into cramps and he allowed himself to shake them independently, trying to get some feeling back into his calves. He was shaking his left leg vigorously, and not paying attention, when he felt a frisson run through the men around to him.

He stopped shaking his leg and looked ahead just as the order to stand to attention came.

There were chariots coming towards them - scores of them.

They were light wickerwork chariots with ironbound wheels and in front of each were two of the small but sturdy British ponies.

Each chariot bore two men, one to drive and the other to fight.

The warriors were amazing; they were more or less naked – some wore a loincloth, most did not – but they were all, to a man, covered in the blue dye which they called 'woad' and had their hair in braids interwoven with feathers. They were armed with spears

239

and swords and carried round shields but these were quite small and would not offer much protection against the Romans' weapons.

The British warriors came streaming into the narrow valley, howling and shouting as they did so, their voices rising above the shrill cries of their war trumpets.

On and on they came, speeding into the valley.

And then they stopped.

Dead.

As if someone had drawn a line in the ground across the valley and they had been told not to cross it.

There were the ranks of chariots, complete with their naked blue warriors screaming and shaking their weapons at the Romans who just stood and waited as they had been ordered so to do by their General who, very visible at the front of the Roman lines atop his horse in his gorgeous purple cloak, was also silently waiting.

The valley was filling up behind the British chariots with men, and some women, on foot. They also were armed, but as far as Graecus could see not very well armed, and it was clear to him that Boudicca had placed her warrior class at the front of her army and the peasants carrying their farm implements as weapons behind them.

And now, behind the peasants, the heavy carts carrying the wives and children, some of them babes in arms, arrived and came to a halt in the mouth of the valley. Graecus strained his eyes to see if he could spot the woman he had met the night before, but although he could see flashes of Iceni sky blue, any one of which might have been her, it was too far away to make out anyone's face – it was just a blur of people, animals and vehicles.

It seemed as if the Britons had had an order to make as much noise as possible and the shape of the landscape had the effect of concentrating the cacophony so that their shouts and screams and taunts and insults came from all directions, bouncing from the walls of the valley into the Romans' ears.

Graecus had seen this kind of display before – the tribes in Germany used a similar technique. It was an attempt to scare the

Romans into surrender or, at the least, undermine their confidence and it often worked when they faced less disciplined, less experienced enemies. Indeed, Graecus could feel the panic rising in a young soldier from his century who was standing limply on the edge of their lines and he was moved to say to him in a stage whisper, 'Steady lad, it's all just for show! They can make as much noise as they like – they're still no match for the Roman Army.'

'Sorry sir,' said the young man, standing up straight now with a ramrod back.

Suddenly the crowds of British chariots parted, and through the avenue thus created came an arresting sight.

It was Boudicca in her gilded chariot pulled by two perfectly matched chestnut ponies who must have been chosen for their colour for their coats had been brushed till they shone in the morning sun just like her hair.

She was magnificent. Standing erect, alone in her chariot, holding the reins herself and in total control, her tawny hair flowing behind her.

She was at the end of the 'avenue' now, and crossing into the no man's land between her troops and those of her enemy, she brought her ponies to a halt with a deft pull on the reins.

She was facing the Roman ranks as if to let them have a very good look at her.

On closer inspection, she was even more striking.

Tall, half a head taller than Graecus, with milk white skin and green/gold eyes she stared at the Roman ranks with an imperious gaze. She wore a long dress over which was a plaid cloak pinned at her shoulder with a large brooch but around her neck glittered a heavy golden torc, a sign of her royal blood.

Boudicca looked at the Romans, moving her eyes slowly along their ranks as if trying to fix each man with her gaze. Then she turned her back on them and, having unpinned her cloak, she unfastened one shoulder of her dress and let it down so that a portion of her bare back was on display.

The skin of her back was pure white except for the livid marks of the Roman lash which had scarred her for life.

She let them have a long look at the damage they had done to her person and then slowly replaced her dress and pinned up her cloak.

Now she pulled on her ponies' reins and neatly turning her chariot round so that she was facing her own people with her back to the Romans she drove towards her army and stopped.

She began to speak.

She had a deep voice for a woman. Deep and resonant, and even though Graecus could not understand what she said, he knew from her phrasing and her cadences that she was a powerful speaker and that her words would stir her people.

She began in a matter of fact manner, using Julius Caesar's name several times, then she changed the rhythm to include repetitious phrases, probably about the losses of freedom and self-determination the Britons had endured under their oppressors, and then she began to raise her voice and use her hands and arms to emphasise her words ending her oration with a bloodcurdling shout and a chopping motion with her sword arm which, Graecus assumed, demonstrated how she wished her troops to deal with the Romans.

Then she crossed her arms across her chest in a humble gesture and lowered her head as if to say that she was the servant of her people as well as their queen, and they gave her a long, loud rousing cheer, rattling their swords in the air and those who had none saluting her with their pikes and axes.

Next, as if they were playing a game according to known rules, she turned her chariot again to face the Romans and nodded at Suetonius who bowed courteously to her from his saddle.

Suetonius too seemed to know the rules of this game and, turning his horse round so he could face his troops, he began to address them in his penetrating, patrician voice.

'Pay no heed to the squeals of these Britons who, being badly armed and ill-disciplined, are more like women than warriors. When they see our courage and resolve – the courage and resolve of those who have beaten them many times before – they will turn and run. When there are many legions fighting in a battle, the chances of winning honours are few, but when, as today, there is only a small number fighting a numerous enemy – then just think of the honours which could be yours! Keep strictly to your ranks, throw your javelins and strike out with your shield bosses and your gladiuses then move on. Do not be distracted by booty. Follow me and follow my orders and the day will be ours.'

Boudicca's chariot now disappeared back down the 'avenue' which closed behind her and the first row of British chariots moved forward.

Graecus felt his men tensing their muscles ready for action but there was no sign of any orders being given and he murmured under his breath, 'Wait for it, wait for it.'

But at this stage, the Britons were more intent on giving an acrobatic display than charging at their enemies. It seemed bizarre to Graecus and, he assumed, to anyone else who had not fought them before, but seven or eight of the chariots were chasing about the empty arena between the two armies and were circling one another then turning very sharply and intersecting each other while the warriors left the relative safety of the wicker-bound platform and nimbly tiptoed along the traces brandishing their swords and spears, shouting and making faces at the Romans.

Then with breathtaking skill, they left the arena and drove some way up the sides of the valley, below the tree line, and deftly turned their chariots round and drove down the hill, back into the valley.

Graecus did not know whether to applaud or to laugh. It was a very clever, skilful display and it must have worked for them in the past, but to his eyes, and probably those of every Roman soldier there that day, this little circus, this little chariot display, had made the Britons look naïve and inexperienced in organised warfare. He could feel confidence growing in the Roman ranks.

The display chariots went back to their places in the front line of Boudicca's army and then began another bout of shouting, jeering, booing, blowing of horns, and rattling of weapons while the Romans just kept silently to their ranks, eyes forward.

Perhaps they expected some response from the Romans, some gesturing and posturing because it seemed to unsettle them that there was no response to their antics and they fizzled out with the men in the chariots ceasing first and then the men behind them and so on until even the peasants at the back had fallen silent.

Graecus could see Boudicca. She had drawn her chariot up to a vantage point on the side of the valley which was to his left and she was standing there looking down at her troops. She had been joined in her chariot by two other women with long tawny hair just like hers and Graecus assumed these younger women were her daughters – the princesses who had been defiled on Catus Decianus's orders – whose presence was another potent reminder to the Britons of what they were fighting for.

Now that there was silence and all eyes were on her, Boudicca picked up her spear, and thrusting it vigorously forward, gave the order for her men to begin the battle.

The chariots with their naked blue warriors began to advance, picking up speed and then, for Graecus, everything went into slow motion for a few seconds as his eyes, ears and nose became mesmerised by the scene unfolding before him.

The British chariots thundered across the open space in the valley, their warriors whooping their war cries while the mid-morning sun glinted off their weapons and he could smell the feral scent of their ponies' sweat but he knew that soon, very soon, all of this would change and there would be blood and mayhem and he willed time to stand still for just a little longer as he contemplated this scene full of drama, tension, colour and… a terrible beauty.

The chariots were almost upon them when the Roman horns sounded the order for the first javelins to be loosed and hundreds of deadly weapons whickered through the air before finding their mark in flesh and bone and then the valley was filled with anguished human cries and the screams of injured ponies.

Down went many of the chariots but some kept coming, some were riderless, yet others carried their armed warriors – brandishing their spears – and then the horn sounded the order for second javelins and the men in the Roman front line threw the javelins they had been handed by the men behind them and again the air went dark with flying death and again the javelins found their mark piercing arms, legs, bellies and necks and reducing the ranks of charioteers to a handful who kept on coming.

The Romans now faced a line of dead and injured men and horses littering the space between them and the Britons but there were still gaps in the barrier, places where the Britons could advance and still they came and still they were picked off while inflicting minimal harm on the Roman forces.

The few warriors who had been protected from the Roman *pila* by their shields soon had to discard them because behind the sharp spear tip of the Roman javelin was a collar of soft metal specially designed to dig itself into an opponent's shield and render it useless.

And so these brave men, naked except for their swords and their woad came towards the Romans, sometimes clambering over the fallen to reach their enemies, making themselves easy targets for the javelins thrown by the men who had been to the rear of the ranks but had, in their long practised way, changed places with their colleagues at the front, some of whom had been wounded by British spears.

There were no more chariots now and there was a lull in the battle – an unnatural cessation of activity.

Graecus looked to his left and saw Suetonius, still sitting quietly on his horse. Graecus knew he was waiting for the right moment to give the order to move forward.

In the far distance was Boudicca's chariot carrying its trio of royal women looking onto the mangled mess of injured men and corpses interspersed with broken bits of wickerwork and downed ponies which had been their crack troops.

Some of the maimed Britons were screaming. One man stood up and tottered a few steps pulling out the javelin embedded in his belly but spilling his guts with it and his cries filled the valley with pain until a Roman legionary took pity on him, and with a well-aimed throw, dispatched him with a *pilum* between the shoulder-blades.

But there were still many thousands of Britons crowding the valley and now, with another forward thrust of her spear, Boudicca gave them the order to advance.

This was that part of the battle which would most involve Graecus's men and he made a short prayer to Gideon's God to keep them all safe (with the possible exception of Solitarius).

The Britons were making their way across no man's land, negotiating the ground littered with the cream of their fighters, but there were thousands of them and the sight of them with their wild hair, woad striped faces and their blood-curdling cries was impressive and a reminder that this battle had a long way to go.

The Britons were less than a hundred yards away when Suetonius gave the order and the next volley of javelins whistled through the gap between them and the Romans and fell onto their massed ranks bringing many of them down and making the ground beneath the survivors less easy to negotiate.

But still they kept coming, even after another javelin volley.

Now, the Britons who had managed to survive the javelins and the obstacle course were too near for another volley and the Roman horns sounded the order to close ranks.

With the sound of clanking metal and creaking leather, the two front lines of legionaries and auxiliaries all moved as one man to obey this order and it was as if each one was a moving part of a larger organism, shoulder to shoulder and hip to hip with the man next to him, their long shields in front of them, protecting them far better than the Britons' inferior equipment.

The horns sounded again – with the order to advance, and after all those weeks of waiting, the moment Graecus had both desired and dreaded had come.

There was another deafening sound – the thud of thousands of pairs of feet stepping together and the metallic ring of thousands of deadly gladiuses being unsheathed as the Roman killing machine moved forward.

Graecus's senses were still heightened and he could smell the scent of ale on the breath of the Britons coming towards him and he could feel urgency in their approach.

There was a solid wall of the Britons now, jostling with one another to keep their ground as their countrymen crowded behind them eager for their chance of killing a Roman.

Thirty feet, twenty feet, ten feet, the Romans moved forward, poised in every sinew to demonstrate the superiority of a disciplined army against a rabble, no matter how numerous and how highly motivated they might be.

Then there was no distance between them and the blood rang in Graecus's ears as a surge of energy coursed through him and he confronted the first of the men he must kill that day if he were to survive and the Romans were to win this battle.

The man was not very tall and was unremarkable – clothed and not painted blue.

But he came at Graecus with a savagery which would have done credit to a lioness protecting her cubs.

And he was strong.

He thrust a long heavy sword at Graecus and nearly connected with his shin but Graecus managed to jump sideways while aiming a blow at the man's arm.

These were preliminary moves while each man gauged the other's skill and decided how much of his precious energy he would need to use on trying to kill or maim the other.

When he had first looked at the man, Graecus had thought that it would be easy to dispatch him and had not put all his strength and skill into the fight, but now that he had witnessed the man's deadly resolve, Graecus knew that he would need to put his back into it.

Graecus came back at the man with a straight thrust to his unprotected torso but the man sidestepped and went for Graecus again with his sword which had a longer reach than Graecus's gladius but was less easy to manoeuvre by being heavy. Graecus also noticed that the man's sword was blunt at the end – it was a slicing weapon rather than a sticking weapon and this made a difference to the way they would fight.

They were looking at one another now, weighing up the situation and then the man went for a blow at Graecus's neck, thinking he could take off his head but Graecus was too quick for him and stuck him in the belly while he had his hands raised to strike.

The man fell forward onto Graecus's sword which thrust deep into his gizzards with a soft wet squelching sensation and then he had to withdraw it, glistening with the man's giblets and gastric juices, the acrid smell of which always turned Graecus's stomach, before he could go on to the next man who wanted to kill him.

Graecus did not know how many Britons there were but he reckoned that he and every other Roman fighting on these front lines would need to kill at least ten of Boudicca's men in order to swing the battle in their favour. Given the Romans' superior weapons, armour and training, this *was possible,* but the problem from their point of view was that each Briton needed to kill only one Roman in order to make his contribution to Boudicca's victory.

This meant that, even with the help of the reserve troops from the anterior lines, the Romans would get tired long before the Britons and then they would become careless and make mistakes and every Roman corpse would be a potent encouragement to the Britons to fight on.

From where he was standing, Graecus could see many British dead but about ten Roman corpses. If there were a similar number of Roman dead on all the other areas of the battlefield, the Britons were making headway, and by attrition, they might win the day.

All around Graecus, the men of his century were engaged in the ritual dance of death – smash the face of the enemy with your shield and then stick your gladius in his guts and pull it out then let him fall to the ground.

Bish, smash, thrust, crash. Bish, smash, thrust, crash.

Now the numbers of the fallen were becoming so great that the wall of death was in the Romans' way and they had to give ground in order to have ground on which to stand but this was also a problem for the Britons who, the cavalry still being in place on the wings of the Roman formation, had to climb over the dead in order to reach the enemy.

It was about mid-day, the sun was high in the sky and it was getting hot.

Graecus could feel sweat running down his spine under the padded jerkin and his heavy cuirass. It was undoubtedly better to have proper protective clothing but, as the sweat ran down his brow and stung his eyes, Graecus envied the Britons their lack of heavy clothing.

For Graecus and his men the hand to hand fighting had been going for about a couple of hours now, interspersed with intervals when the men behind relieved them at the front line, and the ground was wet and slippery with blood and slime making it all the more difficult for the Romans to keep ahead of the Britons who were fresher and whose bare feet gripped the ground better.

Graecus felt that it was more than possible that they could lose and was wearily pulling his gladius out of yet another Briton's guts when he heard the sound of their horn – his century's horn. But the noise it made was not a signal he recognised. And it seemed to be coming from some way off.

He turned and, out of the corner of his eye saw a wild eyed Solitarius, horn to his lips, but he was not where he should be. Why was he not with the rest of the century? Why was he standing away from the rest of them, halfway up the hill behind them? And what was the meaning of this strange signal?

Graecus tried to think of an answer to all these questions while fending off a big, hairy Briton and then their horn sounded again. It sounded like that rarest of signals – the retreat - but this time its call was strangled in mid flow and fell away in a diminuendo farting sound as Solitarius hit the ground, writhing, transfixed by a spear. A Roman spear.

Graecus quickly looked in the direction from which the spear had come and saw Germanicus.

His son had a wide, very satisfied grin on his face and winked at his father.

Graecus now needed to pay attention to the next wave of Britons and could give no more thought to Solitarius except the fleeting one that he would not be missed.

On and on the Britons came. On and on the Romans fought

getting hotter and hotter in their heavy armour and more and more tired as the afternoon sun beat down.

Then there was a new twist to the steady flow of Britons and the monotonous cut and thrust of the fighting as, all of a sudden, there appeared to be many more enemy and this situation which the Romans had, with difficulty, been controlling now threatened to slip away from them, and with it, the battle.

This new stream of Britons had come from within the wall of death – Graecus saw that they had been organised enough to use their carts to clear away enough of the fallen and the pieces of broken chariots to make a pathway and now they streamed down it.

This was an unforeseen event but there was no panic among the Roman ranks –just a palpable feeling of resigned exhaustion.

The Britons poured down this new 'avenue' and began to lay into the Romans with renewed vigour. The horns sounded for more Roman reserves to come forward and the battle area was thick with fighting men.

The Romans needed to keep their nerve – this battle would be won on confidence as much as on skill and stamina.

Graecus started to sing their battle song and soon the men around him joined in.

But still the Britons kept on coming and some of them kept the avenue free of bodies to enable the flow of fresh fighters against the tired Romans.

Graecus began to fear that all would be lost and hoped that their deaths would be swift when he saw, out of the corner of his eye, Germanicus's bare blonde head, alone, isolated in the midst of a group of Britons at the bottom of the avenue.

This gave him more cause for fear than anything else which had happened that day – the Britons would be fresh troops and Germanicus had lost his wobbly helmet so was both unprotected and, with his bright head, a lure for the enemy.

Graecus could see that Germanicus was busy with two swords and was making a valiant effort to hold off the Britons but it was only a matter of time before one of them would do him great harm and Graecus could not allow this to happen – life without Germanicus was unthinkable.

Graecus called on all his reserves of energy and became a frenzied madman as he hacked, cut, stuck, smashed and thrust his way through the enemy, large and small, to enable him to get to his son.

'Welcome father!' said Germanicus when his Centurion managed to make his way through the murderous Britons and stand next to him, gladius and shield at the ready.

Now there were two of them and, if they perished, at least they would die together.

Cut, thrust, bish, crash, cut, thrust, bish, crash – together they fought for their lives while Zig assisted their endeavours by biting the ankles of their opponents – deftly severing their tendons.

But even Germanicus was tiring and Graecus had cramp in his legs and their movements were slower and more careless as the heat and dehydration took their toll.

In a spat with a gigantic red-headed Briton, Graecus took a cut to his left leg and almost went down but recovered himself in time to prevent decapitation by another big man who, suddenly, turned and was pierced by someone new to the fray.

It was Felix. Wonderful Felix who could not have been more welcome had he been carrying Falernian wine and hare and apple pies.

Then Pneumaticus appeared.

Then Magnus.

Then Impedimentus.

Then Incitatus, who, with his usual stamina, still appeared energetic.

Then Acerbus joined their group of fighters and more men from Graecus's century came.

Followed by men from Acerbus's century.

Soon there were over a hundred Romans holding their position at the bottom of the 'Avenue' and the flow of Britons slowed to a trickle.

The horns sounded.

It was the prearranged and much longed for signal for the

cavalry to withdraw and allow the infantry to make its way round the wall of death. Suetonius must have seen from his observation point that the Romans now had the advantage.

The orders were to use the corridor of space vacated by the cavalry to advance in a pincer movement but this unexpected opening up of the Avenue, and their position at the foot of it, seemed to Graecus to be an opportunity which must be grasped, and glancing at Acerbus who was nodding to him, he saw that his colleague was of the same mind.

Calling their men forward, Graecus and Acerbus started down the Avenue towards the thick of the Britons.

CHAPTER SIXTEEN

Germanicus joined his father at the front of the thin Roman line making its way through the wall of death.

'What was Solitarius doing half way up the hill behind us?'

'He was running away father. He saw that the battle was not going our way at that point and he was trying to save his skin.'

'Hah! A coward just like his master,' said Graecus. 'But why was he sounding the retreat?'

'I can only guess that he wanted to clothe his own cowardice with a veil of confusion.'

'You did exactly the right thing in killing him then– he could have lost us the battle by sowing the seeds of doubt in our men's minds,' said Graecus.

Thank you, father, I did it for the good of the army but I *did* enjoy it.'

Graecus smiled at his son as they reached the end of the Avenue and joined the melee of Britons.

The Britons were lightly armed but, if they were surprised by the appearance of the Centurions and their men at the mouth of the Avenue, they gave no sign of it, being very determined and ferocious in their assaults on the Romans.

Graecus and Acerbus and their men fought them in their disciplined, almost ritualistic way and began to make ground although the press of Britons before them was still very great and each of them, even Incitatus, was dog tired.

The sun showed that it was about three hours past the midday and Graecus was wondering what had happened to the pincer movement which the legionaries had been ordered to carry out when he suddenly felt a change of attitude in the Britons around him – instead of confident resolve, there was a whiff of panic in their ranks.

In that moment, Graecus knew that the battle was theirs.

Panic in an army is fatal – it is utterly contagious and spreads like wildfire.

The thicket of Britons around them began to thin out and Graecus could see that the legionaries had been successful in making their way through the British ranks.

The Britons were facing a strong wall of Roman troops now and began to retreat. Graecus watched as, in minutes, they turned from a strong fighting force into a keening rabble trying to run for their lives.

The Britons were trying to flee from the advancing legionaries and auxiliaries but they were throwing themselves back onto the massed ranks of their own carts and wagons filled with their wives, children and livestock sitting in the mouth of the valley and they were trapped.

Graecus could see some of them trying to escape via the sloping sides of the valley but these men were easily picked off by the cavalry whose advance Suetonius had ordered for this very purpose.

It was all over for the Britons.

Systematically, methodically, the Romans advanced, and even though they started to move the baggage wagons away, those Britons who escaped the valley by this route were dispatched by the cavalry and those who could not escape the valley simply perished in the path of the deadly wedge of the Roman infantry advance.

By the late afternoon the valley was filled with the dead and the dying and Boudicca's chariot was nowhere to be seen.

Those Britons who were left standing began to sing a mournful tune which, Graecus thought, must be their death song.

He admired their bravery as, unlike some Romans he could name, once they saw it was hopeless, they stood their ground as long as they could and still hoped to take an enemy with them when they died.

And then, finally, there was not a man or woman standing. They were all down. But many of them were not dead and the Roman soldiers went about the field finishing off those whose cries alerted them to their agony while their medical colleagues searched for the Roman wounded.

The sickly smell of blood mingled with the acid stench of

spilled gizzards filled the air and crows began to call to each other over the valley.

It would not be long before they settled on this gargantuan feast and, as he went searching for the still living fallen, Graecus pondered that he hated the crows' delight in the suffering of others.

He did not relish this task anyway; it was so different from the heat of battle when the desire to preserve one's own life made it easy to pierce an enemy but now the proud blue warriors were maimed and broken and there were thousands of them piled all over the valley.

Some of them were women and they had fought as bravely as their menfolk.

As he walked the battlefield, Graecus hoped that he would not find any wounded women as he did not know if he would be able to dispatch a wounded woman and he hoped, all the more, that he would not find the lovely Iceni noblewoman.

The shrieks and cries on the battlefield were becoming fewer and Graecus had just dispatched a man with a severe leg wound when he saw a skinny knee sticking out from under the corpse of a burly Briton and his heart stopped in his chest.

'Over here!' he called. 'Get some help over here now!' as he bent and tried to dislodge the dead weight of the red-headed six-footer.

'We're getting some help for you,' he said to the owner of the knee. 'Just hang on, you will soon be in the *infirmarium*.'

Felix and a legionary whom he did not know appeared and when Felix saw the skinny knee he said, 'Oh no, not him, please make it someone else. Please let it not be him.'

Graecus said, 'At the count of three, we'll all lift the corpse together. Ready? One, two, three, HEAVE!'

They threw the dead Briton to one side and Graecus hardly dared look at what, or who, was underneath but his love for his friend overcame his fear and he forced himself to lower his gaze.

It was Acerbus. He was lying on his back, his arms outstretched and his head thrown back. His little legs were bent, exaggerating the skinniness of his knees. There was a dark cloud of blood on the lower part of his tunic where he had been pierced in the belly.

He was moaning.

'Get Magnus!' Graecus said urgently to Felix while he cradled Acerbus's head in his hands. Then to Acerbus, 'Magnus will soon have you on the mend. He is on his way now, just hang on my friend!' The legionary, sensing that he could do no more to help, left the scene to carry on his deadly work.

Acerbus was delirious. He was railing against the foreman of his Aunt's farm and how he cheated her at harvest time by stealing some of the crop for himself. He thought that Graecus was the foreman and said to him, 'Don't try to fool me, I know what tricks you're up to. Don't try to sweet talk me, you blackguard!' while trying to raise himself to his feet.

Graecus knew this could be dangerous and told Acerbus not to agitate himself but to no avail and the flow of blood through his tunic was renewed.

Where was Magnus?

'I know what a thief you are, you scum!' shouted Acerbus at Graecus and tried again to get to his feet.

'You'll answer to ME!' he shouted in a surprisingly strong voice for such a badly wounded man but the blood stain grew larger and Graecus knew that he must do *something* to stop Acerbus from agitating himself further.

'Forgive me, my friend,' he said, 'I have no alternative but to do this,' as he squatted over him, lifted his fist and delivered a blow to Acerbus's jaw which laid him out cold.

Graecus knelt on the ground and cradled Acerbus's head again, as he had been taught by Magnus, so that he would not choke on his tongue, and waited.

It was a summer's evening now. Warm and balmy and, in other circumstances, Graecus would have thought it a beautiful evening but kneeling on the bloody ground, in this valley which had become a charnel house, holding the head of one of his most treasured friends, his only thought was to wish for an end to this day.

He heard anxious voices speaking Latin and called, 'Over here! We're over here!'

Magnus, Felix and Germanicus appeared with a medical

orderly from one of the Legions who was carrying a stretcher onto which they loaded Acerbus very carefully.

Felix and Germanicus carried the stretcher while Magnus and the orderly looked at the wound.

The orderly shook his head and Magnus looked grave.

'I am not hopeful,' he said. 'It is a stomach wound and you know as well as I do that they are usually fatal. We will make him as comfortable as we can but I have seen younger men die from less serious wounds.'

'But you *must* save him!' said Graecus and was horrified by the panic in his voice.

'We will do our best,' said Magnus very quietly and Graecus, ashamed of his outburst, said, 'I know you will, you always do.'

They reached the collection of tents which was the field *infirmarium* where the surgeons were working on the wounded.

Magnus saw one of them whom he had known years ago in Judea – an Egyptian auxiliary of rare skill – and said to Graecus, 'He's the man we want for Acerbus, if anyone can heal him, it's Ptolemy.'

Graecus approached the surgeon, his arms bloody to the elbow, and said, 'I hear from Magnus that you are the best surgeon he knows and I take that as a rare recommendation. Please look after our colleague, Acerbus, he is a good soldier and a better friend. We do not wish to lose him.'

'There are many calls on my time today but I have just finished sewing up a young legionary who had lost the lower part of his leg. Bring your friend over here and I will assess him now,' said Ptolemy.

'Thank you, a thousand times thank you,' said Graecus as Felix and Germanicus laid the comatose Acerbus on Ptolemy's table.

'You may go now,' he said, 'I work better without an audience.'

They left the tent and went back to the noisome task of killing wounded people.

* * *

At about the tenth hour of the day, as the sun was beginning to get low in the sky, the horns sounded the mustering notes and they gathered to one side of the valley.

Suetonius appeared on his horse, the legates flanking him.

'Men,' he said, 'brothers in arms, my friends, you have won a great victory today and as I speak to you now, the messages telling of your valour are on their way to Rome, Our Emperor will soon know of your steadfastness and your bravery. I am proud of you all. You have fought with stout hearts all this day and I wish you now to rest a while. Food is coming from our camp and I wish that you would eat and drink and regain your strength for, later this evening, we shall begin to dig the trenches to bury the enemy dead – I don't want to leave them lying about as food for the crows, nor as a rallying point for any other tribe which might fancy starting a rebellion. That's all for now. Rest for two hours. Dismissed.'

The food came and, after he had washed his hands and face in clean water and rinsed his feet, Graecus realised that he was ravenous and he and his men found a place on the hillside where they could sit and eat and gratefully drink the wine which had come from their camp while trying to make sense of the battle and wondering how they had managed to win against such a numerous enemy.

Then they went back to work.

The legionary engineers told them where to dig and they began digging.

They dug huge straight trenches, about five feet deep, at the valley's sides where there were fewer bodies to move out from their way.

The digging continued by torchlight, long after it was dark but their efforts were helped by the moon which was again bright, albeit on the wane.

They finished at about four hours short of the dawn when the order came to stop and to rest for the remainder of the night.

Graecus and his men chose a place as far away as possible from the noise made by the brassy Batavians who were celebrating victory as if it had been their efforts alone which had secured it.

Graecus lay on the ground and silently thanked Gideon's God for the safe delivery of his son. Then he asked Gideon's God for the recovery to full health of his friend and mentor Acerbus.

Graecus was just drifting off to sleep when he heard someone call his name:

'Centurion Graecus, Centurion Graecus!' There it was again. He sat up and looked about him.

There was a party of legionaries walking about the auxiliary lines, calling *his* name.

'I am here!' he shouted and waited as they approached him.

The man in front was a legionary Centurion with a mean set to his face.

'Centurion Graecus,' he said, 'it is my unpleasant duty to give you this,' handing a scroll to Graecus, who unrolled it but was having difficulty reading it in the semi-darkness.

'It is a warrant for the arrest of your standard bearer, Germanicus. He is to answer a charge of murder.'

Graecus could make no sense of this – his mind froze while Germanicus looked puzzled and the rest of the contubernium gasped in horror. What the legionary had said was ridiculous – Germanicus had been killing people all day but it was in the service of Rome – that was his job – how could it be murder?

Graecus stood up in the hope that he might be better able to comprehend this nasty turn of events if he were on his feet, facing the legionary who was reading from a scroll he was holding.

'He is to be charged with the murder of your horn-blower, who was found with an auxiliary spear embedded in him. And these men,' here he read out two very strange sounding names which meant nothing to Graecus, 'saw your son throw the spear.'

Graecus felt relief flood through him. Germanicus angrily opened his mouth ready to speak but Graecus began before him.

'Ah, I can explain that,' Graecus said smoothly. 'It's quite simple. Solitarius was running away from the battlefield and he started to sound the retreat but my son here saw that he was causing confusion and dealt with him as befits a quick-thinking Roman soldier intent on victory.'

'It is not as simple as you make it out to be. The information given here differs from your version.'

'But that is what my son told me, and he always speaks the truth,' said Graecus.

'That may well be the case but it is not up to me to decide what the truth is in this case – it will be up to the legates and *you* will not be called upon to give evidence.'

'But am I not allowed to speak for a member of my contubernium? A man who would give his life for me?'

'Not when he is your son.'

Graecus's bowels turned to water and he had to steady himself against Felix who was also now standing. Germanicus looked stricken and Zig growled at the legionary.

Incitatus had been listening intently to the exchange between the Centurions, and nimbly raising himself from the ground, smiled pleasantly at the legionary officer and asked if he would kindly repeat the names of the men who had laid the information against Germanicus.

The legionary repeated the odd-sounding names and Incitatus looked thoughtful before saying, 'These men are Batavians, are they not?' And the legionary replied,

'Yes, soldier, they are. They are members of the Batavian cavalry, who were able to see a great deal of what was going on.'

'Do you know these men?' said Graecus.

'Not really, no, but I have seen them,' said the legionary.

'Is one of them missing his front teeth?'

'Yes, that is correct.'

'And does the other have big hands?'

'Yes, like shovels – big red shovels – now I come to think of it.'

Incitatus was gesturing to Graecus that he wished to say something and Graecus nodded to him to speak.

'Domine, our brother here has said that, as Germanicus's father, you cannot speak for him even though you are his commanding officer but our Army Regulations state that an accused man is allowed to have someone to speak for him and I wish to volunteer to defend our standard bearer.'

Graecus was well aware of Incitatus's grasp of military regulations, his eloquence and his sharp mind and could think of no one better so he nodded again and watched with despair in his heart as Germanicus's hands were tied behind his back and he was led away by the legionaries with Incitatus and Zig following behind – the dog's tail hanging limply between his legs.

Graecus tried to sit down but his legs were so weak that he fell to the ground and sat, stunned by this most potent piece of nastiness which came hard on the heels of all the other dreadful things which had befallen them since they had left Lower Germania.

'I will make you some honey water,' said Felix and went to light a fire.

Impedimentus came to sit next to Graecus.

'Domine,' he said, 'this cannot be right. We all know that Germanicus is innocent. He is a good soldier and a good servant of Rome. Those Batavians are slippery customers. They like to make trouble and would lie to their gods if it suited them. We will make sure that the truth is heard.'

Impedimentus rarely, if ever, addressed him as 'Domine' and Graecus knew that his old colleague was concerned for both him and his son and was trying to comfort him.

'Thank you my friend. We will all do our best to help him, I'm sure of that, but what I am not sure of is *how* we can help him.'

'Well, Domine, someone *must* have seen something or heard something which will help Germanicus.'

'I hope you are right – it would be the worst injustice I could contemplate to lose my son for someone as worthless as Solitarius and on the say-so of those slimy Batavians,' said Graecus.

Felix appeared with a steaming beaker of honey water and Graecus drank it gratefully while Impedimentus sat thoughtfully at his side.

'Domine,' he said, 'why *did* Germanicus kill Solitarius?'

'Because he was deserting. Because he thought we'd lost the

battle. Because he was a coward and he was sounding the retreat.'

'Did you hear that?'

'Yes, I did. I heard him sound it and *I* was confused by it as others must also have been,' said Graecus.

'But the Batavians could not have heard it from their position right at the edge of the valley,' Impedimentus pointed out.

'No, you are correct, that is a very good point. But you heard what the legionary said – I am not to be allowed to say that I heard Solitarius sounding the retreat.'

'But someone else must have heard it. Someone other than you.'

'I am trying to think of who else was nearby when I heard it.'

'Where was Norbanus?'

'I do not know where he was precisely at that point, but as Senior Centurion he should have been in a place where he had a good view of what was happening on the battlefield.'

'Exactly. So *he* may be able to help us.'

'That is another very good thought, my friend.'

'Mmm, yes it is,' said Impedimentus. 'I'll go and see if I can find him now.'

Impedimentus rose and walked in the direction of the temporary legionary command post which had been erected in the mouth of the valley following the Romans' victory.

Graecus closed his eyes which were hot, gritty and tired and massaged the bridge of his nose then rubbed his temples vigorously to try to get his brain working.

The difficulty was, though, that his heart was pounding and his emotions were so heightened that he could hardly think at all.

He could make no sense of anything and he decided that he would pray to Gideon's God who had often answered his prayers and because Gideon's God was a god of love and Graecus's love for his son was such that he could not contemplate life without him.

'Dear God of love,' he prayed, 'please deliver my son from this latest threat to his safety and have him released as an innocent man and a good soldier. Oh, and please help Acerbus to recover fully from his wound.'

Someone standing in front of Graecus cleared his throat to

draw the Centurion's attention and Graecus opened his bloodshot eyes to see Impedimentus, shifting impatiently from foot to foot.

'He was not there, Domine. Suetonius sent him back to the main camp and I do not know whether he will be coming back here. But the thing is, the legates' clerk told me that they are planning to try Germanicus later this morning and they want to use him as an example to stiffen discipline – they say there have been too many occasions when a battle has been used to settle old personal scores.'

'My God!' said Graecus and received a strange look from Impedimentus before 'correcting' himself by saying 'I mean, Ye Gods! How much time do we have?'

'Not long. They say they will try him half way through the morning.'

'I need to think. I need to think of something to save him. *Someone* must have seen what really happened.'

Graecus paced up and down and his fevered mind began to clear itself as the blood reached his legs and the cool of the early morning soothed his head.

He did not know where the idea came from – it could have been planted in his head by Gideon's God, or it could just have been his own tired brain, but the idea *did* come and he excitedly said to Impedimentus, 'I have it! I must speak to Suetonius! He more than anyone would have seen the way the battle was going and he may have heard something. Is he here? Do you know where he is?'

'No. But I agree with you that it would make sense to speak to him, if you can get access to him – I mean, he is our General, will he speak to you?'

'If he is here, I am sure he will speak to me. He is a true soldier and a fair man, albeit brusque and demanding. I will go now – there is no time to waste.'

'Do you wish me to come with you?'

'Thank you my friend for the offer of your company but I think it would be best if I did this alone.'

'As you wish. May the gods go with you.'

Graecus began to walk towards the mouth of the valley but found that he needed urgently to visit the latrines where he had to waste twenty precious minutes quietening his bowels. Then he raked his fingers through his hair in an attempt to make himself more presentable as he walked quickly to the temporary command post.

It was no more than a small collection of leather tents but it was guarded, as usual, by the whey faced scribblers.

Luckily for Graecus the scribbler at the front desk was one he recognised and who recognised him – he was the one who had taken him, Pneumaticus and Incitatus into the rehearsal for the *consilium* and he smiled when he saw Graecus.

'Hail, Centurion!' he said cheerfully. 'What business do you have with us today?'

'I need to see Suetonius,' said Graecus.

'Do you, indeed?' said the young man smiling. And then in a mock conspiratorial manner, 'But the trouble is, he is very busy and I have orders not to disturb him – and you can imagine how much I would not wish to disobey his express wishes.'

'Tell him it is Centurion Graecus and that I wish to speak to him, as one father to another.'

The smile left the young man's face as he saw the determined set of Graecus's shoulders and he sat silently for a minute, thinking.

'Please!' said Graecus in a steady voice but one which carried urgency.

'I'll see what I can do,' said the young man, putting down his pen and rising from his stool.

'Thank you,' said Graecus. 'May the gods smile on you and all your family.'

The young man went into the tent and was gone for a long while.

Graecus wiped his face with his neckerchief.

There was no sound coming from the interior of the tent – no shouting, nor the sound of things hitting the floor – just silence.

Eventually the young man reappeared and said, 'He will see you. Follow me.'

They went into the tent, and yet again, there was the tent

within a tent arrangement, but much smaller than at the main camp, and Graecus's eyes had to accustom themselves to the shade after they had been in the sunlight outside.

'He is in here,' said the young man quietly, opening the flap of the inner tent, and Graecus stepped inside.

CHAPTER SEVENTEEN

Suetonius was at his desk, a huge pile of documents in front of him and piles on the floor beside him. He looked up when Graecus entered the tent and, to Graecus's amazement, he stood up and offered him his arm in greeting.

'Hail!' said the General. 'How are you and your men this morning? Did you not win a wonderful victory for Rome yesterday! I am proud of you all, you fought like lions!'

'Thank you my lord. We give thanks that we were led by a man who had faith in us and whose own courage was a great example,' said Graecus.

'Please sit,' said Suetonius indicating a stool in front of his desk. 'Now what is it you wanted to speak to me about? That pasty faced youth said it was something about your being a father. Have you been busy with a local woman?'

'No, my lord – those I have seen are not really to my taste – they are too tall. But I *am* a father already, my lord – some years ago I adopted a boy in Lower Germania. I called him Germanicus and he serves with me now in my contubernium. He is a fierce fighter and loyal to Rome. He fought valiantly yesterday and...'

Graecus's throat was so tight with emotion that he could hardly continue – his heart and his mind rebelled at the thought that his brave, faithful, wonderful son could be sacrificed because the Batavians wanted revenge.

'I am not sure what the problem is, then?' said Suetonius gently.

Graecus swallowed and tried to make his voice steady. 'My lord, as I speak, my son, Germanicus is under close arrest charged with murder and the legates will try him for that offence later this morning.'

'*What?* How has that come about?' said Suetonius.

'My lord, I will tell you as much as I know. Germanicus is charged with the murder of our horn blower, Solitarius, and he does not deny that he transfixed Solitarius with his spear, but the fact of the matter was that Solitarius was in the act of running away from the battlefield when Germanicus threw the spear, and what was worse, he was sounding the retreat.'

Graecus paused to let his words sink in while Suetonius looked grave and said, 'Please continue.'

'My lord, I heard the horn sound the retreat and looked round to see where it was coming from – it distracted me in the midst of the battle and confused me for a moment but then the sound died away and I looked round to see Solitarius falling to the ground, felled by a spear. A spear thrown by my son. But I knew immediately that Germanicus had taken the correct action because Solitarius was well behind our lines and was running away.'

'I see,' said Suetonius, rubbing his chin with his right hand. 'And I suppose you have been denied the opportunity to speak for the man in your century because he is your son.'

'Precisely, my lord.'

'But someone else must have seen what was going on. Someone else must have heard the horn.'

'That is why I have come to see you, my lord. I hoped that, from your vantage point, you might have seen or heard something to help my son.'

Suetonius sat motionless, lost in thought, for quite some time while Graecus's heart somersaulted between hope and despair. Then Suetonius spoke.

'I would like to help you – I *do know how, as a father,* you wish to protect your son and I would not wish for a miscarriage of justice but I do not think I have any memory of such a thing and I cannot be seen to twist military discipline to suit my own ends, any more than you can, Centurion Graecus.

'My lord, my son is young and sometimes rash but he used his initiative in the heat of battle and he did what he thought was the right thing for his colleagues.'

'I hear what you say, Centurion, and I know that you are a good soldier and I am sure that you have brought up your son to follow your example but I cannot have my soldiers killing one another and getting away with it – in the heat of battle or not. If you are to save your son, you will need to find someone else to speak for him.'

Through the depths of his misery and desperation, Graecus became aware that there was a commotion outside the tent, a raising of voices and someone shouting, 'But I *must* see him!' and in strode Norbanus.

Suetonius and Graecus looked up in surprise at the Senior Centurion's unorthodox entry into his General's presence but this gave Norbanus the opportunity to speak.

'My lord,' he said somewhat out of breath, 'I regret my barging in here and I apologise for disturbing you, but I must speak to you to prevent a terrible injustice which is about to take place.'

'Humph!' said Suetonius. 'That seems to be a popular theme this morning.'

'Indeed, my lord, and the injustice which I wish to prevent, concerns this man's son,' said Norbanus.

'Hmm?' said Suetonius. 'Well, you had better get your breath back and tell me about it.'

Norbanus took several deep breaths and then said, 'My lord, you will recall that after the battle, you asked me to identify for you a young soldier with bright blonde hair whom you had seen fighting like a demon at the bottom of the passage the Britons had opened up in the wall of death? You said that you felt that this young man, who had lost his helmet, turned the battle in our favour because he and his colleagues opened up the front we needed to drive a wedge against the Britons.'

'Yes, yes, I remember, I did say that and I want to find this young man because he deserves full battle honours, but what has that to do with miscarriages of justice?'

'My lord, that young man and this man's son are one and the same,' said Norbanus.

'Ohhhh...' said Suetonius trying to work out the implications of what he had just learned.

'Yes, my lord, and what is more, *I* heard the horn blower sound the retreat and I would have transfixed him myself had I been quick enough but this young man, Germanicus, did it for me.'

'I see,' said Suetonius. 'Well, I am heartily glad that you have been able to tell me the whole truth about this matter, but what I don't know is who started this hare running in the first place?'

'A couple of Batavian cavalrymen who have a grudge against Germanicus and who made a complaint to the legates who took it very seriously,' said Norbanus grimly.

'Those fucking Batavians are more trouble than they're worth and the legates need to spend more time thinking about winning battles than they do about pettifogging regulations,' spat Suetonius. And then he said, 'Have Germanicus released immediately and put the Batavians under arrest – I'll deal with them later – after I've given the legates a lesson in where their priorities should lie.'

'Yes, my lord, I will see to it immediately!' said Norbanus, grinning.

'Thank you, my lord, I knew that I would get a fair hearing for my son from you,' said Graecus.

'Well, with Norbanus's help, we have got to the bottom of it,' said Suetonius. 'And I meant what I said – your son and his colleagues, including you, deserve full battle honours and I shall recommend that you receive them – we won an historic victory yesterday and Rome has good reason to be grateful to us.'

'Thank you, my lord,' said Graecus. 'I am deeply honoured.'

'Now you must go and find your son and tell him the good news. You are dismissed,' said Suetonius.

Graecus left the tents and went into the valley to find his men.

They were burying the bodies of the British dead – hauling dead meat to the trenches they had dug the night before.

It was gruelling work both physically and mentally because it was impossible, when faced with such carnage, not to think about the suffering of those who had died and the desolation wrought on those left behind.

Pneumaticus saw Graecus first and hailed him.

'What is the news! Tell us!'

'The news is good. The news is very good – Germanicus is to be released and we are all to be nominated by Suetonius for battle honours.'

'Ye Gods!' said Pneumaticus. 'The Roman Army will never

cease to amaze me – one minute Germanicus is a criminal about to be tried for murder and the next minute he's a war hero!'

Graecus felt that he could not have expressed the morning's events and his thoughts about them any better himself – Pneumaticus had the knack of pithily encapsulating things.

'Yes, it is amazing is it not, how life turns from good to bad and back again,' said Graecus. 'But what was miraculous was that Norbanus turned up just when he did – it would have been very different had he not,' said Graecus.

'Oh, that was no miracle,' said Pneumaticus. 'Felix bribed a wounded cavalryman with the promise of one of his pies to lend his horse to Impedimentus who rode back to the main camp to find Norbanus. Norbanus didn't know that Germanicus had been charged with murder but was furious when he found out and came charging back to put the case to Suetonius.'

'Well I can hardly thank any of them enough,' said Graecus, feeling that he could breathe again now that Germanicus was to be released.

And then he thought about Acerbus.

'I am going to the *infirmarium* to see how Acerbus is this morning,' he said, and without waiting for a reply, set off for the hospital tents.

He found Acerbus easily enough, he was lying on a truckle bed just inside the first of the tents into which Graecus peered.

He was lying on his back, breathing noisily through his nose.

His colour was bad – a yellowy grey, tinged with angry red spots on his cheeks. There was an uneaten bowl of porridge by the side of the bed.

Graecus looked for the medical orderly and found him further inside the tent, attending to a legionary who had a deep wound to his thigh.

The orderly looked up when he saw the officer approach and then went back to dressing the legionary's leg while saying, 'How can I help you, sir?'

'I am enquiring about my colleague, Acerbus. How is he

doing this morning?'

'Well, sir, the wound was deep and penetrated his guts. I cannot promise anything, sir. Our surgeon did his best but sometimes only the gods can help. To be honest with you sir, I do not think he will live.'

At that moment, there was a noise behind them and Graecus recognised Acerbus's voice crying out in pain.

Graecus and the orderly hurried over to Acerbus's bed where he lay writhing in agony, shouting out his father's name, begging him for help to stop the pain.

It was dreadful to witness his friend's torture and Graecus asked the orderly if there was anything he could do to ease his friend's torment.

'Sir, I have given him as much poppy as I can without killing him and I daren't give him any more.'

'But this is terrible, if he is dying, he will not make a good death – he will go to his gods in a frenzied state.'

'That may be so, sir, but it is my job to heal the sick, not to kill them with my medicine.'

Acerbus tossed and turned, trying to get away from the pain in his guts, his hands clawing at his belly, wanting to draw the torment out from his body.

His cries were pitiful. Graecus could not bear to see his strong, brave, wise, funny friend in such agony.

'Brother,' he said to the orderly, 'our own medical man would, I am sure, like to see Acerbus just to make sure that he is as comfortable as possible. I take it that you have no objection?'

'No, sir, if your man can help him, then I will be grateful – his screams are upsetting the rest of my patients.'

'Thank you,' said Graecus and sprinted from the tent in search of Magnus who, luckily, was nearby, attending to several of the wounded from Graecus's century.

Graecus quickly took in the scene and saw that there was no urgency – these soldiers did not need Magnus as badly as did Acerbus – and went to him and whispered, 'Do you have any of the mushroom left? Acerbus is delirious with pain and the legionary orderly will give him no more poppy. We cannot let him suffer.'

'Yes, I have a little left. There is more than enough to have an effect on him, he's not a big man.'

'Good, let us not waste any time – I don't want him to be in this state any longer than is necessary.'

The two men went swiftly back to the hospital tent where they found Acerbus in a worse condition than when Graecus had left – big globules of sweat covered his brow and his eyes were rolling uncontrollably from side to side.

'You fuckers!' he shouted. 'I'll get you for this! Don't think you can get away with cheating me!'

'He's dying,' said Magnus. 'It won't be long but I think we should help him on his way.'

'Just do it, do it quickly,' said Graecus, his throat tightening yet again that morning at the thought that someone he loved was about to be taken from him.

Magnus felt in the pouch at his waist and took out a small leather package from which he carefully extracted a small piece of dried up mushroom and then, without ceremony, he dropped it into Acerbus's open, cursing, mouth.

Acerbus obligingly swallowed the little morsel and his friends watched and waited for it to work its magic.

It did not take long.

Within a few minutes Acerbus had stopped shouting and was lying calmly on his back with his eyes closed. Then he stopped clawing at his belly and put his hands tidily by his sides – as if he were standing to attention but lying down.

Within a few more minutes, the muscles of his face relaxed and he looked peaceful.

Then, to Graecus's relief, Acerbus began to smile.

'Thank God!' he said.

'What did you say?' said Magnus. 'Did you just say, "Thank God"?'

'I may have said that, yes,' said Graecus. 'I have found Gideon's God to be very helpful in times of need.'

'Mmm,' said Magnus. 'Whilst I have no doubt that Gideon's God must be very powerful as he saved his life, you must be careful not to be seen to have anything to do with this Christian God – I mean, you must not forget that Acerbus told us that Nero is blaming the Christians for Rome's ills and he wishes to purge the city of them.'

'Yes, you are correct, I must be careful,' said Graecus.

Acerbus lay quietly on his bed, smiling, breathing steadily, all signs of pain having left his face.

'He will shortly be joining his ancestors,' said Magnus.

'Yes he will, and he will be leaving the world a colder place – he was a good, honest man and a true soldier.'

'You will miss him.'

'Yes, I shall – terribly, he was like the father I never had.'

As Graecus said this, Acerbus gave a deep, contented sigh and died with a broad, almost lascivious grin on his face.

'Life will be difficult without him,' said Graecus. 'He taught me so much.'

'But you can, at least, know that you did your best for him and he died happy.'

'I must tell Norbanus – he and Acerbus went back many years together. You had better get back to your other patients – their need is greater than Acerbus's now,' said Graecus as he carefully and tenderly closed his friend's unseeing eyes.

Graecus left the hospital tent and went to Norbanus's tent.

The Senior Centurion was sitting on a folding stool at his campaign desk, his head in his hands.

Graecus stood silently for a few moments waiting for Norbanus to notice his presence, but after a minute or two he thought that Norbanus must be asleep and was about to leave when Norbanus suddenly woke with a start and looked at Graecus but without recognising him.

'Sir?' said Graecus. 'Sir, are you well? Can I fetch the physician?'

'Oh, it's you,' said Norbanus passing his hands over his grey face. 'I'm afraid that as soon as I sat down, I fell asleep – I'm getting a bit long in the tooth for all this. In the old days, I could stay awake for four days and nights at a time but now the gods no longer favour me with boundless vigour and after only two sleepless nights I'm done in. But that is all by the by, what is it you want?'

'Sir, I have bad news.'

'Not about Germanicus, surely? I thought I'd sorted that little mares' nest out earlier.'

'No sir, it's about our dear friend Acerbus. He died about a quarter of an hour ago.'

'Ye gods. Was it peaceful? Did he die well?'

'Yes, sir, he did, he died with all the dignity which he would have wished.'

'Then I am thankful for that but I shall grieve him for many a month – he was one of the most trustworthy men I have ever known... and one of the best soldiers,' said Norbanus, looking even more weary now than when Graecus had entered his tent.

There was silence for a while as the two men thought of their lost friend and then Norbanus said, 'You can do me a favour. By rights, I should sort through Acerbus's things and arrange for them to be sent to his family, but I haven't the time this morning, and more importantly, I haven't the heart. Would you do it for me – just parcel up his belongings and give them to my second in command – he'll know where to send them.'

'Yes, sir, I will be glad to do that for you and for Acerbus.'

'Thank you and I'm ordering the auxiliaries back to the main camp now for some food and some sleep – you deserve it after your performance yesterday.'

'Thank you sir, we're all relieved it turned out as it did' said Graecus and left Norbanus's tent walking back to the auxiliary lines with a heavy heart.

The order to return to the main camp had preceded him and when he found his men they were busy packing up.

As Graecus approached, Germanicus looked up from replacing the cover on his shield.

'Father, what is the matter? You look very sad.'

'Acerbus died this morning from the wounds he received yesterday.'

'But they operated on him last night.'

'Yes, my son, I know, but the wound was too deep and the gods had decided to call him back.'

'That is terrible for us all. He was loved by all of us.'

'Yes, my son, he was,' said Graecus, and was embarrassed to realise that he had tears in his eyes. 'But he died as he lived – valiantly and in the service of Rome.'

Soon all the auxiliaries were ready to return to the main camp and they left the battlefield camp-site just before the mid-day.

The men were hot, tired and hungry when they reached the main camp and Felix set to immediately with his pots and pans producing hot water for washing and shaving and then hot porridge followed by bread and cheese. Graecus could not eat the cheese – it was too heavy for his stomach – but Felix gave him some honey and he ate that with his bread.

Feeling clean and better-fed, Graecus could now face the task of going through Acerbus's property.

He walked resolutely to his friend's tent and opened the flap.

Sunlight flooded the dark interior and Graecus could see motes of dust dancing in the rays.

Graecus stood in the open flap and looked around. It was strange to be in this tent without Acerbus. It seemed very wrong to be here without his vigorous presence, his deafening laugh and his willingness to help his friends.

Acerbus must have left in a hurry.

There were several open boxes on his bed, their contents strewn carelessly onto both the bed and the floor. And several items of clothing tossed into a corner.

This was odd.

Acerbus was a tidy man – years of army life had taught him that it was best to be that way. And why would he have been looking at documents on the morning before the most important battle of his life? If he'd wanted to check his will, for example, why would he not have done it the day before when he would have had more time to do it properly and leave everything tidy?

Graecus thought about this, and the more he thought about it, the more he smelled a rat.

He began to look around him more carefully. He looked at the tangle of clothes and knew that Acerbus would not have left his things in such a state.

Yes, it was definitely not Acerbus who had left this mess and whoever it was who had made it was up to no good.

But who else would be interested in Acerbus's property? What could there be which would be valuable to someone else? Did whoever it was find what he was looking for?

Graecus looked around again and saw that there were footprints in the dirt floor of the tent.

He got to his knees and looked very carefully at the footprints.

There were two sets of prints – one made by a pair of army boots – the indentations from the studs were quite clear – and the other made by a pair of shoes.

The prints made by the boots could have been Acerbus's own – both he and Graecus preferred to wear boots rather than the shoes to which Centurions were entitled.

As far as Graecus knew, Norbanus, who wore shoes, had not recently been to Acerbus's tent, so who, of the officer class had been? He looked again at the shoe prints and now noticed that they were very small.

Could they have been made by a woman? Possibly. It would be very odd if they were a woman's footprints but it was all odd anyway.

Graecus stood up, his mind a jumble of uncomfortable thoughts, but he had come to do a job for Norbanus and he must do it so he began to sort through the documents on Acerbus's bed.

They were a mixture of old orders, personal letters and some letters relating to the family estates and Graecus began by sorting these into piles.

He recognised the old orders as he had received similar orders himself (except from the orders sent him by the legate) and he dealt with these first – folding them carefully and then tying them together with a piece of string he found on the tent floor.

The letters relating to Acerbus's family estates were next. Graecus did not want to read them – they were none of his business, but he needed to glance at them to ensure that he was putting them in the correct pile and he noticed that they were mostly from Acerbus's cousin, Sextus Caelius Caldus – the Roman Senator.

Graecus sat on Acerbus's bed as he put these letters in order. He thought that putting them in order of the date they were written would be best and, as he began to open the correspondence, he smiled.

He smiled because he was remembering what Acerbus had said about his cousin, the Senator.

He had said that he was a man of such honesty and conscience that his nickname in the Senate was 'Integritus' but that he was so long-winded in his speeches and his declamations that his other, more common, nickname was 'Interminatus.'

Graecus remembered this and could hear again Acerbus's explosion of laughter and how he had had to stand back to avoid being covered in spittle as Acerbus split his sides at his own joke.

He began to sort the letters, noting the dates as he did so.

The letters seemed to follow a pattern.

Integritus would write three times a year giving Acerbus news of the family estates – Graecus was not reading the letters but he could not help noticing the general drift of them as he unfolded the parchment and looked for the dates.

The first of the letters was dated eight years before – about the time when Acerbus was first posted to Lower Germania and came into Graecus's life – and seemed to be all about the harvest and the profits which had been made from selling the olives and the grapes. This letter was two pages long and the second page was devoted to family news.

Graecus went back to the pile of letters to find the second in the sequence and saw that it was dated three months after the first. He refolded it and put it on top of the first letter.

Now he looked for the third letter in the sequence and found it; it was dated six months after the previous letter.

Graecus was trying very hard not to read the letters but it was difficult not to notice their contents and, keen student of calligraphy that he was, it was impossible not to notice Integritus's very strange handwriting which would be flowing and as normal as any other hand and then there would suddenly be a letter on its side or back to front or even upside down. This peculiarity was not uniform in that it was not always the same letters which were wrongly placed – in fact, it appeared that all the letters of the alphabet at one time or another, suffered from this misalignment.

Graecus now had six epistles in date order in his pile and picked up the seventh letter.

It was written from Rome and dated from the spring four years previously. The first paragraph appeared to be news about close relatives and, in trying not to read it, Graecus decided to pay attention to the odd lettering.

The first odd letter was an 'n' on its side, the next was an 'e' which was written backwards, the third was an 'r' upside down and the fourth was a squashed 'o.'

Graecus felt a prickle of fear at the back of his neck.

'n-e-r-o.'

'Nero.'

It was a code.

He quickly scanned the rest of the letter.

'n-e-r-o-m-a-d-d-e-r-t-h-a-n-e-v-e-r-b-u-r-r-u-s-d-e-s-p-a-i-r-s-b-u-t-o-u-r-p-l-a-n-g-o-i-n-g-b-a-d-l-y'

It was definitely a code and a stupidly unsophisticated one at that. Graecus threw the letter to one side and moved on to the next, reading the coded letters: 'n-o-h-o-p-e-o-f-s-e-n-a-t-e-b-a-c-k-i-n-g-f-o-r-c-o-u-p.'

This was worse than he could have imagined; Acerbus and his cousin were plotting to depose Nero. But surely Burrus, his long standing adviser, could not be involved?

Graecus put this letter aside and moved onto the next in the sequence, a letter written in the autumn, four years previously.

He paid no attention to the details of the harvest and its handsome profits but read the coded words feverishly: 't-h-e-b-o-y-i-s-o-u-r-b-e-s-t-c-h-a-n-c-e'.

'The boy is our best chance.'

The boy is our best chance?

A horrible thought entered Graecus's mind.

He went on to the next letter, dated the following spring and read the code: 'p-l-e-b-s-l-a-c-k-f-a-i-t-h-i-n-N-a-t-r-u-e-r-u-l-e-r-n-e-e-d-e-d.

The horrible thought stayed in Graecus's mind.

He went on to the next letter where the code read: 'm-a-k-e-s-u-r-e-b-o-y-h-a-s-a-l-l-s-k-i-l-l-s.'

Graecus could read no more. He threw the letter aside with disgust.

He saw now what had been going on between Acerbus and his cousin.

He saw that they were plotting to oust Nero and that the 'boy' was Germanicus –everyone knew that Nero's claim to the imperial throne was tenuous, he was Claudius's son by adoption only, and his popularity was wearing thin – perhaps the people would be persuaded to take an honest young soldier as their ruler, especially if his claim was one of the true blood...

Graecus's disgust ebbed away as his thoughts strayed to the possibility of Germanicus becoming Emperor of Rome. He day-dreamed of how wonderful Rome could be if it were ruled by a fair, just, decent man and how Germanicus could be relied upon not to allow all that power to corrupt his ideals. Graecus saw himself as the young Emperor's adviser and fondly imagined himself dispensing wise counsel to his son.

His son.

Well, there was the problem. Germanicus was his son, but only by adoption... the identity of his blood father would be the source of his claim but was also the greatest threat to his safety.

This was madness. Graecus could not allow these letters to be sent back to Acerbus's family – the less that was known about Germanicus's real father and the fewer the people who knew the better. Graecus could not take the risk that the secret he and Acerbus had shared for so long would be brought out into the open in Rome.

No, he must destroy the letters.

He bundled them up and tied them with string. He would burn them himself later but he began to think about what Acerbus might have said in *his* letters to Integritus and was deeply concerned that a cache of letters could be lying in Nero's hands at that moment and that they would signal his son's doom.

Graecus passed a hand wearily over his brow. Why was life so complicated? Why did people feel the need to lie and cheat and to clamber over other people in order to fulfil their vaunting ambitions? Why were the rulers of the greatest empire the world had ever seen so corrupt, so depraved, so venal? Why could they not be more like Flavius who was powerful but fair and decent and honest?

He realised that he felt angry with Integritus and even angrier with Acerbus for having gambled with his son's future. How could Acerbus have so callously sought to use him as a political pawn?

Graecus was suddenly so incensed with Acerbus that the bile rose in his throat and, had his old friend been present, he would have put his hands round his scraggy little neck and throttled him. He realised that he was muttering the words 'How *dare* he, how *could* he?' over and over again and tried to calm himself by breathing deeply. He listened to the sound of his own breath coming and going, in and out for a few seconds and closed his eyes.

'Graecus, I wanted what was best for Rome. I never wanted to harm Germanicus, I just wanted fair government to be restored to Rome,' said a loud voice.

Graecus opened his eyes expecting, by some miracle, to see Acerbus standing in front of him but there was no one there – the tent was empty apart from him.

Who had spoken, then?

'*I* spoke to you,' said Acerbus's voice.

'But you died this morning.'

'Yes, I did but just because I stopped breathing, doesn't mean that I can allow you to think badly of me. I want you to understand why I did what I did. I want you to understand that Rome is greater than any one person, even an Emperor, particularly if that Emperor is Nero, and that Rome needs a Germanicus so that she can be truly great.'

'I am very confused. I seem to be hearing you perfectly clearly but there is no one else here, and anyway, you're dead.'

'Well, I can hear you clearly and you're not speaking – we're having this conversation in your head – it's possible for me to speak to you from beyond the grave by talking straight into your head and what I want you to know is that I did it with the best of intentions and I do not wish you to think badly of me.'

'I am angry that you did this behind my back and without thought for Germanicus's safety. You, more than anyone, know how dangerous Rome and the Imperial Court are for my son and yet you plotted with your cousin to oust Nero and replace him with Germanicus.'

'Yes, we did, but we had not gone any further than just have the actual idea. We knew that he was still too young and that he needed to have more experience of life before he could seriously be considered as a candidate so we knew we would have to wait a while and we had not yet involved anyone else in our plan.'

'Well, I am grateful for that at least. When would you have tried to make Germanicus Emperor, then?'

But there was no answer. Acerbus had gone. If he had been there, that is. Maybe this 'conversation' was just a figment of an exhausted mind. Maybe Acerbus had not communicated with him at all but it *had* been his voice and it had been his way of putting things, and in any event, it had been a very useful 'conversation.' Maybe Acerbus could still be Graecus's mentor even from the afterlife.

Graecus found this very comforting and his anger melted; he could afford to feel proud that patrician Romans wanted *his* son for their Emperor. Yes, he could afford to feel proud because, now that he knew of their hatchling plot, he could make sure that it was never going to happen – he could make sure that Germanicus would never set foot in Rome.

CHAPTER EIGHTEEN

Graecus quickly sorted the rest of the letters, the personal ones, without looking at anything in them but the date – if Acerbus had had sixteen children by different women (which, granted, was unlikely) Graecus really did not wish to know – then he tied them into a bundle and, picking up the rest of Acerbus's correspondence, he left the tent and went back to his own section of the auxiliary lines.

Felix was standing in front of a blazing brazier on which sat a steaming pot while many of Graecus's men stood around inhaling the glorious smell of boiling fowl, onions, carrots and leeks which Felix was busily stirring while humming to himself.

Graecus was anxious to burn the incriminating letters and so told his men to stop loitering and find something useful to do. Then he waited until Felix had one of his coughing fits and was distracted from the job in hand so that Graecus could quickly slip the letters into the brazier without Felix knowing – the less anyone knew about this, the better.

The parchment of the offending correspondence was compatible with the wood and the coals in the brazier and was soon blazing merrily away while Felix was still standing there, wooden spoon in his hand, eyes closed, coughing and spluttering.

Eventually, Felix stopped coughing and opened his eyes.

'It smells wonderful, my friend,' said Graecus.

'Well, I hope it smells better than rotting Britons,' said Felix. 'I'd like to get *that* smell out of my nostrils – there's nothing worse, it sticks to you longer than the smell of a cheap whore.'

'Indeed,' said Graecus, wondering whether this unusually sharp observation from Felix meant that Acerbus was whispering in his ear also.

The letters had disappeared without trace in the brazier and Graecus silently gave thanks to any god who was listening that he had been able to dispose of the evidence so cleanly and effectively. Now he must take the rest of the letters to Norbanus's *optio*, his second in command, and he went to find the tent where the Legion's administrative staff did whatever it was that they did all day. When he got to the tent, he went straight to the *optio*, introduced himself and offered him the letters.

'Just put them there,' the man said, almost without looking up from his columns of figures. 'I'll deal with them later. You may go.'

Graecus felt this was unnecessarily rude and dismissive and thought, not for the first time, that those who were second in command in a unit were often more arrogant than the Commander himself. Then he went back to his own unit where he had a very satisfying supper from Felix's pot and, after a few cupfuls of wine and a few songs, he went to bed and slept soundly for what seemed like days.

The following morning, Graecus and his men were ordered back to the battlefield where there was still work to do disposing of enemy corpses and he had cause to recollect Felix's remark from the night before.

The battlefield was beginning to be cleared and grass was now visible in between what had been a carpet of dead Britons but it was horrible work. No one, not one soldier ever in the history of combat ever liked this job. It was heavy work – some of the fallen were giants of men and while you were carrying them across the field to the mass graves, you could not help but look at their faces and wonder who they had been in life – whose son, whose father, whose brother, whose husband? And where the fallen were women, it was even more poignant.

And they stank. They stank of dried blood and congealed gizzards, and sometimes, where a fallen warrior had suffered a deep abdominal wound, they stank of shit, but it was the worst smelling shit you had ever encountered.

This was all bad enough, but where the crows had found the corpse before the burial party, then there was also the fact that its eyes could have been taken as a tasty morsel by the ever present carrion wheeling over the valley or its face could have been torn to shreds by their vicious beaks and, to Graecus, this seemed much more revolting than any damage inflicted by a Roman gladius.

Graecus, ever a stickler for cleanliness, hated this job more than any other and was pleased when he saw Norbanus striding across the field in his direction.

'Hail, Centurion!' Norbanus called to Graecus from a few yards away.

'Good morning, sir,' said Graecus.

'I just wanted to ask you a quick question,' said Norbanus. 'Those letters, Acerbus's letters, which you left with my *optio*, were they the only ones you could find? Were they the only letters in our late brother's tent?'

Graecus's heart had been pounding with the physical exertion of moving large corpses all morning but now his heart stopped dead in his chest. What was Norbanus asking him, did he know about Integritus's letters? If so, how much did he know about the letters?

'The thing is,' continued Norbanus cheerfully, 'I wonder what happened to all those letters he used to get from his cousin – I mean, they wrote to each other several times a year, about family business and all of that.'

'Humph,' thought Graecus, 'about family business and about deposing Nero so that they could replace him with my son.' But what he said was, 'Were they important, then, the letters from Integritus?'

'Not especially as far as I know, but now that Acerbus is dead, his family will expect to have the letters returned. Did you see them, then? Have you got them?'

Graecus did not know what to say and pretended to remove a non-existent fly from his eye while he thought about his reply. 'I need to relieve myself,' he said. 'Let us walk to the bushes.'

At the edge of the valley, Graecus turned to face Norbanus and looked at him searchingly for a full minute. Then he said, 'I found Integritus's letters but I have burned them.'

'*Burned them?* Why on earth did you do that? How am I to explain to a Senator that we've burned his letters?'

'If you had seen them yourself you would have understood

that I burned them for the Senator's own protection.'

'What? Because he could have been blackmailed or something, is that what you mean?'

'Up to a point but it was worse, much worse than that. Integritus is in great danger and the letters were evidence against him.'

Norbanus was silent, turning what Graecus had said over and over in his mind.

'It's something to do with Germanicus, isn't it?' he said suddenly and, thought Graecus, a little triumphantly, as if pleased by his own forensic powers.

Graecus needed to decide whether he could trust Norbanus with this latest piece of dangerous information – he had not liked Norbanus's note of triumph just now but, in the past few months, he and the Senior Centurion had shared other secrets and Norbanus *had* saved Germanicus from being tried for murder.

There was no real choice. 'Integritus and Acerbus were plotting to overthrow Nero,' said Graecus in a low voice.

'And replace him with Germanicus?' said Norbanus incredulously.

Graecus nodded.

'Ye gods!' said Norbanus letting out a long slow whistle. 'But why Germanicus? What's so special about him, other than that he's now a war hero, that is? I mean, he's a wonderful example of what the flower of Rome should be but he has no connections in Rome, he's an auxiliary. He probably doesn't even know who his real father is...'

Graecus could see that Norbanus's mind was casting about trying to make sense of what seemed incomprehensible, but then Norbanus had another thought. 'Wait a minute!' he said. 'That useless creep Verus was interested in your son, wasn't he? He had the unlovely Solitarius spying on him, didn't he? What's going on here? You must tell me!'

'I cannot tell you as it will put you in danger and widen the circle of those who can harm my son.'

'But he isn't really your son is he? He's your son by adoption. Whose son is he? *That* is what this is all about really isn't it?' said Norbanus.

'Your powers of deduction do you great credit,' said Graecus wearily.

'So, I am on the right track. So, he must be the blood son of someone very important, someone who would given him a good claim to the empire... well, that would need to be someone who could give him a better claim than Nero's... someone in the Julio-Claudian dynasty...' said Norbanus, pacing up and down between the bushes.

Then: 'I've got it! He has to be Claudius's son! That's the only deduction which makes sense, and the timing fits. It's very unlikely that he's Caligula's because he preferred boys or his own sisters, and anyway, he was hated by the end of his reign so it *has to be Claudius.*'

'Please keep your voice down,' said Graecus. 'The lives of those I love depend on this fact being known by as few people as possible.'

'Yes, I see that,' said Norbanus. 'But doesn't Verus know already? Isn't that why he was spying on your boy?'

'Yes, that sadly is true, and – I hate to say it – but his ghastly cousin Vulponia knows it also.'

Norbanus groaned and put his head in his hands saying, 'Your boy is as good as dead, then. You know as well as I do that those two are pure poison.'

'Yes, I know their evil natures well enough but all is not lost – Flavius has used his influence these last seven or eight years to keep us well away from any power struggles and, as long as we have his protection and Germanicus does not draw attention to himself, I feel there is hope for my boy's future.'

Oh, my dear fellow, you are so naïve – do you not see that Germanicus has already drawn attention to himself – he is a war hero! He is a war hero at a time when Rome needs heroes; when Nero wants good news to keep the plebs sweet.'

'But we are mere auxiliaries, we are nobodies – Rome will not be interested in us,' said Graecus.

'For an intelligent man, you are remarkably stupid at times,' said Norbanus. 'Do you not see that the fact that you are nobodies would make you all the more attractive to Nero for then he could make much of you, make you his little pets, showing how generous he is, without at the same time putting himself in any danger of being outclassed... Well, on the face of it that would be true, but if it became known that Germanicus is Claudius's blood son, then Nero would have to find a way of dealing with his popularity... this is a very knotty problem indeed and the best you can hope for is that you can stay well away from Nero and Roman politics.'

'That is what I intend to do,' said Graecus.

'But tell me, why are you and the others so convinced that Germanicus actually *is* Claudius's son?'

'Because of the resemblance. It was Acerbus who noticed it first – when Germanicus happened to be standing next to a bust of our late Emperor – and then Flavius noticed it for the same reason but, by then, I had already had an indication that both Vulponia and Verus had noticed it themselves and since then, since we came to this infernal island which seems to be littered with busts of Claudius, I've worked hard to ensure that Germanicus is never seen standing next to one of them.'

'Oh my dear fellow,' said Norbanus, 'life is not easy, is it?'

'No. it is not. But I know that in many ways I am a rich man for unlike the glittering, ambitious thrusting new men of Rome, I know that I am genuinely loved by my son and my friends, any one of whom would take the sword's blow for me. There are not many men in Rome who could say the same.'

No, there are not, and there are days when I have to give unpopular orders, usually from one of the legates, when I know that my men would rather kill me than die for me so you are richer than me.'

Another thought dropped into Graecus's head. 'There is something else I must tell you,' he said. 'Something about those letters.'

'Yes? What about them?'

'Well, we are not the only people interested in them. Someone else must have wanted them, or wanted something from Acerbus's tent, anyway, because when I got there, the place had been ransacked – Acerbus was a tidy man and his tent was in chaos.'

'But who could have wanted to go through his things, and if they did, did they find what they wanted?'

'I do not know. All I know is that there were footprints in the dust on the floor – some of them came from Acerbus's nailed boots but there was another set – from someone wearing shoes – someone with very small feet – so small, they could even have been a woman's footprints.'

'This is beginning to sound very far-fetched. The only women in camp now are slaves – most of whom cannot read so I do not see how they could be wanting to see Acerbus's letters from his cousin,' said Norbanus.

'Nor do I,' said Graecus. 'And, in any event, the incriminating passages in the letters, the passages about replacing Nero with Germanicus, were in code so I doubt that an illiterate slave girl would have been any the wiser had she looked at them for weeks on end.'

'My mind is reeling with what you have told me and I need time to think about it,' said Norbanus. 'I am going back to my tent, farewell.'

'Farewell,' said Graecus and went back to the ghastly job of clearing the battlefield.

* * *

The valley where thousands of brave men and women lost their lives and where Boudicca's hopes of freedom for the Britons were dashed was cleared by the middle of the following afternoon and Graecus was relieved that he would now be able to wash the smell of death from his hair, his body and his nose.

The following few days were taken up with administrative duties – reviewing supplies with Impedimentus, checking on the wounded with Magnus and, with Incitatus, ensuring that the century's records were up to date. After the excitement of the battle and its aftermath, this period of calm was a welcome respite to Graecus and his men who could allow their exhausted minds and bodies to rest and recuperate.

But this peaceful period could not last for long.

Rumours filtered through the camp that new orders had come from Rome and there was the usual speculation as to what they were. One of the more incredible stories was that they were all to be posted to the far north of Britannia to quell the Scots and, at the other extreme, that they would be shipped to North Africa. Graecus had heard wild rumours before and decided that it was best not to think about what would happen next until the orders were actually given.

They came soon enough – on the seventh day after the battle.

It was the legions who had their orders first.

Norbanus told them that Nero had personally ordered them to seek out the leaders of the rebellious Britons and kill them and their families – man, woman and child – then burn their houses and any crops so that no Briton would ever be tempted to defy Rome again. Reinforcements would be coming from Germany to assist in this task.

Graecus and his men were still waiting for their orders but then Graecus was told to attend a meeting with Suetonius.

When he entered Suetonius's tent within a tent, he was relieved to see Norbanus sitting to one side of their General, but the legates sat on the other.

'Welcome!' said Suetonius. 'Have a seat. I have good news for you.'

'Yes, my lord?'

'Yes, your century is to be given a special task.'

'Yes, my lord?'

'Hmm, indeed; we have it on good authority that the Iceni have much treasure – gold and silver – and we want you to find it. We've been looking at that fool, Catus Decianus's, books of account and he states that old Prasutagus had more wealth, much more, than was mentioned in his will and, now that Boudicca is out of the way, Nero hopes to be able to get his hands on the whole of his rightful inheritance.'

'I see, my lord. Does Catus Decianus give us any information about where this treasure can be found.'

'Yes, he does,' said Clueless, butting in while his commanding officer drew breath. Clueless was more animated than Graecus had ever seen before and it was obvious that gold excited him much more than battle. 'He tells us that it is hidden at the Iceni Great Temple so all you need to do is to go there, find it and bring it back and Nero will be even more delighted with us than he is already,' Clueless said, his eyes shining like those of an enthusiastic puppy keen to please its master.

There was much that Graecus disliked about Clueless, so he addressed his next remark to Suetonius. 'And what has happened to Boudicca? Do we know where she has gone?'

'No,' said Suetonius, 'she vanished into thin air. No one can recall seeing her after the battle turned against her – she and her daughters left the battlefield, but there is a rumour that she took poison and, given her situation, that was probably the best choice – a proud woman like that wouldn't want to be paraded through Rome as Nero's captive, would she now?'

'Probably not, my lord. When do we leave for this Great Temple?'

'Tomorrow morning,' said Clueless, his lust for gold again ousting the good manners he should have accorded to his General.

Graecus thought for a few moments of the task that lay ahead and then said, 'My lord, is it possible for me to see Catus's records – I feel it would make our task easier if I knew exactly what our Procurator said.'

'I see no reason why not. Do you not have the records here?' said Suetonius, looking at Clueless.

'Yes, I do, my lord. The Centurion may come to get them. They are here beside me on the floor.'

Graecus knew he was being kept very strictly in his place by the legate – he was only an auxiliary, after all, and of no importance – so he stood and went to the table where the legates sat and bent down to pick up the pile of documents lying on the floor at Clueless's feet.

It was a large pile and it took Graecus several moments to bundle the documents into his arms, trying not to smear them with dust, and then, just as he rose from the floor, he glanced at the legate's feet to make sure that he had picked up all the documents.

Clueless had very small feet. Just like a woman's feet, really, in their neat little leather shoes.

* * *

Graecus and his men set off early the following day, with a small escort of infantry cavalry. Graecus and Incitatus had spent several hours the previous evening poring over Catus's records then they and Impedimentus had worked out the route they would take to this place deep in Iceni lands, about sixty miles north west of Camoludunum.

It was a glorious, golden late summer's day, with the sun glinting through the canopies of trees and bouncing back from the rocks which sometimes lined their way, and as they passed through mile after mile of rolling countryside, Graecus thought that this island was not really as poisonous as it had seemed when they first landed. In fact, in the sunlight, it was very calming, and now that the road ahead had been cleared by the legionaries, Graecus could just amble peacefully along on Perdix and observe the scenery.

Of course, it was lonely without Acerbus and Graecus spent several hours thinking about his friend and colleague and, at the end of this long contemplation, he realised that he had fully forgiven Acerbus and his cousin for wanting to make Germanicus Emperor – they only wanted what was best for Rome, and it *was* flattering that they thought that his son, brought up in accordance with his principles, would be the best leader for the greatest empire the world had ever known.

Then his mind turned to more immediate matters and he recalled the hurried conversation he had had with Norbanus at first light that morning when he had told Norbanus that he strongly suspected that it had been Clueless who had been fishing about in Acerbus's tent.

Norbanus had not been surprised and had said, 'Oh, he's another in the same mould as Verus – all ambition and no balls. I'll keep an extra vigilant eye on him from now on.'

As he rode, Graecus tried to work out the meaning of Clueless's interest in Acerbus's belongings and, after turning it over in his mind several times, was forced to come to the uncomfortable conclusion he had reached many times before – that much of Roman government was rotten and that Clueless was hoping to find something which he could use to his own advantage. Graecus hoped that it was nothing more than that – that Clueless was clueless as far as the plot to depose Nero and replace him with Germanicus was concerned – but he could not be sure.

The journey to the Great Temple took five and a half days, all of them dry and bright and Graecus and his companions saw the amazing structure from far away, long before they were standing in front of it.

From a distance it looked like a series of enormous wooden palisades surrounded by a huge ditch. It was rectangular with just one entrance and Graecus signalled to the horsemen and his men to make for that point.

They arrived as the late afternoon sun began to cast shadows and, as Graecus brought Perdix to a halt, he could feel the relief of his men behind him that, after this long hard march, they had come to their destination.

Graecus dismounted and told his men to stand easy and refresh themselves while he took the leather pouch from his waist and poured its contents over his head, gratefully gulping some of the water into his mouth as it ran over his closed eyes down his face.

'Centurion?' said a voice.

Graecus quickly opened his eyes and looked ahead of himself to see who had addressed him but there was no one there.

'Centurion' said the voice again and Graecus thought for just a moment that it was Acerbus again but it did not sound like him – the voice was accented, not Roman.

'Centurion!' said the voice again and Graecus realised that it was coming from his elbow.

He looked down and into a pair of sky blue eyes.

The eyes were laughing and Graecus laughed too.

'Brother,' said the legionary, 'you did not expect to see me down here, did you? You expected someone taller. Well, it happens all the time – I think I must be the shortest man in the cavalry.'

Graecus could believe it – the man was fully two heads shorter than him and had a brown, very lined face but it bore the sunniest of smiles and Graecus felt pleased that, after all the intrigues of the past few months and the horrors of the battle, this place seemed to be open and friendly.

'Welcome!' said the little man. 'We are delighted to see you. It has been a lonely time here for me and my men.'

Graecus now saw that the man was a Decurion – a cavalry officer in charge of ten horses. Indeed, now that he looked at him again, Graecus saw that the little man might have been born in the saddle as his legs were so bowed that a forearm's length of daylight was visible through his splayed thighs.

'Is it just you and your men, here then? Is there no one else?'

'No, we were sent here six days ago – as soon as it became clear that we'd won the battle against Boudicca – and we were told that it was our job to stop the Iceni from reclaiming some treasure or something, something that's buried here.'

'That's why we've come, we're supposed to find it and send it to Rome for Nero. Have you seen any Iceni since you've been here?'

'No. I must admit that, before you came, we were feeling very undermanned for the task given to us but we've seen no sign of trouble.'

'Well, the legions were given the order to kill any Iceni rebels they could find, man, woman and child and they've probably been doing their job with their usual efficiency.'

'That is it for us here then. We leave tomorrow. We have orders to return to our fort.'

'Well, brother, that will not stop you and your men enjoying the best supper you have had in a long time – our cook is the best in all the Army and you must eat with us tonight!' said Graecus who liked the look of the Decurion and was always very proud of Felix's skills – and always very good at producing other mouths for him to feed.

Felix was soon busy with his knives, skinning hare, chopping turnips and onions adding herbs and his own culinary magic to his boiling pots while the soldiers set up their camp and looked around them at this new place which was to be their home... for how long?

For as long as it took to find what Nero wanted... as long as it took to find the buried 'treasure' in this isolated place.

* * *

The Decurion and his men left early the following day together with the horsemen who had escorted Graecus's century there – setting off in a cloud of dust and a clatter of hooves – leaving Graecus and his men in charge of the Great Temple.

When the sound of the hooves had disappeared into the distance, there was a deep silence broken only by the gentle twitterings of songbirds and Graecus looked around him at the vastness of the temple and tried to begin to plan how he and his men would find the 'treasure' in this huge place.

He thought of it as 'treasure' in his mind as he had no idea exactly for what he was looking – Catus Decianus's records merely said that Prasutagus, while he was a client king of Rome, had not revealed the full extent of his wealth and Catus had surmised that this meant that the half of his kingdom which he left to Nero was a meagre part of his true estate. Catus had then gone on to extrapolate from this that Prasutagus probably had valuables, gold and silver, hidden somewhere and that they would most likely be found at the Great Temple.

Really it was no more than that. It was a supposition made by a greedy tax collector who would have wanted to get his own hands on the money had he not been forced to flee the country first. This was not helpful from Graecus's viewpoint as he felt he had been sent on a wild goose chase and that it was likely that he would upset some very powerful people when he failed to find the 'treasure.'

With these thoughts in his head, he looked around again, trying to put himself into the minds of the Iceni and where they would bury their treasure, if they had had any to bury.

It was difficult. One of his problems was that this 'Temple' was nothing like any temple he had ever seen – there was no altar, there seemed to be no particular spot where the priests would perform their rites – in fact it just looked like a big open-air theatre, dotted with trees enclosed by the wooden fences with standing space for many, many people.

Then he thought that the 'treasure' must have been buried fairly recently – after all, Prasutagus had been dead for only two years, and if it had been buried at the time of his death, surely there would be some sign of disturbance of the ground. Yes, that would be the first thing they would do, they would survey this huge space for signs of the soil having been moved.

Graecus called his men and allotted to each of them a portion of the site which was his to observe and investigate – if any man found anything of interest he was to call Graecus immediately.

The men set off to their plots, each carrying a spade, and began their investigations, walking carefully in straight lines along the land looking for anything which might indicate something unusual.

Graecus knew from the expressions on his men's faces that they also felt this was a waste of time – Pneumaticus in particular gave him a withering look and Graecus had to raise an eyebrow at him to remind him that he had been given an order by his Centurion and he should obey it. But he still felt foolish and ineffectual.

Some of the men came back before the end of the morning to say that they had found nothing and Graecus told them that they could not have looked properly in that short time and they must look again.

Graecus felt more and more discomfited as he watched his men patrolling the land, walking backwards and forwards on their allotted plots as if it were some kind of offering to the gods and he wished he could think of a better way to find the 'treasure', if it existed.

But, in the middle of the afternoon, Impedimentus left his plot and came to Graecus to tell him, with his usual attention to detail, that there was a patch of earth which felt different underfoot from the ground around it and he thought that the grass over this patch looked a brighter green. Graecus told him to start digging and Impedimentus went back to his patch to begin work with his spade while the other men continued to patrol their plots.

Graecus had no great hopes that Impedimentus would find anything and was not paying any attention to his labours. He was surprised therefore when his baggage master called him over to view his work.

'I think there is something buried here,' said Impedimentus. 'Look at the way the soil is freely falling from my spade, and it seems to be a different colour from the surrounding earth.'

'Yes, I agree,' said Graecus and went to fetch a spade so that he could feel useful.

The two men dug for the remainder of the afternoon and the soil became darker and darker as they dug. By the time the light failed they had dug a pit several feet wide and deep enough to require shuttering at its sides but there was no sign of anything buried in it, only the dark soil and a strong, musky, mossy smell.

Graecus did not know what to make of this but it was the only piece of ground so far which had thrown up anything interesting, and when he called a halt to the day's work, he told Impedimentus that they would resume their digging the following day.

Graecus was sure that there was no 'treasure' to be found in Impedimentus's pit and did not post a guard there overnight thinking that the presence of the century's camp just outside the walls of the palisade would suffice.

* * *

Graecus's century spent a peaceful night in their camp at the Temple and woke to a dry sunny day – ideal for digging.

After breakfast, Graecus attended to a few administrative tasks, reviewing manpower with Incitatus and was looking at the sorry list of men lost since they left Lower Germania when a flushed Impedimentus appeared.

'Domine,' he said breathlessly, and attracted Graecus's full attention for Impedimentus, with his Roman ways, normally found it hard to give Graecus his full rank.

'Domine, come and look at the hole we dug yesterday – we must have had visitors in the night!'

'What do you mean?'

'There are footprints in the earth.'

Graecus groaned inwardly. Footprints again. More intrigue.

'I will return later,' Graecus said to Incitatus and went with Impedimentus back to the hole.

'See here!' said Impedimentus. 'Look, there are three sets of footprints.'

The baggage master was crouching down next to the one of the mounds of earth which he and Graecus had excavated from the ground the previous day and he was correct – there were footprints and it was clear that they had not been made by soldiers.

Graecus squatted next to Impedimentus and looked more closely at the footprints. They had been made by shod feet but the shoes were not of the strong leather type worn by Romans or the 'civilised' world. The shoes must have been very soft, prob- ably made from some type of fabric or animal skin tied around the feet and this made the footprints more indistinct than they would have been otherwise but it was still possible to see that there, indeed, were three sets of prints – small, medium and large – as if a man, a woman and a child had been there.

'You are correct,' said Graecus to Impedimentus, 'but what is puzzling me is that whoever was here last night did not disturb the hole – whatever is in there, if anything, is still intact.'

'Maybe there is nothing there.'

'That is what is worrying me.'

'What happens if we do not find anything here?'

'Our current popularity will be short lived.'

'But we cannot find what is not here.'

'My views entirely but I suspect that the legates will find our failure unacceptable so it is best if you continue to dig. I will send three other men to help you,' said Graecus, walking away with a resigned sigh.

The digging recommenced and, with four men working at it, there was soon a large hole but still no sign of anything having been buried although the excavated earth looked as if it had recently been disturbed.

Then, in the middle of the afternoon, a spade struck metal.

CHAPTER NINETEEN

On getting the exciting news, Graecus rushed over to the hole and jumped down into it next to Pneumaticus who was leaning on his spade.

'Well?' said the Centurion. 'What happened?'

'Oh, I just did this,' said Pneumaticus striking hard at the ground and producing a ringing note from the earth. 'And it did that – made that noise.'

'Go and get Incitatus immediately – tell him to stop whatever he is doing and come here now. Impedimentus, get me some brushes, the softest brushes that we have – I need as many as you can find.'

Pneumaticus and Impedimentus ran off to fulfil their orders and Graecus dropped to his knees at the spot where Pneumaticus's spade had struck.

He began rubbing away the earth with his hands, filling his finger nails with the moist brackish dirt, wishing all the while that he would discover that what lay beneath was gold.

He could feel cold metal under his hands. It was curved, like a dome, and so far, he could feel no edge to it.

Now he could see something glinting in the earth - just a glint of metal, nothing more than that but it was an encouragement that there really was something there. Graecus moved quickly, digging away with his dirty bare hands trying to reveal the earth's secret store.

Now he could see an edge to the metal. It too was curved and it looked as if the metal could be bronze. It was tarnished and could not be gold, but if whatever it was were bronze, then that could be encouraging – grave goods were often a mixture of metals – bronze, silver and gold. Could this be Prasutagus's treasure?

Graecus dug faster and soon revealed a rim – whatever this was had a rim. Well, a cooking pot had a rim but then so did a helmet and, so far, it was not clear that this hidden thing was either of those but, if asked, Graecus would have preferred that it were a helmet.

Now the others had returned, standing at the edge of the hole, staring intently down at their Centurion scrabbling away in the dirt with his bare hands trying by some obscure kind of alchemy to make treasure for Nero appear out of the ground.

Incitatus spoke first. 'Domine, do you wish us to come down to you?'

Graecus was irritated at his men's lack of urgency and said sharply, 'No, I do not. I wish to leave this hole and I want you to come down here, all of you, and free this object so that I can see what it is.'

The soldiers all recognised his exasperated tone and quickly jumped into the hole while Graecus scaled the ladder which was the way out of it. They set to work with their brushes and cleared away more earth from around the object.

There was a ridge between the halves of the dome which led to the rim… It was beginning to look much more like a helmet than a cooking pot.

But the Britons wore hardly any armour and Graecus had seen no evidence that they wore helmets. Then, as more dirt was cleared away, Graecus could see that it was indeed a helmet, possibly a fine helmet and of a type he did not know.

Graecus could not stand the suspense and, after saying to his men that they should continue to brush away and let him know when they had freed the object, he went to his tent and asked Felix for some honeyed water to calm himself.

He lay on his bed and thought about what could be done if this object were not part of the treasure and what he would do if they did not find the treasure but it was too difficult to see beyond the freeing of the helmet and, anyway, he was tired and he fell asleep.

He dreamed of Arminia, as he often did when he slept well and, in this dream, he and she were married and living with Germanicus and his wife and children and were all happy and contented together in a villa filled with sunshine and laughter surrounded by good vines and olive groves. It was a delicious dream and was so much what Graecus wanted for his later life that he was very displeased to be woken from it by Incitatus shaking him by the shoulder and telling him to wake up.

'Domine, domine, wake up, look at what we have unearthed!' he said.

Graecus rubbed his eyes and sat up, looking first at Incitatus whose face was a picture of excitement and then he looked at what he had in his hands.

'We need to clean it up but it is magnificent, is it not?' said Incitatus.

It *was* magnificent – a most wonderfully shaped, majestic helmet, fit for a prince, even in this dishevelled state.

Graecus took it in his hands, marvelled at its sweeping curves and was impressed by its reassuring weight. He somehow felt it was important to him personally and tried to feel a connection with the man who had worn it.

'Do you think it was Prasutagus's?' he said

'No, I do not,' said Incitatus softly. 'This helmet was not made here and it is much older than Prasutagus. I would bet a month's wages that this is Thracian and that it was made at least three hundred years ago.'

Graecus was astonished by this. He let his jaw drop and sat on his bed with the helmet in his hands, open-mouthed for a few minutes while he stared at it and saw that there could be truth in what Incitatus had just said. 'How do you know?' he asked.

'The Thracians are my countrymen's near neighbours and I have seen pictures in frescoes and statues of their warriors – warriors from their heroic past. I recognise this as being of the shape and design shown in those pictures, but even covered in dirt, you can see that this was made for a high born person.'

'Yes, I agree. Please clean all the dirt from it, I need to see it in all its glory. Do it now but do it carefully.'

'Yes, Domine, it will be a great pleasure for me to restore something like this. But what, in the names of all the gods was it doing lying in the ground at the Iceni Great Temple?'

'I have no idea and was hoping that you might have had one – the Thracians were your neighbours, after all,' said Graecus still uncertain as to the best way to search for the treasure but feeling buoyed by the discovery of the helmet.

'Well, you speak Greek, Domine, they could have been your ancestors,' said Incitatus lightly to Graecus's back as he left the tent to see what was happening in the hole.

Graecus quickly descended the ladder to where Germanicus and Impedimentus were on all fours, diligently brushing at the ground. Pneumaticus, who was older than them, stood shaking his legs saying, 'These creaky knees of mine are not happy squatting in a hole,' while Zig sniffed busily at the spot where Germanicus was working.

'Ah, father,' said Germanicus, 'I am glad you have come. I think I may have something here. It seems to be a collection of old bones.'

Graecus went and knelt next to his son and saw several small bones pointing up from the earth.

'Yes, I see what you mean. Go and get Magnus and we shall see if he can tell us what these are. I will keep brushing away at the soil around them while you are gone,' said Graecus.

Germanicus got to his feet with the agility of an acrobat and went to find Magnus while Graecus picked up the soft brush and began sweeping dirt from the bones but he knew well before his son's reappearance that what he was excavating was a human hand. There was no flesh on it and the bones were yellowed. Graecus stared at it, wondering how this hand was connected with the helmet. Freed from the soil which had been its resting place, the hand was pointing upwards and looked very vulnerable and fragile.

Graecus knew all about death and its aftermath, he had lived with it as a constant companion for all his adult life but there was something poignant about this relic of a hand, posed almost in greeting, something which he recognised, which caught his breath and brought an unexpected and unwanted lump to his throat. If this was not Prasutagus, who was it?

By the time that Germanicus returned with Magnus, Graecus had uncovered the whole of the skeletal hand, wrist and some of the forearm.

'Well,' said Magnus, 'what do we have here? Or whom, to be precise, as it is undoubtedly human, but whoever it was has been dead and buried these many years. But the soil has been disturbed recently. That is strange.'

'Yes, it is,' said Graecus. 'I do not know any more than you do at the moment, but we need to disinter our late friend here in case there are more clues. So far, he and his helmet are all we have. Carry on, men, and keep me informed of any developments.'

Graecus climbed out of the hole and stood for a few moments calming his pounding heart. The sun was high in the sky on this glorious late summer's afternoon with the sound of the breeze soughing gently through the oak trees as the background chorus for the singing of the birds. Standing at the edge of the hole, on this balmy day Graecus looked around him and suddenly saw loveliness.

This puzzled him because he had so often thought of this island as terrible and dreadful and inhospitable, but when it was quiet like this and peaceful and no one was trying to kill or main you or those you love, then it was really quite staggeringly beautiful – more subtle in its contours than much of the Mediterranean and more varied in its vegetation than Lower Germania, it had a quiet confidence which whispered grace. Graecus enjoyed this feeling for a while, breathing in the pure air of Britannia, marvelling at the gentle curves and bright greenness of her countryside and allowed his soul to rejoice in this foreign land. Now he really understood why Boudicca and her people would want to have their freedom, why they would want to have this land for themselves and live in it in their own way, in the ways of their forebears without interference from 'civilised' Rome with its insistence on taxes and tribute.

A little later, Graecus went back to his tent where Incitatus was working on the helmet but he found the atmosphere in the tent oppressive and could not stay, thinking that he could more usefully walk around the remainder of the site observing what the other men were doing and spent the rest of the afternoon encouraging them to keep looking and to start digging if they thought they saw something different. He knew that his men thought it was all a waste of time but they were good natured about it and probably felt that, after all the dramas of the past months, it was better than the alternatives.

The smell of cooking began to permeate the camp and realising that he was hungry Graecus went back to his tent in search of water to wash his dirty hands before supper. When he got to the tent, Incitatus was sitting on his bed polishing the helmet.

It took Graecus's breath away.

It was bright bronze, glinting in the shaft of light coming through the open tent flap, its smooth dome catching the early evening's rays and sending them back to Graecus who was temporarily blinded by its flashing light.

The smoothness of the dome was offset by the depth of detail of the creatures – fabulous sea-serpents with undulating tails like the waves of a boiling sea – which were emblazoned on the high cheek-pieces and rested on the curve of the neckpiece.

'It would have had a plume here,' said Incitatus indicating the ridge on the top of the dome. 'Look, there are holes in which it would have fitted. I have seen pictures of them and it would have been a tall, coloured plume, rather like the one you wear on your helmet now, but going from the front to back of the head. The workmanship is superb. Look at these serpents – they even have flames coming from their mouths and you can see their eyes.'

Graecus could hardly speak. He found the helmet over-whelming and, much to his embarrassment, it brought tears to his eyes. He pretended to remove a piece of grit from the corner of his left eye to give himself time to think and to try to understand why this helmet, this old helmet which had belonged to someone long dead, should make him feel so full of emotion. It made no sense. It was nonsense. He must calm himself.

Happily, Incitatus was not looking at him, he was examining the helmet, turning it round and round in his hands, murmuring, 'Magnificent, just magnificent.'

'Yes, it is. We are privileged to be able to see something so old and so well preserved. Please put it on my desk when you have finished,' said Graecus leaving the tent, grateful that the fresher air of the evening was cooling his face.

Pneumaticus appeared. 'We've cleared all the way around the skull,' he said, 'and there's something else down there. Magnus thinks it might be a horse.'

'Oh yes, they were great horsemen,' said Incitatus, coming out of the tent from behind Graecus. 'The Thracians were renowned for their horsemanship.'

'*Thracians?*' cried Pneumaticus. 'What have Thracians got to do with anything?'

'Incitatus is sure that the helmet we found here is Thracian and must be three hundred years old,' said Graecus feeling again the lump in his throat.

'But *why-y-y?*' said Pneumaticus, screwing up his face and wrinkling his nose in disbelief, saying yet again exactly what Graecus thought but in fewer words.

'We do not know and I cannot think how we would find the answer but we must keep digging, it is our only hope of finding the treasure,' said Graecus.

'Oh yes, the digging, we must keep digging,' said Pneumaticus in a voice which would have resulted in a month's latrine duty had it been used by anyone else.

The men were beginning to settle in this place and an essential part of their normal routine was re-established that evening with singing and story-telling after supper around the camp-fires. Graecus joined in and sang several of the plaintive songs which suited his clear tenor voice and was given a rapturous reception by his audience but he was disturbed that the lump in his throat kept intruding.

When it finally got dark, the men went to their tents and Graecus settled into his bed, but as he closed his eyes, he glanced at the helmet on the desk at his bedside and it seemed to glow in the moonlight.

* * *

Graecus dreamed. He dreamed of being in a softly rolling, green land dotted with oak trees and running streams which were misty in the early mornings. It was very beautiful. In the dream, he was himself but he looked different – his dark hair was long and straight and was caught in a knot on the top of his head. He was more muscled and shorter than his present body with deep olive skin but it was him and the grey eyes were the same.

The dream was of an earthly paradise where he and his red-headed comrades hunted the beasts out from the trees and across broad plains and tended to their prized horses, but best of all in the dream, Graecus made love to a blonde princess lying on top of her sky blue cloak and when, in calling out in her ecstasy she turned her face fully to him, he saw that she was the beautiful Iceni woman and he knew that they were sworn to each other as man and wife.

* * *

Graecus woke with tears in his eyes. It was not quite light and he lay on his back for some time remembering the dream and the wonderful feeling it had given him. The dream had been of a glorious life lived freely among gallant comrades and with a loving, lovely wife. But it was nothing to do with Rome. The country was not Italy, nor was it Lower Germania and the man seemed to be him – he saw the dream through the man's eyes – but the man looked different – squat and swarthy, even though he had grey eyes. It was very confusing and added to Graecus's discomfort at the strange feelings he experienced when he looked at the helmet.

Graecus squeezed his eyes shut and tried to blot out the dream and the helmet. He was a Centurion in the service of Rome and he had an important job to do. He was also responsible for the lives of eighty men; he could not afford to have his head turned by mystical dreams which were, he thought with a shudder, the stuff of the Druids in the land of the Druids. Graecus shook his head vigorously and sat up on his bed determined to be as hard-headed an officer as Nero would require.

The helmet sat on his desk, luminous in the morning light, and without his knowing that it was coming, a sob sprang from Graecus's mouth.

'Father!' said Germanicus. 'Are you ill?'

Graecus coughed and said, 'No, my son, I think I may have swallowed a small fly in my sleep and I was trying to dislodge it, that is all.'

'Oh, thank Jupiter. We never know what ills await us in this barbarian land,' said Germanicus, and then – from nowhere, without his knowing that he would say it, Graecus said very sharply, 'If you care to look closely at this land, through your own eyes and not through those of ambitious politicians and tax collectors, you might see that it had its own civilisation long before Caesar came.'

Each of them was astonished at this outburst and each looked at the other with amazement during the shocked silence between them.

Graecus's mind was reeling. What was the matter with him? It seemed as if he had been possessed by some alien force. He must *control* himself!

'My son, I do apologise most humbly to you,' he said. 'I spoke out of turn and too vehemently. My only defence is that I feel the weight of the responsibility of finding this so-called treasure and I have not the faintest idea where it may be.'

'Yes, father, I understand.'

'I am not sure that you do, Germanicus. You have not yet experienced the burden of command and the real weight of it. Sometimes, I feel it is more than I can bear,' said Graecus, aware that he had said more than he meant to say but that it was true – the loneliness was unbearable for him at times and he really missed Acerbus's wisdom and camaraderie.

Graecus sat with his head in his hands feeling both wretched and useless – wretched because he had been brusque with his son and useless because he could not find the treasure. He was vaguely aware that his men had tactfully left the tent and was grateful to be alone with his misery.

A beaker of hot honeyed water was thrust under his face.

'Drink that, you need the sweetness,' said Felix standing in front of Graecus, proffering the beaker with a stern face which brooked no argument. 'I am worried about you, Domine,' he continued. 'You have been very distant and a little strange these last few days. What is the matter with you?'

'Oh, my old friend, has it been so obvious? I had hoped that I was keeping my lack of good humour to myself.'

'Well, not everyone would notice but I have known you these many years. Have you had bad news – is it something you could tell me?' said Felix in a softer voice.

Graecus did not know where to start and, for one of the few times in his life, was lost for words.

How did you tell your oldest friend that you were losing your mind? That you had been bewitched by an old helmet? That a set of dusty yellow bones had reduced you to tears? That you had dreamed of being in Britannia three hundred years before and that you were then a Thracian married to the Iceni woman you had met the night before the battle with Boudicca?

Felix misinterpreted Graecus's silence and said, 'Is it a secret? I thought that we did not have secrets from one another.'

'No, my friend it is not a secret, rather it is that I do not know where to start to try to explain what it is that ails me. It is inexplicable.'

'Am I not clever enough to understand? Is that it?'

'No, not at all. It is that I fear that am not clever enough to explain but I will try, as long as you swear not to laugh at me.'

'On Jupiter's altar, I swear,' said Felix solemnly.

'Well, ever since we found this,' said Graecus, picking up the helmet and handing it to Felix, 'I have had the strongest feeling that it is, in some way, connected with me. I know that sounds far-fetched but the feeling became even stronger when I saw the bones of the hand of the man to whom the helmet probably belonged. His fingers were the same length as mine and his hands were the same breadth as mine and touching them brought a lump to my throat. Then last night I had a vivid dream that I, Graecus, had been here, living with the Britons as my comrades, but it was three hundred years ago and I was then a Thracian married to an Iceni princess.'

Graecus finished his earnest address and looked at Felix for his reaction.

Felix stared at his Centurion and then threw back his head and laughed for several minutes, fanning his face with his neck-erchief as he rocked backwards and forwards with mirth while Graecus resisted the urge to pour the honey water over his head.

'It is *not* funny,' said Graecus. 'It is most disturbing and it is unsettling me when I need to have all my wits about me.'

'No, no, you misunderstand me,' said Felix, his laughter ending in a coughing fit which made his eyes water and required the use of his neckerchief to dry them. 'I am not laughing at you, I am laughing with relief. When I have seen you so distressed these last few days, I thought it might have been something to do with your health and I could not bear to have another fright like the one we had just before the battle. What you have told me is a great relief and it is fascinating. So you think you have lived before?'

'Thinking seems to be the least of it. I am trying very hard not to think about it – it is much more what I *feel*. It is as if my body remembers – my body is reliving what I felt when I was here in this country before.'

'But if that is all true, then this helmet was yours!' said Felix triumphantly. 'You must put it on to see if it fits,' he said, doing what Graecus had not dared to do – placing the helmet over the Centurion's head.

It fitted perfectly. Graecus felt the pleasure of the accustomed weight and looked out at the world through a diminished view whose pattern he knew as well as the back of his own hand. It was shocking that it all felt so familiar; his body sang with recognition and long-held memories came flooding back.

In the leather contubernium tent in Britannia in Nero's Empire, Felix was gesturing animatedly to Graecus, saying that the helmet seemed to have been made for him, but Graecus had gone elsewhere – on a journey through time, back to when he had been the friend and ally of the Britons in his adopted country and had been the husband of the lovely Iceni woman. His heart ached for the happiness they had had and the joy of the freedom of his life then when he was his own master and had served no man. He heard voices in his head – the voices of his long dead friends calling to him, telling him that he was too slow in the hunt, urging him on to ride harder and faster, laughing with him around a fire in the depths of the winter with the furs soft and warm about his body and the embers smoking in the crisp, cold air.

Felix had stopped talking but now there was another voice in his head, a more recently remembered voice. It was Acerbus saying in his clear, loud way, 'Oh, so you put it on in the end! Your helmet, I mean. It took you long enough. Fits you like a glove – just like it did when it was made for you three hundred odd years ago. When you were Argoraax.'

'I do not understand any of this,' said Graecus in his head.

'Well, I do not profess to be an expert but I do have the advantage of being dead so I can tell you without fear of contradiction that the helmet is yours, or was yours when you were Argoraax the Thracian.'

'But that means that I have lived before.'

'Yes, you have, many times, and you will live many more lives after this one, as do we all.'

'But why?' thought Graecus, remembering Pneumaticus's pithy way of getting to the point.

'As I said, I am not an expert but from what I have learned here, in the place we go to between lives, we come and go and have different experiences in our various lives so that we can learn. It's like being part of a very special school.'

'But what is the subject we are learning?'

'Love. We are learning how to love.'

'And when have we learned enough about love?' Graecus asked in his head, pleased with his brevity, but Acerbus had gone.

Graecus felt faint, there was so much he needed to try to understand and he needed to clear his head. He took off the helmet and handed it to Felix while he pushed back the lock of hair which fell over his brow.

Felix opened his mouth to speak, but at that moment Incitatus came into the tent with a letter bearing a large, important-looking seal.

'This has just come,' he said. 'And the riders are waiting for a reply. It's urgent, they say.'

Graecus sat at his desk and opened the letter. It was from Clueless, and after the usual greetings, asked him to report on the progress he had made in finding the treasure, reminding him that Nero was relying on him to find Prastagus's hidden gold and silver. The body of the letter had been written by a scribe but the signature was Clueless's own – a large, formless scrawl which did nothing to enhance Graecus's opinion of him.

'Felix, give the riders food and wine and ask Germanicus to keep them amused while we make our reply,' said Graecus as he and Incitatus settled down to decide what to say to the legate.

'We've had only a few days in this vast area, and there were no clues as to what we are really looking for, nor where it is,' sighed Incitatus. 'He is very impatient.'

'Well, it is always possible that he has exaggerated to someone important our chances of finding anything. He may have wished to impress someone close to Nero, or even Nero himself.'

'But what shall we say?'

'We shall tell the truth.'

'What, that we've found an old helmet?'

'No, that we've found a priceless antique artefact,' said Graecus and began to dictate the letter to Incitatus beginning with warm greetings and delight that the legate had taken the trouble to write and enquire after progress. Then he went on to say that they had been very encouraged to find a valuable Thracian helmet which he felt was a sign that there was more to be unearthed; he chose his words carefully so that he was not telling lies but he knew it was a very particular form of the truth and was not how he would have expressed himself to Norbanus or Flavius.

Incitatus finished writing the Centurion's words in his precise, neat hand and Graecus wrote the final sentence, sending hopes for the good health of the legate, in his own bold hand and then signed the letter and gave it to Incitatus to hand to the riders so that Clueless would have the reply as soon as possible.

Graecus now sat on his bed, more concerned than ever that they would find no treasure and that Clueless's wrath would lead to vengeance. He picked up the helmet to remind himself of a life when he had been free of the need to pacify scum like that and sat, turning it in his hands trying to make some meaning of what Acerbus had said. His fingers played with the rim and he was asking the gods (and God) for understanding when he noticed that there was a rough patch on the inside of the brass dome, just above the rim and thought Incitatus had missed a piece of mud so he wet his finger with spit, and looking within the helmet, began to rub away at it.

But it was not mud, it was writing. It was very small writing and Graecus could not make it out so he went to the tent flap to view it in the sunlight. It was a Greek-looking script but he did not recognise the words. He called Incitatus over to have a look.

'Can you read this? You are our best scholar, what does it say?'

Incitatus squinted at it and turned the helmet round to get a better look at the tiny letters but he seemed to be having difficulty.

'I need to sit down and study it carefully,' he said.

'Do it now!' ordered Graecus. 'I want to know what it says.'

Incitatus was surprised by the urgency in Graecus's voice but went back into the tent and set to work with a wax tablet and stylus trying out various interpretations of the script. He made funny little noises while he was doing this – talking to himself and huffing and puffing, saying, 'No, that's not right, silly boy,' just as his tutors may have done years before when he was studying in Mediolanum, while Graecus hopped from foot to foot with impatience, and in the end, Incitatus had to tell him that he would do the job more quickly if he were left alone.

Graecus went to view the digging in the hole where the helmet had been found and saw that the body had been almost completely excavated. Magnus was also standing at the edge of the hole looking down.

'He was not very tall, not as tall as we are,' he said. 'But the bones look strong and I think he cannot have been very old when he died. The mystery is what he was doing here.'

Graecus could have enlightened his colleague as to some of what the Thracian had been doing but felt it was best to keep to a minimum the number of those who knew that the mysterious Thracian was none other than their Centurion in a life three hundred years earlier. But was it true? Was it really him or had he, by some means, found a way of entering the heart and mind of this long dead foreigner?

Incitatus came up behind them carrying the helmet.

'I have translated it, Domine. Do you wish to know what it says?'

'More than you can imagine,' said Graecus.

'Well, this is a rough translation, I would need to look at some old records to be sure but I think what it says is: 'Behold the helmet of Argoraax. Evil comes to him who steals it',' said Incitatus and wondered why Graecus had gone so pale so suddenly.

Graecus thought he would faint and fall into the hole and grabbed tightly onto Magnus's arm to steady himself. 'Did you say that the name was Argoraax?' he said.

'Yes,' said Incitatus, 'the lettering is quite clear, the man's name was Argoraax.'

'Remarkable, remarkable, utterly remarkable!' whispered Graecus.

There was a silence while the others wondered what their leader was finding so remarkable and he was saying silently to himself 'It *is* true, it *is* true. I am he and he is me.'

Magnus cleared his throat loudly to rouse them all from their reveries and Graecus looked carefully into the hole at the remains of what he had been.

'What is that on the top of his head?'

'Oh we think it is his hair,' said Impedimentus from the hole. 'We will see it properly when we finish uncovering his head, but it looks as if he had straight black hair and he wore it in a knot on top of his head. What a stupid fashion that must have been.'

'It was a sign of virility,' said Graecus, walking quickly away before anyone could ask him how he knew.

CHAPTER TWENTY

Graecus decided that he needed to know who the nocturnal visitors were who had left their footprints near the hole – they could have vital information. He persuaded himself that whatever information they might have would be useful in the search for the 'treasure' but he knew that what he really wanted from them was information about Argoraax –who was he and how he came to be in Britannia all those years ago?

He decided that he and Felix would keep watch on the hole that night and, to lure the visitors to the hole, he would place the helmet at its side. This was risk in this, he knew, but he had no other ideas and, if the visitors were only a man, woman and child, then he and Felix were more than a match for them.

They had a light supper and went to bed for a few hours before it was fully dark so that they might be refreshed and awake by the time that they took their places behind the oaks next to the hole. Neither of them had done sentry duty for many years and, at first, it was almost enjoyable for them to be sitting on their little stools on a fine, dry, moonlit night each one thinking of similar nights when they were young men on watch together. In the old days the most difficult thing had been not to giggle when one caught the other's eye and motioned to something funny but now the difficulty, despite the light supper and the nap, was to stay awake.

Graecus felt his eyelids drooping and, in the silence of the night, would have sworn that he heard Felix's eyes close. Even if he had not, the gentle snoring of his friend, soon made clear his restful state.

Graecus did not wish to make a noise in waking Felix, nor did he wish to allow him to keep on snoring as it was getting louder. He needed to poke him awake and so looked for a branch to use as a stick but there was none anywhere nearby. He rose from his stool, thinking that this had been a very stupid idea of his when he could be lying in his bed fast asleep rather than trying to find sticks in the dark to stop someone snoring, when he heard the sound of soft voices coming from beyond the curtain of trees.

Felix woke with a start and made a throat clearing noise which sounded deafening to Graecus but there was no pause in the sound of the voices which continued to make their way around the perimeter of the open space contained by the oak trees.

Graecus signalled to Felix to follow him to the edge of the tree-curtain where they positioned themselves behind a large, old oak from where they could see the progress of the owners of the voices.

There was a tall, thin man, a shorter woman and a child of about eight years of age. This much was clear from their restricted view. The woman had long blonde hair and Graecus felt a catch in his throat.

The trio came nearer and Graecus saw that it was the Iceni woman holding the child, a girl by the look of it, by the hand. Even in the moonlight the woman looked careworn and prematurely aged – she held herself as if she had the cares of the world on her shoulders and Graecus's heart went out to her.

The man did not appear to be a warrior, he looked more like a peasant and his attitude towards the woman was deferential. Graecus had not expected this. He did not wish to startle them nor to increase the woman's burdens. He did not know what to do.

'You can come out now,' said the woman in a loud voice, in quaint Latin, into the trees. 'We know you are there, we have been watching you.'

There was nothing for it but to comply with her wishes and Graecus signalled to Felix to accompany him in stepping forward out of the trees into the large clearing.

'I thought it was you,' she said to Graecus. 'Welcome to the lands of the Iceni, welcome to the lands of my ancestors.'

'My lady, I am deeply grateful that you survived the rout of your people,' said Graecus, bowing to the woman.

'Save your soft words for those who will be moved by them!' she hissed at him. 'As soon as it is light tomorrow you Romans will go back to your job of skewering Iceni babies and sowing our fields with salt.'

'We are not Romans, my lady, we are auxiliaries and we have had no part in reprisals against your people.'

'Only because you have been sent here on another task.'

'That may be true my lady but we try to live our lives as honourably as soldiery will allow, you have my word on that.'

'What are you doing here?'

'We are looking for Prasutagus's treasure, the treasure he hid from Rome.'

'Ha!' she snorted. 'Well, I wish you the best of luck in finding it because there isn't any.'

'Well, we have found a wonderful helmet so far,' said Graecus levelly, even though his heart was beating as loudly as a drum at the Circus, 'and it appears to be Thracian.'

'Yes, and I know that you've been studying it because I've watched you,' said the woman, whose spiritedness was animating her face, making the signs of fatigue disappear and renewing her beauty. Graecus could hardly bear to look at her but then he could hardly take his eyes off her either – he felt like an awkward young man awash with competing emotions, disturbed by her presence but stupidly elated that she had been *watching* him. Did she have some comprehension of what he knew about their shared past?

'I have been studying it in the hope of finding a clue as to why a Thracian might have found himself in Iceni lands three hundred years ago,' he managed to say without mangling his words, although his heart was beating in time to a horse's hooves at the gallop.

'And why would that interest you?' the woman said.

'I am curious as to how Argoraax the Thracian came to be buried here, that is all,' he said, concerned that he was not being entirely truthful.

'Oh, so you have found his name in the helmet and your scholar worked out what it said. How clever you Romans are! Well, you should take heed of the curse written there. It is powerful.'

'But would it be powerful against the man whose helmet it had been in a previous life?' thought Graecus, but what he said was, 'I have no intention of stealing it madam. It is yours for the taking if you wish to have it.'

Graecus heard Felix's sharp intake of breath at this mad gamble, but it paid off handsomely for what she replied was, 'It is not the helmet I seek.'

'What is it that you seek, then, my lady?' said Graecus casually.

'You cannot think that I would tell you.'

'No, I cannot say that I do but I hoped that you might.'

'You speak as if I should trust you,' she said witheringly and wrinkled her nose in disbelief which wounded Graecus more than she could imagine.

'Again, I say that I hoped that you might. *I am not a Roman.* In truth, I do not know where I came from and I have served Rome for many years but I have come to respect the ways of your people and, although I am a soldier, I try to perform my duties with honour and integrity.' At the end of this little speech, Graecus looked towards Felix who bowed his head to the woman in a courtly manner while Graecus added, 'My old friend here is in a similar position and knows that our century tries to uphold the best of Rome, not the worst.'

Felix nodded again, smiling his best sunny smile at the woman, but she was not moved by their words and spat at them, 'But we are at war! My people are fighting for survival and you try to trick me into trusting you!'

'But why did you come here now, tonight, with your child, if you knew we were watching you and could have taken you?'

'Because I wanted to tell you that the helmet belonged to one of my ancestors and that if you steal it then the curse will be fulfilled.'

'Argoraax was your ancestor?'

'Yes, he was shipwrecked here many generations ago and married one of my Iceni forebears. He taught us horsemanship and became one of us. He was an important warrior and we revere his memory. He died in battle defending us against the Catuvellauni so, you see, not all foreigners have to be our enemies.'

Her Latin was quaint and spoken with a soft accent but her words were eloquent and Graecus desperately wanted to tell her what his heart knew about their history. But his head told him that it would be met with disbelief or ridicule and he could not bear that.

Another thought struck him and it was a blow greater than any he had experienced on the battlefield – he had been an Iceni hero three hundred years before, one of their champions, but now it was his job to rob them of their treasure and, he almost sobbed when he thought of this, put them to the sword if they resisted.

He furiously tried to conjure up Acerbus to ask him how this dilemma was a lesson in love and, more to the point, what was the answer. It seemed cruel to him that he should be brought to this place and to a situation where his joy in meeting someone so dear to him in the past was poisoned by the fact that, because of Nero's greed, she must now be his enemy.

Felix sensed that Graecus was in difficulty and said, 'My lady, your child looks hungry and cold, I will fetch some bread and cheese for her and I have an old blanket which can be cut down for her – it will not be long before the winter is upon us.'

Graecus felt ashamed. Felix's kind thoughts for the child were what was needed here – that was more important than his intellectual agonising over his soul's heritage; the little girl did look underfed and was shivering in a thin dress in the cool night.

'No, I will go,' said Graecus. 'Felix, please look after our guests while I am gone.'

Graecus knew that had he offered the woman any help for herself she would have refused it but she also looked hungry as did the man and he went straight to Felix's stores and found bread, cheese and bacon for them before rummaging through Felix's chest for the old blanket. The chest contained old letters, drawings of places to which they had been posted, bits of ornaments – mementoes of a soldier's life – but nestling at the bottom, under the blanket, was a little charcoal drawing of Graecus done many years before by their old colleague Litigiosus, now dead. It was a sketchy portrait dashed off in a few moments and showed the Centurion laughing at some shared joke. Graecus remembered it now and that it had been done when they all lived in Lower Germania shortly after his elevation from the ranks. He had thought it had been put on the fire long ago and it touched him deeply to think that Felix had saved this memento of him. Perhaps he was not so useless after all.

Graecus bundled up the blanket with the food and hurried back to Felix and the Iceni. They were standing in silence – the little girl holding tightly onto her mother's hand while the man stood to one side, staring at Felix.

'He does not know what to make of us,' said Felix to Graecus, assuming that the man, who had, so far, said nothing, spoke only the Iceni language.

'Indeed, I do not,' said the man in a surprisingly deep voice and good Latin. 'I cannot decide whether you are good men doing a bad job or bad men trying to deceive us for your gain.'

'Well,' said Graecus, 'events may have to help you decide, but in the meantime, the child is cold, hungry and tired as are all three of you. Take this food and go to your home to eat it before getting some sleep.'

'We have no home, it has been destroyed by the legionaries,' said the woman in an exhausted voice.

'Take my cloak,' said Graecus. 'Here, take it, it will keep you warm, I have another.'

The woman took the cloak and Graecus was absurdly happy that she would be wearing his cloak.

'Goodnight,' said Graecus, 'I wish you well.'

'Much good it will do us,' said the woman, but she was fastening the cloak around her with some pleasure as she said it.

The Iceni left, and when they were out of earshot, Felix said, 'Phew! She is a brave woman! Who is she? Do you know her?'

'What a difficult question… I met her the night before the battle when I went for a walk and became lost. I stumbled across her feeding her baby some distance from Boudicca's camp. She could have killed me but she did not – she spared my life. But that was not the first time I met her – I knew her three hundred years ago when she was my wife – she is the woman I dreamed about.'

'Ye gods,' said Felix, 'what a complicated life you lead!'

'And I could not say whether it is a blessing or a curse,' said Graecus. 'The only thing I really know at this moment is that I too am cold and tired and I want my bed. Come, let us go back to the camp.'

The two old soldiers walked quickly back to their tent and were in their beds in minutes. The night's revelations were too much for Graecus to grasp and he fell immediately into a deep, dreamless sleep.

* * *

For two more days it was more of the same, more close scrutiny of the ground, more digging, more concern that nothing would be found, more heart-searching for Graecus.

Then the following night it rained very hard and the men all sat grumpily in their tents complaining that Britannia was bad enough in the sunshine but intolerable in the rain and Graecus busied himself with a close reading of Army Regulations lest his tongue should get the better of him and launch into a stout defence of the beauty of this land.

There were no footprints near the hole the next day and Graecus assumed that the heavy rain had kept even weather-hardened Britons under shelter overnight and the grass squelched beneath everyone's boots as they set out yet again to patrol the temple grounds.

Graecus watched his men with a heavy heart as he did not know whether he wanted the 'treasure' to be found so that he could keep Clueless at bay or for it not to be found so that the Iceni would have *something* left to call their own. He was being pulled in two directions and found it most uncomfortable, and on top of that, he was beginning to have a sore throat.

Graecus went back to his tent and asked Magnus to make him a tincture and requested some very hot honey water from Felix. Then he sat on his bed watching Magnus working away with his pestle and mortar crushing herbs for the tincture while he sipped carefully at the scalding honey water.

Impedimentus came into the tent in rather a hurry.

'Oh, there you are. I have been looking for you all over the camp. This heavy rain we have had has made the ground look different in some places – three large rings and two smaller ones have appeared.'

'Are they gold?' said Graecus, hopefully… but then in dread.

'No, they are not,' said Impedimentus testily as if Graecus had just said something very stupid, 'they are rings in the earth and it would appear that they were enclosures of some sort.'

Graecus did not know whether he was disappointed or elated. Either way, he would need to investigate and, picking up his bone beaker, he followed Impedimentus to the far end of the site, away from the entrance, where he saw immediately that there were, indeed, three large and two smaller rings in the grass where, after the soil had been refreshed by the rain, the grass was bright green, in contrast with the darker grass which covered the rest of the area.

Graecus looked carefully at the rings, the larger of which were the size of the large round houses beloved of the Britons and then he sent for Pneumaticus.

Pneumaticus came strolling over the enclosure as if he were out on an evening's promenade. He was whistling and had thrown his spade nonchalantly over his shoulder. Graecus watched his progress and saw the changed look on his face as he noticed the rings.

'But they were not there yesterday!' he said when he reached Graecus.

'I suspect that they were but we could not see them – last night's rain made them more obvious. But what I want to know from you is, what are they?'

'Why are you asking me?' said Pneumaticus.

'Because you are a Briton,' Graecus said patiently. 'And I was hoping that something about these rings would jog your memory – something from your childhood perhaps?'

'Oh, I don't know about that,' said Pneumaticus scratching his head and nearly injuring himself with the shovel. 'My childhood was a very long time ago… and I spent my time running wild in the woods chasing things… girls mostly, I wasn't all that interested in architecture.'

'But could these rings show where the walls of roundhouses have been?' said Graecus in desperation.

'Well, they *could*,' said Pneumaticus. 'They are round, after all. But why would you want three roundhouses in the middle of this place, and what are the two smaller rings for?'

'I could not have put it better myself but I was hoping for answers from you and you have posed more questions.'

'Shall I go now?'

'No, I want you to start digging here, I will call some of the other men over and we shall see if there is anything to be learned from this part of the temple.'

Graecus called Germanicus and two others then watched as the four of them set about digging the ground around the circles where he had indicated he wished them to start.

It was not long before post holes began to appear at regular intervals and, just before mid-day, some buckles and a brooch were found.

By the middle of the afternoon, Graecus's throat was not responding to either the honey water or Magnus's tincture and it began to ache even when he was not speaking and he was less alert than usual so that the horsemen who were approaching the temple were almost upon it by the time that he looked up and saw them.

His heart stopped dead in his chest and his throat tightened even more.

Big Red Hands and No Teeth were approaching the temple, the visors of their shiny helmets thrown open so that Graecus would know they came without shame.

They made straight for him, bringing their sweated horses to a halt and jumping down from them with all the enthusiasm of a bridegroom on his wedding night. Had they been anyone else,

Graecus would have felt that their exuberance was charming but, as it was, he knew that it meant trouble.

Graecus felt it was important that he should speak first – he was the senior officer after all – so he composed himself to make some commanding opening remark but his throat was raging and all that came out of his mouth was a croak and his strong words died on his lips.

'Oh, so it's you!' said Germanicus with a sneer. 'Come to make mischief, have you?'

'Oh no,' said Big Red Hands, lisping slightly in parody of Germanicus's voice, 'We have come on the orders of our friend, our esteemed legate. Look, he has written you a letter,' he said, handing to Graecus a document bearing Clueless's seal.

'My father has lost his voice,' said Germanicus. 'But I am sure that he will keep a close eye on you and, even if his back is turned, then rest assured that I shall be watching your every move.'

'And how *is* your little dog?' said Big Red Hands. 'I hear that he acquitted himself with valour on the battlefield. More than can be said for some people. Some people, that is, who prefer murdering their own colleagues to killing the enemy.'

His recklessness was amazing. Graecus could feel the white heat of Germanicus's anger and was trying to say something soothing to him but his voice would not work and he feared that there would be bloodshed before the Batavians' horses had even stopped panting but Incitatus arrived at that moment and took the letter from Graecus's hand saying calmly, 'We need to read this immediately, Domine, it looks important.'

Graecus signalled to Impedimentus to approach and croaked into his ear 'Watch these two like a hawk. Ask Felix to feed them and water their horses. Do not let them out of your sight and make sure that Germanicus is not left alone with them – you know why,' and then went into his tent so that he and Incitatus could read the unwelcome communication.

Graecus sat at his desk, undid the seal with his small knife and gingerly unfolded the document as if it were a snake.

Although it was not a reptile, its slithering purpose was just as dangerous – the letter was a deceptive masterpiece where the words said one thing but Graecus knew their meaning was wildly different.

'Most worthy colleague,' it read, *'We are greatly pleased to receive your letter and to learn of the progress you are making in seeking the hidden treasure of Prasutagus. Your news of the finding of the Thracian helmet has excited us all. We know that you will, with your customary efficiency, be investigating every possible clue to the whereabouts of the gold and silver but we are concerned that you may not have sufficient men of proper calibre to assist you in your diligent search. Although we are suffering manpower shortages ourselves, we are mindful of the interest being shown by our most beloved and gracious Emperor Nero in your activities and we are, therefore, sending these two valorous cavalrymen to assist you. Our Batavian brothers fought with the great Emperor Claudius when he won this island for Rome and are skilled in dealing with native populations. We trust that you will find them helpful and look forward soon to be able to send happy news to Rome.'*

It ended with the amorphous scrawl which passed for Clueless's signature.

Graecus would have spat at it had his throat not been as dry as the African desert but the best he could do was to throw it onto his desk in disgust and run his fingers through his hair.

Incitatus knew the true meaning of the letter and had groaned softly when he read it over Graecus's shoulder. 'Ye gods,' he said, 'how can we be expected to find something which is not here? And now we have those two thugs fixing us with their beady little eyes, reporting on us to the legate. It is just not fair!'

'It is not fair but it *is* politics,' whispered Graecus, who was feeling calmer now that he had had time to think.

'Well, they have been sent here to help and I shall make sure that they do. I shall keep them digging – all day, and all night if necessary!' he hissed.

Graecus left the tent and went to find the Batavians.

They were sitting next to one of Felix's burning field braziers, their helmets thrown to the ground beside them next to their long cavalry swords. They were laughing loudly at some private joke and the gaps in No Teeth's mouth were plainly visible – Germanicus had taken out five of his front teeth.

The sight of No Teeth's shattered mouth gave Graecus quiet satisfaction and he found enough voice to be able to tell them to report to Pneumaticus and to start digging and keep on until he told them to stop.

'Oh, so you want us to do the dirty work, do you?' said Big Red Hands – No Teeth seemed to have been dumbstruck – 'Even though all *you've* managed to find so far is a stupid old helmet!'

'I expect you to follow my orders just as everyone else here does. You are no different,' whispered Graecus wishing that his voice did not sound like that of an adolescent boy.

'Oooh, listen to him, listen to the big Centurion, telling us what to do! Anyone would think he was important.'

'Well, he fucking is important!' said Felix, pulling Big Red Hands roughly to his feet and holding him by the edge of his tunic. 'He is the Centurion round here and you're just cavalry. You do as he says or you'll feel the weight of this!' he said, shoving his large clenched fist in the Batavian's face.

Felix was a strong man and Big Red Hands knew from the determined look on the cook's face that he meant what he said.

'All right, all right, don't get your knickers in a twist' he said. Felix let go of him and Graecus pointed to where the Batavians should go.

They slunk away, their departing backs a picture of insolence, walking very slowly as if picking up each foot was the most difficult thing they had ever done.

'Thank you, my friend,' whispered Graecus. 'Your intervention was well-timed and very effective. You must have been holding his collar very tightly – I saw that he had tears in his eyes.'

'Oh, I don't think it was that,' said Felix snorting, 'I've just been chopping onions,' and then collapsed into laughter which was so infectious that Graecus joined in despite his throat, and the two of them laughed and laughed until their stomachs hurt just as they had done when they were carefree young men.

Laughing with Felix was good medicine for, when he returned to his tent afterwards, Graecus realised that, although Big Red Hands's words had angered him, he was by far the more fortunate of the two – to the Batavian, the helmet was a worthless old piece of junk, but to him it was a priceless reminder of a glorious life, lived to the full with a beautiful woman among brave colleagues; yes, this knowledge was confusing to him in the life he was leading now, but it was also enriching.

CHAPTER TWENTY-ONE

As dusk approached Graecus became agitated again. He dreaded what might happen if the Iceni woman and her companions came back to the temple now that the Batavians were here. Clueless's words 'They are skilled in dealing with native populations' kept running through his mind. It was back to the bad old days of Solitarius – being spied on by the lackeys of an unscrupulous politician but this time there were two of them and Germanicus was intent on sending them both to their ancestors but how would they explain that this time?

To make matters worse, his throat was agony – it was so swollen that he could not swallow and his voice had gone completely – not even a croak emerged when he tried to speak.

Graecus had told the Batavians to pitch their tent next to that of his contubernium so that he would be aware of their movements and, now that it was dark, he kept opening the flap so that he could hear their guttural voices and their coarse laughter and be sure that they were where they had been told to stay.

It was a fine night and the stars were out all over the sky, flittering like jewels against a dark cloth. Graecus paused to look at them and to wonder if the Iceni woman was watching them also. He did not even know her name but he knew so much else about her. He knew that she was brave and that they had loved each other deeply three hundred years before.

The Batavians were still making a din in their tent and Graecus felt very tired so he lay on his bed, thinking about when he and the Iceni woman had been lovers. This was intoxicating and he fell asleep with a smile.

* * *

Graecus dreamed that Acerbus came to him.

He was insistent. There was no doubt that what he said was urgent. 'Look for the rum fire. That is the key. That is the answer! Find the rum fire and all will be well.'

* * *

Germanicus was shaking him awake.

'Father, father, they've left the tent. The Batavians have gone.'

Graecus was awake in a moment and, picking up his gladius, followed Germanicus who was following the Batavians towards the temple.

They ran swiftly in the velvet night, swords at the ready. An owl flew overhead but the rest was silence and Graecus felt a deep familiarity – his body remembered other nights long ago in Britannia when he and his Iceni friends had gone hunting and, through long practice, they had moved as one man. Now he was running with his son, whom he loved more than life and their tie was such that they breathed as one.

But the silence was broken by voices. Graecus could hear the girl's voice speaking quickly and excitedly.

The Batavians had stopped in their tracks. They were listening to the child's voice and now the man had joined in, speaking urgently in a low tone. Graecus did not speak their language but it sounded as if he were telling the girl to keep quiet. And now the woman said something. Something in a dismissive tone. Through the gaps in the trees, Graecus could see them clearly and the woman was wearing his cloak.

The Batavians were also watching the Iceni and Graecus could see that they were wondering why or how it was that the woman had acquired a Centurion's cloak; in the depths of the night, where the darkness blanketed them and seemed to connect them all, Graecus felt he could hear the Batavians' thoughts and could not understand how they did not know that they were being followed.

The Iceni had stopped walking and were standing just to one side of the centre of the large clearing. Graecus saw that the man was carrying a stout stick which he was using to draw a circle around himself and his companions. He was muttering something in a rhythmic, repetitive way and the woman was joining in at certain points while the child remained silent.

Graecus could feel that the Batavians were becoming impatient but then the man produced a small shovel from beneath his battered tunic and, falling to his knees, began to dig into the grassy surface of the clearing muttering his imprecations all the while.

The child sat on the ground, and her blonde hair glistened in the starlight. She was a beautiful child, as beautiful as her mother and Graecus's heart hammered at the thought that she was in some way related to him.

The shovel shone like silver as the man dug away. Now he was uncovering something.

Slowly and with reverence the man lifted a small cup from the ground. It was covered in earth but it was still possible to see that it was gold in colour.

Graecus's heart was in his mouth and Germanicus took a sharp intake of breath as he watched the man try to clean the dirt from the cup with his shabby sleeve.

The woman was weeping now. Sobbing. Graecus wanted to leave his hiding place and take her in his arms and hold her tightly to his chest to comfort her but that would be madness.

The Batavians drew their long cavalry swords and moved to enter the clearing.

'Those bastards!' spat Germanicus. 'They can't leave anything alone.'

The woman had covered her face with her hands in an attempt to comfort herself and then she turned her back on the child and the man but Graecus could see that her shoulders were heaving with grief.

The Batavians moved swiftly into the clearing and within seconds had overpowered the girl and the man. The girl screamed and the man bellowed, alerting the woman to the Batavians' ugly presence.

The woman was staring at the Batavians as if they were dirt. She knew that they and their countrymen had been vital to the success of Claudius's invasion of Britannia and she hated them as deeply as she hated any Roman.

The Batavians raised the girl and the man to their feet, pointing their swords to their chests. They were grinning – Graecus could see what was left of No Teeth's yellow fangs glinting darkly in the starlight – and they were asking questions in Latin, their harsh voices making the words sound even more threatening.

'We know there's treasure here, so don't deny it,' said Big Red Hands. 'Tell us where it is and the child will come to no harm.'

The woman said nothing and the man followed her example.

Big Red Hands picked up the cup and, sticking it right under the woman's nose, said, 'It's gold, isn't it? Don't try to fool me. And there's lots more round here. We know that your stupid old king was hiding it from our Emperor, the great Nero.'

He paused for breath and the woman spat in his face. Graecus could feel Germanicus's wrath rising to danger point and saw that Big Red Hands had his dagger at the woman's throat.

Graecus knew that the woman would make no sound. Not even if they cut her to ribbons – she would not give them the satisfaction – she would stand with her head held high and look at them, fixing them with her proud gaze until her life's blood drained away. His wife was like that.

'And where did you get this?' asked Big Red Hands, fingering the scarlet cloak which accentuated the woman's lovely long hair. 'How come you, a piece of Iceni scum, have got your hands on a Centurion's cloak?'

Big Red Hands had dropped his heavy cavalry sword and was stroking the wool of the cloak as he said this, then – casually at first but with increasing attention – cupping the woman's breast as he spoke.

Graecus knew that Germanicus was incensed and he shared his feelings but he did not see how they could intervene without Germanicus losing his temper and killing another of Rome's soldiers.

Big Red Hands was now paying great attention to the woman's breast and No Teeth was grinning widely, enjoying the spectacle.

The woman showed no emotion and Big Red Hands said, 'Enjoying it, are you?' laughing in her face as he assaulted her.

They were the last words he spoke.

The woman brought a dagger from under her cloak and stabbed her attacker straight through the heart so quickly that he fell with a smile still on his face and a swelling under his tunic.

No Teeth now had hold of the girl's neck and was holding his dagger to her throat. 'Stay where you are!' he hissed to the woman, 'And don't you move either!' he said to the man. Then: 'Tell me where the treasure is,' to them both.

The child began to cry and her sobs were pitiful.

Graecus could feel Germanicus's boiling anger and tried to say something to calm him but his voice failed and then his son was on his feet running behind the trees.

'There is no treasure,' said the woman. 'We've told you before. Nero has taken all our gold and our silver, as well as our lands. We have nothing left.'

'What about this then?' said No Teeth, pointing at the little gold cup lying on the ground at his feet.

'That was the cup given to our gods to celebrate the birth of my son five months ago.'

Germanicus appeared in the clearing, gladius drawn, running silently towards No Teeth's back.

The child was sobbing loudly and No Teeth slapped her face hard saying, 'Stop that wailing, you little bitch.'

Germanicus tapped No Teeth on the shoulder and said, 'Leave her alone. Try picking on me instead. Here, take your sword,' handing the cavalry weapon to No Teeth who took it and began circling Germanicus.

Graecus came into the clearing wanting to break up the fight but his voice would not work and within a few seconds Germanicus had closed in on No Teeth.

The cavalry sword was longer than the gladius and in theory this gave No Teeth an advantage but it was heavier and was less easy to use on foot than on horseback. In any case, No Teeth was no match for Germanicus being older and heavier, and it seemed to Graecus that this was only ever going to end with No Teeth on the point of Germanicus's gladius.

How would he explain that to Clueless? Then again, if he intervened and took No Teeth back to the camp, he would need to take the Iceni woman, the child and the man and No Teeth would tell Clueless what had happened which would probably end in their crucifixion or worse.

Graecus's throat was swelling with anxiety and he was finding it hard to breathe. No Teeth had noticed him and Graecus could see his mind working – trying, and failing, to understand why he had not arrested the Iceni.

The pain and swelling in Graecus's throat were unbearable and he realised just as he was falling to the ground that he was going to faint.

* * *

Her hands were cool as she put them to his forehead and whispered in her musical voice, 'You have a fever. You are burning.'

Graecus's throat was raging but he felt he was in Elysium being tended to by the woman of his dreams.

He opened his eyes and saw the Iceni woman bending over him, her hand now touching his cheek, feeling its heat. She looked deeply into Graecus's eyes and even in the starlight, he saw that she recognised something in him – something that she knew and loved. He saw that she did not understand it but that she was grateful for it – that it gave her some succour in this time of unspeakable horror.

Graecus smiled at her and croaked, 'My lady!' while she smiled back as if she knew that she had once, long ago, been his lady.

'My lady, your hand is calming my fever,' he said, remembering the soft touch of her fingers in other times.

Germanicus appeared, towering over his father, peering anxiously at him as he lay on the hard ground.

'Father, what is it?' he said. 'Is it your throat? Do you have a fever?'

Graecus struggled to sit up and saw that No Teeth's lifeless body was lying a few feet away, a large pool of blood seeping from his belly. He did not look peaceful.

Germanicus followed his father's gaze and said, 'It didn't take long, I –' but Graecus cut him off sharply, saying in a voice whose strength surprised him,

'I do not wish to know what happened – that way I will not need to tell any lies. It is quite possible that he met his death at the hands of those whose lands he sought to plunder. We will leave the Batavians here and allow others to find them in the morning. Now, please help me to my feet.'

The woman was holding the little gold cup, cradling it to her chest, weeping.

'My lady, where is your baby?' said Graecus, thinking to distract the woman from her grief.

'Dead,' she said. 'Run through with a Roman sword, just as many other Iceni babies. Your Emperor sees danger in suckling infants.'

'My lady, I am truly sorry to hear of your loss – I saw how tenderly you cared for your child.'

'He was my hope. He was my future after my husband died. Now there is nothing.'

'There is always hope, my lady, your people need to have hope.'

'What hope can we have? We have no future.'

'My lady, you must be strong for your people. They need to have thoughts of a better time to carry on with the present. You must be strong for them.'

'I see that you are an honourable man but those you serve are not. They seek to destroy us and all that we stand for. They seek to force us into their way of life.'

'My lady, you speak the truth about Rome's intentions but your people will survive, I feel it in my bones and in my heart. But they need *you* to be strong for them.'

'I do not know why but I take comfort from what you say. There is a quality about you which is familiar to me. It is very strange but I trust you.'

The woman laughed wryly at this thought and said, 'How odd it is that I am standing here in front of your dead colleagues and you are asking me to be strong for the sake of your enemies.'

'Your people are not my enemies – I see that they had their reasons for defying Rome.'

'And so I survive, to fight on,' said the woman wearily.

'Fighting is not the only answer,' whispered Graecus, remembering what Acerbus had said.

'What other answer is there?' said the woman.

'Love,' said Graecus. 'Love is an answer.'

The woman stared at him with incredulity at first but he held her gaze and she saw that he meant it, that in some way he loved her.

'I will not forget you,' she said softly. 'But now I must go. My people need me.'

'And I shall remember you, my lady,' said Graecus bending over her hand and kissing it for a long moment, marvelling at the scent of her skin.

Then she was gone, walking away into the distance with the girl and the tall man. Graecus watched her go with sadness in his heart but also a feeling of contentment that he had met her again and that they had both remembered the love they had shared three hundred years before.

'Do you know her father?' said Germanicus.

'I do not know her name. But I have met her several times and I admire her courage, her truth and her desire to protect her people. They are qualities which would be useful in Rome. Now let us leave these two here and go back to our beds. I am very tired.'

* * *

Graecus's throat was raging again the following morning and neither Magnus's nor Felix's ministrations helped to ease it. He lay on his bed listening to the sounds of the camp going on around him, waiting for the moment when someone would discover the Batavians' bodies and come running to his tent with the news.

No one came running. Instead, Pneumaticus brought the news at a very slow amble.

He came to the contubernium tent just after breakfast and put his head round the open flap saying, 'I don't suppose you'll be too upset by this but it looks as if those fools, the Batavians, were out snooping last night and the wolves got them.'

'Wolves?' said Graecus, all other thoughts gone from his mind.

'Yes, wolves. Their carcasses have been picked so bare so that they're almost unrecognisable – it's only because their swords were there that we knew who they were. The young lad who found them had a proper nasty turn – he's never seen damage like it before. There must have been a big pack of them. Funny that nobody heard anything though.'

'Oh, wolves can work very silently when they need to,' said Graecus sagely. 'Well, we had better bury the remains and give them a proper military send-off. Send Incitatus to me, we need to write to Clueless to give him the sad news of the premature demise of his crack troops,' he added before falling back on his pillows.

Pneumaticus left and Graecus let a slow smile to spread across his face – how wonderful were the ways of nature! How marvellous that the wolves were out in force last night and how splendid that they liked the taste of Batavians! How glorious that he would now be able to write carefully but truthfully to Clueless!

Incitatus came in and Graecus sat up saying, 'You have heard the news?'

'Yes, it is dreadful, is it not?' said Incitatus grinning.

'Oh, just too awful for words,' said Graecus laughing out loud even though it hurt his throat. 'But we must overcome our grief and write to our legate with the terrible news.'

'Yes, we must,' said Incitatus settling himself down on his stool waiting for his Centurion's grave words.

'Greatly esteemed leader,' he began, 'sad greetings! It is my solemn duty to be the bringer of most dreadful news. I have the burden of informing you that your faithful and brave servants What's-his-name and His Sidekick (you will get their full names from the century's records) last night perished in the furtherance of their duties. They were savaged by a pack of wolves while they were following their own investigations into the whereabouts of Prasutagus's treasure and, it is thought, in pursuit of native intelligence. So violent was the wolves' attack and so extensive were the injuries suffered by our beloved colleagues (here Graecus broke into giggles at his own audacity in telling the story in this way, knowing that Clueless would know that he was playing him at his own game) that their bodies were virtually unrecognisable. We will accord them all military honours possible in this barbarous land and know that you will inform their relatives in your official capacity as their commander. May they be feasting in Elysium as I write!

'With all good wishes for your honour's health and that of your family, I remain your humble servant, etc, etc.'

By the time Graecus had finished dictating this letter both he and Incitatus were giggling helplessly at the empty words, knowing that Clueless could do nothing about it.

Then Graecus thought of another thing. It had been at the back of his mind but now it came to the fore.

'Incitatus, do you know anything about a "rum fire"?' he asked.

'Oh, yes, you obviously know more about the Thracians than you think. The rhomphaia was their best weapon. Our man here would have been very familiar with its use. It was a long pole with a curved blade on the end. The Thracians used them to great effect in battle.'

'Do you think our friend Argoraax brought one with him? Could there be one here, I wonder.'

'It is possible, I suppose. It could even be likely.'

Incitatus went away to copy out the letter onto parchment in his best handwriting and Graecus lay back, smiling again, happy that they had been relieved of the Batavians' horrible presence and he had not needed to lie on Germanicus's behalf.

Incitatus brought in the letter and Graecus signed it with his best pen, then folded it and said, 'Get one of our best riders to take it. He can use one of the Batavians' horses – they are used to being ridden hard. Please send Felix to me.'

Incitatus left and soon after Graecus heard the sound of urgent hooves leaving the camp then Felix entered the tent.

'Old friend,' said Graecus, 'I need your help. I have shared with you and you alone the secret of my former connection with this land and with the Iceni woman and now I need to share with you the secret that Acerbus speaks to me.'

'But he's dead,' said Felix reasonably.

'Yes, I know that but he has a way of speaking to me inside my head. His words are as clear as your voice is now but it is *his* voice and his manner of speaking.'

'Well, I am your oldest friend and I do not yet see other signs of your having lost your mind so I suppose I must believe you. What does Acerbus say?'

'Well, for one thing he told me the name of the owner of the helmet, my name as it were, before Incitatus translated it for us.'

'Phew!' said Felix, 'I always knew that Acerbus was well connected but to know someone from three hundred years ago takes some doing.'

'As you say, he knew all the best people. But he told me something very interesting the other night – he told me to look for the rhomphaia. That was my weapon when I was Argoraax. It is a long wooden pole with a curved blade on the end.'

'Why would we want that?' said Felix.

'Because Acerbus said all would be well if we found it.'

'But why?' said Felix prompting Graecus to think that he must have been spending too much time with Pneumaticus.

'If I knew the answer to that I would be a very happy man. Suffice it to say that Acerbus has not let me down yet, ever, and it is the only clue I have now – it is all we have to go on.'

'What do you want me to do?'

'I want you to walk round this site, bearing in mind what I have just said and ask Acerbus where the rhomphaia is. Ask him to help us find it.'

'Um, just so that I understand this,' said Felix, 'you want me to walk aimlessly about this huge place, asking a dead man to help me find the long lost weapon of another dead man, a shipwrecked Thracian, who happened to have been you in a previous life? And if I do, everything will be fine?'

'Yes.'

'Oh, all right then. It *is* a nice day. Perfect for a walk.'

'Yes. Off you go.'

'Just one more thing.'

'What is it?'

Why am I looking? Why are you not doing it yourself? I mean, Acerbus has been talking to you not to me.'

'Exactly. And if he talks to you now, then I am not imagining it – I'm not losing my sanity.'

'When you put it like that, I can hardly refuse, can I?'

'No. Off you go.'

Graecus sat at his desk and busied himself with the century's records. It was peaceful work and required only the use of his brain not his voice. He realised that his breathing had become more rhythmic and that the tension in his shoulders was easing.

He put down his pen and closed his eyes.

He spoke to God. Gideon's God.

'Dear God, please let us emerge from this situation with honour. Please let us find the treasure but let the Iceni not be completely destroyed. Please let my wife and her people have a future. Please keep my son and my friends safe. Thank you.'

He felt foolish but it was no more foolish than speaking to Acerbus nor any more foolish than thinking, well, *knowing* actually, that he had lived here before and had loved, still loved, the Iceni woman. He thought about how he *knew* about his life as Argoraax and concluded that he knew with his heart and that it was different from thinking with his head and he knew that the heart was by far the more powerful of the two.

Germanicus came into the tent, his blonde hair glowing in the shaft of light cast by the open flap, and Graecus's heart turned over with love for his wonderful son.

'Father, Felix wants you to come to see something. Please come with me immediately.

Felix was kneeling on the ground in the middle of the largest of the circles which had appeared after the heavy rain. He looked hot and bothered.

'Oh, there you are. We need to dig here.'

The other men in the vicinity were watching Felix with interest and Graecus had to get down on the grass next to him so that he could whisper in his ear, 'Why? Why here?'

'Because Acerbus told me to dig here, that's why.'

Graecus laughed out loud – a great bellow of joy.

'Did it sound just like him? Did it sound as if it were him speaking but it was inside your head?'

'Yes, exactly like that. I thought the others must also be able to hear him – he was so loud and clear – but they just carried on with their work. It was very strange, but he also said it was just like you to want the Iceni woman to be safe.'

'Oh, he's listening to my prayers, now, is he?'

'There are worse things,' said Felix, and Graecus nodded in agreement while beckoning to three young soldiers and telling them to pick up their shovels and begin to dig where Felix was pointing.

CHAPTER TWENTY-TWO

It did not take long. About three feet down, there was the rhomphaia. It was wrapped in sheepskin and was in good condition – the shaft was intact and still strong and the blade was razor sharp. Graecus picked it up with reverence and made some testing passes with it, slicing the air with ease and gauging the power of the weapon. It felt wonderful. The knowledge of how to use this ancient instrument of death prickled up his arm and coursed through his veins, transporting him back to simpler times when he had lived the life of a free warrior. But 'What do we do now?' said one of the young men, bringing Graecus back to the present.

'Keep digging. Keep digging where Felix tells you to dig,' said Graecus and went back to his tent to clean his rhomphaia.

This was pleasurable work – rubbing olive oil into the wooden shaft, polishing the blade with ground pumice before shining it with a soft cloth – and Graecus was immersed in his task, whistling softly to himself, when he heard Acerbus's unmistakeable voice.

'It's not yours,' he said.

'So why did you tell Felix where to find it?'

'Because she needs it. The Iceni woman needs it. It is a sacred symbol of their tribe.'

'What should I do with it, then?'

'Leave it on the ground. Leave it for her tonight.'

'I am sure that you know best. I will do as you say but I do it with reluctance – it is wonderful to feel this weapon in my hands again.'

'You were a great warrior. But you were also a good man. That was why the Iceni loved you and took your rhomphaia as the symbol of power tempered with fairness.'

'You make it sound as if I were a wise man.'

'Oh, in that case I exaggerate! You were just a very human man,' said Acerbus breaking into his loud, snorting, spitting laugh.

Graecus began laughing too, but seeing the young soldier come into his tent, he had to pretend that he was coughing in order to cover up the fact that he was laughing while alone in an empty tent.

'What is it?' he said.

'Oh, sir, Felix asked me to come to get you. We think there are other objects buried near to that spot. Felix is getting excited.'

Graecus went back to the grass circle with the young soldier, trying to quieten his own pounding heart.

Felix was down a hole shovelling feverishly at the dark soil. There was a dirty object lying to one side of a new hole adjacent to the first hole and the object was shaped like a jug with a long slender handle. Graecus picked it up and rubbed at it with his sleeve.

Some of the dirt came away and revealed a shiny metal surface beneath. It looked like gold. Graecus could not be quite sure, but it really did look like gold to him.

'There's a lot more down here!' shouted Felix. 'Perhaps there is some treasure. Perhaps old Prasutagus was more cunning than we thought.'

Graecus looked down into the hole and saw what Felix meant – there were little mounds within the earth where other objects were buried. 'Get Germanicus and Impedimentus – oh, and Incitatus!' he shouted to the men who were staring down into Felix's hole while he began scrabbling at the earth with his hands.

'I must give the rhomphaia back,' he whispered to Felix. 'Acerbus says that although it was mine, it is no longer mine. The Iceni people need it as a sort of talisman for them for the future.'

'Well, you could never say that your life is dull, could you,' said Felix, laughing and coughing at the same time.

'I often wish that it could be peaceful and tranquil,' said Graecus. 'It would be wonderful to have a wife and a home and to watch Germanicus's children grow up.'

'Perhaps you will have children of your own,' said Felix, concentrating on pulling a muddy bracelet out of the ground.

'Oh, I have given up all hope of that,' said Graecus. 'I feel I am too old now, never mind when I leave the army, and no young woman would want me.'

'Rubbish!' said Felix. 'You still have a spring in your step and all your hair and teeth. Many a woman would be glad of your company.'

'But would these women who would be glad to meet me, be the kind of women I would like to meet?' said Graecus.

'Oh fiddle faddle!' said Felix. 'Just stop it, will you? Just stop being so modest!'

'I have much to be modest about,' said Graecus.

'Well, if we get *donativa* for this lot, we could all be very rich and *then* the women will flock to us,' said Felix.

The others arrived and Graecus told Germanicus to help Felix but to be very careful with the objects. Then he asked Incitatus to examine the jug with the slender handle. Incitatus rubbed off more of the dirt with a wet finger and said, 'I would welcome Impedimentus's opinion but I think it is gold – and the carvings are very fine. This is a jug fit for a king.'

Impedimentus took the jug from Incitatus and turned it over in his hands several times before saying 'Yes, in my mind there is no doubt, no doubt whatsoever – it is gold.'

'Good!' said Graecus. 'Now, Impedimentus, I want you to keep a tally of what is being unearthed and I want you, Incitatus, to clean the objects.

Graecus went to fetch a stool and sat on it to watch progress.

During the course of the afternoon a great mound of beautiful objects emerged from the hole and, as Incitatus began to clean them, it became clear that they were treasure – gold and silver cups embedded with stones, heavy torcs wrought in the most gorgeous swirling waves to adorn the necks of the Iceni nobility, silver plates and knives with ivory handles. A pile of objects sat in front of Impedimentus waiting for him to list them.

* * *

As dusk began to descend, Graecus had to think about how the trove of objects should be guarded. There was no stronghold at the camp – only the leather tents. And then a stray thought crept into his mind. From whom would they be guarding the treasure?

From those to whom it belonged.

This thought would not go away and then it was joined by another uncomfortable thought – how could he in all conscience, knowing of his past with the Iceni, rob them of all this and give it to Nero who had no right to it, other than that gained by victory in a battle fought by other men?

As it became darker, Graecus wrestled with this conundrum and tied his mind in knots trying to find a way in which he could satisfy his conscience but still be able to deliver up sufficient treasure to satisfy the greed of both Clueless and Nero.

He sat with his supper cooling in front of him, while all around him, his men were full of excitement at the prospect of *donativa* – a share of what they had found. For them, even a small trinket would represent more riches than they could earn in many years in Rome's service and would mean that they could marry when they finally left the army.

This thought was helpful in that it meant there was *some* good in handing at least some of the treasure over to Rome; his men – hardworking, faithful and reliable – would benefit if Nero saw fit to declare that they warranted *donativa* and it was likely that their Emperor would so as to appear generous and attract the loyalty of the legions. There was also the point that he would have Clueless off his back, for the moment at least.

He did not know what to do as far as the treasure was concerned but he did have to fulfil his promise to Acerbus to return the rhomphaia to the Iceni. He went to his tent and picked up his weapon. He held it tenderly, remembering his happy life as Argoraax when the twists and turns of politics were absent and he could make decisions based simply on what was good for those he loved.

'Come on now,' said Acerbus, 'that was then, this is now. You have work to do.'

'But where should I put it?' said Graecus. 'Where should I put it so that the Iceni woman will find it?'

'I will tell you. Firstly, you need to leave the camp by the main gate, then turn left and walk straight ahead for five hundred paces to the large oak tree. You can put it there. It will be safe and the woman will find it because she often sits there.'

'I will do as you say.'

Graecus walked quickly to the gate and smiled to the guards as he walked away into the darkening evening.

He found the oak tree and gently placed the rhomphaia under it, imagining the Iceni woman's joy when she found it. He imagined her sitting there sometimes, looking at the moon, talking to her goddess and decided he would sit there for a while, just to feel close to her again.

The night was glorious, dry and fine and Graecus sat for some time, watching the stars emerge from their dark blanket.

He heard a light step coming towards the tree over the dusty grass. It was her. His heart leapt and his throat went dry. Should he leave? Should he warn her that he was there?

'*Salve,*' she said in her soft voice as he stood to greet her. 'You have found my tree.'

'Yes, my lady, I was brought here to give you this,' said Graecus, handing her the rhomphaia from under his cloak.

Her face broke into a wide smile and she gave a little 'Whoop' of joy. 'How did you know where it was? How did you find it?'

'My lady, I can only say that I was guided to find it by someone who was very dear to me in life and who watches over me in death.'

'You have poetry in your soul, Centurion,' she said, coming very close to him and kissing his cheek, pressing her warm body next to his.

Graecus gulped for air. He could smell her hair and see her eyes glistening with invitation under the moonlight. His blood sang with sweet desire but he could not be sure – she was a grieving woman – he would not wish to force himself on her. He looked questioningly at her and saw her smile of agreement.

It was enough. He pulled her close to him and gently put his mouth on hers while she settled into the contours of his body and their lips and tongues began to explore hidden delights.

Graecus thought he would explode with happiness to be reunited with his beautiful wife and she was as passionate and giving now as she had been three hundred years before. They made love under the moon and the stars lying on his cloak and then snugly beneath it as they held each other in a tender embrace, whispering their wonder at what had just happened.

'Was that wrong?' he said. 'To the world we are enemies.'

'No, it could not be wrong. You have brought back the sign my people need. You have given me the rhomphaia and now I will bear your son.'

'My son! How can you be sure?'

'Because it is that time of the moon when I am fertile and I know you will give me a son.'

'How will you explain that to your people? You have no husband.'

'I will tell them the truth. I will tell them that I was visited by the spirit of Argoraax and he gave me back our people's symbol. Then when our son is born they will know that Argoraax visited me in more ways than one.'

'How wonderfully true that is,' said Graecus kissing her, and feeling again desire welling up, visiting her once more.

'I must go,' she said some time later. 'I must go and give my people this wondrous gift. I carry a child in my belly and that will also give them joy.'

'But what of the treasure?' Graecus asked. 'Will there not be fury that we have stolen your gold and silver?'

'Oh no,' the woman said, 'that is not even a tithe of what there is. The rest is hidden where you will not find it. Prasutagus buried that other stuff so that the Romans would find it and that arrogant pig Decianus would think that he'd found our all our gold and silver.'

She stood and brushed down her dress then put on her cloak – the Centurion's cloak he had given her.

'You have given me life,' she said with tears in her eyes.

'Where there was only death and suffering we now have hope and a new life. Thank you Centurion.'

'My lady,' he said bending to kiss her, 'this has been the most magical night of my life.'

'We must part now before the rest of the world intrudes on our magic,' she said, and turned to walk away.

He watched her light step as she walked away out of his life but he knew she would live in his heart.

Graecus walked back to the camp, past the guards and back to his tent. He got into bed and just before he fell asleep he remembered to say 'Thank you' to Gideon's God.

* * *

The treasure was cleaned and a careful list was made by Impedimentus of what it comprised; Graecus grinned to himself every time he looked at the pile of glittering metal thinking that the Iceni had so much more – squirreled away out of Nero's reach.

Nevertheless, it was with a happy smile that Graecus wrote to Clueless telling him of the find and asking that his century be relieved of their duties in guarding so many valuable objects in this wild place.

Clueless arrived within days, his horse almost dead from fatigue but its rider alive with excitement at the thought of gold and lavish praise from Nero.

Graecus and Felix did their best to make Clueless and his retinue comfortable in the camp but it was too primitive for their tastes and it was clear that the auxiliaries were all very much surplus to requirements now that they had found Prasutagus's fabled treasure. Within a few days they were all tripping over each other and tempers were becoming frayed – Graecus's men wished to know where they would be posted next and if they would be given bounty but Clueless and his retinue wished only to ensure that they took most of the credit for unearthing the treasure. Graecus cared about none of these matters, being carried about his daily duties on a cloud of wonderment at his encounter with the Iceni woman.

Then came a letter from Norbanus telling Graecus that he and his men were to be sent to Deva to reinforce the legion there in case the Welsh tribes were feeling rebellious. Norbanus's letter was formal and correct but Graecus read between its lines that the Senior Centurion was keeping them away from all the vengeful retribution being visited on Boudicca's allies by the legates as he knew it would not be to their taste.

The century left for Deva in the autumn and spent the winter there.

It was a very long, cold, dark time when the snow covered the ground for many weeks and smothered sound. The legionaries were friendly, the fort's walls thick enough to withstand the weather and, in the extreme quiet of their surroundings, Graecus and his men rested, recovering their health and vigour after the privations of the previous months.

Often, sitting by the fire, after supper, his men around him busy with their pursuits, Graecus would wonder how the Iceni woman was progressing with her pregnancy and hoped that she was getting enough food to make a strong son. He sent her loving thoughts and felt that she was sending them to him.

Then, in the spring, after the snow had melted and the weather again favoured travel, came a letter, a very official letter for Graecus.

It was from Suetonius and bore his great seal. Graecus opened it with awe – the heavy red seal clanking against his fingers as he unfolded the parchment. Its contents were also awesome.

Greetings, valorous colleague,' it began, *'I, Suetonius Paulinus, am instructed by our most beloved and gracious Emperor, Nero Claudius Caeser Augustus Germanicus, to advise you that he has, in his benevolence, granted me and those of my men whom I deem fitted by their actions on that day, the inestimable honour of an Ovation to be held at Rome with all attendant processions and Games to demonstrate the gratitude of our Emperor, the Senate and the people of Rome for the deliverance of the island of Britannia from the threat caused to our Empire by the harridan Boudicca. You, your son and your men fought like lions on the day of the great battle against Boudicca's hordes and it is my pleasant duty to inform you that you and your century will join me in Rome for the celebrations and will receive battle honours and donativa for the decisive part you played in defeating our enemies.*

With all good wishes for a safe journey to Rome,

Suetonius'

Graecus sat with the letter in his hand for some time, stunned by what it meant. It was the most glorious news that any soldier could receive, especially for a Roman soldier and even more so for a humble auxiliary – to be singled out for honours at an *ovation* was something most men would only achieve in their daydreams but here it was being offered to him and to his men. They would also receive bounty and that would make them wealthy but, as far as Graecus was concerned, this would all be achieved at a great cost.

He had striven to keep Germanicus out of the public eye all these years and now he was to be displayed as one of the centres of attention before the Imperial Court at the very centre of all the intrigues and plotting which Graecus had tried so hard to avoid. Germanicus was young and outstandingly handsome – he would draw all eyes and some of them would look at him with a special glance and draw their own conclusions.

'What is in the letter, father?' said Germanicus.

'Yes, tell us what is in the important-looking letter!' said the others.

'We are invited to Rome to receive full battle honours and *donativa* as part of Suetonius Paulinus's *ovation*. There will be processions and Games,' said Graecus, his voice barely more than a whisper.

'But father, that is wonderful, no one deserves it more than you!' said Germanicus, his eyes shining. 'But why do you look so dark?'

Graecus struggled to find the words. How could he tell his son that this, their finest hour, was also that which he least wanted? How could he say to his boy that going to Rome as the hero of a regime he had come largely to despise, and as a student of a religion whose followers were liable to be persecuted in the name of entertainment, was the thing he most feared?

But, most important of all, how would he keep Germanicus – and himself – safe?

CHRONICLES OF ETERNITY III

A CAPITAL TIME

We hope you have enjoyed reading *The Weight of Time*. On the follow-ing page is a taste of its sequel – *A Capital Time* – due for publication in Autumn 2010.

In this third book Graecus and his men experience the excitement and exhaustion of being in Rome, the largest and busiest city of the Ancient World and among all the glitter of its marbled buildings, its riches and its alluring women they encounter not only danger and threat but also courage and poignant reunions.

PROLOGUE

It was dark now and the candles had burned too low. The woman rose to her feet and said, 'Rest for few moments, this is a momentous journey for you', while she took two new candles from the box by the fireside, lit them and put them carefully in the hearth where their soft light played upon the face of the subject lying peacefully on the sofa and the only sound breaking the silence was the measured breathing of the subject's hound stretched elegantly across its owner.

The woman sat opposite and said, 'You are still in the life as Graecus, the Centurion. you have defeated Boudicca, you are with your century and with your beloved son, Germanicus. take me to the next important scene in that life. Where do you wish to go now?'

The subject stirred and the dog became more alert. The woman could see that the subject was quickly scanning scenes under closed eyelids and muttering, 'Yes, that's what happened, we went to Deva but it was peaceful and tranquil, yes, we were content while we were there, but then there was the letter from Suetonius.......the letter which changed our lives.......'

'Tell me what happened,' said the woman softly,'How did the letter change your lives?'